The Night Has a Thousand Eyes

Books by Ruskin Bond

Fiction
The Gold Collection: The Master's Greatest Stories
The Last Tiger: My Favourite Animal Stories
Song of the Forest: Tales from Here, There, and Everywhere
The Shadow on the Wall: My Favourite Stories of Ghosts, Spirits, and Things that Go Bump in the Night
Miracle at Happy Bazaar: My Very Best Stories for Children
Rhododendrons in the Mist: My Favourite Tales of the Himalaya
A Gallery of Rascals: My Favourite Tales of Rogues, Rapscallions, and Ne'er-do-wells
Unhurried Tales: My Favourite Novellas
Small Towns, Big Stories
Upon an Old Wall Dreaming
A Gathering of Friends
Tales of Fosterganj
The Room on the Roof & Vagrants in the Valley
The Night Train at Deoli and Other Stories
Time Stops at Shamli and Other Stories
Our Trees Still Grow in Dehra
A Season of Ghosts
When Darkness Falls and Other Stories
A Flight of Pigeons
Delhi Is Not Far
A Face in the Dark and Other Hauntings
The Sensualist
A Handful of Nuts
Maharani
Secrets

Non-fiction
It's a Wonderful Life: Roads to Happiness
Rain in the Mountains
Scenes from a Writer's Life
Landour Days
Notes from a Small Room
The India I Love

Anthologies
A Town Called Dehra
Classic Ruskin Bond: Complete and Unabridged
Classic Ruskin Bond Volume 2: The Memoirs
Dust on the Mountain: Collected Stories
Friends in Small Places
Ghost Stories from the Raj
Great Stories for Children
Tales of the Open Road
The Essential Collection for Young Readers
Ruskin Bond's Book of Nature
Ruskin Bond's Book of Humour
The Writer on the Hill

Poetry
Hip-Hop Nature Boy & Other Poems
Ruskin Bond's Book of Verse

The Night Has a Thousand Eyes

MY FAVOURITE STORIES OF LOVE, WARMTH, AND FRIENDSHIP

RUSKIN BOND

ALEPH

ALEPH BOOK COMPANY
An independent publishing firm
promoted by *Rupa Publications India*

First published in India in 2023
by Aleph Book Company
7/16 Ansari Road, Daryaganj
New Delhi 110 002

ISBN: 978-93-95853-89-7

3 5 7 9 10 8 6 4 2

Printed in India.

To
Shrishti
in gratitude for looking after me so wonderfully when your
parents were away in their village.
Strawberry milkshakes forever!

CONTENTS

INTRODUCTION
FACES IN THE MIST

The first thing I do when I get up in the morning is to look through my window to see the sun come up. But this morning the sun did not break through, there was only a thick, heavy mist pressing against the windowpanes.

As I stood there, peering into this shifting curtain, I began to see faces—the faces of those I had known and sometimes loved, and the faces of those I had written about: a girl in a train, a girl on a railway platform; Sushila with her gentle smile; Binya showing off her new umbrella; an old lady who knew a lot about plants and flowers; a backward boy who attached himself to me; an eccentric rani in her room of many colours; school friends—'the four feathers' and others; a boy who leaves his village to earn a few rupees; Prem as a youth, Rakesh, a small boy planting a cherry seed; my father, leading me by the hand as we went up the hill to my new school; childhood memories.... Friends, familiars, companions, lovers.... And some who came and went, like ships passing each other, sending out a greeting, a message of goodwill, and then disappearing in the mist.

And here are many of them, embedded in some of my favourite stories. Some have come and gone, a few remain. I have tried to give them a little permanence by writing about them, catching their personalities on paper. I do not write plots, I write people. And there are still so many people to write about....

The mist is moving on. The sun filters through, and I remember the voyage home, long long years ago though it might have been yesterday—is it Time that's passing, or just

you and I?—and I sit down to write about a starry night that I
shared with someone special on an old passenger liner.

Ruskin Bond

Landour
28 April 2023

THE NIGHT HAS A THOUSAND EYES

The Polish passenger liner *Batory* had a poor reputation. During the war, it had been captured by the Germans and was used to transport troops to North Africa. Now it was a cruise ship again. But things kept going wrong—fires broke out, there was a collision, sailors deserted, a mutiny was suppressed. It seldom sailed on time. So, when on an impulse, I decided to return to India, I was able to obtain a berth at short notice. The ship was only half full and I had a cabin to myself.

It was tourist class of course. There was no first class on the *Batory*. But the facilities weren't bad. There was a bar, a shower room, a small lounge and library, an upper deck with lots of deckchairs, and several lifeboats which looked as though they might once have been required.

I'd been two years in London, working as a junior clerk; but I'd managed to save enough for the voyage and something for my homecoming. I'd written a novel and been lucky enough to find a publisher. But the actual publication was a long way off, and I was anxious to return to India. The fifty-pound advance would cover the cost of the voyage.

We left London in a fog and arrived at Gibraltar in bright sunshine. There were no alarms, and no one fell overboard. It was rather a dull two days. The crew kept to themselves, the passengers looked a bit seedy—the seas had been rough in the Channel. Now we were in calmer waters.

The only person I'd noticed was a girl—a schoolgirl by the looks of her attire—white blouse, knee-length skirt, gym shoes; her hair short, gamine-like, reminding me of Leslie Caron in *Lili*. She was in the process of turning into a woman—all legs and arms and nowhere to put them. No make-up, her eyes fresh, darting here and there. Green eyes, or so I noticed when I saw her close-up in the little perfume shop in Gibraltar.

I was looking through a selection of cheap perfumes, with the intention of buying a present for my mother, when a voice behind me said, 'Don't take those. Take the eau-de-cologne.'

I turned to look into the green eyes of this awkward-looking girl who smiled and said, 'Buying something for your girlfriend?'

'I don't have a girlfriend. It's for my mother. I know nothing about perfume.'

'Then play safe and buy the eau-de-cologne.'

Behind her stood a large formidable-looking woman who must have been in her fifties.

'This is my aunt, Mrs Bhushan. Aunt Shanti is an expert on perfumes. What do you think, aunty?'

Aunt Shanti said, 'Let him decide for himself. It's none of your business.'

'Oh, but I am grateful for the advice,' I said, and bought the eau-de-cologne. Two bottles, in fact.

We parted. They were doing a round of The Rock (as Gibraltar was called) in a local cab, and I wasn't invited to join them. I wandered through the small market and back to the ship.

ᠸ

That evening and the next day, the girl and I passed each other occasionally while strolling about the upper deck. She was almost always accompanied by her aunt, the stout lady. I noticed that she would sometimes give her aunt the slip, dodging behind a lifeboat or darting into the saloon, but the guardian was soon after her.

Once she stopped to greet me with a quizzical smile. 'Hullo again. Are you enjoying the voyage?'

'So far so good,' I said. 'The old ship isn't playing any tricks.'

'Is it supposed to?'

'At least once, during a voyage. Just for luck.'

The aunt intervened. 'Come along, Nina. It's lunch time and I'm hungry.'

So her name was Nina.

'You're always hungry, aunty,' she said, but they made for the dining room and I made for the saloon bar and ordered a vodka. The Polish vodka was supposed to be good, as good as the Russian, and I felt I was duty-bound to make a comparison.

At the bar I met a young man, Praveen Kapadia, who was returning to India after taking his degree from the London School of Economics. He was well connected and knew something or the other about several of our fellow passengers, including the girl.

'She's a lively girl,' I said. 'But under surveillance. Who is she, do you know?'

'Oh, she's the ambassador's daughter.'

I was startled. As far as I knew, our ambassador was a bachelor.

'Not Menon,' said Praveen. 'Another ambassador. He's posted in Estonia or Latvia or one of those places where no one goes to study. So he sent his daughter to school in England.'

'So what is she doing on this ship?'

'Going home like me. She's finished school, but her father doesn't want her running about with a lot of party-going teenagers. So he's sending her home to absorb some real Indian culture. Instead of pop music, she'll learn Bharatanatyam. Probably take Sanskrit classes too. Otherwise she'll never get rid of her Cockney accent.'

'She doesn't have a Cockney accent. She's quite polished.'

'So you've spoken to her?'

'Only briefly. Her aunt wouldn't let her out of sight.'

'Instructions from the ambassador. Make sure she doesn't pick up a boyfriend in the course of the voyage.'

The next day we were well into the Mediterranean. Blue skies and calm seas. I sunned myself in a deckchair. The small ship's library had a set of Conrad and I was reading *Typhoon*, about a tramp steamer caught up in a storm at sea. I hoped we weren't going to experience typhoons, cyclones, or hurricanes. But I loved Conrad. He knew the sea in all its moods.

There was a vacant deckchair next to mine. Someone settled down in it. Absorbed in my book, I took no notice.

'Do you read a lot?' The voice had a musical quality. It was the ambassador's daughter. Best to be respectful.

'I read a lot,' I said. 'It takes me out of myself.'

'I wish I was a reader. But I can't concentrate for long. My father says I have a grasshopper mind.'

'Well, it must be fun to be a grasshopper,' I said. 'On the move all the time. Hopping about, chirping merrily in the garden. I'm the opposite. My teachers said I had a sluggish mind. I'm a snail.'

She laughed and clapped her hands. 'That's nice. The grasshopper and the snail. We should be friends. How old are you?'

'Twenty-one. And you must be seventeen or eighteen.'

'Just about. And what takes you to India?'

'I'm going home. I've had enough of the West. Are you going home too?'

'I don't know where my real home is…. I've grown up in Europe with my father. Mother passed away when I was six. Now I'm supposed to discover my homeland—go to Santiniketan and learn to sing, dance, and act in Tagore's plays. Do you like Tagore?'

'Love him.'

'Maybe you could read some Tagore to me.'

'Love to…. Tomorrow perhaps. But here comes your aunt.'

Mrs Bhushan stood over us, blotting out the sun. 'There's nowhere to sit,' she said pointedly.

I got up, offered her my chair, and she took it without hesitation. As I turned to leave, Praveen Kapadia strolled up, and said, 'We'll be passing Stromboli this evening, at about eight. It's active these days. Don't forget to come up and watch it.'

I glanced at the girl. She nodded vigorously. 'Stromboli! We can't miss it, aunty.'

Later that evening most of the passengers were on the deck to watch the distant volcano. It was too dark to see the volcano itself, but every now and then it would emit a plume of crimson which would light up the night sky. Stromboli, the 'lighthouse' of the Mediterranean.

Stromboli in all its glory, belching fire and reminding us that in the long run it was Nature that decided the fate of the universe and not the endless conflicts of humankind.

Nina was standing beside me, but so was Mrs Bhushan, determined to see that her extrovert niece did not fall into the hands of a young man who looked far from prosperous. I think I looked respectable enough, but my clothes were readymade, not tailor-made, and that indicated a working-class background. But my accent was still pure Anglo-Indian, and that confused her a little.

'I've got a headache,' she said after sometime. 'I think I'll go to bed. Are you coming, Nina?'

'I'll come with you, aunty. There are some aspirins in my suitcase.'

Dutifully, she followed her escort down to their cabin on the lower deck. The crowd on the upper deck was beginning to disperse. Stromboli had put on a show, and now the old ship was ploughing a calm sea, leaving the small volcanic island far behind. I wandered about the deck. The night sky was clear, the stars were out, millions of sparkling diamonds ranged across the

heavens. How did they get there, and what did we mean to them
and they to me. I stood at a railing, pondering on the mysteries
of our existence. Presently, I felt a hand slip into mine. A warm
soft hand, resting gently against my palm.

'Where's your aunt?' I asked.

'In bed,' she said. 'I gave her a sleeping tablet.'

'I thought you said aspirin.'

'She needed to sleep. Tell me about the stars.'

'Well, I am not into astronomy. Or even astrology. But that's
the Milky Way, that cluster of stars right above us. And that's
the Great Bear, that formation that looks like a bear. And that's
Orion—' I did not know anything about Orion, so I just looked
into her eyes and saw the starlight there. And then I remembered
the opening lines of a poem, and I spoke them aloud:

'"The night has a thousand eyes, and the day but one...."
Millions of stars looking down at us, just you and I, and we are
all that matters at the moment.' I put her hand to my lips and
kissed her gently on the soft of her palm.

'Let's take a walk,' she said. And hand in hand we walked
around the deserted deck. In the distance a passing steamer hooted
in acknowledgement of our presence. The *Batory* was not alone.

'Ships that pass in the night,' I said. 'Saying goodnight and
goodbye.'

'We'll say goodbye in three or four days from now.'

'It's not really goodbye,' I said. 'The word is short for God-
be-with-you.'

The night has a thousand eyes,
    And the day but one;
Yet the light of the bright world dies
    With the dying sun.*

*From the poem by Francis William Bourdillon.

I would have changed the line to the 'rising sun' because a couple of mornings later we were at Port Said, and a hot desert sun was pouring down on us.

Soon the deck was swarming with peddlers. Somehow they'd got permission to come on board. Some were selling packets of dates. Some were selling exotic perfumes. Bags made of camel hide were also on sale. And aphrodisiacs and love potions!

An Arab wearing a fez and clad in a dusty burnous was trying to interest Mrs Bhushan in a vial of 'Spanish fly'—a powerful and dangerous sexual stimulant. Aunty did not know this.

'Is it a fragrance? Is it a cure for headaches?'

'Cure for everything,' gushed the colourful salesman. 'Gives you much excitement, much love, much fun. Only a few drops and madam will make love to a camel!'

Mrs Bhushan threatened to have the man thrown off the ship, and he slunk away, in search of more promising clients.

'Does it really do all those things for you?' asked Nina innocently.

'I've heard it does,' I said. 'But people have died from overdosing.'

'Overexcitement is bad for you,' said Mrs Bhushan.

We went ashore. The ship was moored at the canal entrance for a certain period—it was a very busy Suez Canal in those days—and we had to be back in two or three hours.

The main thoroughfare of Port Said was a busy one, thronged with seafarers, tourists on day trips, traders of many nationalities, and conmen out to take innocent tourists for a ride. Conmen the world over do much the same thing.

We resisted the blandishments of a young man who was determined to take us to see Salome doing the dance of the seven veils, and sought shelter in a dingy restaurant where we drank syrupy sweet 'sherbets' priced as though it were cognac.

'Back to the ship,' ordered Aunt Shanti. 'This is no place for us.'

But on our way back to the landing-stage a donkey cart collided with a cyclist right in front of us, and in the ensuing melee Aunt Shanti's purse vanished. Then, on the gangway, she slipped and sprained her ankle. It wasn't a good day for aunty.

Nina applied Sloan's Liniment to aunty's ankle, bandaged it, and gave her two aspirins. We went in search of a doctor, but there wasn't one on the ship.

'Don't worry,' I said. 'There no swelling. And we'll soon be in Bombay. Just another three nights.'

That night we were out of the canal and ploughing through the Red Sea. The stars were still with us. Not a cloud in the sky. Nina stayed with her aunt, and I walked the decks alone. I knew I wouldn't sleep. I saw the dawn break, the sun come up over to the horizon, and the sea burning bright.

Later that day, Nina and I watched the flying fish, as they leapt in and out of a placid sea.

'How's aunty?' I asked.

'Much better.'

'Keep her on her bunk till we reach Bombay.'

'And then we'll all go our different ways. I'll be met by many people. Officials mostly.'

'And I'll be met by no one.' I sang a snatch of an old ballad— *"'I'll take the low road and you'll take the high road, but I'll be in Scotland before ye!"*—Instead of Scotland, say Himachal.'

'And I'll be in Santiniketan, learning classical dance. And will we meet again?'

'Probably not—voyagers go their different ways—ships that pass us in the night…. And you're the ambassador's daughter and I'm the struggling writer.'

That night the *Batory* did its best to live up to its reputation. Around midnight, alarm bells sounded. A voice on the intercom said: 'Everyone up on deck—wear your life jackets!'

I looked around for my life jacket. There wasn't one. I hurried up on deck. People were milling around, none of them wearing life jackets. The jackets were still in the ship's hold.

Fortunately, they were not required. The ship wasn't sinking. But someone had fallen overboard. Or been thrown overboard. A sailor, we were told. The ship had shut its engines and slowed down, and a searchlight was played over the surrounding waves, but whoever had gone overboard had been left far behind in the ship's wake.

'I'll never travel by this ship again,' declared Aunt Shanti, limping back to her cabin.

'You won't,' said Praveen Kapadia. 'This is her last voyage. After this she goes to the scrapyard.'

And so, next day, we sailed into the Arabian Sea. It was our last night in the old *Batory*.

It was a night different from the others. The stars were hidden by storm clouds and a strong wind ruffled the sea. The old ship ploughed gamely on through the rising waves, rolling as it did so—rolling like a drunk on his way home. Nina and I were the only ones on deck apart from a couple of the ship's crew.

'Would you like to go down?' I asked.

'No, I'm enjoying it. I like the wind. I like the waves. But where are the stars?'

'No stars tonight. But look!'

Through a rift in the clouds, we caught a glimpse of the crescent moon, riding the sky.

'You sang about the stars,' said Nina. 'Now sing something about the moon!'

'"It steals the sleep from baby's eyes, it steals the smiles from baby's lips." Tagore wrote that, although I think I've got it mixed up. But it's from *The Crescent Moon*.'

I looked into her eyes. The moon was there, playing tricks in her eyes; green one moment, silver the next.

'Close your eyes,' I said.

She closed her eyes and I kissed them one by one.

She opened her eyes. 'You *kissed* me!'

'I'm sorry,' I said, and I kissed her on her nose.

'You kissed my nose!'

'It's a beautiful nose.'

'How can a nose be beautiful?'

'If it adorns a beautiful person.' And I kissed her on her ear lobes. 'Your ears are beautiful too.'

'Is that all? Can't you kiss me properly?'

So I kissed her on her sweet and salty lips, and then it began to rain, and still I kissed her, and the rain ran down our cheeks and became part of the kiss. The kiss of the sea.

'You'd better get below decks, you two,' a sailor called out. 'Or you'll be washed overboard!'

⌣

I delivered Nina to Aunt Shanti, who had been worried at her absence. The ship shuddered a bit, as it braced against the storm.

'Are we going to sink?' asked aunty. 'There are no life jackets.'

'Don't worry,' I said. 'These old ships are used to storms and typhoons. They just bob about like corks.'

By morning, the storm had passed and the sea was calm again. Nina saw a flying-fish. A good omen.

As we approached Ballard Pier, she said, 'It's time to say goodbye. There'll be people to meet me. Officials mostly.'

'That's all right,' I said. 'You go along with aunty. Just wave to me from the pier. I'll leave the ship after everyone else.'

And that's what happened.

Aunt Shanti limped down the gangway, resting on Nina's arm. I stood above them, leaning against the ship's railings. When they were half-way down, Nina turned to me and called 'Goodbye!'

'Goodbye,' I called. 'God-be-with-you!'

And then they were down on the pier, surrounded by family, friends, and officials. The ambassador's daughter.

I caught a glimpse of her as they moved towards a waiting car. She waved to me again, then disappeared in the crowd.

I never saw her again.

It happened a long time ago, and my memory is fading, but I wanted to recall and capture the kiss again, before it faded away forever.

HIGH WATER

The island of Jersey, in the Channel Islands, was blessed with numerous bays, coves, and inlets. I spent two years of my life on the island, when I was just eighteen. It was an insular place in more ways than one, and I was restless, eager to move to London, to the world of books, theatre, music, and a cosmopolitan atmosphere. I had a job, I had my aunt's home; but I was lonely, and I missed my school and college friends.

On weekends, or on holidays, I would explore the island's bay and beaches, and there was one particular cove that I liked because it was a little difficult to get to, and the tourists usually gave it a miss. It had a pebbled beach (unsuitable for sun bathing), and when the tide came in the sea waves beat up against the cliff wall. When the tide was out, you could walk or paddle a considerable distance before reaching any great depth.

In swimming shorts, I would venture quite far out, my limit being a group of rocks that were exposed when the tide was out, but submerged when the tide had turned and was approaching high water.

Those lonely rocks attracted me in some strange way. No one else visited them, and I felt they belonged to me and to the seagulls that were forever wheeling overhead, their mournful calls contending with the sound of the waves lapping against the base of the rocks.

One morning towards the end of April, when the tide was out, I walked out to the rocks, now fully exposed, and settled down on one of the them in order to absorb some of the spring sunshine. It was a flattish rock, and I stretched out in a languid, sensuous mood. The sky was a tent of blue. The sea was relatively calm. All was well. Only the gulls complained.

I dozed off. In fact, I fell fast asleep; dreamt of tropical lagoons, coconut palms, and jungle princesses. I don't know how long I slept—two hours or more—but when I woke up, the sun had disappeared and a heavy mist had drifted in over the sea. I couldn't see the beach. I could only see the neighbouring rocks. And now the level of water had risen. A wave dashed against the rocks, sending its spray over my shivering body.

I felt trapped. I would have to swim back to the shore, and I was a poor swimmer. Before long, the sea would cover the rocks, and I would be swept off them. The sea was rough now, and the sound of the waves striking the rocks drowned out the cries of the gulls.

I stood there, naked to the elements, shivering in the cold salt spray.

I decided to call for help. The beach seemed very far away, but perhaps a passing boat would pick up my cries.

'Help, help!' I called, and I was answered by the cries of the gulls, as though they were mocking me.

'No one will hear you. Don't tire yourself by shouting.'

Someone had spoken to me. It was a human voice, not a bird.

Standing on another rock, a few feet away, was a girl in a red bathing-suit. It's hard for me to describe her. She was about my age, or perhaps a little younger; fifteen or sixteen. She had short curly hair. She stood barefooted on a flat rock, her arms on her hips, as though defying the wind and waves.

'I haven't seen you before,' she said, her accent that of the island people. 'You were sleeping for some time. You overslept. Now it's too late.'

'Why didn't you wake me?'

'I couldn't get across to you. There's a strong current between the rocks.'

'Who are you?'

'I'm Alice. From the village in the bay.'

'How did *you* get here?'

'I was bathing and collecting mussels. I am always collecting mussels. You can find them on the rocks when the tide is out.'

'But what are we going to do now?' I asked fearfully. 'The water will soon be over the rocks.'

'Yes, the tide is coming in fast. And there's a storm coming up too. Can you swim?'

'Very little.'

'Don't try. You'll be swept against the rocks.'

The sky was grey, the waves ominous. It had begun to rain, and the wind swept the cold rain across my face and exposed body. I shivered from a surge of fear.

'What do we do now?' I called out to the girl.

'Nothing. Hold my hand if you can reach across.'

I stretched my arm as far I could, but I could only touch her fingers.

'I'm Alice,' she said.

'I know. Hello, Alice.'

'It's only a dream,' she said. 'We'll wake up soon.'

But it wasn't a dream for me. It was real, and we were going to drown or be dashed to death against the rocks.

And then, through the gathering darkness of the storm, I heard someone calling out: 'Ahoy there, ho! Is anyone there? Ahoy!'

A small fishing boat was approaching us, tossing about on the turbulent sea.

'Here!' I called. 'Help! Here on the rocks.'

The boat came nearer. Two men were in it. Fishermen or, possibly lifeguards.

'We're stranded,' I called. 'Come nearer. Take us off!'

'Can't get too close!' called one of the men. 'I'm throwing you a rope.'

He tossed me a rope, and I grabbed it, stepped into deep water and was hauled across to the boat. The two men got me

into the boat and were about to pull away from the rocks when
I remembered the girl.

'Wait, wait!' I cried. 'There's a girl on the rocks.'

'Can't see anyone,' said the younger man. 'Can you see
anyone, Bill?'

'Your eyes are better than mine,' said the older man, but
he peered into the gathering mist and called out: 'Halloo! Is
anyone there?'

He was answered by the crash of the waves as they struck
the rocks.

'Her name's Alice,' I said. 'She was talking to me. Alice,
Alice!' I called, adding my shouts to theirs. Did I hear a faint
cry carried away by the wind?

'There's no one there now,' said the younger man, starting
to row towards the shore.

'She was standing on the next rock,' I pleaded. 'She touched
my hand.'

'Did you say Alice?' asked Bill. 'There was a girl called Alice
who drowned here many years ago. You weren't here then, Jim.
Like you, son, she came out to the rocks just as the tide was
turning and a storm brewing. She was swept away by the currents.
We never found her.'

'Are you saying he saw her ghost?' laughed Jim, now pulling
vigorously on the oars. The rocks were slipping away, now under
high water, out of our vision.

'Could be,' said Bill. 'Others have sometimes seen her.'

'But she was real,' I said. 'She touched me.'

'Maybe she did,' said Bill. 'Maybe she gave you a helping
hand. Those rocks are not for sunbathers. Don't go out there
again, son. We won't always be around to rescue you.'

He took the other pair of oars, and we went skimming over
the leaping waves towards the safety of the shore.

I kept staring back towards the now invisible outcrop of

rocks, but I could see nothing. Above the sound of the rushing waves I heard only the mournful cries of the gulls as they circled above us.

'She touched me,' I said to myself. 'She must have been real.'

MRS BHUSHAN TO THE RESCUE

'The school's a zoo!' shouted Mr Bhushan, the new headmaster, banging his desk so vigorously that his secretary, Miss Thimble, dropped her tea cup. There was tea all over the floor, but at that moment, Ginger, the school cat, walked in and licked up the spilt tea.

'Get that cat out of here!' shouted the Headmaster. 'I've seen enough of animals in this school! Someone has a dog, someone keeps birds, the boys keep white rats and other rodents. I won't have it. Type out a notice for the school board. Are you listening, Miss Thimble? Stop stroking that cat, and do what I tell you!'

Miss Thimble shooed the cat out of the office and returned to her desk. An hour later, a notice went up on the school's notice board: 'As from next week, no student and no member of the staff will be permitted to keep pets on the school premises. This applies to dogs, cats, birds, and other forms of wildlife.'

There was consternation in the corridors of Corbet Memorial, a residential school for boys straddling the slopes of one of our hill stations. Previous headmasters had been fairly tolerant about staff members keeping pets, as long as they didn't adopt snakes, reptiles, and Himalayan bears. Mr Oliver, who taught English, had a dachshund called Wendy. Man and dog were devoted to each other. They never missed their early morning walks together. Mr Oliver was a bachelor, a lonely man, and Wendy was his only companion.

Mr Tuli had a pigeon. He was a familiar sight, walking about the school grounds with the pigeon perched on his shoulder, sometimes on his bald head. Mr Tuli, who taught math, was in his late fifties, approaching retirement. His wife disliked pigeons, so the pigeon stayed with Mr Tuli most of the time.

Miss Khanna, who taught French (she'd even been to France), had an aquarium full of pretty goldfish. Would she be allowed to keep her goldfish? They didn't bother anyone. They didn't bark, they didn't enter classrooms, they didn't get in anyone's way. But rules were rules, and Headmaster Bhushan was a stickler for rules.

Ginger the cat did not belong to anyone in particular. In other words, he belonged to everyone. He had been the school cat for several years, spending most of his time in the vicinity of the dining room and kitchen. The cook and his assistants gave him titbits from time to time, and he repaid their friendship by keeping down the mice and rat population. When the nights grew cold, he would make his way up to the first-floor dormitories, and curl up at the foot of one of the beds. He knew that young Tata (class eight) kept a pet squirrel, but he left it alone. Ginger didn't think much of squirrels, but he was a tolerant and good-natured cat.

What are you going to do with your squirrel? Tata's friends, having seen the notice board, kept asking him this question. Most of the time, the squirrel lived in his pockets, coming out from time to time to partake potato chips that came his way.

'Can't take it to class anymore,' said Tata philosophically. 'He'll have to stay in my locker.'

Mr Oliver strode into the headmaster's office and thrust his letter of resignation under the headmaster's beaky nose.

'What's this?' asked Mr Bhushan.

'My resignation,' said Mr Oliver. 'A month's notice. And while I'm here, don't think for a moment that I'll send my dog away. We leave together.'

'Why all this fuss over a dog?' Mr Bhushan was puzzled.

'When I came to this school seven years ago, Wendy was with me. When she leaves, I leave. You can get yourself another English teacher.'

Mr Oliver rose and made a dignified exit from the office.

On his way to his rooms, he stopped at the school canteen and bought several chicken patties. Equipped with these, he entered his quarters to be greeted with leaps and bounds by his faithful companion. Together, they settled down on an old sofa, consumed their patties, and contemplated the future.

'We'll go to Goa,' said Mr Oliver. 'There's a school there that will take me. It's near a beach, and you'll love playing about in the sand. And they make great sausages in Goa.'

Wendy licked Mr Oliver all over his bald head. She would be happy with him in Goa or Greenland or anywhere he went.

Mr Tuli couldn't afford to put in his resignation. He was approaching retirement, and he would have difficulty in getting another teaching job. And his wife would be loath to leave the hill station. Her evening perambulations on Mall Road would come to an end. So would her presidency of the ladies' Gymkhana Club.

'Get rid of that pigeon,' she told her husband, and dutifully he handed it over to the school's baker who lived in the bazaar and who promised to keep it with his own pigeon.

'Well, at least it's going to a good home,' he said with an air of resignation. Mr Tuli wasn't the sort of person to take on the headmaster.

Nor was Miss Khanna. She decided to do nothing. How could anyone object to her goldfish? They weren't troubling anyone. On the contrary, she had to protect them from Ginger the cat, who had tried more than once to pluck one of the fish out of the tank and had nearly fallen, as a result.

And now Ginger was going. The headmaster had sent for the school chowkidar, Ram Singh, and ordered him to get hold of the cat and transport it to some distant village or hilltop—preferably the next mountain.

'I don't want to see it here again!' he ranted. 'No cats, no dogs, no birds, no porcupines!'

'There isn't a porcupine,' said Miss Thimble, although she did think the headmaster was a bit like a porcupine, all prickly, and with his oily hair standing on end.

'Miss Khanna keeps goldfish,' Miss Thimble remarked. She did not get along very well with Miss Khanna; they were both competing for the attention of the handsome young games master.

'Goldfish!' exclaimed the headmaster with a guffaw, 'I love fish. Fried with fingers chips. We'll have them for dinner.'

And so things stood a day or two later. Ginger had been placed in a basket and taken to an unknown destination. Tata's squirrel was lodged in the gloomy box room, where his owner visited him from time to time with glucose biscuits and pieces of toast. Mr Tuli looked rather forlorn without his pigeon. And Mr Oliver was busy writing applications for teaching jobs in different schools, always emphasizing the fact that he had a canine companion who would also be in residence.

The headmaster's wife, Mrs Bhushan, did not take much interest in school activities and was unaware of the rule about pets. She came from an affluent family, her father having made a fortune manufacturing plastic buttons and plastic flowers. He was known as the plastic king of the Doab and could have bought Corbet Memorial and several others like it.

Mrs Bhushan had her own interests. She collected old silver jewellery, and in the old bazaar there were several shops dealing in silver and costume jewellery worn by the village folk.

Mrs Bhushan, a large florid woman in her early forties, sent for her driver and set out for the old bazaar, a twenty-minute drive from the school. She was soon having a lively conversation with a silversmith, who was showing her a pair of silver anklets designed for someone slimmer and younger than Mrs Bhushan.

Presently, there was a diversion.

Just outside the shop, in the middle of the road, an irate individual was cursing and shouting as he belaboured a small donkey who was overloaded with sacks of potatoes. The donkey, barely a grown animal, was down on its knees, unable to rise. Its owner was beating it with a stick, and the little donkey brayed pathetically.

Mrs Bhushan saw what was happening. She was a soft-hearted person and hated seeing any form of cruelty. She strode out of the shop and confronted the furious donkey owner.

'Leave that poor creature alone,' she called out. 'Put that stick away!'

The angry man stood back and stared at the plump lady. 'What is it to you?' he demanded. 'I have to deliver these potatoes.'

'Then use a cart,' said Mrs Bhushan. 'Or get a mule, or carry them yourself!'

There was a furious argument. A crowd collected.

'What do you want for your donkey?' demanded Mrs Bhushan. 'I'll buy it from you!'

'One thousand rupees,' said the man without any hesitation. 'In cash!'

Mrs Bhushan had the money. She would go without those silver anklets, at least for today.

She counted out the required notes and handed them over to the donkey owner. 'Bobby!' she called out to her driver. 'Bring the car here!' she turned to the donkey owner (no longer the owner) and snapped out an order: 'Now remove those sacks of potatoes!' Soon the little donkey was upon his wobbly legs. Mrs Bhushan gazed into the luminous, appealing eyes and fell in love with the helpless creature.

Bobby blew on his horn and drove up in the car. Mrs Bhushan opened the rear door. 'Now help me get it on to the back seat,' she said.

'The seat will be spoilt,' objected Bobby.

'Never mind,' said Mrs Bhushan, 'it's only plastic.'

Together they got the donkey on to the back seat. Mrs Bhushan sat up front beside the driver. And the three of them drove away in triumph.

Mr Bhushan left his office at five o'clock sharp. It was time for tea and a dish of hot, fresh paneer pakoras. As he walked down the gravel path to his house, a strange sight met his protruding eyes. On the veranda were Mrs Bhushan and the maidservant, a bucket of water between them, and they were giving a bath to—surely it wasn't a donkey?

'What on earth is that?' he exclaimed, goggling.

'A donkey,' said Mrs Bhushan, 'Isn't it beautiful? Just look at those wonderful ears—and soulful eyes! A donkey in the house brings good luck!'

'In the house!'

'Well, the back veranda, I've already placed some mattresses there.'

'You're keeping this—this creature!'

'Well, of course, dear, I've paid a thousand rupees for it. But he must have a name. We can't keep calling him "it".'

'Nonsense!' exclaimed Mr Bhushan.

'No, we can't call it nonsense. Think of something nice.'

'Rubbish!'

'That's worse! Rubbish won't do.'

'Good heavens!' said Mr Bhushan, throwing up his arms.

'That's better, Good Heavens is a bit long for a name, but we can call him Heavenly. Do you like the name, dear?' she said, addressing the donkey.

Heavenly gave a loud bray.

Mr Bhushan had no choice but to cancel his orders prohibiting the keeping of pets by members of the staff. How could he ban pets when his wife was the proud owner of a donkey? And whenever he tried to oppose her, he had visions of his father-in-law's millions and his own ambition to own a school or schools of his own one day.

So Miss Thimble put another notice on the notice board to the effect that staff members were permitted to keep pets—but only one pet per teacher. Tata's squirrel had always been outlawed, but Tata was confident that it would be able to slip into class with him, provided it did not try exploring Miss Khanna's dupatta.

Mr Oliver took back his resignation, and Mr Tuli got back his pigeon. Ginger the cat had no difficulty in finding his way back to the school, and was given a warm welcome by the cook and his assistants.

Everyone was happy and the school team proceeded without any major mishap. But there was one small tragedy. Ginger got into Miss Khanna's room and was seen exiting with the tail fin of a goldfish protruding from his mouth. He had already swallowed a couple, leaving Miss Khanna with just one goldfish.

Miss Khanna was heartbroken. And Miss Thimble made things worse by saying, 'Well, you're only allowed one pet, anyway.'

But the handsome young games master felt sorry for Miss Khanna and gave her a present of several rainbow-coloured goldfish.

So Miss Khanna had the last laugh, as well as the attentions of the games master for a few weeks. But Miss Thimble had youth on her side, and she was determined to vanquish her rival in the young man's affections.

But that's another story....

THE YELLOW UMBRELLA

The postman knocks, or used to, in the old days when I lived in Maplewood Lodge, down in the forest on the outskirts of Mussoorie. Now the courier services have taken over, and the postman is something of a rarity, but back in the sixties and seventies, I would always be looking out for him, because he brought me cheques from publishers and magazines, and in those days, it was the only mode of payment apart from the occasional money order. I was making a living entirely from my writing, and those 'cheques in the mail' were essential for my survival.

Prakash was my postman for two or three years. His daily beat brought him from the post office on the Mall to the school on the ridge above my cottage, a walk of about two and a half miles. He was nearing sixty, on the verge of retirement, and the long walk would tire him out.

I had been in the cottage just three or four days when he came trudging down the forest path with a couple of letters for me. I was at my desk on the veranda when I heard a stentorian voice calling: 'Postman, postman!' I got up from my desk. He looked at my typewriter.

'This is your work, your office?' he asked.

'Yes, I am a writer,' I said.

'No, you are a typer,' he said.

'You mean a typist? I do my writing on this typewriter.' (In those days I used to type my stories.)

'So you are a typer-writer,' he insisted.

And from that day on he always addressed me as Mr Typer-writer.

Well, I didn't mind as long as I got my letters. And he was

very regular, turning up every day (except holidays) around noon, calling out, 'Postman! Letters for Mr Typer-writer!' He had some difficulty pronouncing my real name.

He would usually find me at my desk or in the tiny garden where I was trying to grow snapdragons and petunias. On hot days he would ask me for a glass of water, and after he had quenched his thirst, he would sit on the low garden wall for five or ten minutes and bring me up to date on what was happening in the town. A movie was being made on the Mall, and there was much excitement because the beautiful Hema Malini was in town. Or something more mundane such as a leopard having been seen on Camel's Back Road, or a beauty contest underway at the Savoy. I seldom went into town, so Prakash the postman was my local newspaper.

The months passed quietly, the seasons changed, my work progressed. Those all-important cheques arrived from time to time, so did the winter rains and a fall of snow. Prakash had a rough voice but he wasn't very strong, and in his old, frayed overcoat he was beginning to look older than his years. Instead of a glass of water, I would give him a glass of hot, sweet tea, and he would perk up and plod back up the hill to his quarters in the town. He was married, but his wife lived in their village on the next range. She had to look after his old mother and a cow and a couple of goats.

'I will retire soon,' he told me, 'and then I will get another cow and maybe a mule to bring our milk and vegetables to Mussoorie. Big business!'

When summer came again he abandoned his overcoat and started wearing a cap to shield him from the sun. When the monsoon arrived, he started carrying an umbrella. It was shabby and torn and did not give him much protection. And the rains were heavy that year.

'Won't the post office give you a decent umbrella?' I asked.

'They gave me this one five years ago,' he said. 'Now they don't have a budget for umbrellas.'

'Well, I'll get you one,' I said 'I'm going into town tomorrow, and I'll get you a good umbrella.'

'That's very kind of you,' said Prakash. 'I would like a blue umbrella.'

'Why blue?'

He told me that he had often seen a little village girl, Binya, coming from or going to school, and she had a pretty blue umbrella. He wanted one just like it!

'Well, I'll see what I can find,' I said. And I walked into town, looking for a blue umbrella.

But the umbrella shops had all run out of blue umbrellas. Suddenly they had become very popular.

I didn't think Prakash would care for an ordinary black umbrella. So I settled for a bright yellow umbrella, and the following day, when he arrived with his old umbrella blown inside out by a strong wind, I presented him with the yellow umbrella.

'Yellow is the colour of the sun,' I said. 'It will keep you sunny and cheerful!'

He accepted it graciously and carried it about wherever he went, even when the rains were over. You could tell when he was coming because of that blob of bright yellow moving about on the hillside.

Then one day, in the middle of October, someone else arrived with my post.

He was a young man, neatly dressed, very polite. 'Your letters, sir, I'm the new postman.'

It was quite a shock.

'What happened to Prakash?' I asked anxiously, 'I hope he isn't sick.'

'He's fine, sir. He took his retirement pension and went back to his village.'

'Oh, I see.' I was a little disappointed that he hadn't told me he was going, but he was probably in a hurry to buy that cow. The new postman was fine, and I did not expect to see Prakash again.

It was late October. I'd been working hard, and I felt like getting away from typewriter, even if it was only for a couple of days. I was a good walker and had done some trekking over the years. I decided to take a long walk to Dhanaulti, where there was an old forest rest house set amidst deodars and horse chestnuts.

In those days there was no motor road to Dhanaulti, just a footpath used by pilgrims on their arduous trek to Gangotri. Dhanaulti was about twenty miles from my cottage, and I expected to be there by evening if I walked at a steady pace. My friend and helper, Pran Singh, made some sandwiches for me and filled a water bottle with lemon juice; these went into my haversack (the modern backpack had yet to be invented), and I set off cheerfully, hoping to enjoy the sparkling autumn air and the wonderful views from the winding path to Dhanaulti.

I'd covered about five miles, past the village of Suakholi, when I found the path blocked by a herd of goats, and in order to avoid them I left the narrow path and scrambled up the slope of the hill, made slippery by fallen pine needles. On my way down I slipped and fell, twisting my ankle. I wasn't badly hurt, but the ankle was painful, and I continued limping along, wishing I'd brought along a stout walking stick.

Still, I struggled on, as I was now about half way to Dhanaulti, and when I saw some wayside huts about half a mile distant, I decided I'd rest in the village and then decide whether to go or not.

As I approached, I noticed a large yellow blob outside one of the shacks. It was a yellow umbrella! And beneath it, sheltering from the sun was Prakash, my old postman.

As soon as he saw me, he got up, exclaiming: 'Typer-writer sir! What are you doing here?'

'Just taking a walk. Is this your village?'

'Yes, my fields are just below. But you have hurt yourself, come and sit down. Better still, come inside and rest.'

His small tile-roofed dwelling was the first off the road. It was two-storeyed, the ground floor being reserved for his cows. Yes, there were now two of them.

He took me upstairs and made me comfortable on an old cane chair. He called for his wife and asked her to make us some tea. She was a round, plump, jolly woman who was delighted to have an unexpected visitor. The tea was followed by hot pakoras and walnuts from their own walnut tree.

'You have sprained your ankle,' said Prakash. 'See, it is quite swollen. You should not walk any further. Better to stay the night.'

But I knew that Prakash would not have a spare cot or even a spare mattress, so I said, 'I'll manage, it's not too bad.'

Just then a pack of mules arrived, on its way to Mussoorie; the mules were loaded with sacks of beans and radishes. The mule driver was singing the latest Hindi hit song.

'Hey, Melaram!' shouted Prakash. 'Do you have space on one of your mules?'

'For a friend of yours, there will be space,' answered the mule driver.

'Then deliver my friend, the Typer-writer, to the first doctor you find in Mussoorie.'

'At your command,' said Melaram. 'It shall be done.' He brought over one of his mules, transferred its load to another mule, and made a saddle of sorts out of empty gunny bags. They were straggled onto the patient animal, and I was helped onto it by the two men, while Prakash's wife looked on with unconcealed amusement.

It was the first time I had taken a ride on a mule, and I hoped there would not be another. Two hours of riding a mule can give you a very sore bottom.

'Come again, Typer-writer sir,' said Prakash, and we trotted off, the mule driver in the lead, followed by my mount and several others. I looked back to see Prakash waving to me, holding up the yellow umbrella, which had turned to burnished gold in the setting sun.

There's an old saying, 'One good turn deserves another'. A bit of a cliché but true. There's such a thing as the law of compensation, a sort of Karma, that works best in this life. Kindness begets kindness, and never mind the sore bottom.

WHO KISSED ME IN THE DARK?

This chapter, or story, could not have been written but for a phone call I received last week. I'll come to the caller later. Suffice to say that it triggered off memories of a hilarious fortnight in the autumn of that year (can't remember which one) when India and Pakistan went to war with each other. It did not last long, but there was plenty of excitement in our small town, set off by a rumour that enemy parachutists were landing in force in the ravine below Pari Tibba.

The road to this ravine led past my dwelling, and one afternoon I was amazed to see the town's constabulary, followed by hundreds of concerned citizens (armed mostly with hockey sticks) taking the trail down to the little stream where I usually went birdwatching. The parachutes turned out to be bedsheets from a nearby school, spread out to dry by the dhobis who lived on the opposite hill. After days of incessant rain the sun had come out, and the dhobis had finally got a chance to dry the school bedsheets on the verdant hillside. From afar they did look a bit like open parachutes. In times of crisis, it's wonderful what the imagination will do.

There were also blackouts. It's hard for a hill station to black itself out, but we did our best. Two or three respectable people were arrested for using their torches to find their way home in the dark. And of course, nothing could be done about the lights on the next mountain, as the people there did not even know there was a war on. They did not have radio or television or even electricity. They used kerosene lamps or lit bonfires!

We had a smart young set in Mussoorie in those days, mostly college students who had also been to convent schools and some of them decided it would be a good idea to put on a show—or an old-fashioned theatrical extravaganza—to raise funds for the war effort. And they thought it would be a good idea to rope me in, as I was the only writer living in Mussoorie in those innocent times. I was thirty-one and I had never been a college student, but they felt I was the right person to direct a one-act play in English. This was to be the centrepiece of the show.

I forget the name of the play. It was one of those drawing room situation comedies popular from the 1920s, inspired by such successes as *Charley's Aunt* and *Tons of Money*. Anyway, we went into morning rehearsals at Hakman's, one of the older hotels, where there was a proper stage and a hall large enough to seat at least two hundred spectators.

The participants were full of enthusiasm, and rehearsals went along quite smoothly. They were an engaging bunch of young people—Guttoo, the intellectual among them; Ravi, a schoolteacher; Gita, a tiny ball of fire; Neena, a heavy-footed Bharatanatyam exponent; Nellie, daughter of a nurse; Chameli, who was in charge of make-up (she worked in a local beauty saloon); Rajiv, who served in the bar and was also our prompter; and a host of others, some of whom would sing and dance before and after our one-act play.

The performance was well attended, Ravi having rounded up a number of students from the local schools; and the lights were working, although we had to cover all doors, windows, and exits with blankets to maintain the regulatory blackout. But the stage was old and rickety, and things began to go wrong during Neena's dance number when, after a dazzling pirouette, she began stamping her feet and promptly went through, while the rest of her remained above board and visible to the audience.

The schoolboys cheered, the curtain came down, and we rescued Neena, who had to be sent to the civil hospital with a sprained ankle, Mussoorie's only civilian war casualty.

There was a hold-up, but before the audience could get too restless the curtain went up on our play, a tea party scene, which opened with Guttoo pouring tea for everyone. Unfortunately, our stage manager had forgotten to put any tea in the pot and poor Guttoo looked terribly put out as he went from cup to cup, pouring invisible tea. 'Damn. What happened to the tea?' muttered Guttoo, a line, which was not in the script. 'Never mind,' said Gita, playing opposite him and keeping her cool. 'I prefer my milk without tea,' she said and proceeded to pour herself a cup of milk.

After this, everyone began to fluff their lines and our prompter had a busy time. Unfortunately, he'd helped himself to a couple of rums at the bar, so that whenever one of the actors faltered, he'd call out the correct words in a stentorian voice which could be heard all over the hall. Soon there was more prompting than acting, and the audience began joining in with dialogue of their own.

Finally, to my great relief, the curtain came down—to thunderous applause. It went up again, and the cast stepped forward to take a bow. Our prompter, who was also curtain-putter, released the ropes prematurely and the curtain came down with a rush, one of the sandbags hitting poor Guttoo one the head. He has never fully recovered from the blow.

The lights, which had been behaving all evening, now failed us, and we had a real blackout. In the midst of this confusion, someone—it must have been a girl, judging from the overpowering scent of jasmine that clung to her—put her arms around me and kissed me.

When the light came on again, she had vanished.

Who had kissed me in the dark?

As no one came forward to admit to the deed, I could only make wild guesses. But it had been a very sweet kiss, and I would have been only too happy to return it had I known its ownership. I could hardly go up to each of the girls and kiss them in the hope of reciprocation. After all, it might even have been someone from the audience.

Anyway, our concert did raise a few hundred rupees for the war effort. By the time we sent the money to the right authorities, the war was over. Hopefully they saw to it that the money was put to good use.

We went our various ways, and although the kiss lingered in my mind, it gradually became a distant, fading memory and as the years passed it went out of my head altogether. Until the other day, almost forty years later....

'Phone for you,' announced Gautam, my seven-year-old secretary.

'Boy or girl? Man or woman?'

'Don't know. Deep voice like my teacher, but it says you know her.'

'Ask her name.'

Gautam asked.

'She's Nellie, and she's speaking from Bareilly.'

'Nellie from Bareilly?' I was intrigued. I took the phone.

'Hello,' I said. 'I'm Bonda from Golconda.'

'Then you must be wealthy now.' Her voice was certainly husky. 'But don't you remember me? Nellie? I acted in that play of yours, up in Mussoorie a long time ago.'

'Of course, I remember now.' I was remembering. 'You had a small part, the maidservant I think. You were very pretty. You had dark, sultry eyes. But what made you ring me after all these years.'

'Well, I was thinking of you. I've often thought about you. You were much older than me, but I liked you. After that show, when the lights went out, I came up to you and kissed you. And then I ran away.'

'So it was you! I've often wondered. But why did you run away? I would have returned the kiss. More than once.'

'I was very nervous. I thought you'd be angry.'

'Well, I suppose it's too late now. You must be happily married with lots of children.'

'Husband left me. Children grew up, went away.'

'It must be lonely for you.'

'I have lots of dogs.'

'How many?'

'About thirty.'

'Thirty dogs! Do you run a kennel club?'

'No, they are all strays. I run a dog shelter.'

'Well, that's very good of you. Very humane.'

'You must come and see it sometime. Come to Bareilly. Stay with me. You like dogs, don't you?'

'Er—yes, of course. Man's best friend, the dog. But thirty is a lot of dogs to have about the house.'

'I have lots of space.'

'I'm sure... well, Nellie, if ever I'm in Bareilly, I'll come to see you. And I'm glad you phoned and cleared up the mystery. It was a lovely kiss, and I'll always remember it.'

We said our goodbyes and I promised to visit her someday. A trip to Bareilly to return a kiss might seem a bit far-fetched, but I've done sillier things in my life. It's those dogs that worry me. I can imagine them snapping at my heels as I attempt to approach their mistress. Dogs can be very possessive.

'Who was that on the phone?' asked Gautam, breaking in on my reverie.

'Just an old friend.'

'Dada's old girlfriend. Are you going to see her?'

'I'll think about it.'

And I'm still thinking about it and about those dogs. But bliss it was to be in Mussoorie forty years ago, when Nellie kissed me in the dark.

Some memories are best left untouched.

THE GARDEN OF DREAMS

It wasn't so long ago that I found myself in Kathmandu, the colourful capital of Nepal, attending one of those literary festivals that have caught on in countries where books are still written, published, and sometimes read. I had a day or two to myself and I was wandering about in the streets looking for quaint corners—for I am a collector of quaint corners—when I came across a walled enclosure, a long, high wall with just an entrance, a heavy door over which was painted the following legend: 'Garden of Dreams'.

Naturally I was curious. If there was a garden it was behind that wall. And since it had advertised itself, presumably it was open to the public.

On the pavement, not far from the entrance, sat an old woman who was selling trinkets, costume jewellery, and semi-precious stones.

'Mother,' I said, for she seemed older than me, 'What's in that garden of dreams?'

'Flowers,' she said, 'And running water. And dreams.'

Her face was furrowed with the passage of time but she had a cheerful, winning smile and her forearms were covered with the colourful bangles, her fingers with rings of onyx and jade.

'I suppose I can go in,' I said.

'It will open any minute,' she said. 'But first, why don't you buy something? A bracelet for your lady love?'

'I don't have a lady love.' But I bought a tiny mirror from her. It was ringed with different coloured stones and crowned with a gaudily painted wooden parrot. As I pocketed my purchase, the door to the garden opened and the old lady said, 'You can go in now and look for your dream.'

There was no one at the door and I couldn't see anyone in the garden, although there were signs of activity at the other end, where a couple of gardeners were pruning a rose bush.

There were roses everywhere—lush golden roses, and pink lollipops, and roses that opened like a woman's labia, and roses that shone in the early morning sun, and some that still held dewdrops between their petals.

I had the garden to myself for almost half an hour, and in that time I followed little paths that meandered between beds of crimson poppies, scented petunias of every shade, carpets of multi-coloured phlox, pansies with their funny faces that looked like Oliver Hardy's larkspur, wallflowers, snapdragons....

There was a small waterfall at one end of the garden and it fed a small stream that ran in and out of the spaces between the flower beds. Here and there you could cross the stream by means of small bridges. They gave the garden a distinct Japanese or Oriental look.

I sat down on a bench and tried to take it all in. I am a sensualist by nature, but here there was so much to absorb— colour, fragrance, sunshine and shade, the flow of water, the pattern of leaves, the twitter of small birds, the passage of a butterfly.... And presently other people were trickling into the garden—some Japanese tourists, laden with cameras; a stout Indian lady in a pink sari, accompanied by a brood of children; a bearded, bespectacled artist with a sketch pad; an English-looking woman lurking beneath a large hat.

The woman in the hat stopped beside me and said, 'Lovely garden, isn't it? So very English....'

'They say the late Rana was inspired by a garden he saw in France,' I commented.

'But French gardens are so formal, aren't they? And this one has something of everything. Even a bit of the willow pattern plate. Was that Chinese or Japanese?'

'Probably a bit of both,' I said. 'Let's just say it's uniquely Nepalese!'

The lady in the hat moved on and the woman in the pink sari plonked herself down on the bench. She was soon joined by two of her noisy children and I made way for them and strolled across to the far end of the garden. Here a fountain was playing and in the pool surrounding it there were several goldfish. Nearby there was a girl on a swing. She could have been sixteen or twenty-six, I couldn't guess her age, she was young and pretty but she was also quite adult in her poise and manner. She made me think of *Alice in Wonderland*. She was dressed all in green, but there was a purple hibiscus in her hair.

'Do you like goldfish?' she asked.

'I do,' I said. 'There is something very restful about them. I can watch them for hours. How they silently glide around in their watery world.'

'And they don't bark,' she said. 'Or make any noise at all.'

I laughed. 'Do you come here often?'

'Quite often,' she said. 'It's your first visit, isn't it?'

'Yes, and I'm only here for a day or two. This garden belonged to a princess, I'm told. Does anyone live there now, in the old palace?'

'Sometimes the princess comes. But she's very old now—she doesn't come down from her tower.'

'And you—are you a princess too?'

She laughed, and I noticed that her eyes were dark like hazelnuts. There were silver anklets on her feet and a daisy chain around her throat.

'No,' she said, 'I'm just a—' She broke off and looked away and there was a touch of sadness on her face. 'I do all sorts of things,' she said, sounding quite cheerful again. 'Have you seen the birds?'

'You mean the sparrows?'

'No, the aviary. There are lots of small birds. Come, I'll show you.'

She jumped off the swing and beckoned and I found myself by her side, holding her hand.

Had she taken my hand or had I taken hers? I wasn't sure. It was just something that had happened.

The touch of her hand sent a strange thrill through my entire person. It wasn't like any hand that I'd ever held. It was a young hand, the palms soft and the fingers strong; but it was also the hand of her ancestors and I felt that it had stories to tell. It was also taking something out of me. I felt younger, even reckless. I clung to her hand as though I was clinging to life itself; I did not want to let go.

A variety of small, colourful birds flitted about the spacious aviary, some on swings, some on the branches of a small blossoming plum tree. Plum blossoms were flung far and wide. There was a great amount of birdsong, if you could call it that. Really just twittering and chirping, like a bunch of cocktail party humans having a gossip session. A pair of lovebirds appeared to be enamoured of each other; they kept kissing each other with their tiny beaks.

'See, they are making love!' exclaimed my companion, her hand pressing into mine. Her hazel eyes were excited. I was tempted to kiss her but at that moment the large-hatted lady loomed over us and we became self-conscious.

'Sexy little creatures, aren't they?' she said. 'Just like a couple of teenagers.'

She was obviously referring to the lovebirds, for I was no teenager; but my companion led me away, still holding me by the hand.

She took me into a shady arbour, and we sat there for some time, and she told me her name, Kiran, and that she lived close by and came to the garden almost every day. I did not ask her too many questions. Conscious that I was much older than her and that she knew nothing about me, I did not want to frighten her off with too much familiarity. A gazelle will come to you if you are very still but if you move towards it, the beautiful creature will dart away. And this was a gazelle I was talking to.

She asked me questions and I told her about myself, that I worked for an Indian publishing firm and that I was in Kathmandu for a few days—with just a day or two to go.

'Will you come again tomorrow?' she asked.

'If you like,' I said, 'And then perhaps you can show me the marketplace. It's close by, isn't it?'

'Yes, quite close. But I like it here in the garden.' She had released my hand and I felt that something was going from me. And then the lady in the pink sari barged in with her kids, and the spell was broken.

She walked with me as far as the garden door. I looked back at the tall, old building behind the garden.

'Do you live there?' I asked.

She nodded, smiling wistfully.

'It looks very old,' I said. 'So you really are a princess?'

She laughed and her dark eyes lit up in the sunshine. 'I am anything I want to be.'

'Till tomorrow, then,' I said.

'Till tomorrow....'

And so we parted. Out on the street I bought another trinket, and the old lady noticed that I looked happy and she gave me a toothless grin and asked, 'Did you find your dream?'

'Better than a dream,' I said and made my way back to the hotel where I had a meeting with local publishers.

⟋

I forget how I spent the rest of that day. I kept thinking about the girl in the garden. We had struck up a good rapport and I wanted to see her again and take our friendship forward.

So next morning, after breakfast, I sallied forth to the garden of dreams.

She wasn't there.

I walked around the garden several times. I hung about near the pool and the aviary and sat on a bench for at least an hour. Visitors came and went. Tourists from China and Japan; talking, admiring. Loud-voiced Americans. Some quiet, reserved Africans. A writer from India came up to me and thrust a folder into my hands. 'For you to publish,' he said. 'It will sell in millions!' He must have followed me into the garden. I promised to read his masterpiece.

Then I paced about, studying rose bushes, herbaceous borders, lovebirds. No one came.

It was getting on to noon when I gave up and left the garden.

No, I did not buy any trinkets.

The old woman looked up at me and said, 'No good dream today?'

I shook my head and said, 'Yesterday I met a girl in the garden. She said her name was Kiran. She was to meet me again today. She was a princess, I think. Do you know her?'

The old woman shook her head. 'There is no princess living here. Kiran? I do not know the name. Perhaps she could not come today. Why not try tomorrow?'

'But I must leave tomorrow.'

'It is sad, then. She means much to you, this girl?'

'I think so.'

She nodded wisely. 'Many hearts have been broken in the garden of dreams.' And she said no more.

⁔

I wandered the streets of Kathmandu. I wasn't looking for anyone. I just couldn't stand being alone in my hotel room or in the company of writers and publishers.

Towards evening I passed the garden of dreams. The door was shut, the walls were too high to see anything. I supposed she did not want to see me again. That overture of friendship, the pressure of her hand, the tenderness in her eyes, her every gesture had spoken of liking, if not of love. Perhaps it meant nothing after all. Just a way of passing the time.... And here I was, a middle-aged moron, fretting like an adolescent who had just fallen in love!

My plane was to leave at noon.

There was time for one last visit to the garden, albeit a hurried one.

It was far too early. The street was deserted. The garden door was locked from within. The old lady with her wares was yet to arrive. The sun was only just coming up.

Further along the street, where the garden enclosure ended, someone was sweeping the pavement using a long-handled broom. Fallen leaves and plastic waste were being swept into an imposing heap—all so symbolic of the new century.

I approached the early morning sweeper. Perhaps he could help me.

It wasn't a 'he'. The person, dressed in a uniform of sorts, turned to me when I spoke and I was shocked into silence; for it was none other than Kiran.

She was as surprised as I was. She dropped the broom. A look of panic crossed her face and then vanished just as quickly.

'You are here—so early—it does not open till ten.'

'I came to see you, not the garden,' I said. 'And you promised to meet me yesterday.'

'I could not come. I was sent into town on some work. My father works for the old king's family. But as you can see, I am not a princess. That was just a game.' She gave me an enigmatic smile.

'So let the game continue,' I said and held out my hand.

She took it, held it for a moment, then let it fall. 'You are a good person,' she said simply.

'And you are a princess,' I said, 'and I want to see you again. But my plane leaves shortly. If I come again in a few months' time, will you be here?'

'In the garden or outside?' Her good humour was returning.

'Near the aviary. Where the lovebirds sing.'

'They don't sing,' she said, laughing. 'They kiss each other all the time.'

Well, I didn't kiss her, although I longed to do so. The street was filling up, people were staring at us. There were no cell phones then, but I gave her my home address and asked her to write to me. Then I rushed back to the hotel, collected my bag, sent for a taxi, and headed for the airport.

Soon the garden and Kiran were just a dream.

*

But it was a dream that wouldn't go away.

The monsoon rains came and went and an autumn breeze swept across the hills and knocked over the windows of my hilltop home. There was no word from Kiran. Perhaps she did not write letters. Perhaps she did not write at all!

On my desk was the little mirror I'd bought from the old lady outside the garden. It sparkled in the morning sun; it glowed at the time of sunset. A little bird—just a sparrow—flew in at the open window—examined the wooden parrot, pecked at the mirror and flew away. Sometimes I thought I saw someone in the mirror—just a figure, a slight figure in green, but she was always walking away. Mirrors can play tricks.

And this planet, this earth and its hidden fires, can be cruel.

An earthquake struck the Himachal.

It ran through the heart of Nepal, razing towns, villages, palatial buildings, and humble dwellings. Thousands perished.

Thousands lost their homes, their living, their loved ones. These sudden horrific natural calamities almost always strike the poorest, most vulnerable countries—Haiti, Mozambique, small island nations, landlocked mountain lands, Nepal....

As the news came through on my television, I feared the worst. Would Kiran have survived? And what of other friends and associates? I phoned them, made enquires, but news trickled through very slowly. People were too busy salvaging what was left of their homes. And many slept in the open as aftershocks ran through the country, bringing down structures already weakened by the earth's convulsions.

And then there was a period of quiet as things began to settle. Normalcy could not return, but the resilient people of this small nation went about rebuilding their homes and shattered lives.

There was no news of Kiran or the garden or the old lady on the street. They were not people who normally made the news. I would have to visit Kathmandu again, to see if the garden and its occupants were still there.

But before I could do that I had a visitor.

The steps to my room are steep and uneven and I was struggling up them after a visit to the bazaar when I noticed someone sitting on the top step, a backpack by her side.

It was Kiran. She looked tired and weak, but more beautiful than ever.

'I've come to see you,' she said.

'For a long, long time, I hope.' And I took her by the hand and led her into my home, my garden of books.

And that was how Kiran came into my life.

If you meet her, she will tell you about the garden of dreams (it's still there) and the old lady on the street (she's still there) and the lovebirds and the goldfish and the little stream. And perhaps she will take you there some day; for she is a girl who can make dreams come true.

THE EYES HAVE IT

I had the train compartment to myself up to Rohana, then a girl got in. The couple who saw her off was probably her parents. They seemed very anxious about her comfort and the woman gave the girl detailed instructions as to where to keep her things, when not to lean out of windows, and how to avoid speaking to strangers.

They called their goodbyes, and the train pulled out of the station. As I was totally blind at the time, my eyes sensitive only to light and darkness, I was unable to tell what the girl looked like. But I knew she wore slippers from the way they slapped against her heels.

It would take me some time to discover something about her looks and perhaps I never would. But I liked the sound of her voice and even the sound of her slippers.

'Are you going all the way to Dehra?' I asked.

I must have been sitting in a dark corner because my voice startled her. She gave a little exclamation and said, 'I didn't know anyone else was here.'

Well, it often happens that people with good eyesight fail to see what is right in front of them. They have too much to take in, I suppose. Whereas people who cannot see (or see very little) have to take in only the essentials, whatever registers tellingly on their remaining senses.

'I didn't see you either,' I said. 'But I heard you come in.'

I wondered if I would be able to prevent her from discovering that I was blind. Provided I keep to my seat, I thought, it shouldn't be too difficult.

The girl said, 'I'm getting off at Saharanpur. My aunt is meeting me there.'

'Then I better not get too familiar,' I replied. 'Aunts are usually formidable creatures.'

'Where are you going?' she asked.

'To Dehra and then to Mussoorie.'

'Oh, how lucky you are. I wish I was going to Mussoorie. I love the hills. Especially, in October.'

'Yes, this is the best time,' I said, calling on my memories. 'The hills are covered with wild dahlias, the sun is delicious, and at night you can sit in front of a log fire and drink a little brandy. Most of the tourists have gone and the roads are quiet and almost deserted. Yes, October is the best time.'

She was silent. I wondered if my words had touched her or whether she thought me a romantic fool. Then I made a mistake.

'What is it like outside?' I asked.

She seemed to find nothing strange in the question. Had she noticed already that I could not see? But her next question removed my doubts.

'Why don't you look out of the window?' she asked.

I moved easily along the berth and felt for the window ledge. The window was open and I faced it, making a pretence of studying the landscape. I heard the panting of the engine, the rumble of the wheels, and in my mind's eye, I could see telegraph posts flashing by.

'Have you noticed,' I ventured, 'that the trees seem to be moving while we seem to be standing still?'

'That always happens,' she said. 'Do you see any animals?'

'No,' I answered quite confidently. I knew that there were hardly any animals left in the forests near Dehra.

I turned from the window and faced the girl, and for a while we sat in silence.

'You have an interesting face,' I remarked. I was becoming quite daring but it was a safe remark. Few girls can resist flattery. She laughed pleasantly—a clear, ringing laugh.

'It's nice to be told I have an interesting face. I'm tired of people telling me I have a pretty face.'

Oh, so you do have a pretty face, thought I. And aloud I said, 'Well, an interesting face can also be pretty.'

'You are a very gallant young man,' she said. 'But why are you so serious?'

I thought, then, that I would try to laugh for her, but the thought of laughter only made me feel troubled and lonely.

'We'll soon be at your station,' I said.

'Thank goodness it's a short journey. I can't bear to sit in a train for more than two or three hours.'

Yet, I was prepared to sit there for almost any length of time, just to listen to her talk. Her voice had the sparkle of a mountain stream. As soon as she left the train she would forget our brief encounter. But it would stay with me for the rest of the journey and for some time after.

The engine's whistle shrieked, the carriage wheels changed their sound and rhythm, and the girl got up and began to collect her things. I wondered if she wore her hair in a bun or if it was plaited. Perhaps it was hanging loose over her shoulders. Or was it cut very short?

The train drew slowly into the station. Outside, there was the shouting of porters and vendors and a high-pitched female voice near the carriage door. That voice must have belonged to the girl's aunt.

'Goodbye,' the girl said.

She was standing very close to me. So close that the perfume from her hair was tantalizing. I wanted to raise my hand and touch her hair, but she moved away. Only the scent of perfume still lingered where she had stood.

There was some confusion in the doorway. A man, getting into the compartment, stammered an apology. Then the door banged, and the world was shut out again. I returned to my berth. The guard blew his whistle and we moved off. Once again I had a game to play and a new fellow traveller.

The train gathered speed, the wheels took up their song, the carriage groaned and shook. I found the window and sat in front of it, staring into the daylight that was darkness for me.

So many things were happening outside the window. It could be a fascinating game guessing what went on out there.

The man who had entered the compartment broke into my reverie.

'You must be disappointed,' he said. 'I'm not nearly as attractive a travelling companion as the one who just left.'

'She was an interesting girl,' I said. 'Can you tell me—did she keep her hair long or short?'

'I don't remember,' he said sounding puzzled. 'It was her eyes I noticed, not her hair. She had beautiful eyes but they were of no use to her. She was completely blind. Didn't you notice?'

LOVE IS A SAD SONG

I sit against this grey rock, beneath a sky of pristine blueness, and think of you, Sushila. It is November, and the grass is turning brown and yellow. Crushed, it still smells sweet. The afternoon sun shimmers on the oak leaves and turns them a glittering silver. A cricket sizzles its way through the long grass. The stream murmurs at the bottom of the hill—that stream where you and I lingered on a golden afternoon in May.

I sit here and think of you and try to see your slim brown hand resting against this rock, feeling its warmth. I am aware again of the texture of your skin, the coolness of your feet, the sharp tingle of your fingertips. And in the pastures of my mind I run my hand over your quivering mouth and crush your tender breasts. Remembered passion grows sweeter with the passing of time.

You will not be thinking of me now, as you sit in your home in the city, cooking or sewing or trying to study for examinations. There will be men and women and children circling about you, in that crowded house of your grandmother's, and you will not be able to think of me for more than a moment or two. But I know you do think of me sometimes, in some private moment which cuts you off from the crowd. You will remember how I wondered what it is all about, this loving, and why it should cause such an upheaval. You are still a child, Sushila—and yet you found it so easy to quieten my impatient heart.

On the night you came to stay with us, the light from the street lamp shone through the branches of the peach tree and made leaf patterns on the walls. Through the glass panes of the front door I caught a glimpse of little Sunil's face, bright and questing, and then—a hand—a dark, long-fingered hand that could only have belonged to you.

It was almost a year since I had seen you, my dark and slender girl. And now you were in your sixteenth year. And Sunil was twelve; and your uncle, Dinesh, who lived with me, was twenty-three. And I was almost thirty—a fearful and wonderful age, when life becomes dangerous for dreamers.

I remember that when I left Delhi last year, you cried. At first I thought it was because I was going away. Then I realized that it was because you could not go anywhere yourself. Did you envy my freedom—the freedom to live in a poverty of my own choosing, the freedom of the writer? Sunil, to my surprise, did not show much emotion at my going away. This hurt me a little, because during that year he had been particularly close to me, and I felt for him a very special love. But separations cannot be of any significance to small boys of twelve who live for today, tomorrow, and—if they are very serious—the day after.

Before I went away with Dinesh, you made us garlands of marigolds. They were orange and gold, fresh and clean and kissed by the sun. You garlanded me as I sat talking to Sunil. I remember you both as you looked that day—Sunil's smile dimpling his cheeks, while you gazed at me very seriously, your expression very tender. I loved you even then....

Our first picnic.

The path to the little stream took us through the oak forest, where the flashy blue magpies played follow-my-leader with their harsh, creaky calls. Skirting an open ridge (the place where I now sit and write), the path dipped through oak, rhododendron, and maple, until it reached a little knoll above the stream. It was a spot unknown to the tourists and summer visitors. Sometimes a milkman or woodcutter crossed the stream on the way to town or village but no one lived beside it. Wild roses grew on the banks.

I do not remember much of that picnic. There was a lot of

dull conversation with our neighbours, the Kapoors, who had come along too. You and Sunil were rather bored. Dinesh looked preoccupied. He was fed up with college. He wanted to start earning a living: wanted to paint. His restlessness often made him moody, irritable.

Near the knoll the stream was too shallow for bathing, but I told Sunil about a cave and a pool further downstream and promised that we would visit the pool another day.

That same night, after dinner, we took a walk along the dark road that goes past the house and leads to the burning ghat. Sunil, who had already sensed the intimacy between us, took my hand and put it in yours. An odd, touching little gesture!

'Tell us a story,' you said.

'Yes, tell us,' said Sunil.

I told you the story of the pure in heart. A shepherd boy found a snake in the forest and the snake told the boy that it was really a princess who had been bewitched and turned into a snake, and that it could only recover its human form if someone who was truly pure in heart gave it three kisses on the mouth. The boy put his lips to the mouth of the snake and kissed it thrice. And the snake was transformed into a beautiful princess. But the boy lay cold and dead.

'You always tell sad stories,' complained Sunil.

'I like sad stories,' you said. 'Tell us another.'

'Tomorrow night. I'm sleepy.'

We were woken in the night by a strong wind which went whistling round the old house and came rushing down the chimney, humming and hawing and finally choking itself.

Sunil woke up and cried out, 'What's that noise, Uncle?'

'Only the wind,' I said.

'Not a ghost?'

'Well, perhaps the wind is made up of ghosts. Perhaps this wind contains the ghosts of all the people who have lived and died in this old house and want to come in again from the cold.'

You told me about a boy who had been fond of you in Delhi. Apparently he had visited the house on a few occasions, and had sometimes met you on the street while you were on your way home from school. At first, he had been fond of another girl but later he switched his affections to you. When you told me that he had written to you recently, and that before coming up you had replied to his letter, I was consumed by jealousy—an emotion which I thought I had grown out of long ago. It did not help to be told that you were not serious about the boy, that you were sorry for him because he had already been disappointed in love.

'If you feel sorry for everyone who has been disappointed in love,' I said, 'you will soon be receiving the affections of every young man over ten.'

'Let them give me their affections,' you said, 'and I will give them my chappal over their heads.'

'But spare my head,' I said.

'Have you been in love before?'

'Many times. But this is the first time.'

'And who is your love?'

'Haven't you guessed?'

Sunil, who was following our conversation with deep interest, seemed to revel in the situation. Probably he fancied himself playing the part of Cupid, or Kamadeva, and delighted in watching the arrows of love strike home. No doubt I made it more enjoyable for him. Because I could not hide my feelings. Soon Dinesh would know, too—and then?

A year ago my feelings about you were almost paternal! Or so I thought.... But you are no longer a child and I am a little older too. For when, the night after the picnic, you took my hand and held it against your soft warm cheek, it was the first time that a girl had responded to me so readily, so tenderly. Perhaps it was just innocence but that one action of yours, that acceptance of me, immediately devastated my heart.

Gently, fervently, I kissed your eyes and forehead, your small round mouth, and the lobes of your ears, and your long smooth throat; and I whispered, 'Sushila, I love you, I love you, I love you,' in the same way that millions and millions of love-smitten young men have whispered since time immemorial. What else can one say? I love you, I love you. There is nothing simpler; nothing that can be made to mean any more than that. And what else did I say? That I would look after you and work for you and make you happy; and that too had been said before, and I was in no way different from anyone. I was a man and yet I was a boy again.

We visited the stream again, a day or two later, early in the morning. Using the rocks as stepping stones, we wandered downstream for about a furlong until we reached a pool and a small waterfall and a cool dark cave. The rocks were mostly grey but some were yellow with age and some were cushioned with moss. A forktail stood on a boulder in the middle of the stream, uttering its low pleasant call. Water came dripping down from the sides of the cave, while sunlight filtered through a crevice in the rock ceiling, dappling your face. A spray of water was caught by a shaft of sunlight and at intervals it reflected the colours of the rainbow.

'It is a beautiful place,' you said.

'Come, then,' I said, 'let us bathe.'

Sunil and I removed our clothes and jumped into the pool while you sat down in the shade of a walnut tree and watched us disport ourselves in the water. Like a frog, Sunil leapt and twisted about in the clear, icy water; his eyes shone, his teeth glistened white, his body glowed with sunshine, youth, and the jewels made by drops of water glistening in the sun.

Then we stretched ourselves out beside you and allowed the

sun to sink deep into our bodies.

Your feet, laved with dew, stood firm on the quickening grass. There was a butterfly between us: its wings red and gold and heavy with dew. It could not move because of the weight of moisture. And as your foot came nearer and I saw that you would crush it, I said, 'Wait. Don't crush the butterfly, Sushila. It has only a few days in the sun and we have many.'

'And if I spare it,' you said, laughing, 'what will you do for me, what will you pay?'

'Why, anything you say.'

'And will you kiss my foot?'

'Both feet,' I said and did so willingly. For they were no less than the wings of butterflies.

Later, when you ventured near the water, I dragged you in with me. You cried out, not in alarm but with the shock of the cold water, and then, wrenching yourself from my arms, clambered on to the rocks, your thin dress clinging to your thighs, your feet making long patterns on the smooth stone.

Though we tired ourselves out that day, we did not sleep at night. We lay together, you and Sunil on either side of me. Your head rested on my shoulders, your hair lay pressed against my cheek. Sunil had curled himself up into a ball but he was far from being asleep. He took my hand, and he took yours, and he placed them together. And I kissed the tender inside of your hand.

I whispered to you, 'Sushila, there has never been anyone I've loved so much. I've been waiting all these years to find you. For a long time I did not even like women. But you are so different. You care for me, don't you?'

You nodded in the darkness. I could see the outline of your face in the faint moonlight that filtered through the skylight. You never replied directly to a question. I suppose that was a feminine quality; coyness, perhaps.

'Do you love me, Sushila?'

No answer.

'Not now. When you are a little older. In a year or two.'

Did you nod in the darkness or did I imagine it?

'I know it's too early,' I continued. 'You are still too young. You are still at school. But already you are much wiser than me. I am finding it too difficult to control myself, but I will, since you wish it so. I'm very impatient, I know that, but I'll wait for as long as you make me—two or three or a hundred years. Yes, Sushila, a hundred years!'

Ah, what a pretty speech I made! Romeo could have used some of it; Majnu, too.

And your answer? Just a nod, a little pressure on my hand. I took your fingers and kissed them one by one. Long fingers, as long as mine.

After some time I became aware of Sunil nudging me.

'You are not talking to me,' he complained. 'You are only talking to her. You only love her.'

'I'm terribly sorry. I love you too, Sunil.'

Content with this assurance, he fell asleep; but towards morning, thinking himself in the middle of the bed, he rolled over and landed with a thump on the floor. He didn't know how it had happened and accused me of pushing him out.

'I know you don't want me in the bed,' he said.

It was a good thing Dinesh, in the next room, didn't wake up.

∽

'Have you done any work this week?' asked Dinesh with a look of reproach.

'Not much,' I said.

'You are hardly ever in the house. You are never at your desk. Something seems to have happened to you.'

'I have given myself a holiday, that's all. Can't writers take holidays too?'

'No. You have said so yourself. And anyway, you seem to have taken a permanent holiday.'

'Have you finished that painting of the Tibetan woman?' I asked, trying to change the subject.

'That's the third time you've asked me that question, even though you saw the completed painting a week ago. You're getting very absent-minded.'

There was a letter from your old boyfriend; I mean your young boyfriend. It was addressed to Sunil, but I recognized the sender's name and knew it was really for you.

I assumed a look of calm detachment and handed the letter to you. But both you and Sunil sensed my dismay. At first you teased me and showed me the boy's photograph, which had been enclosed (he was certainly good looking in a flashy way); then, finding that I became gloomier every minute, you tried to make amends, assuring me that the correspondence was one sided and that you no longer replied to his letters.

And that night, to show me that you really cared, you gave me your hand as soon as the lights were out. Sunil was fast asleep.

We sat together at the foot of your bed. I kept my arm about you, while you rested your head against my chest. Your feet lay in repose upon mine. I kept kissing you. And when we lay down together, I loosened your blouse and kissed your small firm breasts, and put my lips to your nipples and felt them grow hard against my mouth.

The shy responsiveness of your kisses soon turned to passion. You clung to me. We had forgotten time and place and circumstance. The light of your eyes had been drowned in that lost look of a woman who desires. For a space we both struggled against desire. Suddenly, I had become afraid of myself—afraid for you. I tried to free myself from your clasping arms. But you cried in a low voice, 'Love me! Love me! I want you to love me.'

Another night you fell asleep with your face in the crook of my arm, and I lay awake a long time, conscious of your breathing, of the touch of your hair on my cheek, of the soft warm soles of your feet, of your slim waist and legs.

And in the morning, when the sunshine filled the room, I watched you while you slept—your slim body in repose, your face tranquil, your thin dark hands like sleeping butterflies and then, when you woke, the beautiful untidiness of your hair and the drowsiness in your eyes. You lay folded up like a kitten, your limbs as untouched by self-consciousness as the limbs of a young and growing tree. And during the warmth of the day a bead of sweat rested on your brow like a small pearl.

I tried to remember what you looked like as a child. Even then, I had always been aware of your presence. You must have been nine or ten when I first saw you—thin, dark, plain-faced, always wearing the faded green skirt that was your school uniform. You went about barefoot. Once, when the monsoon arrived, you ran out into the rain with the other children, naked, exulting in the swish of the cool rain. I remembered your beautiful straight legs and thighs, your swift smile, your dark eyes. You say you do not remember playing naked in the rain but that is because you did not see yourself.

I did not notice you growing. Your face did not change very much. You must have been thirteen when you gave up skirts and started wearing the salwar kameez. You had few clothes but the plainness of your dress only seemed to bring out your own radiance. And as you grew older, your eyes became more expressive, your hair longer and glossier, your gestures more graceful. And then, when you came to me in the hills, I found that you had been transformed into a fairy princess of devastating charm.

We were idling away the afternoon on our beds and you were reclining in my arms when Dinesh came in unexpectedly. He said nothing, merely passed through the room, and entered his studio.

Sunil got a fright and you were momentarily confused. Then you said, 'He knows already,' and I said, 'yes, he must know.'

Later I spoke to Dinesh. I told him that I wanted to marry you; that I knew I would have to wait until you were older and had finished school—probably two or three years—and that I was prepared to wait although I knew it would be a long and difficult business. I asked him to help me.

He was upset at first, probably because he felt I had been deceptive (which was true), and also because of his own responsibility in the matter. You were his niece, and I had made love to you while he had been preoccupied with other things. But after a little while when he saw that I was sincere and rather confused, he relented.

'It has happened too soon,' he said. 'She is too young for all this. Have you told her that you love her?'

'Of course. Many times.'

'You're a fool, then. Have you told her that you want to marry her?'

'Yes.'

'Fool again. That's not the way it is done. Haven't you lived in India long enough to know that?'

'But I love her.'

'Does she love you?'

'I think so.'

'You think so. Desire isn't love, you must know that. Still, I suppose she does love you, otherwise she would not be holding hands with you all day. But you are quite mad, falling in love with a girl half your age.'

'Well, I'm not exactly an old man. I'm thirty.'

'And she's a schoolgirl.'

'She isn't a girl any more, she's too responsive.'

'Oh, you've found that out, have you?'

'Well…' I said, covered in confusion. 'Well, she has shown

that she cares a little. You know that it's years since I took any interest in a girl. You called it unnatural on my part, remember? Well, they simply did not exist for me, that's true.'

'Delayed adolescence,' muttered Dinesh.

'But Sushila is different. She puts me at ease. She doesn't turn away from me. I love her, and I want to look after her. I can only do that by marrying her.'

'All right, but take it easy. Don't get carried away. And don't, for God's sake, give her a baby. Not while she's still at school! I will do what I can to help you. But you will have to be patient. And no one else must know of this or I will be blamed for everything. As it is Sunil knows too much, and he's too small to know so much.'

'Oh, he won't tell anyone.'

'I wish you had fallen in love with her two years from now. You will have to wait that long, anyway. Getting married isn't a simple matter. People will wonder why we are in such a hurry, marrying her off as soon as she leaves school. They'll think the worst!'

'Well, people do marry for love you know, even in India. It's happening all the time.'

'But it doesn't happen in our family. You know how orthodox most of them are. They wouldn't appreciate your outlook. You may marry Sushila for love, but it will have to look like an arranged marriage!'

Little things went wrong that evening.

First, a youth on the road passed a remark which you resented; and you, most unladylike, but most Punjabi-like, picked up a stone and threw it at him. It struck him on the leg. He was too surprised to say anything and limped off. I remonstrated with you, told you that throwing stones at people often resulted in a fight, then realized that you had probably wanted to see me fighting on your behalf.

Later you were annoyed because I said you were a little absent-minded. Then Sunil sulked because I spoke roughly to him (I can't remember why), and refused to talk to me for three hours, which was a record. I kept apologizing, but neither of you would listen.

It was all part of a game. When I gave up trying and turned instead to my typewriter and my unfinished story, you came and sat beside me and started playing with my hair. You were jealous of my story, of the fact that it was possible for me to withdraw into my work. And I reflected that a woman had to be jealous of something. If there wasn't another woman, then it was a man's work, or his hobby, or his best friend, or his favourite sweater, or his pet mongoose that made her resentful. There is a story in Kipling about a woman who grew insanely jealous of a horse's saddle because her husband spent an hour every day polishing it with great care and loving kindness.

Would it be like that in marriage, I wondered—an eternal triangle: you, me, and the typewriter?

But there were only a few days left before you returned to the plains, so I gladly pushed away the typewriter and took you in my arms instead. After all, once you had gone away, it would be a long, long time before I could hold you in my arms again. I might visit you in Delhi but we would not be able to enjoy the same freedom and intimacy. And while I savoured the salty kiss of your lips, I wondered how long I would have to wait until I could really call you my own.

Dinesh was at college and Sunil had gone roller skating and we were alone all morning. At first you avoided me, so I picked up a book and pretended to read. But barely five minutes had passed before you stole up from behind and snapped the book shut.

'It is a warm day,' you said. 'Let us go down to the stream.'

Alone together for the first time, we took the steep path down to the stream, and there, hand in hand, scrambled over the rocks until we reached the pool and the waterfall.

'I will bathe today,' you said; and in a few moments you stood beside me, naked, caressed by sunlight and a soft breeze coming down the valley. I put my hand out to share in the sun's caress, but you darted away, laughing, and ran to the waterfall as though you would hide behind a curtain of gushing water. I was soon beside you. I took you in my arms and kissed you, while the water crashed down upon our heads. Who yielded—you or I? All I remember is that you had entwined yourself about me like a clinging vine, and that a little later we lay together on the grass, on bruised and broken clover, while a whistling thrush released its deep sweet secret on the trembling air.

Blackbird on the wing, bird of the forest shadows, black rose in the long ago of summer, this was your song. It isn't time that's passing by, it is you and I.

It was your last night under my roof. We were not alone, but when I woke in the middle of the night and stretched my hand out, across the space between our beds, you took my hand, for you were awake too. Then I pressed the ends of your fingers, one by one, as I had done so often before, and you dug your nails into my flesh. And our hands made love, much as our bodies might have done. They clung together, warmed and caressed each other, each finger taking on an identity of its own and seeking its opposite. Sometimes the tips of our fingers merely brushed against each other, teasingly, and sometimes our palms met with a rush, would tremble and embrace, separate, and then passionately seek each other out. And when sleep finally overcame you, your hand fell listlessly between our beds, touching the ground. And I lifted it up, and after putting it once to my lips, returned it gently to your softly rising bosom.

And so you went away, all three of you, and I was left alone with the brooding mountain. If I could not pass a few weeks without you how was I to pass a year, two years? This was the question I kept asking myself. Would I have to leave the hills and take a flat in Delhi? And what use would it be—looking at you and speaking to you but never able to touch you? Not to be able to touch that which I had already possessed would have been the subtlest form of torture.

The house was empty, but I kept finding little things to remind me that you had been there—a handkerchief, a bangle, a length of ribbon—and these remnants made me feel as though you had gone forever. No sound at night, except the rats scurrying about on the rafters.

The rain had brought out the ferns, which were springing up from tree and rock. The murmur of the stream had become an angry rumble. The honeysuckle creeper winding over the front windows was thick with scented blossom. I wish it had flowered a little earlier, before you left. Then you could have put the flowers in your hair.

At night I drank brandy, wrote listlessly, listened to the wind in the chimney, and read poetry in bed. There was no one to tell stories to and no hand to hold.

I kept remembering little things—the soft hair hiding your ears, the movement of your hands, the cool touch of your feet, the tender look in your eyes, and the sudden stab of mischief that sometimes replaced it.

Mrs Kapoor remarked on the softness of your expression. I was glad that someone had noticed it. In my diary I wrote: 'I have looked at Sushila so often and so much that perhaps I have overlooked her most compelling qualities—her kindness (or is it just her easygoingness?), her refusal to hurt anyone's feelings (or is it just her indifference to everything?), her wide tolerance (or is it just her laziness?)... Oh, how absolutely ignorant I am of women!'

Well, there was a letter from Dinesh and it held out a lifeline, one that I knew I must seize without any hesitation. He said he might be joining an art school in Delhi and asked me if I would like to return to Delhi and share a flat with him. I had always dreaded the possibility of leaving the hills and living again in a city as depressing as Delhi but love, I considered, ought to make any place habitable....

And then I was on a bus on the road to Delhi.

The first monsoon showers had freshened the fields and everything looked much greener than usual. The maize was just shooting up and the mangoes were ripening fast. Near the larger villages, camels and bullock carts cluttered up the road, and the driver cursed, banging his fist on the horn.

Passing through small towns, the bus driver had to contend with cycle rickshaws, tonga ponies, trucks, pedestrians, and other buses. Coming down from the hills for the first time in over a year, I found the noise, chaos, dust, and dirt a little unsettling.

As my taxi drew up at the gate of Dinesh's home, Sunil saw me and came running to open the car door. Other children were soon swarming around me. Then I saw you standing near the front door. You raised your hand to your forehead in a typical Muslim form of greeting—a gesture you had picked up, I suppose, from a film.

For two days Dinesh and I went house hunting, for I had decided to take a flat if it was at all practicable. Either it was very hot, and we were sweating, or it was raining and we were drenched. (It is difficult to find a flat in Delhi, even if one is in a position to pay an exorbitant rent, which I was not. It is especially difficult for bachelors. No one trusts bachelors, especially if there are grown-up daughters in the house. Is this because bachelors are wolves or because girls are so easily seduced these days?)

Finally, after several refusals, we were offered a flat in one of those new colonies that sprout like mushrooms around the capital. The rent was two hundred rupees a month and although I knew I couldn't really afford so much, I was so sick of refusals and already so disheartened and depressed that I took the place and made out a cheque to the landlord, an elderly gentleman with his daughters all safely married in other parts of the country.

There was no furniture in the flat except for a couple of beds, but we decided we would fill the place up gradually. Everyone at Dinesh's home—brothers, sister-in-law, aunts, nephews, and nieces—helped us to move in. Sunil and his younger brother were the first arrivals. Later the other children, some ten of them, arrived. You, Sushila, came only in the afternoon, but I had gone out for something and only saw you when I returned at tea time. You were sitting on the first-floor balcony and smiled down at me as I walked up the road.

I think you were pleased with the flat; or at any rate, with my courage in taking one. I took you up to the roof, and there, in a corner under the stairs, kissed you very quickly. It had to be quick, because the other children were close on our heels. There wouldn't be much opportunity for kissing you again. The mountains were far and in a place like Delhi, and with a family like yours, private moments would be few and far between.

Hours later when I sat alone on one of the beds, Sunil came to me, looking rather upset. He must have had a quarrel with you.

'I want to tell you something,' he said.

'Is anything wrong?'

To my amazement he burst into tears.

'Now you must not love me anymore,' he said.

'Why not?'

'Because you are going to marry Sushila, and if you love me too much it will not be good for you.'

I could think of nothing to say. It was all too funny and all too sad.

But a little later he was in high spirits, having apparently forgotten the reasons for his earlier dejection. His need for affection stemmed perhaps from his father's long and unnecessary absence from the country.

Dinesh and I had no sleep during our first night in the new flat. We were near the main road and traffic roared past all night. I thought of the hills, so silent that the call of a nightjar startled one in the stillness of the night.

I was out most of the next day and when I got back in the evening it was to find that Dinesh had had a rumpus with the landlord. Apparently the landlord had really wanted bachelors, and couldn't understand or appreciate a large number of children moving in and out of the house all day.

'I thought landlords preferred having families,' I said.

'He wants to know how a bachelor came to have such a large family!'

'Didn't you tell him that the children were only temporary and wouldn't be living here?'

'I did, but he doesn't believe me.'

'Well, anyway, we're not going to stop the children from coming to see us,' I said indignantly. (No children, no Sushila!) 'If he doesn't see reason, he can have his flat back.'

'Did he cash my cheque?'

'No, he's given it back.'

'That means he really wants us out. To hell with his flat! It's too noisy here anyway. Let's go back to your place.'

We packed our bedding, trunks, and kitchen utensils once more, hired a bullock cart, and arrived at Dinesh's home (three miles distant) late at night, hungry and upset.

Everything seemed to be going wrong.

Living in the same house as you, but unable to have any real contact with you (except for the odd, rare moment when we were left alone in the same room and were able to exchange a word or a glance) was an exquisite form of self-inflicted torture: self-inflicted, because no one was forcing me to stay in Delhi.

Sometimes you had to avoid me and I could not stand that. Only Dinesh (and, of course, Sunil and some of the children) knew anything about the affair—adults are much slower than children at sensing the truth—and it was still too soon to reveal the true state of affairs and my own feelings to anyone else in the family. If I came out with the declaration that I was in love with you, it would immediately become obvious that something had happened during your holiday in the hill station. It would be said that I had taken advantage of the situation (which I had), and that I had seduced you—even though I was beginning to wonder if it was you who had seduced me! And if a marriage was suddenly arranged, people would say: 'It's been arranged so quickly. And she's so young. He must have got her into trouble.' Even though there were no signs of your having got into that sort of trouble.

And yet I could not help hoping that you would become my wife sooner than could be foreseen. I wanted to look after you. I did not want others to be doing it for me. Was that very selfish? Or was it a true state of being in love?

There were times—times when you kept your distance and did not even look at me—when I grew desperate. I knew you could not show your familiarity with me in front of others and yet, knowing this, I still tried to catch your eye, to sit near you, to touch you fleetingly. I could not hold myself back. I became morose, I wallowed in self-pity. And self-pity, I realized, is a sign of failure, especially of failure in love.

It was time to return to the hills.

Sushila, when I got up in the morning to leave, you were still asleep and I did not wake you. I watched you stretched out on your bed, your dark face tranquil and untouched by care, your black hair spread over the white pillow, your long thin hands and feet in repose. You were so beautiful when you were asleep.

And as I watched, I felt a tightening around my heart, a

sudden panic that I might somehow lose you.

The others were up and there was no time to steal a kiss. A taxi was at the gate. A baby was bawling. Your grandmother was giving me advice. The taxi driver kept blowing his horn.

Goodbye, Sushila!

We were in the middle of the rains. There was a constant drip and drizzle and drumming on the corrugated tin roof. The walls were damp and there was mildew on my books and even on the pickle that Dinesh had made.

Everything was green, the foliage almost tropical, especially near the stream. Great stag ferns grew from the trunks of trees, fresh moss covered the rocks, and the maidenhair fern was at its loveliest. The water was a torrent, rushing through the ravine and taking with it bushes and small trees. I could not remain out for long, for at any moment it might start raining. And there were also the leeches who lost no time in fastening themselves on to my legs and feasting on my blood.

Once, standing on some rocks, I saw a slim brown snake swimming with the current. It looked beautiful and lonely. I dreamt a dream, very disturbing dream, which troubled me for days.

In the dream, Sunil suggested that we go down to the stream. We put some bread and butter into an airbag, along with a long bread knife, and set off down the hill. Sushila was barefoot, wearing the old cotton tunic which she had worn as a child, Sunil had on a bright yellow T-shirt and black jeans. He looked very dashing. As we took the forest path down to the stream, we saw two young men following us. One of them, a dark, slim youth, seemed familiar. I said 'Isn't that Sushila's boyfriend?' But they denied it. The other youth wasn't anyone I knew.

When we reached the stream, Sunil and I plunged into the pool, while Sushila sat on the rock just above us. We had been bathing for a few minutes when the two young men came down the slope and began fondling Sushila. She did not resist, but Sunil climbed out of the pool and began scrambling up the slope. One of the youths, the less familiar one, had a long knife in his hand. Sunil picked up a stone and flung it at the youth, striking him on the shoulder. I rushed up and grabbed the hand that held the knife. The youth kicked me on the shins and thrust me away and I fell beneath him. The arm with the knife was raised over me, but I still held the wrist. And then I saw Sushila behind him, her face framed by a passing cloud. She had the bread knife in her hand, and her arm swung up and down, and the knife cut through my adversary's neck as though it were passing through a ripe melon.

I scrambled to my feet to find Sushila gazing at the headless corpse with the detachment and mild curiosity of a child who has just removed the wings from a butterfly. The other youth, who looked like Sushila's boyfriend, began running away. He was chased by the three of us. When he slipped and fell, I found myself beside him, the blade of the knife poised beneath his left shoulder blade. I couldn't push the knife in. Then Sunil put his hand over mine and the blade slipped smoothly into the flesh.

At all times of the day and night I could hear the murmur of the stream at the bottom of the hill. Even if I didn't listen, the sound was there. I had grown used to it. But whenever I went away, I was conscious of something missing and I was lonely without the sound of running water.

I remained alone for two months and then I had to see you again, Sushila. I could not bear the long-drawn-out uncertainty of the situation. I wanted to do something that would bring everything nearer to a conclusion. Merely to stand by and wait was intolerable. Nor could I bear the secrecy to which Dinesh had sworn me. Someone else would have to know about my intentions—someone would have to help. I needed another ally to sustain my hopes; only then would I find the waiting easier.

You had not been keeping well and looked thin, but you were as cheerful, as serene as ever.

When I took you to the pictures with Sunil, you wore a sleeveless kameez made of purple silk. It set off your dark beauty very well. Your face was soft and shy and your smile hadn't changed. I could not keep my eyes off you.

Returning home in the taxi, I held your hand all the way.

Sunil (in Punjabi): 'Will you give your children English or Hindi names?'

Me: 'Hindustani names.'

Sunil (in Punjabi): 'Ah, that is the right answer, Uncle!'

And first I went to your mother.

She was a tiny woman and looked very delicate. But she'd had six children—a seventh was on the way—and they had all come into the world without much difficulty and were the healthiest in the entire joint family.

She was on her way to see relatives in another part of the city and I accompanied her part of the way. As she was pregnant, she was offered a seat in the crowded bus. I managed to squeeze in beside her. She had always shown a liking for me and I did not find it difficult to come to the point.

'At what age would you like Sushila to get married?' I asked casually, with almost paternal interest.

'We'll worry about that when the time comes. She has still to finish school. And if she keeps failing her exams, she will never finish school.'

I took a deep breath and made the plunge.

'When the time comes,' I said, 'when the time comes, I would like to marry her.' And without waiting to see what her reaction would be, I continued: 'I know I must wait a year or two, even longer. But I am telling you this, so that it will be in your mind. You are her mother, and so I want you to be the first to know.' (Liar that I was! She was about the fifth to know.

But what I really wanted to say was, 'Please don't be looking for any other husband for her just yet.')

She didn't show much surprise. She was a placid woman. But she said, rather sadly, 'It's all right but I don't have much say in the family. I do not have any money, you see. It depends on the others, especially her grandmother.'

'I'll speak to them when the time comes. Don't worry about that. And you don't have to worry about money or anything—what I mean is, I don't believe in dowries—I mean, you don't have to give me a Godrej cupboard and a sofa set and that sort of thing. All I want is Sushila....'

'She is still very young.'

But she was pleased—pleased that her flesh and blood, her own daughter, could mean so much to a man.

'Don't tell anyone else just now,' I said.

'I won't tell anyone,' she said with a smile.

So now the secret—if it could be called that—was shared by at least five people.

The bus crawled on through the busy streets and we sat in silence, surrounded by a press of people but isolated in the intimacy of our conversation.

I warmed towards her—towards that simple, straightforward, uneducated woman (she had never been to school, could not read or write), who might still have been young and pretty had her circumstances been different. I asked her when the baby was due.

'In two months,' she said. She laughed. Evidently she found it unusual and rather amusing for a young man to ask her such a question.

'I'm sure it will be a fine baby,' I said. And I thought: that makes six brothers-in-law!

I did not think I would get a chance to speak to your Uncle Ravi (Dinesh's elder brother) before I left. But on my last evening in Delhi, I found myself alone with him on the Karol Bagh road.

At first we spoke of his own plans for marriage, and, to please him, I said the girl he'd chosen was both beautiful and intelligent.

He warmed towards me.

Clearing my throat, I went on. 'Ravi, you are five years younger than me and you are about to get married.'

'Yes, and it's time you thought of doing the same thing.'

'Well, I've never thought seriously about it before—I'd always scorned the institution of marriage—but now I've changed my mind. Do you know whom I'd like to marry?'

To my surprise Ravi unhesitatingly took the name of Asha, a distant cousin I'd met only once. She came from Ferozepur, and her hips were so large that from a distance she looked like an oversized pear.

'No, no,' I said. 'Asha is a lovely girl but I wasn't thinking of her. I would like to marry a girl like Sushila. To be frank, Ravi, I would like to marry Sushila.'

There was a long silence and I feared the worst. The noise of cars, scooters, and buses seemed to recede into the distance, and Ravi and I were alone together in a vacuum of silence.

So that the awkwardness would not last too long, I stumbled on with what I had to say. 'I know she's young and that I will have to wait for some time.' (Familiar words!) 'But if you approve, and the family approves, and Sushila approves, well then, there's nothing I'd like better than to marry her.'

Ravi pondered, scratched himself, and then, to my delight, said: 'Why not? It's a fine idea.'

The traffic sounds returned to the street, and I felt as though I could set fire to a bus or do something equally in keeping with my high spirits.

'It would bring you even closer to us,' said Ravi. 'We would like to have you in our family. At least I would like it.'

'That makes all the difference,' I said. 'I will do my best for her, Ravi. I'll do everything to make her happy.'

'She is very simple and unspoilt.'

'I know. That's why I care so much for her.'

'I will do what I can to help you. She should finish school by the time she is seventeen. It does not matter if you are older. Twelve years difference in age is not uncommon. So don't worry. Be patient, and all will be arranged.'

And so I had three strong allies—Dinesh, Ravi, and your mother. Only your grandmother remained, and I dared not approach her on my own. She was the most difficult hurdle because she was the head of the family, and she was autocratic and often unpredictable. She was not on good terms with your mother and for that very reason I feared that she might oppose my proposal. I had no idea how much she valued Ravi's and Dinesh's judgement. All I knew was that they bowed to all her decisions.

How impossible it was for you to shed the burden of your relatives! Individually, you got on quite well with all of them; but because they could not live without bickering among themselves, you were just a pawn in the great joint family game.

You put my hand to your cheek and to your breast. I kissed your closed eyes and took your face in my hands, and touched your lips with mine; a phantom kiss in the darkness of a veranda. And then, intoxicated, I stumbled into the road and walked the streets all night.

I was sitting on the rocks above the oak forest when I saw a young man walking towards me down the steep path. From his careful manner of walking, and light clothing, I could tell that he was a stranger, one who was not used to the hills. He was about my height, slim, rather long in the face; good looking in a delicate sort of way. When he came nearer, I recognized him as the young man in the photograph, the youth of my dream—your late admirer! I wasn't too surprised to see him. Somehow, I had always felt that we would meet one day.

I remembered his name and said, 'How are you, Pramod?'

He became rather confused. His eyes were already clouded with doubt and unhappiness; but he did not appear to be an aggressive person.

'How did you know my name?' he asked.

'How did you know where to find me?' I countered.

'Your neighbours, the Kapoors, told me. I could not wait for you to return to the house. I have to go down again tonight.'

'Well then, would you like to walk home with me, or would you prefer to sit here and talk? I know who you are, but I've no idea why you've come to see me.'

'It's all right here,' he said, spreading his handkerchief on the grass before sitting down on it. 'How did you know my name?'

I stared at him for a few moments and got the impression that he was a vulnerable person—perhaps more vulnerable than myself.

My only advantage was that I was older and therefore better able to conceal my real feelings.

'Sushila told me,' I said.

'Oh. I did not think you would know.'

I was a little puzzled but said, 'I knew about you, of course. And you must have known that or you would hardly have come here to see me.'

'You knew about Sushila and me?' he asked, looking even more confused.

'Well, I know that you are supposed to be in love with her.'

He smote himself on the forehead. 'My God! Do the others know, too?'

'I don't think so.' I deliberately avoided mention of Sunil.

In his distraction he started plucking at tufts of grass. 'Did she tell you?' he asked.

'Yes.'

'Girls can't keep secrets. But in a way I'm glad she told you.

Now I don't have to explain everything. You see, I came here for your help. I know you are not her real uncle but you are very close to her family. Last year in Delhi she often spoke about you. She said you were very kind.'

It then occurred to me that Pramod knew nothing about my relationship with you, other than that I was supposed to be the most benevolent of 'uncles'. He knew that you had spent your summer holidays with me—but so had Dinesh and Sunil. And now, aware that I was a close friend of the family, he had come to make an ally of me—in much the same way that I had gone about making allies!

'Have you seen Sushila recently?' I asked.

'Yes. Two days ago, in Delhi. But I had only a few minutes alone with her. We could not talk much. You see, Uncle—you will not mind if I also call you uncle? I want to marry her but there is no one who can speak to her people on my behalf. My own parents are not alive. If I go straight to her family, most probably I will be thrown out of the house. So I want you to help me. I am not well off, but I will soon have a job and then I can support her.

'Did you tell her all this?'

'Yes.'

'And what did she say?'

'She told me to speak to you about it.'

Clever Sushila! Diabolical Sushila!

'To me?' I repeated.

'Yes, she said it would be better than talking to her parents.'

I couldn't help laughing. And a long-tailed blue magpie, disturbed by my laughter, set up a shrill creaking and chattering of its own.

'Don't laugh, I'm serious, Uncle,' said Pramod. He took me by the hand and looked at me appealingly.

'Well, it ought to be serious,' I said. 'How old are you, Pramod?'

'Twenty-three.'

'Only seven years younger than me. So please don't call me uncle. It makes me feel prehistoric. Use my first name, if you like. And when do you hope to marry Sushila?'

'As soon as possible. I know she is still very young for me.'

'Not at all,' I said, 'Young girls are marrying middle-aged men every day! And you're still quite young yourself. But she can't get married as yet, Pramod, I know that for a certainty.'

'That's what I feared. She will have to finish school, I suppose.'

'That's right. But tell me something. It's obvious that you are in love with her and I don't blame you for it. Sushila is the kind of girl we all fall in love with! But do you know if she loves you? Did she say she would like to marry you?'

'She did not say—I do not know....'

There was a haunted, hurt look in his eyes and my heart went out to him. 'But I love her—isn't that enough?'

'It could be enough—provided she doesn't love someone else.'

'Does she, Uncle?'

'To be frank, I don't know.'

He brightened up at that. 'She likes me,' he said. 'I know that much.'

'Well, I like you too, but that doesn't mean I'd marry you.'

He was despondent again. 'I see what you mean.... But what is love, how can I recognize it?'

And that was one question I couldn't answer. How do we recognize it?

I persuaded Pramod to stay the night. The sun had gone down and he was shivering. I made a fire, the first of the winter, using oak and thorn branches. Then I shared my brandy with him.

I did not feel any resentment against Pramod. Prior to meeting him, I had been jealous. And when I first saw him coming along the path, I remembered my dream, and thought,

'Perhaps I am going to kill him, after all. Or perhaps he's going to kill me.' But it had turned out differently. If dreams have any meaning at all, the meaning doesn't come within our limited comprehension.

I had visualized Pramod as being rather crude, selfish, and irresponsible, an unattractive college student, the type who has never known or understood girls very well and looks on them as strange exotic creatures who are to be seized and plundered at the first opportunity. Such men do exist, but Pramod was never one of them. He did not know much about women; neither did I. He was gentle, polite, unsure of himself. I wondered if I should tell him about my own feelings for you.

After a while he began to talk about himself and about you. He told me how he fell in love with you. At first he had been friendly with another girl, a class fellow of yours but a year or two older. You had carried messages to him on the girl's behalf. Then the girl had rejected him. He was terribly depressed and one evening he drank a lot of cheap liquor. Instead of falling dead, as he had been hoping, he lost his way and met you near your home. He was in need of sympathy and you gave him that. You let him hold your hand. He told you how hopeless he felt and you comforted him. And when he said the world was a cruel place, you consented. You agreed with him. What more can a man expect from a woman? Only fourteen at the time, you had no difficulty in comforting a man of twenty-two. No wonder he fell in love with you!

Afterwards you met occasionally on the road and spoke to each other. He visited the house once or twice, on some pretext or other. And when you came to the hills, he wrote to you.

That was all he had to tell me. That was all there was to tell. You had touched his heart once and touching it, had no difficulty in capturing it.

Next morning I took Pramod down to the stream. I wanted to

tell him everything, and somehow I could not do it in the house.

He was charmed by the place. The water flowed gently, its music subdued, soft chamber music after the monsoon orchestration. Cowbells tinkled on the hillside and an eagle soared high above.

'I did not think water could be so clear,' said Pramod. 'It is not muddy like the streams and rivers of the plains.'

'In the summer you can bathe here,' I said. 'There is a pool further downstream.'

He nodded thoughtfully. 'Did she come here too?'

'Yes, Sushila and Sunil and I…. We came here on two or three occasions.' My voice trailed off and I glanced at Pramod standing at the edge of the water. He looked up at me and his eyes met mine.

'There is something I want to tell you,' I said.

He continued staring at me and a shadow seemed to pass across his face—a shadow of doubt, fear, death, eternity, was it one or all of these, or just a play of light and shade? But I remembered my dream and stepped back from him. For a moment both of us looked at each other with distrust and uncertainty. Then the fear passed. Whatever had happened between us, dream or reality, had happened in some other existence. Now he took my hand and held it, held it tight, as though seeking assurance, as though identifying himself with me.

'Let us sit down,' I said. 'There is something I must tell you.'

We sat down on the grass and when I looked up through the branches of the banj oak, everything seemed to have been tilted and held at an angle, and the sky shocked me with its blueness, and the leaves were no longer green but purple in the shadows of the ravine. They were your colour, Sushila. I remembered you wearing purple—dark smiling Sushila, thinking your own thoughts and refusing to share them with anyone.

'I love Sushila too,' I said.

'I know,' he said naively. 'That is why I came to you for help.'

'No, you don't know,' I said. 'When I say I love Sushila, I mean just that. I mean caring for her in the same way that you care for her. I mean I want to marry her.'

'You, Uncle?'

'Yes. Does it shock you very much?'

'No, no.' He turned his face away and stared at the worn face of an old grey rock and perhaps he drew some strength from its permanency. 'Why should you not love her? Perhaps, in my heart, I really knew it, but did not want to know—did not want to believe. Perhaps that is why I really came here—to find out. Something that Sunil said....'

'But why didn't you tell me before?'

'Because you were telling me!'

'Yes, I was too full of my own love to think that any other was possible. What do we do now? Do we both wait and then let her make her choice?'

'If you wish.'

'You have the advantage, Uncle. You have more to offer.'

'Do you mean more security or more love? Some women place more value on the former.'

'Not Sushila.'

'I mean you can offer her a more interesting life. You are a writer. Who knows, you may be famous one day.'

'You have your youth to offer, Pramod. I have only a few years of youth left to me—and two or three of them will pass in waiting.'

'Oh, no,' he said. 'You will always be young. If you have Sushila, you will always be young.'

Once again I heard the whistling thrush. Its song was a crescendo of sweet notes and variations that rang clearly across the ravine. I could not see the bird but its call emerged from the forest like some dark sweet secret and again it was saying, 'It isn't time that's passing by, my friend. It is you and I.'

Listen. Sushila, the worst has happened. Ravi has written to say that a marriage will not be possible—not now, not next year; never. Of course he makes a lot of excuses—that you must receive a complete college education ('higher studies'), that the difference in our age is too great, that you might change your mind after a year or two—but reading between the lines, I can guess that the real reason is your grandmother. She does not want it. Her word is law and no one, least of all Ravi, would dare oppose her. But I do not mean to give in so easily. I will wait my chance. As long as I know that you are with me, I will wait my chance.

I wonder what the old lady objects to in me. Is it simply that she is conservative and tradition-bound? She has always shown a liking for me and I don't see why her liking should change because I want to marry her grandniece. Your mother has no objection.

Perhaps that's why your grandmother objects. Whatever the reason, I am coming down to Delhi to find out how things stand.

Of course the worst part is that Ravi has asked me—in the friendliest terms and in a most roundabout manner—not to come to the house for some time. He says this will give the affair a chance to cool off and die a natural (I would call it an unnatural) death. He assumes, of course, that I will accept the old lady's decision and simply forget all about you. Ravi is yet to fall in love.

Dinesh was in Lucknow. I could not visit the house. So I sat on a bench in the Talkatora Gardens and watched a group of children playing gulli danda. Then I recalled that Sunil's school got over at three o'clock and that if I hurried I would be able to meet him outside the St Columba's gate.

I reached the school on time. Boys were streaming out of the compound and as they were all wearing green uniforms—a young forest on the move—I gave up all hope of spotting Sunil. But he saw me first. He ran across the road, dodged a cyclist, evaded a bus, and seized me about the waist.

'I'm so happy to see you, Uncle!'

'As I am to see you, Sunil.'

'You want to see Sushila?'

'Yes, but you too. I can't come to the house, Sunil. You probably know that. When do you have to be home?'

'About four o'clock. If I'm late, I'll say the bus was too crowded and I couldn't get in.'

'That gives us an hour or two. Let's go to the exhibition grounds. Would you like that?'

'All right, I haven't seen the exhibition yet.'

We took a scooter rickshaw to the exhibition grounds on Mathura Road. It was an industrial exhibition and there was little to interest either a schoolboy or a lovesick author. But a cafe was at hand, overlooking an artificial lake, and we sat in the sun consuming hot dogs and cold coffee.

'Sunil, will you help me?' I asked.

'Whatever you say, Uncle.'

'I don't suppose I can see Sushila this time. I don't want to hang about near the house or her school like a disreputable character. It's all right lurking outside a boys' school; but it wouldn't do to be hanging about the Kanyadevi Pathshala or wherever it is she's studying. It's possible the family will change their minds about us later. Anyway, what matters now is Sushila's attitude. Ask her this, Sunil. Ask her if she wants me to wait until she is eighteen.

She will be free then to do what she wants, even to run away with me if necessary—that is, if she really wants to. I was ready to wait two years. I'm prepared to wait three. But it will help if I know she's waiting too. Will you ask her that, Sunil?'

'Yes, I'll ask her.'

'Ask her tonight. Then tomorrow we'll meet again outside your school.'

We met briefly the next day. There wasn't much time. Sunil had to be home early and I had to catch the night train out of

Delhi. We stood in the generous shade of a peepul tree and I asked,

'What did she say?'

'She said to keep waiting.'

'All right, I'll wait.'

'But when she is eighteen, what if she changes her mind? You know what girls are like.'

'You're a cynical chap, Sunil.'

'What does that mean?'

'It means you know too much about life. But tell me—what makes you think she might change her mind?'

'Her boyfriend.'

'Pramod? She doesn't care for him, poor chap.'

'Not Pramod. Another one.'

'Another! You mean a new one?'

'New,' said Sunil. 'An officer in a bank. He's got a car.'

'Oh,' I said despondently. 'I can't compete with a car.'

'No,' said Sunil. 'Never mind, Uncle. You still have me for your friend. Have you forgotten that?'

I had almost forgotten, but it was good to be reminded.

'It is time to go,' he said. 'I must catch the bus today. When will you come to Delhi again?'

'Next month. Next year. Who knows? But I'll come. Look after yourself, my friend.'

He ran off and jumped on to the footboard of a moving bus. He waved to me until the bus went round the bend in the road.

It was lonely under the peepul tree. It is said that only ghosts live in peepul trees. I do not blame them, for peepul trees are cool and shady and full of loneliness.

I may stop loving you, Sushila, but I will never stop loving the days I loved you.

BREAKFAST AT BAROG

It's well over seventy years that I actually breakfasted at Barog, that little railway station on the Kalka–Simla line; but last night I dreamt of it—dreamt of the station, the dining room, the hillside, and the long dark Barog tunnel—which meant that it had been present in my subconscious all these years and was now striving to come to the fore and revive a few poignant memories.

Should I go there again? The station is still there, and so is the tunnel. I'm told that the area has been built up over the years, so that it is now almost a mini hill station. That wouldn't surprise me. Our villages have become towns, our towns have become cities, and in a few years' time our country will be one vast megacity with a few parks here and there to remind us that this was once a green planet.

I don't remember any dwellings around Barog, just that one little station and its one little restaurant with a cook and a waiter and its one little stationmaster. No, such a small station couldn't have had someone as important as a stationmaster. Someone quite junior must have been in charge.

Never mind. It was the breakfast that was important. And that I was with my father and on my way to Simla and a boarding school. The boarding school was the least desirable part of the journey. It was almost two years since I had been in a school and I was perfectly happy to continue living in an ideal world where schools need not exist. The breakup of my parents' marriage had resulted in my being withdrawn from a convent school in Mussoorie and taken over by my father who was on active service with the RAF. It was 1942 and World War II was at its peak. Against all regulations he kept me with him, but to do this he had to rent a flat in New Delhi. Most of the day, he was at work and I would have the flat to myself, surrounded by books, gramophone records, and stamp albums. Evenings I would help him with his stamp collection, for he was an avid collector. On weekends he would take me to see Delhi's historic monuments; there was no dearth of them. From the stamps I learned geography, from the monuments history, from the books literature. I learnt more in two years at home than I did in a year at school.

But finally he was transferred—first Colombo, then Karachi, then Calcutta—and it was no longer possible for me to share his quarters. I was admitted to Bishop Cotton's in Simla.

We took the railcar from Kalka. It glided over the rails without any of the huffing and puffing of the steam engine that dragged the little narrow gauge train up the steep mountain. I would be travelling in that train in the years to come, but on this, my first to Simla, I was given the luxury of the railcar.

It glided into the Barog station punctually at 10 a.m., in time for breakfast.

The Barog breakfast was already well known and I did full justice to it. I skipped the cornflakes and concentrated on the scrambled eggs and buttered toasts. There was bacon too, and honey and marmalade.

'Tuck in, Ruskin,' said my father, 'school breakfasts won't be half as good.'

He didn't eat much himself. There was a lot on his mind in those days, apart from his work. There was his estranged wife, my mother; my invalid sister, now with his mother in Calcutta; his frequent transfers; his own frequent attacks of malaria; and our future in India, once the War was over—for India's Independence was just around the corner.

'When do we get to Simla?' I asked, quite happy to remain in Barog forever.

'In a little over an hour. But first we go through the longest of all the tunnels on this line. It will take about five minutes. Time for you to make a wish.'

The railcar plunged into the tunnel, and we were enveloped in the darkness of the mountain. I held my father's hand. A couple of soldiers sitting behind us broke into a song from an earlier war.

> *'Pack up your troubles in your old kitbag,*
> *And smile, smile, smile!'*

A glimmer of daylight appeared at the end of the tunnel and then we were out in the sunshine and the pine-scented air.

'Did you make your wish?' asked my father.

I nodded, 'I wished that my mother would come back.'

He was silent for a few moments. 'Do you miss her a lot?'

'I don't miss her,' I said firmly. 'I'm always happy with you. But you miss her all the time. I don't like to see you so sad.'

'I've often asked her to come back,' he said. 'But it's up to her. She wants a different kind of life.'

And that was true. She was still very young—in her late twenties—and she enjoyed parties and dances and a busy social life. My father was in his forties. He liked staying at home, listening to classical music. When he took a holiday, he went in search of rare butterflies. My mother was a butterfly too— pretty, merry, fluttering here and there—but most unwilling to be displayed in a butterfly museum.

I suppose for most of us, big or small, life is just a succession of making mistakes and we spend most of our time trying to rectify them. Marriage was a mistake for both my parents. And I was a product of that mistake!

In the time he had, my father did his best for me. And how proud I was of him when he accompanied me down to my new school! He was wearing his dark blue RAF uniform with its flying officer's stripes, and uniforms, especially officers' uniforms, made a great impression amongst schoolboys in those wartime days. I was received with respect and curiosity. Word went around that my father was a fighter pilot and that he'd shot down dozens of Japanese planes! He was another Biggles, that fictional aviator. Nothing could have been further from reality. My father did not fly at all. He worked for a unit called Codes and Cyphers, helping to create new codes or breaking down enemy codes. It was important work and secret work, but there was no glamour about it.

Not that I was averse to the glamour of being Biggles Junior. In my previous school I'd been something of an outsider and the Irish nuns hadn't cared much for a quiet, sensitive boy. Here I was made to feel I belonged and in no time at all I made a number of friends. It was already halfway through the school year, but I had no difficulty in catching up with my classmates.

This was 'prep' school—junior school—and certainly more fun than senior school, still a couple of years away, would ever be…. Still, I was always looking forward to the winter break, when I would be with my father again, for at least three months. And there he was, waiting at the Old Delhi railway station, as my train drew alongside the platform. He was still in Delhi, at Air Headquarters, and I made the most of my time with him. Connaught Place was close by, and two or three evenings every week, we would go to the cinema. There were four to choose from—the Regal, the Rivoli, the Odeon, and the Plaza, all very new and smart and showing the latest films from Hollywood. I became a regular film buff. The bookshops were there too, and the record shops, and Wenger's with its confectionery and the Milk Bar with its milkshakes and Kwality with its ice creams. It was hard to believe that there was a world war going on in Europe and Asia and North Africa and the Pacific; or that the Quit India Movement was at its height and that my father and

I might have to leave the country in the near future. He spoke about it sometimes and of the possibility of my going to a school in England. We did not talk about my mother, but I noticed that he still kept a photograph of her in his desk drawer.

It was back to school in March, when the rhododendrons were in bloom. This time I went up with the school party, in the small train with its steam engine chugging slowly up the steep inclines. The journey took all day. We did stop briefly at Barog, but we were not allowed to get down from the train; one or two boys were certain to be left behind. I looked longingly at the little restaurant on the far side of the platform; but it was already teatime. Breakfast was for the railcar!

The school year rolled on. My father was transferred to Karachi and then to Calcutta. He had grown up in Calcutta and knew the city well. He wrote to me every week and in his last letter he told me what I could look forward to during the winter holidays—the New Market with its bookshops, the botanical gardens with its ancient banyan tree, the zoo, the riverfront, the great maidan where hundreds of people would be taking in the evening air.... I was hoping he would come up to see me during the autumn break, but instead I had news of another kind.

It must be difficult for a young schoolmaster, as yet untouched by tragedy, to tell a ten-year-old that he has just lost his father. Mr Murtough was given this onerous duty. And he did his best, mumbling something ridiculous about God needing my father more than I did and so on and so on....

My friends were more natural in expressing this sympathy—giving me their sweets or chocolates, offering to play games with me, talking to me in the middle of the night when they discovered I wasn't asleep.... For the future did look bleak. I wasn't sure where I would be going next—my Calcutta granny or my Dehra granny, or my mother and stepfather.... I did receive a letter from my mother, telling me that my father had died of the malaria that had plagued him for years; but it was an unemotional letter and it did little to bring me comfort.

But I did go to her when school closed for the winter and I was to spend the next few years in my stepfather's home. But that's another story.

I continued my school in Simla, and every year in March, the small train would take me and my schoolmates up the mountain, through numerous tunnels and winding gradients, forests of pine and deodar, and we always stopped at Barog, before the biggest tunnel of all. But I never made another wish when passing through that tunnel.

That was over seventy years ago.

Is the railcar still running on that line? And do they still serve breakfast at Barog?

They say you should see Venice before you die. Or better still, Varanasi. But I'll settle for that little station among the pines. And if my father is standing on the platform, waiting for me, ready to take me by the hand, I'll be a small boy again and that railcar will take us to a different destination altogether.

THE BLUE UMBRELLA

'Neelu! Neelu!' cried Binya.

She scrambled barefoot over the rocks, ran over the short summer grass, up and over the brow of the hill, all the time calling 'Neelu, Neelu!' Neelu—Blue—was the name of the blue-grey cow. The other cow, which was white, was called Gori, meaning Fair One. They were fond of wandering off on their own, down to the stream or into the pine forest, and sometimes they came back by themselves and sometimes they stayed away—almost deliberately, it seemed to Binya.

If the cows didn't come home at the right time, Binya would be sent to fetch them. Sometimes her brother, Bijju, went with her, but these days he was busy preparing for his exams and didn't have time to help with the cows.

Binya liked being on her own, and sometimes she allowed the cows to lead her into some distant valley, and then they would all be late coming home. The cows preferred having Binya with them, because she let them wander. Bijju pulled them by their tails if they went too far.

Binya belonged to the mountains, to this part of the Himalayas known as Garhwal. Dark forests and lonely hilltops held no terrors for her. It was only when she was in the market town, jostled by the crowds in the bazaar, that she felt rather nervous and lost. The town, five miles from the village, was also a pleasure resort for tourists from all over India.

Binya was probably ten. She may have been nine or even eleven, she couldn't be sure because no one in the village kept birthdays; but her mother told her she'd been born during a winter when the snow had come up to the windows, and that was just over ten years ago, wasn't it? Two years later, her father had died, but his passing had made no difference to their way of life. They had three tiny terraced fields on the side of the mountain, and they grew potatoes, onions, ginger, beans, mustard, and maize: not enough to sell in the town, but enough to live on.

Like most mountain girls, Binya was quite sturdy, fair of skin, with pink cheeks and dark eyes, and her black hair tied in a pigtail. She wore pretty glass bangles on her wrists and a necklace of glass beads. From the necklace hung a leopard's claw. It was a lucky charm, and Binya always wore it. Bijju had one, too, only his was attached to a string.

Binya's full name was Binyadevi, and Bijju's real name was Vijay, but everyone called them Binya and Bijju. Binya was two years younger than her brother.

She had stopped calling for Neelu; she had heard the cowbells tinkling, and knew the cows hadn't gone far. Singing to herself, she walked over fallen pine needles into the forest glade on the spur of the hill. She heard voices, laughter, the clatter of plates and cups, and stepping through the trees, she came upon a party of picnickers.

They were holidaymakers from the plains. The women were dressed in bright saris, the men wore light summer shirts, and the children had pretty new clothes. Binya, standing in the shadows between the trees, went unnoticed; for some time she watched the picnickers, admiring their clothes, listening to their unfamiliar accents, and gazing rather hungrily at the sight of all their food. And then her gaze came to rest on a bright blue umbrella, a frilly thing for women, which lay open on the grass beside its owner.

Now Binya had seen umbrellas before, and her mother had a big black umbrella which nobody used anymore because the field rats had eaten holes in it, but this was the first time Binya had seen such a small, dainty, colourful umbrella and she fell in love with it. The umbrella was like a flower, a great blue flower that had sprung up on the dry brown hillside.

She moved forward a few paces so that she could see the umbrella better. As she came out of the shadows into the sunlight, the picnickers saw her.

'Hello, look who's here!' exclaimed the older of the two women. 'A little village girl!'

'Isn't she pretty?' remarked the other. 'But how torn and dirty her clothes are!' It did not seem to bother them that Binya could hear and understand everything they said about her.

'They're very poor in the hills,' said one of the men.

'Then let's give her something to eat.' And the older woman beckoned to Binya to come closer.

Hesitantly, nervously, Binya approached the group.

Normally she would have turned and fled, but the attraction was the pretty blue umbrella. It had cast a spell over her, drawing her forward almost against her will.

'What's that on her neck?' asked the younger woman.

'A necklace of sorts.'

'It's a pendant—see, there's a claw hanging from it!'

'It's a tiger's claw,' said the man beside her. (He had never seen a tiger's claw.) 'A lucky charm. These people wear them to keep away evil spirits.' He looked to Binya for confirmation, but Binya said nothing.

'Oh, I want one too!' said the woman, who was obviously his wife.

'You can't get them in shops.'

'Buy hers, then. Give her two or three rupees, she's sure to need the money.'

The man, looking slightly embarrassed, but anxious to please his young wife, produced a two-rupee note and offered it to Binya, indicating that he wanted the pendant in exchange. Binya put her hand to the necklace, half afraid that the excited woman would snatch it away from her. Solemnly she shook her head.

The man then showed her a five-rupee note, but again Binya shook her head.

'How silly she is!' exclaimed the young woman.

'It may not be hers to sell,' said the man. 'But I'll try again. How much do you want—what can we give you?' And he waved his hand towards the picnic things scattered about on the grass.

Without any hesitation Binya pointed to the umbrella.

'My umbrella!' exclaimed the young woman. 'She wants my umbrella. What cheek!'

'Well, you want her pendant, don't you?'

'That's different.'

'Is it?'

The man and his wife were beginning to quarrel with each other.

'I'll ask her to go away,' said the older woman.

'We're making such fools of ourselves.'

'But I want the pendant!' cried the other, petulantly.

And then, on an impulse, she picked up the umbrella and held it out to Binya.

'Here, take the umbrella!'

Binya removed her necklace and held it out to the young woman, who immediately placed it around her own neck. Then Binya took the umbrella and held it up. It did not look so small in her hands; in fact, it was just the right size.

She had forgotten about the picnickers, who were busy examining the pendant. She turned the blue umbrella this way and that, looked through the bright blue silk at the pulsating sun, and then, still keeping it open, turned and disappeared into the forest glade.

II

Binya seldom closed the blue umbrella. Even when she had it in the house, she left it lying open in a corner of the room. Sometimes Bijju snapped it shut, complaining that it got in the way. She would open it again a little later. It wasn't beautiful when it was closed.

Whenever Binya went out—whether it was to graze the cows, or fetch water from the spring, or carry milk to the little tea shop on the Tehri road—she took the umbrella with her. That patch of sky-blue silk could always be seen on the hillside.

Old Ram Bharosa (Ram the Trustworthy) kept the tea shop on the Tehri road. It was a dusty, un-metalled road. Once a day, the Tehri bus stopped near his shop and passengers got down to sip hot tea or drink a glass of curd. He kept a few bottles of Coca-Cola too, but as there was no ice, the bottles got hot in the sun and so were seldom opened. He also kept sweets and toffees, and when Binya or Bijju had a few coins to spare, they would spend them at the shop. It was only a mile from the village.

Ram Bharosa was astonished to see Binya's blue umbrella.

'What have you there, Binya?' he asked.

Binya gave the umbrella a twirl and smiled at Ram Bharosa. She was always ready with her smile, and would willingly have lent it to anyone who was feeling unhappy.

'That's a lady's umbrella,' said Ram Bharosa. 'That's only for memsahibs. Where did you get it?'

'Someone gave it to me—for my necklace.'

'You exchanged it for your lucky claw!'

Binya nodded.

'But what do you need it for? The sun isn't hot enough, and it isn't meant for the rain. It's just a pretty thing for rich ladies to play with!'

Binya nodded and smiled again. Ram Bharosa was quite

right; it was just a beautiful plaything. And that was exactly why she had fallen in love with it.

'I have an idea,' said the shopkeeper. 'It's no use to you, that umbrella. Why not sell it to me? I'll give you five rupees for it.'

'It's worth fifteen,' said Binya.

'Well, then, I'll give you ten.'

Binya laughed and shook her head.

'Twelve rupees?' said Ram Bharosa, but without much hope.

Binya placed a five-paise coin on the counter.

'I came for a toffee,' she said.

Ram Bharosa pulled at his drooping whiskers, gave Binya a wry look, and placed a toffee in the palm of her hand. He watched Binya as she walked away along the dusty road. The blue umbrella held him fascinated, and he stared after it until it was out of sight.

The villagers used this road to go to the market town. Some used the bus, a few rode on mules, and most people walked. Today, everyone on the road turned their heads to stare at the girl with the bright blue umbrella.

Binya sat down in the shade of a pine tree. The umbrella, still open, lay beside her. She cradled her head in her arms, and presently she dozed off. It was that kind of day, sleepily warm and summery.

And while she slept, a wind sprang up.

It came quietly, swishing gently through the trees, humming softly. Then it was joined by other random gusts, bustling over the tops of the mountains. The trees shook their heads and came to life. The wind fanned Binya's cheeks. The umbrella stirred on the grass.

The wind grew stronger, picking up dead leaves and sending them spinning and swirling through the air. It got into the umbrella and began to drag it over the grass. Suddenly it lifted the umbrella and carried it about six feet from the sleeping girl. The sound woke Binya.

She was on her feet immediately, and then she was leaping down the steep slope. But just as she was within reach of the umbrella, the wind picked it up again and carried it further downhill.

Binya set off in pursuit. The wind was in a wicked, playful mood. It would leave the umbrella alone for a few moments but as soon as Binya came near, it would pick up the umbrella again and send it bouncing, floating, dancing away from her.

The hill grew steeper. Binya knew that after twenty yards it would fall away in a precipice. She ran faster. And the wind ran with her, ahead of her, and the blue umbrella stayed up with the wind.

A fresh gust picked it up and carried it to the very edge of the cliff. There it balanced for a few seconds, before toppling over, out of sight.

Binya ran to the edge of the cliff. Going down on her hands and knees, she peered down the cliff face. About a hundred feet below, a small stream rushed between great boulders. Hardly anything grew on the cliff face—just a few stunted bushes, and, halfway down, a wild cherry tree growing crookedly out of the rocks and hanging across the chasm. The umbrella had stuck in the cherry tree.

Binya didn't hesitate. She may have been timid with strangers, but she was at home on a hillside. She stuck her bare leg over the edge of the cliff and began climbing down. She kept her face to the hillside, feeling her way with her feet, only changing her handhold when she knew her feet were secure. Sometimes she held on to the thorny bilberry bushes, but she did not trust the other plants, which came away very easily.

Loose stones rattled down the cliff. Once on their way, the stones did not stop until they reached the bottom of the hill; and they took other stones with them, so that there was soon a cascade of stones, and Binya had to be very careful not to start a landslide.

As agile as a mountain goat, she did not take more than five minutes to reach the crooked cherry tree. But the most difficult task remained—she had to crawl along the trunk of the tree, which stood out at right angles from the cliff. Only by doing this could she reach the trapped umbrella.

Binya felt no fear when climbing trees. She was proud of the fact that she could climb them as well as Bijju. Gripping the rough cherry bark with her toes, and using her knees as leverage, she crawled along the trunk of the projecting tree until she was almost within reach of the umbrella. She noticed with dismay that the blue cloth was torn in a couple of places.

She looked down, and it was only then that she felt afraid. She was right over the chasm, balanced precariously about eighty feet above the boulder-strewn stream. Looking down, she felt quite dizzy. Her hands shook, and the tree shook too. If she slipped now, there was only one direction in which she could fall—down, down, into the depths of that dark and shadowy ravine.

There was only one thing to do; concentrate on the patch of blue just a couple of feet away from her. She did not look down or up, but straight ahead, and willing herself forward, she managed to reach the umbrella.

She could not crawl back with it in her hands. So, after dislodging it from the forked branch in which it had stuck, she let it fall, still open, into the ravine below.

Cushioned by the wind, the umbrella floated serenely downwards, landing in a thicket of nettles.

Binya crawled back along the trunk of the cherry tree. Twenty minutes later, she emerged from the nettle clump, her precious umbrella held aloft. She had nettle stings all over her legs, but she was hardly aware of the smarting. She was as immune to nettles as Bijju was to bees.

III

About four years previously, Bijju had knocked a hive out of an oak tree, and had been badly stung on the face and legs. It had been a painful experience. But now, if a bee stung him, he felt nothing at all: he had been immunized for life!

He was on his way home from school. It was two o'clock and he hadn't eaten since six in the morning. Fortunately, the kingora bushes—the bilberries—were in fruit, and already Bijju's lips were stained purple with the juice of the wild, sour fruit.

He didn't have any money to spend at Ram Bharosa's shop, but he stopped there anyway to look at the sweets in their glass jars.

'And what will you have today?' asked Ram Bharosa.

'No money,' said Bijju.

'You can pay me later.'

Bijju shook his head. Some of his friends had taken sweets on credit, and at the end of the month they had found they'd eaten more sweets than they could possibly pay for! As a result, they'd had to hand over to Ram Bharosa some of their most treasured possessions—such as a curved knife for cutting grass, or a small hand-axe, or a jar for pickles, or a pair of earrings—and these had become the shopkeeper's possessions and were kept by him or sold in his shop.

Ram Bharosa had set his heart on having Binya's blue umbrella, and so naturally he was anxious to give credit to either of the children, but so far neither had fallen into the trap.

Bijju moved on, his mouth full of Kingora berries. Halfway home, he saw Binya with the cows. It was late evening, and the sun had gone down, but Binya still had the umbrella open. The two small rents had been stitched up by her mother.

Bijju gave his sister a handful of berries. She handed him the umbrella while she ate the berries.

'You can have the umbrella until we get home,' she said. It was her way of rewarding Bijju for bringing her the wild fruit.

Calling 'Neelu! Gori!' Binya and Bijju set out for home, followed at some distance by the cows.

It was dark before they reached the village, but Bijju still had the umbrella open.

⌣

Most of the people in the village were a little envious of Binya's blue umbrella. No one else had ever possessed one like it. The schoolmaster's wife thought it was quite wrong for a poor cultivator's daughter to have such a fine umbrella while she, a second-class BA, had to make do with an ordinary black one. Her husband offered to have their old umbrella dyed blue; she gave him a scornful look, and loved him a little less than before. The pujari, who looked after the temple, announced that he would buy a multi-coloured umbrella the next time he was in the town. A few days later he returned looking annoyed and grumbling that they weren't available except in Delhi. Most people consoled themselves by saying that Binya's pretty umbrella wouldn't keep out the rain, if it rained heavily; that it would shrivel in the sun, if the sun was fierce; that it would collapse in a wind, if the wind was strong; that it would attract lightning, if lightning fell near it; and that it would prove unlucky, if there was any ill luck going about. Secretly, everyone admired it.

Unlike the adults, the children didn't have to pretend. They were full of praise for the umbrella. It was so light, so pretty, so bright a blue! And it was just the right size for Binya. They knew that if they said nice things about the umbrella, Binya would smile and give it to them to hold for a little while—just a very little while!

Soon it was the time of the monsoon. Big black clouds kept piling up, and thunder rolled over the hills.

Binya sat on the hillside all afternoon, waiting for the rain. As soon as the first big drop of rain came down, she raised the umbrella over her head. More drops, big ones, came pattering down. She could see them through the umbrella silk, as they broke against the cloth.

And then there was a cloudburst, and it was like standing under a waterfall. The umbrella wasn't really a rain umbrella, but it held up bravely. Only Binya's feet got wet. Rods of rain fell around her in a curtain of shivered glass.

Everywhere on the hillside people were scurrying for shelter. Some made for a charcoal burner's hut, others for a mule shed, or Ram Bharosa's shop. Binya was the only one who didn't run. This was what she'd been waiting for—rain on her umbrella—and she wasn't in a hurry to go home. She didn't mind getting her feet wet. The cows didn't mind getting wet either.

Presently she found Bijju sheltering in a cave. He would have enjoyed getting wet, but he had his schoolbooks with him and he couldn't afford to let them get spoilt. When he saw Binya, he came out of the cave and shared the umbrella. He was a head taller than his sister, so he had to hold the umbrella for her, while she held his books.

The cows had been left far behind.

'Neelu, Neelu!' called Binya.

'Gori!' called Bijju.

When their mother saw them sauntering home through the driving rain, she called out: 'Binya! Bijju! Hurry up, and bring the cows in! What are you doing out there in the rain?'

'Just testing the umbrella,' said Bijju.

IV

The rains set in, and the sun only made brief appearances. The hills turned a lush green. Ferns sprang up on walls and tree trunks. Giant lilies reared up like leopards from the tall grass. A white mist coiled and uncoiled as it floated up from the valley. It was a beautiful season, except for the leeches.

Every day, Binya came home with a couple of leeches fastened to the flesh of her bare legs. They fell off by themselves just as soon as they'd had their thimbleful of blood, but you didn't know they were on you until they fell off, and then, later, the skin became very sore and itchy. Some of the older people still believed that to be bled by leeches was a remedy for various ailments. Whenever Ram Bharosa had a headache, he applied a leech to his throbbing temple.

Three days of incessant rain had flooded out a number of small animals who lived in holes in the ground. Binya's mother suddenly found the roof full of field rats. She had to drive them out; they ate too much of her stored-up wheat flour and rice. Bijju liked lifting up large rocks to disturb the scorpions who were sleeping beneath. And snakes came out to bask in the sun.

Binya had just crossed the small stream at the bottom of the hill when she saw something gliding out of the bushes and coming towards her. It was a long black snake. A clatter of loose stones frightened it. Seeing the girl in its way, it rose up, hissing, prepared to strike. The forked tongue darted out, the venomous head lunged at Binya.

Binya's umbrella was open as usual. She thrust it forward, between herself and the snake, and the snake's hard snout thud twice against the strong silk of the umbrella. The reptile then turned and slithered away over the wet rocks, disappearing into a clump of ferns.

Binya forgot about the cows and ran all the way home to tell her mother how she had been saved by the umbrella. Bijju had to put away his books and go out to fetch the cows. He carried a stout stick, in case he met with any snakes.

First the summer sun, and now the endless rain, meant that the umbrella was beginning to fade a little. From a bright blue it had changed to a light blue. But it was still a pretty thing, and tougher than it looked, and Ram Bharosa still desired it. He did not want to sell it; he wanted to own it. He was probably the richest man in the area—so why shouldn't he have a blue umbrella? Not a day passed without his getting a glimpse of Binya and the umbrella; and the more he saw the umbrella, the more he wanted it.

The schools closed during the monsoon, but this didn't mean that Bijju could sit at home doing nothing. Neelu and Gori were providing more milk than was required at home, so Binya's mother was able to sell a kilo of milk every day: half a kilo to the schoolmaster, and half a kilo (at a reduced rate) to the temple pujari. Bijju had to deliver the milk every morning.

Ram Bharosa had asked Bijju to work in his shop during the holidays, but Bijju didn't have time—he had to help his mother with the ploughing and the transplanting of the rice seedlings. So Ram Bharosa employed a boy from the next village, a boy called Rajaram. He did all the washing-up, and ran various errands. He went to the same school as Bijju, but the two boys were not friends.

One day, as Binya passed the shop, twirling her blue umbrella, Rajaram noticed that his employer gave a deep sigh and began muttering to himself.

'What's the matter, Babuji?' asked the boy.

'Oh, nothing,' said Ram Bharosa. 'It's just a sickness that has come upon me. And it's all due to that girl Binya and her wretched umbrella.'

'Why, what has she done to you?'

'Refused to sell me her umbrella! There's pride for you. And I offered her ten rupees.'

'Perhaps, if you gave her twelve....'

'But it isn't new any longer. It isn't worth eight rupees now. All the same, I'd like to have it.'

'You wouldn't make a profit on it,' said Rajaram.

'It's not the profit I'm after, wretch! It's the thing itself. It's the beauty of it!'

'And what would you do with it, Babuji? You don't visit anyone—you're seldom out of your shop. Of what use would it be to you?'

'Of what use is a poppy in a cornfield? Of what use is a rainbow? Of what use are you, numbskull? Wretch! I, too, have a soul. I want the umbrella, because—because I want its beauty to be mine!'

Rajaram put the kettle on to boil, began dusting the counter, all the time muttering: 'I'm as useful as an umbrella,' and then, after a short period of intense thought, said: 'What will you give me, Babuji, if I get the umbrella for you?'

'What do you mean?' asked the old man.

'You know what I mean. What will you give me?'

'You mean to steal it, don't you, you wretch? What a delightful child you are! I'm glad you're not my son or my enemy. But look, everyone will know it has been stolen, and then how will I be able to show off with it?'

'You will have to gaze upon it in secret,' said Rajaram with a chuckle. 'Or take it into Tehri, and have it coloured red! That's your problem. But tell me, Babuji, do you want it badly enough to pay me three rupees for stealing it without being seen?'

Ram Bharosa gave the boy a long, sad look. 'You're a sharp boy,' he said. 'You'll come to a bad end. I'll give you two rupees.'

'Three,' said the boy.

'Two,' said the old man.

'You don't really want it, I can see that,' said the boy.

'Wretch!' said the old man. 'Evil one! Darkener of my doorstep! Fetch me the umbrella, and I'll give you three rupees.'

V

Binya was in the forest glade where she had first seen the umbrella. No one came there for picnics during the monsoon. The grass was always wet and the pine needles were slippery underfoot. The tall trees shut out the light, and poisonous-looking mushrooms, orange and purple, sprang up everywhere. But it was a good place for porcupines, who seemed to like the mushrooms, and Binya was searching for porcupine quills.

The hill people didn't think much of porcupine quills, but far away in southern India, the quills were valued as charms and sold at a rupee each. So Ram Bharosa paid a tenth of a rupee for each quill brought to him, and he in turn sold the quills at a profit to a trader from the plains.

Binya had already found five quills, and she knew there'd be more in the long grass. For once, she'd put her umbrella down. She had to put it aside if she was to search the ground thoroughly.

It was Rajaram's chance.

He'd been following Binya for some time, concealing himself behind trees and rocks, creeping closer whenever she became absorbed in her search. He was anxious that she should not see him and be able to recognize him later.

He waited until Binya had wandered some distance from the umbrella. Then, running forward at a crouch, he seized the open umbrella and dashed off with it.

But Rajaram had very big feet. Binya heard his heavy footsteps and turned just in time to see him as he disappeared between the trees. She cried out, dropped the porcupine quills, and gave chase.

Binya was swift and sure-footed, but Rajaram had a long stride. All the same, he made the mistake of running downhill. A long-legged person is much faster going uphill than down. Binya reached the edge of the forest glade in time to see the thief scrambling down the path to the stream. He had closed the umbrella so that it would not hinder his flight.

Binya was beginning to gain on the boy. He kept to the path, while she simply slid and leapt down the steep hillside. Near the bottom of the hill the path began to straighten out, and it was here that the long-legged boy began to forge ahead again.

Bijju was coming home from another direction. He had a bundle of sticks which he'd collected for the kitchen fire. As he reached the path, he saw Binya rushing down the hill as though all the mountain spirits in Garhwal were after her.

'What's wrong?' he called. 'Why are you running?'

Binya paused only to point at the fleeing Rajaram.

'My umbrella!' she cried. 'He has stolen it!'

Bijju dropped his bundle of sticks, and ran after his sister. When he reached her side, he said, 'I'll soon catch him!' and went sprinting away over the lush green grass. He was fresh, and he was soon well ahead of Binya and gaining on the thief.

Rajaram was crossing the shallow stream when Bijju caught up with him. Rajaram was the taller boy, but Bijju was much stronger. He flung himself at the thief, caught him by the legs, and brought him down in the water. Rajaram got to his feet and tried to drag himself away, but Bijju still had him by a leg. Rajaram overbalanced and came down with a great splash. He had let the umbrella fall. It began to float away on the current. Just then Binya arrived, flushed and breathless, and went dashing into the stream after the umbrella.

Meanwhile, a tremendous fight was taking place. Locked in fierce combat, the two boys swayed together on a rock, tumbled on to the sand, rolled over and over the pebbled bank until they were again thrashing about in the shallows of the stream. The magpies, bulbuls, and other birds were disturbed, and flew away with cries of alarm.

Covered with mud, gasping and spluttering, the boys groped for each other in the water. After five minutes of frenzied struggle, Bijju emerged victorious.

Rajaram lay flat on his back on the sand, exhausted, while Bijju sat astride him, pinning him down with his arms and legs.

'Let me get up!' gasped Rajaram. 'Let me go—I don't want your useless umbrella!'

'Then why did you take it?' demanded Bijju. 'Come on—tell me why!'

'It was that skinflint Ram Bharosa,' said Rajaram.

'He told me to get it for him. He said if I didn't fetch it, I'd lose my job.'

VI

By early October, the rains were coming to an end. The leeches disappeared. The ferns turned yellow, and the sunlight on the green hills was mellow and golden, like the limes on the small tree in front of Binya's home. Bijju's days were happy ones as he came home from school, munching on roasted corn. Binya's umbrella had turned a pale milky blue, and was patched in several places, but it was still the prettiest umbrella in the village, and she still carried it with her wherever she went.

The cold, cruel winter wasn't far off, but somehow October seems longer than other months, because it is a kind month: the grass is good to be upon, the breeze is warm and gentle and pine-scented. That October, everyone seemed contented—everyone, that is, except Ram Bharosa.

The old man had by now given up all hope of ever possessing Binya's umbrella. He wished he had never set eyes on it. Because of the umbrella, he had suffered the tortures of greed, the despair of loneliness. Because of the umbrella, people had stopped coming to his shop!

Ever since it had become known that Ram Bharosa had tried to have the umbrella stolen, the village people had turned against him. They stopped trusting the old man, instead of buying their soap and tea and matches from his shop, they preferred to walk an extra mile to the shops near the Tehri bus stand. Who would have dealings with a man who had sold his soul for an umbrella? The children taunted him, twisted his name around. From 'Ram the Trustworthy' he became 'Trusty Umbrella Thief'.

The old man sat alone in his empty shop, listening to the eternal hissing of his kettle and wondering if anyone would ever again step in for a glass of tea. Ram Bharosa had lost his own appetite, and ate and drank very little. There was no money coming in. He had his savings in a bank in Tehri, but it was a terrible thing to have to dip into them! To save money, he had dismissed the blundering Rajaram. So he was left without any company. The roof leaked and the wind got in through the corrugated tin sheets, but Ram Bharosa didn't care.

Bijju and Binya passed his shop almost every day. Bijju went by with a loud but tuneless whistle. He was one of the world's whistlers; cares rested lightly on his shoulders. But, strangely enough, Binya crept quietly past the shop, looking the other way, almost as though she was in some way responsible for the misery of Ram Bharosa.

She kept reasoning with herself, telling herself that the umbrella was her very own, and that she couldn't help it if others were jealous of it. But had she loved the umbrella too much? Had it mattered more to her than people mattered? She couldn't help feeling that, in a small way, she was the cause of the sad look on Ram Bharosa's face ('His face is a yard long,' said Bijju) and the ruinous condition of his shop. It was all due to his own greed, no doubt, but she didn't want him to feel too bad about what he'd done, because it made her feel bad about herself; and so she closed the umbrella whenever she came near the shop, opening it again only when she was out of sight.

One day towards the end of October, when she had ten paise in her pocket, she entered the shop and asked the old man for a toffee.

She was Ram Bharosa's first customer in almost two weeks. He looked suspiciously at the girl. Had she come to taunt him, to flaunt the umbrella in his face? She had placed her coin on the counter. Perhaps it was a bad coin. Ram Bharosa picked it up and bit it; he held it up to the light; he rang it on the ground. It was a good coin. He gave Binya the toffee.

Binya had already left the shop when Ram Bharosa saw the closed umbrella lying on his counter. There it was, the blue umbrella he had always wanted, within his grasp at last! He had only to hide it at the back of his shop, and no one would know that he had it, no one could prove that Binya had left it behind.

He stretched out his trembling, bony hand, and took the umbrella by the handle. He pressed it open. He stood beneath it, in the dark shadows of his shop, where no sun or rain could ever touch it.

'But I'm never in the sun or in the rain,' he said aloud. 'Of what use is an umbrella to me?'

And he hurried outside and ran after Binya.

'Binya, Binya!' he shouted. 'Binya, you've left your umbrella behind!'

He wasn't used to running, but he caught up with her, held out the umbrella, saying, 'You forgot it—the umbrella!'

In that moment it belonged to both of them.

But Binya didn't take the umbrella. She shook her head and said, 'You keep it. I don't need it anymore.'

'But it's such a pretty umbrella!' protested Ram Bharosa. 'It's the best umbrella in the village.'

'I know,' said Binya. 'But an umbrella isn't everything.'

And she left the old man holding the umbrella, and went tripping down the road, and there was nothing between her and the bright blue sky.

VII

Well, now that Ram Bharosa has the blue umbrella—a gift from Binya, as he tells everyone—he is sometimes persuaded to go out into the sun or the rain, and as a result he looks much healthier. Sometimes he uses the umbrella to chase away pigs or goats. It is always left open outside the shop, and anyone who wants to borrow it may do so; and so in a way it has become everyone's umbrella. It is faded and patchy, but it is still the best umbrella in the village.

People are visiting Ram Bharosa's shop again. Whenever Bijju or Binya stop for a cup of tea, he gives them a little extra milk or sugar. They like their tea sweet and milky.

A few nights ago, a bear visited Ram Bharosa's shop. There had been snow on the higher ranges of the Himalayas, and the bear had been finding it difficult to obtain food; so it had come lower down, to see what it could pick up near the village. That night it scrambled on to the tin roof of Ram Bharosa's shop, and made off with a huge pumpkin which had been ripening on the roof. But in climbing off the roof, the bear had lost a claw.

Next morning Ram Bharosa found the claw just outside the door of his shop. He picked it up and put it in his pocket. A bear's claw was a lucky find.

A day later, when he went into the market town, he took the claw with him, and left it with a silversmith, giving the craftsman certain instructions. The silversmith made a locket for the claw, then he gave it a thin silver chain. When Ram Bharosa came again, he paid the silversmith ten rupees for his work.

The days were growing shorter, and Binya had to be home a little earlier every evening. There was a hungry leopard at large, and she couldn't leave the cows out after dark.

She was hurrying past Ram Bharosa's shop when the old man called out to her.

'Binya, spare a minute! I want to show you something.'

Binya stepped into the shop.

'What do you think of it?' asked Ram Bharosa, showing her the silver pendant with the claw.

'It's so beautiful,' said Binya, just touching the claw and the silver chain.

'It's a bear's claw,' said Ram Bharosa. 'That's even luckier than a leopard's claw. Would you like to have it?'

'I have no money,' said Binya.

'That doesn't matter. You gave me the umbrella, I give you the claw! Come, let's see what it looks like on you.'

He placed the pendant on Binya, and indeed it looked very beautiful on her.

Ram Bharosa says he will never forget the smile she gave him when she left the shop.

She was halfway home when she realized she had left the cows behind.

'Neelu, Neelu!' she called. 'Oh, Gori!'

There was a faint tinkle of bells as the cows came slowly down the mountain path.

In the distance she could hear her mother and Bijju calling for her.

She began to sing. They heard her singing, and knew she was safe and near.

She walked home through the darkening glade, singing of the stars, and the trees stood still and listened to her, and the mountains were glad.

ANGRY RIVER

In the middle of the big river, the river that began in the mountains and ended in the sea, was a small island. The river swept round the island, sometimes clawing at its banks, but never going right over it. It was over twenty years since the river had flooded the island, and at that time no one had lived there. But for the last ten years a small hut had stood there, a mud-walled hut with a sloping thatched roof. The hut had been built into a huge rock, so only three of the walls were mud, and the fourth was rock.

Goats grazed on the short grass which grew on the island, and on the prickly leaves of thorn bushes. A few hens followed them about. There was a melon patch and a vegetable patch. In the middle of the island stood a peepul tree. It was the only tree there. Even during the Great Flood, when the island had been under water, the tree had stood firm.

It was an old tree. A seed had been carried to the island by a strong wind some fifty years back, had found shelter between two rocks, had taken root there, and had sprung up to give shade and shelter to a small family; and Indians love peepul trees, especially during the hot summer months when the heart-shaped leaves catch the least breath of air and flutter eagerly, fanning those who sit beneath.

A sacred tree, the peepul: the abode of spirits, good and bad.

'Don't yawn when you are sitting beneath the tree,' Grandmother used to warn Sita.

'And if you must yawn, always snap your fingers in front of your mouth. If you forget to do that, a spirit might jump down your throat!'

'And then what will happen?' asked Sita.

'It will probably ruin your digestion,' said Grandfather, who wasn't much of a believer in spirits.

The peepul had a beautiful leaf, and Grandmother likened it to the body of the mighty god Krishna—broad at the shoulders, then tapering down to a very slim waist.

It was an old tree, and an old man sat beneath it. He was mending a fishing net. He had fished in the river for ten years, and he was a good fisherman. He knew where to find the slim silver chilwa fish and the big beautiful mahseer and the long-moustached singhara; he knew where the river was deep and where it was shallow; he knew which baits to use—which fish liked worms and which liked gram. He had taught his son to fish, but his son had gone to work in a factory in a city, nearly a hundred miles away. He had no grandson; but he had a granddaughter, Sita, and she could do all the things a boy could do, and sometimes she could do them better. She had lost her mother when she was very small. Grandmother had taught her all the things a girl should know, and she could do these as well as most girls. But neither of her grandparents could read or write, and as a result Sita couldn't read or write either.

There was a school in one of the villages across the river, but Sita had never seen it. There was too much to do on the island.

While Grandfather mended his net, Sita was inside the hut, pressing her Grandmother's forehead, which was hot with fever. Grandmother had been ill for three days and could not eat. She had been ill before, but she had never been so bad. Grandfather had brought her some sweet oranges from the market in the nearest town, and she could suck the juice from the oranges, but she couldn't eat anything else.

She was younger than Grandfather, but because she was sick, she looked much older. She had never been very strong.

When Sita noticed that Grandmother had fallen asleep, she

tiptoed out of the room on her bare feet and stood outside.

The sky was dark with monsoon clouds. It had rained all night, and in a few hours it would rain again. The monsoon rains had come early, at the end of June. Now it was the middle of July, and already the river was swollen. Its rushing sound seemed nearer and more menacing than usual.

Site went to her grandfather and sat down beside him beneath the peepul tree.

'When you are hungry, tell me,' she said, 'and I will make the bread.'

'Is your grandmother asleep?'

'She sleeps. But she will wake soon, for she has a deep pain.'

The old man stared out across the river, at the dark green of the forest, at the grey sky, and said, 'Tomorrow, if she is not better, I will take her to the hospital at Shahganj. There they will know how to make her well. You may be on your own for a few days—but you have been on your own before....'

Sita nodded gravely; she had been alone before, even during the rainy season. Now she wanted Grandmother to get well, and she knew that only Grandfather had the skill to take the small dugout boat across the river when the current was so strong. Someone would have to stay behind to look after their few possessions.

Sita was not afraid of being alone, but she did not like the look of the river. That morning, when she had gone down to fetch water, she had noticed that the level had risen. Those rocks which were normally spattered with the droppings of snipe and curlew and other water birds had suddenly disappeared.

They disappeared every year—but not so soon, surely?

'Grandfather, if the river rises, what will I do?'

'You will keep to the high ground.'

'And if the water reaches the high ground?'

'Then take the hens into the hut, and stay there.'

'And if the water comes into the hut?'

'Then climb into the peepul tree. It is a strong tree. It will not fall. And the water cannot rise higher than the tree!'

'And the goats, Grandfather?'

'I will be taking them with me, Sita. I may have to sell them to pay for good food and medicines for your grandmother. As for the hens, if it becomes necessary, put them on the roof. But do not worry too much'—and he patted Sita's head—'the water will not rise as high. I will be back soon, remember that.'

'And won't Grandmother come back?'

'Yes, of course, but they may keep her in the hospital for some time.'

Towards evening, it began to rain again—big pellets of rain, scarring the surface of the river. But it was warm rain, and Sita could move about in it. She was not afraid of getting wet, she rather liked it. In the previous month, when the first monsoon shower had arrived, washing the dusty leaves of the tree and bringing up the good smell of the earth, she had exulted in it, had run about shouting for joy. She was used to it now, and indeed a little tired of the rain, but she did not mind getting wet. It was steamy indoors, and her thin dress would soon dry in the heat from the kitchen fire.

She walked about barefooted, barelegged. She was very sure on her feet; her toes had grown accustomed to gripping all kinds of rocks, slippery or sharp. And though thin, she was surprisingly strong.

Black hair streaming across her face. Black eyes. Slim brown arms. A scar on her thigh—when she was small, visiting her mother's village, a hyena had entered the house where she was sleeping, fastened on to her leg and tried to drag her away, but her screams had roused the villagers and the hyena had run off.

She moved about in the pouring rain, chasing the hens into a shelter behind the hut. A harmless brown snake, flooded out of its hole, was moving across the open ground. Sita picked up a stick, scooped the snake up, and dropped it between a cluster of rocks. She had no quarrel with snakes. They kept down the rats and the frogs. She wondered how the rats had first come to the island—probably in someone's boat, or in a sack of grain. Now it was a job to keep their numbers down.

When Sita finally went indoors, she was hungry. She ate some dried peas and warmed up some goat's milk. Grandmother woke once and asked for water, and Grandfather held the brass tumbler to her lips.

It rained all night.

The roof was leaking, and a small puddle formed on the floor. They kept the kerosene lamp alight. They did not need the light, but somehow it made them feel safer.

The sound of the river had always been with them, although they were seldom aware of it; but that night they noticed a change in its sound. There was something like a moan, like a wind in the tops of tall trees and a swift hiss as the water swept round the rocks and carried away pebbles. And sometimes there was a rumble, as loose earth fell into the water.

Sita could not sleep.

She had a rag doll, made with Grandmother's help out of bits of old clothing. She kept it by her side every night. The doll was someone to talk to, when the nights were long and sleep elusive. Her grandparents were often ready to talk—and Grandmother, when she was well, was a good storyteller—but sometimes Sita wanted to have secrets, and though there were no special secrets in her life, she made up a few, because it was fun to have them. And if you have secrets, you must have a friend to share them with, a companion of one's own age. Since there were no other children on the island, Sita shared her secrets with the rag doll whose name was Mumta.

Grandfather and Grandmother were asleep, though the sound of Grandmother's laboured breathing was almost as persistent as the sound of the river.

'Mumta,' whispered Sita in the dark, starting one of her private conversations. 'Do you think Grandmother will get well again?'

Mumta always answered Sita's questions, even though the answers could only be heard by Sita.

'She is very old,' said Mumta.

'Do you think the river will reach the hut?' asked Sita.

'If it keeps raining like this, and the river keeps rising, it will reach the hut.'

'I am a little afraid of the river, Mumta. Aren't you afraid?'

'Don't be afraid. The river has always been good to us.'

'What will we do if it comes into the hut?'

'We will climb on to the roof.'

'And if it reaches the roof?'

'We will climb the peepul tree. The river has never gone higher than the peepul tree.'

As soon as the first light showed through the little skylight, Sita got up and went outside. It wasn't raining hard, it was drizzling, but it was the sort of drizzle that could continue for days, and it probably meant that heavy rain was falling in the hills where the river originated.

Sita went down to the water's edge. She couldn't find her favourite rock, the one on which she often sat dangling her feet in the water, watching the little chilwa fish swim by. It was still there, no doubt, but the river had gone over it.

She stood on the sand, and she could feel the water oozing and bubbling beneath her feet.

The river was no longer green and blue and flecked with white, but a muddy colour.

She went back to the hut. Grandfather was up now. He was getting his boat ready.

Sita milked a goat. Perhaps it was the last time she would milk it.

⌣

The sun was just coming up when Grandfather pushed off in the boat. Grandmother lay in the prow. She was staring hard at Sita, trying to speak, but the words would not come. She raised her hand in a blessing.

Sita bent and touched her grandmother's feet, and then Grandfather pushed off. The little boat—with its two old people and three goats—riding swiftly on the river, moved slowly, very slowly, towards the opposite bank. The current was so swift now that Sita realized the boat would be carried about half a mile downstream before Grandfather could get it to dry land.

It bobbed about on the water, getting smaller and smaller, until it was just a speck on the broad river.

And suddenly Sita was alone.

There was a wind, whipping the raindrops against her face; and there was the water, rushing past the island; and there was the distant shore, blurred by rain; and there was the small hut; and there was the tree.

Sita got busy. The hens had to be fed. They weren't bothered about anything except food. Sita threw them handfuls of coarse grain and potato peelings and peanut shells.

Then she took the broom and swept out the hut, lit the charcoal burner, warmed some milk, and thought, 'Tomorrow there will be no milk....' She began peeling onions. Soon her eyes started smarting and, pausing for a few moments and glancing round the quiet room, she became aware again that she was alone. Grandfather's hookah stood by itself in one corner. It was a beautiful old hookah, which had belonged to Sita's great-grandfather. The bowl was made out of a coconut encased in silver. The long winding stem was at least four feet in length. It was their most valuable possession. Grandmother's sturdy shisham wood walking stick stood in another corner.

Sita looked around for Mumta, found the doll beneath the cot, and placed her within sight and hearing.

Thunder rolled down from the hills. BOOM—BOOM—BOOM....

'The gods of the mountains are angry,' said Sita.

'Do you think they are angry with me?'

'Why should they be angry with you?' asked Mumta.

'They don't have to have a reason for being angry. They are angry with everything, and we are in the middle of everything. We are so small—do you think they know we are here?'

'Who knows what the gods think?'

'But I made you,' said Sita, 'and I know you are here.'

'And will you save me if the river rises?'

'Yes, of course. I won't go anywhere without you, Mumta.'

Sita couldn't stay indoors for long. She went out, taking Mumta with her, and stared out across the river, to the safe land on the other side. But was it safe there? The river looked much wider now. Yes, it had crept over its banks and spread far across the flat plain. Far away, people were driving their cattle through waterlogged, flooded fields, carrying their belongings in bundles on their heads or shoulders, leaving their homes, making for the high land. It wasn't safe anywhere.

She wondered what had happened to Grandfather and Grandmother. If they had reached the shore safely, Grandfather would have to engage a bullock cart, or a pony-drawn carriage, to get Grandmother to the district town, five or six miles away, where there was a market, a court, a jail, a cinema, and a hospital.

She wondered if she would ever see Grandmother again. She had done her best to look after the old lady, remembering the times when Grandmother had looked after her, had gently touched her fevered brow and had told her stories—stories about the gods: about the young Krishna, friend of birds and animals, so full of mischief, always causing confusion among the other gods; and Indra, who made the thunder and lightning; and Vishnu, the preserver of all good things, whose steed was a great white bird; and Ganesh, with the elephant's head; and Hanuman, the monkey god, who helped the young Prince Rama in his war with the King of Ceylon. Would Grandmother return to tell her more about them, or would she have to find out for herself?

The island looked much smaller now. In parts, the mud banks had dissolved quickly, sinking into the river. But in the middle of the island there was rocky ground, and the rocks would never crumble, they could only be submerged. In a space in the middle of the rocks grew the tree.

Sita climbed up the tree to get a better view. She had climbed the tree many times and it took her only a few seconds to reach the higher branches. She put her hand to her eyes to shield them from the rain, and gazed upstream.

There was water everywhere. The world had become one vast river. Even the trees on the forested side of the river looked as though they had grown from the water, like mangroves. The sky was banked with massive, moisture-laden clouds. Thunder rolled down from the hills and the river seemed to take it up with a hollow booming sound.

Something was floating down with the current, something big and bloated. It was closer now, and Sita could make out the bulky object—a drowned buffalo, being carried rapidly downstream.

So the water had already inundated the villages further upstream. Or perhaps the buffalo had been grazing too close to the rising river.

Sita's worst fears were confirmed when, a little later, she saw planks of wood, small trees and bushes, and then a wooden bedstead, floating past the island.

How long would it take for the river to reach her own small hut?

As she climbed down from the tree, it began to rain more heavily. She ran indoors, shooing the hens before her. They flew into the hut and huddled under Grandmother's cot. Sita thought it would be best to keep them together now. And having them with her took away some of the loneliness.

There were three hens and a cock bird. The river did not bother them. They were interested only in food, and Sita kept them happy by throwing them a handful of onion skins.

She would have liked to close the door and shut out the swish of the rain and the boom of the river, but then she would have no way of knowing how fast the water rose.

She took Mumta in her arms, and began praying for the rain to stop and the river to fall. She prayed to the god Indra, and, just in case he was busy elsewhere, she prayed to other gods too. She prayed for the safety of her grandparents and for her own safety. She put herself last but only with great difficulty.

She would have to make herself a meal. So she chopped up some onions, fried them, then added turmeric and red chilli powder and stirred until she had everything sizzling; then she added a tumbler of water, some salt, and a cup of one of the cheaper lentils. She covered the pot and allowed the mixture to simmer. Doing this took Sita about ten minutes. It would take at least half an hour for the dish to be ready.

When she looked outside, she saw pools of water amongst the rocks and near the tree. She couldn't tell if it was rain water or overflow from the river.

She had an idea.

A big tin trunk stood in a corner of the room. It had belonged to Sita's mother. There was nothing in it except a cotton-filled quilt, for use during the cold weather. She would stuff the trunk with everything useful or valuable, and weigh it down so that it wouldn't be carried away— just in case the river came over the island….

Grandfather's hookah went into the trunk. Grandmother's walking stick went in too. So did a number of small tins containing the spices used in cooking—nutmeg, caraway seed, cinnamon, coriander, and pepper—a bigger tin of flour and a tin of raw sugar. Even if Sita had to spend several hours in the tree, there would be something to eat when she came down again.

A clean white cotton shirt of Grandfather's, and Grandmother's only spare sari also went into the trunk. Never mind if they got stained with yellow curry powder! Never mind if they got to smell of salted fish, some of that went in too.

Sita was so busy packing the trunk that she paid no attention to the lick of cold water at her heels. She locked the trunk, placed the key high on the rock wall, and turned to give her attention to the lentils. It was only then that she discovered that she was walking about on a watery floor.

She stood still, horrified by what she saw. The water was oozing over the threshold, pushing its way into the room.

Sita was filled with panic. She forgot about her meal and everything else. Darting out of the hut, she ran splashing through ankle-deep water towards the safety of the peepul tree. If the tree hadn't been there, such a well-known landmark, she might have floundered into deep water, into the river.

She climbed swiftly into the strong arms of the tree, made herself secure on a familiar branch, and thrust the wet hair away from her eyes.

She was glad she had hurried. The hut was now surrounded by

water. Only the higher parts of the island could still be seen—a few rocks, the big rock on which the hut was built, a hillock on which some thorny bilberry bushes grew.

The hens hadn't bothered to leave the hut. They were probably perched on the cot now.

Would the river rise still higher? Sita had never seen it like this before. It swirled around her, stretching in all directions.

More drowned cattle came floating down. The most unusual things went by on the water—an aluminium kettle, a cane chair, a tin of tooth powder, an empty cigarette packet, a wooden slipper, a plastic doll....

A doll!

With a sinking feeling, Sita remembered Mumta.

Poor Mumta! She had been left behind in the hut. Sita, in her hurry, had forgotten her only companion.

Well, thought Sita, if I can be careless with someone I've made, how can I expect the gods to notice me, alone in the middle of the river?

The waters were higher now, the island fast disappearing.

Something came floating out of the hut.

It was an empty kerosene tin, with one of the hens perched on top. The tin came bobbing along on the water, not far from the tree, and was then caught by the current and swept into the river. The hen still managed to keep its perch.

A little later, the water must have reached the cot because the remaining hens flew up to the rock ledge and sat huddled there in the small recess.

The water was rising rapidly now, and all that remained of the island was the big rock that supported the hut, the top of the hut itself and the peepul tree.

It was a tall tree with many branches and it seemed unlikely that the water could ever go right over it. But how long would Sita have to remain there? She climbed a little higher, and as she

did so, a jet-black jungle crow settled in the upper branches, and
Sita saw that there was a nest in them—a crow's nest, an untidy
platform of twigs wedged in the fork of a branch.

In the nest were four blue-green, speckled eggs. The crow
sat on them and cawed disconsolately. But though the crow was
miserable, its presence brought some cheer to Sita. At least she was
not alone. Better to have a crow for company than no one at all.

Other things came floating out of the hut—a large pumpkin;
a red turban belonging to Grandfather, unwinding in the water
like a long snake; and then—Mumta! The doll, being filled with
straw and wood shavings, moved quite swiftly on the water and
passed close to the peepul tree. Sita saw it and wanted to call
out, to urge her friend to make for the tree, but she knew that
Mumta could not swim—the doll could only float, travel with
the river, and perhaps be washed ashore many miles downstream.

The tree shook in the wind and the rain. The crow cawed
and flew up, circled the tree a few times and returned to the
nest. Sita clung to her branch.

The tree trembled throughout its tall frame. To Sita it felt
like an earthquake tremor; she felt the shudder of the tree in
her own bones.

The river swirled all around her now. It was almost up to the
roof of the hut. Soon the mud walls would crumble and vanish.
Except for the big rock and some trees far, far away, there was
only water to be seen.

For a moment or two Sita glimpsed a boat with several people
in it moving sluggishly away from the ruins of a flooded village,
and she thought she saw someone pointing towards her, but the
river swept them on and the boat was lost to view.

The river was very angry; it was like a wild beast, a dragon on
the rampage, thundering down from the hills and sweeping across
the plain, bringing with it dead animals, uprooted trees, household
goods, and huge fish choked to death by the swirling mud.

The tall old peepul tree groaned. Its long, winding roots clung tenaciously to the earth from which the tree had sprung many, many years ago. But the earth was softening; the stones were being washed away. The roots of the tree were rapidly losing their hold.

The crow must have known that something was wrong, because it kept flying up and circling the tree, reluctant to settle in it, and reluctant to fly away. As long as the nest was there, the crow would remain, flapping about and cawing in alarm.

Sita's wet cotton dress clung to her thin body. The rain ran down from her long black hair. It poured from every leaf of the tree. The crow, too, was drenched and groggy.

The tree groaned and moved again. It had seen many monsoons. Once before, it had stood firm while the river had swirled around its massive trunk. But it had been young then. Now, old in years and tired of standing still, the tree was ready to join the river.

With a flurry of its beautiful leaves, and a surge of mud from below, the tree left its place in the earth, and, tilting, moved slowly forward, turning a little from side to side, dragging its roots along the ground. To Sita, it seemed as though the river was rising to meet the sky.

Then the tree moved into the main current of the river, and went a little faster, swinging Sita from side to side. Her feet were in the water but she clung tenaciously to her branch.

The branches swayed, but Sita did not lose her grip. The water was very close now. Sita was frightened. She could not see the extent of the flood or the width of the river. She could only see the immediate danger—the water surrounding the tree.

The crow kept flying around the tree. The bird was in a terrible rage. The nest was still in the branches, but not for long…. The tree lurched and twisted slightly to one side, and the nest fell into the water. Sita saw the eggs go one by one.

The crow swooped low over the water, but there was nothing it could do. In a few moments, the nest had disappeared.

The bird followed the tree for about fifty yards, as though hoping that something still remained in the tree. Then, flapping its wings, it rose high into the air and flew across the river until it was out of sight.

Sita was alone once more. But there was no time for feeling lonely. Everything was in motion—up and down and sideways and forwards. 'Any moment,' thought Sita, 'the tree will turn right over and I'll be in the water!'

She saw a turtle swimming past—a great river turtle, the kind that feeds on decaying flesh. Sita turned her face away. In the distance she saw a flooded village and people in flat-bottomed boats, but they were very far away.

Because of its great size, the tree did not move very swiftly on the river. Sometimes, when it passed into shallow water, it stopped, its roots catching in the rocks; but not for long—the river's momentum soon swept it on.

At one place, where there was a bend in the river, the tree struck a sandbank and was still.

Sita felt very tired. Her arms were aching and she was no longer upright. With the tree almost on its side, she had to cling tightly to her branch to avoid falling off.

The grey weeping sky was like a great shifting dome. She knew she could not remain much longer in that position. It might be better to try swimming to some distant rooftop or tree. Then she heard someone calling.

Craning her neck to look upriver, she was able to make out a small boat coming directly towards her.

The boat approached the tree. There was a boy in the boat who held on to one of the branches to steady himself, giving his free hand to Sita. She grasped it, and slipped into the boat beside him. The boy placed his bare foot against the tree trunk and pushed away. The little boat moved swiftly down the river. The big tree was left far behind. Sita would never see it again.

She lay stretched out in the boat, too frightened to talk. The boy looked at her, but he did not say anything, he did not even smile. He lay on his two small oars, stroking smoothly, rhythmically, trying to keep from going into the middle of the river. He wasn't strong enough to get the boat right out of the swift current, but he kept trying.

A small boat on a big river—a river that had no boundaries but which reached across the plains in all directions. The boat moved swiftly on the wild waters, and Sita's home was left far behind.

The boy wore only a loincloth. A sheathed knife was knotted into his waistband. He was a slim, wiry boy, with a hard flat belly; he had high cheekbones, strong white teeth. He was a little darker than Sita.

'You live on the island,' he said at last, resting on his oars and allowing the boat to drift a little, for he had reached a broader, more placid stretch of the river.

'I have seen you sometimes. But where are the others?'

'My grandmother was sick,' said Sita, 'so Grandfather took her to the hospital in Shahganj.'

'When did they leave?'

'Early this morning.'

Only that morning—and yet it seemed to Sita as though it had been many mornings ago.

'Where have you come from?' she asked. She had never seen the boy before.

'I come from...' he hesitated, '...near the foothills. I was in my boat, trying to get across the river with the news that one of the villages was badly flooded, but the current was too strong. I was swept down past your island. We cannot fight the river, we must go wherever it takes us.'

'You must be tired. Give me the oars.'

'No. There is not much to do now, except keep the boat steady.'

He brought in one oar, and with his free hand he felt under the seat where there was a small basket. He produced two mangoes, and gave one to Sita.

They bit deep into the ripe fleshy mangoes, using their teeth to tear the skin away. The sweet juice trickled down their chins. The flavour of the fruit was heavenly—truly this was the nectar of the gods!

Sita hadn't tasted a mango for over a year. For a few moments she forgot about the flood—all that mattered was the mango!

The boat drifted, but not so swiftly now, for as they went further away across the plains, the river lost much of its tremendous force.

'My name is Krishan,' said the boy. 'My father has many cows and buffaloes, but several have been lost in the flood.'

'I suppose you go to school,' said Sita.

'Yes, I am supposed to go to school. There is one not far from our village. Do you have to go to school?'

'No—there is too much work at home.'

It was no use wishing she was at home—home wouldn't be there any more—but she wished, at that moment, that she had another mango.

Towards evening, the river changed colour. The sun, low in the sky, emerged from behind the clouds, and the river changed slowly from grey to gold, from gold to a deep orange, and then, as the sun went down, all these colours were drowned in the river, and the river took on the colour of the night.

The moon was almost at the full and Sita could see across the river, to where the trees grew on its banks.

'I will try to reach the trees,' said the boy, Krishan.

'We do not want to spend the night on the water, do we?'

And so he pulled for the trees. After ten minutes of strenuous rowing, he reached a turn in the river and was able to escape the pull of the main current. Soon they were in a forest, rowing between tall evergreens.

⌁

They moved slowly now, paddling between the trees, and the moon lighted their way, making a crooked silver path over the water.

'We will tie the boat to one of these trees,' said Krishan.

'Then we can rest. Tomorrow we will have to find our way out of the forest.'

He produced a length of rope from the bottom of the boat, tied one end to the boat's stern and threw the other end over a stout branch which hung only a few feet above the water. The boat came to rest against the trunk of the tree.

It was a tall, sturdy toon tree—the Indian mahogany—and it was quite safe, for there was no rush of water here; besides, the trees grew close together, making the earth firm and unyielding.

But the denizens of the forest were on the move.

The animals had been flooded out of their holes, caves and lairs, and were looking for shelter and dry ground.

Sita and Krishan had barely finished tying the boat to the tree when they saw a huge python gliding over the water towards them. Sita was afraid that it might try to get into the boat; but it went past them, its head above water, its great awesome length trailing behind, until it was lost in the shadows.

Krishan had more mangoes in the basket, and he and Sita sucked hungrily on them while they sat in the boat.

A big sambar stag came thrashing through the water. He did not have to swim; he was so tall that his head and shoulders remained well above the water. His antlers were big and beautiful.

'There will be other animals,' said Sita. 'Should we climb onto the tree?'

'We are quite safe in the boat,' said Krishan.

'The animals are interested only in reaching dry land. They will not even hunt each other. Tonight, the deer are safe from the panther and the tiger. So lie down and sleep, and I will keep watch.'

Sita stretched herself out in the boat and closed her eyes, and the sound of the water lapping against the sides of the boat soon lulled her to sleep. She woke once, when a strange bird called overhead. She raised herself on one elbow, but Krishan was awake, sitting in the prow, and he smiled reassuringly at her. He looked blue in the moonlight, the colour of the young god Krishna, and for a few moments Sita was confused and wondered if the boy was indeed Krishna; but when she thought about it, she decided that it wasn't possible. He was just a village boy and she had seen hundreds like him—well, not exactly like him; he was different, in a way she couldn't explain to herself....

And when she slept again, she dreamt that the boy and Krishna were one, and that she was sitting beside him on a great white bird which flew over mountains, over the snow peaks of the Himalayas, into the cloudland of the gods. There was a great rumbling sound, as though the gods were angry about the whole thing, and she woke up to this terrible sound and looked about her, and there in the moonlit glade, up to his belly in water, stood a young elephant, his trunk raised as he trumpeted his predicament to the forest—for he was a young elephant, and he was lost, and he was looking for his mother.

He trumpeted again, and then lowered his head and listened. And presently, from far away, came the shrill trumpeting of another elephant. It must have been the young one's mother, because he gave several excited trumpet calls, and then went stamping and churning through the flood water towards a gap in the trees. The boat rocked in the waves made by his passing.

'It's all right now,' said Krishan. 'You can go to sleep again.'

'I don't think I will sleep now,' said Sita.

'Then I will play my flute for you,' said the boy, 'and the time will pass more quickly.'

From the bottom of the boat he took a flute, and putting it to his lips, he began to play. The sweetest music that Sita had ever heard came pouring from the little flute, and it seemed to fill the forest with its beautiful sound. And the music carried her away again, into the land of dreams, and they were riding on the bird once more, Sita and the blue god, and they were passing through clouds and mist, until suddenly the sun shot out through the clouds. And at the same moment, Sita opened her eyes and saw the sun streaming through the branches of the toon tree, its bright green leaves making a dark pattern against the blinding blue of the sky.

Sita sat up with a start, rocking the boat. There were hardly any clouds left. The trees were drenched with sunshine.

The boy Krishan was fast asleep at the bottom of the boat. His flute lay in the palm of his half-opened hand. The sun came slanting across his bare brown legs. A leaf had fallen on his upturned face, but it had not woken him, it lay on his cheek as though it had grown there.

Sita did not move again. She did not want to wake the boy. It didn't look as though the water had gone down, but it hadn't risen, and that meant the flood had spent itself.

The warmth of the sun, as it crept up Krishan's body, woke him at last. He yawned, stretched his limbs, and sat up beside Sita.

'I'm hungry,' he said with a smile.

'So am I,' said Sita.

'The last mangoes,' he said, and emptied the basket of its last two mangoes.

After they had finished the fruit, they sucked the big seeds until they were quite dry. The discarded seeds floated well on the water. Sita had always preferred them to paper boats.

'We better move on,' said Krishan.

He rowed the boat through the trees, and then for about an hour they were passing through the flooded forest, under the dripping branches of rain-washed trees.

Sometimes they had to use the oars to push away vines and creepers. Sometimes drowned bushes hampered them. But they were out of the forest before noon.

Now the water was not very deep and they were gliding over flooded fields. In the distance they saw a village. It was on high ground. In the old days, people had built their villages on hilltops, which gave them a better defence against bandits and invading armies.

This was an old village, and though its inhabitants had long ago exchanged their swords for pruning forks, the hill on which it stood now protected it from the flood.

The people of the village—long-limbed, sturdy Jats—were generous, and gave the stranded children food and shelter. Sita was anxious to find her grandparents, and an old farmer who had business in Shahganj offered to take her there. She was hoping that Krishan would accompany her, but he said he would wait in the village, where he knew others would soon be arriving, his own people among them.

'You will be all right now,' said Krishan.

'Your grandfather will be anxious for you, so it is best that you go to him as soon as you can. And in two or three days, the water will go down and you will be able to return to the island.'

'Perhaps the island has gone forever,' said Sita.

As she climbed into the farmer's bullock cart, Krishan handed her his flute.

'Please keep it for me,' he said. 'I will come for it one day.'

And when he saw her hesitate, he added, his eyes twinkling, 'It is a good flute!'

⸪

It was slow going in the bullock cart. The road was awash, the wheels got stuck in the mud, and the farmer, his grown son and Sita had to keep getting down to heave and push in order to free the big wooden wheels.

They were still in a foot or two of water. The bullocks were bespattered with mud, and Sita's legs were caked with it.

They were a day and a night in the bullock cart before they reached Shahganj; by that time, Sita, walking down the narrow bazaar of the busy market town, was hardly recognizable.

Grandfather did not recognize her. He was walking stiffly down the road, looking straight ahead of him, and would have walked right past the dusty, dishevelled girl if she had not charged straight at his thin, shaky legs and clasped him around the waist.

'Sita!' he cried, when he had recovered his wind and his balance.

'But how are you here? How did you get off the island? I was so worried—it has been very bad these last two days....'

'Is Grandmother all right?' asked Sita.

But even as she spoke, she knew that Grandmother was no longer with them. The dazed look in the old man's eyes told her as much. She wanted to cry, not for Grandmother, who could suffer no more, but for Grandfather, who looked so helpless and bewildered; she did not want him to be unhappy. She forced back her tears, took his gnarled and trembling hand, and led him down the crowded street. And she knew, then, that it would be on her shoulder that Grandfather would have to lean in the years to come.

They returned to the island after a few days, when the river was no longer in spate. There was more rain, but the worst was over. Grandfather still had two of the goats; it had not been necessary to sell more than one.

He could hardly believe his eyes when he saw that the tree had disappeared from the island—the tree that had seemed as permanent as the island, as much a part of his life as the river itself. He marvelled at Sita's escape.

'It was the tree that saved you,' he said.

'And the boy,' said Sita.

Yes, and the boy.

She thought about the boy, and wondered if she would ever see him again. But she did not think too much, because there was so much to do.

For three nights they slept under a crude shelter made out of jute bags. During the day she helped Grandfather rebuild the mud hut. Once again, they used the big rock as a support.

The trunk which Sita had packed so carefully had not been swept off the island, but the water had got into it, and the food and clothing had been spoilt. But Grandfather's hookah had been saved, and, in the evenings, after their work was done and they had eaten the light meal which Sita prepared, he would smoke with a little of his old contentment, and tell Sita about other floods and storms which he had experienced as a boy.

Sita planted a mango seed in the same spot where the peepul tree had stood. It would be many years before it grew into a big tree, but Sita liked to imagine sitting in its branches one day, picking the mangoes straight from the tree, and feasting on them all day. Grandfather was more particular about making a vegetable garden and putting down peas, carrots, gram, and mustard.

One day, when most of the hard work had been done and

the new hut was almost ready, Sita took the flute which had been given to her by the boy, and walked down to the water's edge and tried to play it.

But all she could produce were a few broken notes, and even the goats paid no attention to her music.

Sometimes Sita thought she saw a boat coming down the river and she would run to meet it; but usually there was no boat, or if there was, it belonged to a stranger or to another fisherman. And so she stopped looking out for boats. Sometimes she thought she heard the music of a flute, but it seemed very distant and she could never tell where the music came from.

Slowly, the rains came to an end. The flood waters had receded, and in the villages people were beginning to till the land again and sow crops for the winter months. There were cattle fairs and wrestling matches. The days were warm and sultry. The water in the river was no longer muddy, and one evening Grandfather brought home a huge mahseer fish and Sita made it into a delicious curry.

♪

Grandfather sat outside the hut, smoking his hookah. Sita was at the far end of the island, spreading clothes on the rocks to dry. One of the goats had followed her. It was the friendlier of the two, and often followed Sita about the island. She had made it a necklace of coloured beads.

She sat down on a smooth rock, and, as she did so, she noticed a small bright object in the sand near her feet. She stooped and picked it up. It was a little wooden toy—a coloured peacock—that must have come down on the river and been swept ashore on the island. Some of the paint had rubbed off, but for Sita, who had no toys, it was a great find. Perhaps it would speak to her, as Mumta had spoken to her.

As she held the toy peacock in the palm of her hand, she

thought she heard the flute music again, but she did not look up. She had heard it before, and she was sure that it was all in her mind. But this time the music sounded nearer, much nearer. There was a soft footfall in the sand. And, looking up, she saw the boy, Krishan, standing over her.

'I thought you would never come,' said Sita.

'I had to wait until the rains were over. Now that I am free, I will come more often. Did you keep my flute?'

'Yes, but I cannot play it properly. Sometimes it plays by itself, I think, but it will not play for me!'

'I will teach you to play it,' said Krishan.

He sat down beside her, and they cooled their feet in the water, which was clear now, reflecting the blue of the sky. You could see the sand and the pebbles of the riverbed.

'Sometimes the river is angry, and sometimes it is kind,' said Sita.

'We are part of the river,' said the boy.

'We cannot live without it.'

It was a good river, deep and strong, beginning in the mountains and ending in the sea. Along its banks, for hundreds of miles, lived millions of people, and Sita was only one small girl among them, and no one had ever heard of her, no one knew her—except for the old man, the boy, and the river.

MOST BEAUTIFUL

I don't quite know why I found that particular town so heartless. Perhaps because of its crowded, claustrophobic atmosphere, its congested and insanitary lanes, its weary people.... One day I found the children of the bazaar tormenting a deformed, retarded boy.

About a dozen boys, between the ages of eight and fourteen, were jeering at the retard, who was making things worse for himself by confronting the gang and shouting abuses at them. The boy was twelve or thirteen, judging by his face, but had the height of an eight or nine-year-old. His legs were thick, short, and bowed. He had a small chest but his arms were long, making him rather ape-like in his attitude. His forehead and cheeks were pitted with the scars of smallpox. He was ugly by normal standards, and the gibberish he spoke did nothing to discourage his tormentors. They threw mud and stones at him, while keeping well out of his reach. Few can be crueller than a gang of schoolboys in high spirits.

I was an uneasy observer of the scene. I felt that I ought to do something to put a stop to it, but lacked the courage to interfere. It was only when a stone struck the boy on the face, cutting open his cheek, that I lost my normal discretion and ran in amongst the boys, shouting at them and clouting those I could reach. They scattered like defeated soldiery.

I was surprised at my own daring, and rather relieved when the boys did not return. I took the frightened, angry boy by the hand, and asked him where he lived. He drew away from me, but I held on to his fat little fingers and told him I would take him home. He mumbled something incoherent and pointed down a narrow lane. I led him away from the bazaar.

I said very little to the boy because it was obvious that he had some defect of speech. When he stopped outside a door set in a high wall, I presumed that we had come to his house.

The door was opened by a young woman. The boy immediately threw his arms around her and burst into tears. I had not been prepared for the boy's mother. Not only did she look perfectly normal physically, but she was also strikingly handsome. She must have been about thirty-five.

She thanked me for bringing her son home, and asked me into the house. The boy withdrew into a corner of the sitting room, and sat on his haunches in gloomy silence, his bow legs looking even more grotesque in this posture. His mother offered me tea, but I asked for a glass of water. She asked the boy to fetch it, and he did so, thrusting the glass into my hands without looking me in the face.

'Suresh is my only son,' she said. 'My husband is disappointed in him, but I love my son. Do you think he is very ugly?'

'Ugly is just a word,' I said. 'Like beauty. They mean different things to different people. What did the poet say?—"Beauty is truth, truth is beauty." But if beauty and truth are the same thing, why have different words? There are no absolutes except birth and death.'

The boy squatted down at her feet, cradling his head in her lap. With the end of her sari, she began wiping his face.

'Have you tried teaching him to talk properly?' I asked.

'He has been like this since childhood. The doctors can do nothing.'

While we were talking the father came in, and the boy slunk away to the kitchen. The man thanked me curtly for bringing the boy home, and seemed at once to dismiss the whole matter from his mind. He seemed preoccupied with business matters. I got the impression that he had long since resigned himself to having a deformed son, and his early disappointment had changed to indifference. When I got up to leave, his wife accompanied me to the front door.

'Please do not mind if my husband is a little rude,' she said. 'His business is not going too well. If you would like to come again, please do. Suresh does not meet many people who treat him like a normal person.'

I knew that I wanted to visit them again—more out of sympathy for the mother than out of pity for the boy. But I realized that she was not interested in me personally, except as a possible mentor for her son.

After about a week I went to the house again.

Suresh's father was away on a business trip, and I stayed for lunch. The boy's mother made some delicious parathas stuffed with ground radish, and served it with pickle and curds. If Suresh ate like an animal, gobbling his food, I was not far behind him. His mother encouraged him to overeat. He was morose and uncommunicative when he ate, but when I suggested that he come with me for a walk, he looked up eagerly. At the same time a look of fear passed across his mother's face.

'Will it be all right?' she asked. 'You have seen how other children treat him. That day he slipped out of the house without telling anyone.'

'We won't go towards the bazaar,' I said. 'I was thinking of a walk in the fields.'

Suresh made encouraging noises and thumped the table with his fists to show that he wanted to go. Finally his mother consented, and the boy and I set off down the road.

He could not walk very fast because of his awkward legs, but this gave me a chance to point out to him anything that I thought might arouse his interest—parrots squabbling in a banyan tree, buffaloes wallowing in a muddy pond, a group of hermaphrodite musicians strolling down the road. Suresh took a keen interest in the hermaphrodites, perhaps because they were grotesque in their own way: tall, masculine-looking people dressed in women's garments, ankle bells jingling on their heavy feet, and their long, gaunt faces made up with rouge and mascara. For the first time, I heard Suresh laugh. Apparently he had discovered that there were human beings even odder than he. And like any human being, he lost no time in deriding them.

'Don't laugh,' I said. 'They were born that way, just as you were born the way you are.'

But he did not take me seriously and grinned, his wide mouth revealing surprisingly strong teeth.

We reached the dry riverbed on the outskirts of the town and crossing it entered a field of yellow mustard flowers. The mustard stretched away towards the edge of a subtropical forest. Seeing trees in the distance, Suresh began to run towards them, shouting and clapping his hands. He had never been out of town before. The courtyard of his house and, occasionally, the road to the bazaar, were all that he had seen of the world. Now, the trees beckoned him.

We found a small stream running through the forest and I took off my clothes and leapt into the cool water, inviting Suresh to join me. He hesitated about taking off his clothes, but after watching me for a while, his eagerness to join me overcame his self-consciousness, and he exposed his misshapen little body to the soft spring sunshine.

He waded clumsily towards me. The water which came only to my knees reached up to his chest.

'Come, I'll teach you to swim,' I said. And lifting him up from the waist, I held him afloat. He spluttered and thrashed around, but stopped struggling when he found that he could stay afloat.

Later, sitting on the banks of the stream, he discovered a small turtle sitting over a hole in the ground in which it had laid its eggs. He had never watched a turtle before, and watched it in fascination, while it drew its head into its shell and then thrust it out again with extreme circumspection. He must have felt that the turtle resembled him in some respects, with its squat legs, rounded back, and tendency to hide its head from the world.

After that I went to the boy's house about twice a week, and we nearly always visited the stream. Before long Suresh was able to swim a short distance. Knowing how to swim—this was something the bazaar boys never learnt—gave him a certain confidence, made his life something more than a one-dimensional existence.

The more I saw Suresh, the less conscious was I of his deformities. For me, he was fast becoming the norm; while the children of the bazaar seemed abnormal in their very similarity to each other. That he was still conscious of his ugliness—and how could he ever cease to be—was made clear to me about two months after our first meeting.

We were coming home through the mustard fields, which had turned from yellow to green, when I noticed that we were being followed by a small goat. It appeared to have been separated from its mother, and now attached itself to us. Though I tried driving the kid away, it continued tripping along at our heels, and when Suresh found that it persisted in accompanying us, he picked it up and took it home.

The kid became his main obsession during the next few days. He fed it with his own hands and allowed it to sleep at the foot of his bed. It was a pretty little kid, with fairy horns and an engaging habit of doing a hop, skip, and jump when moving about the house. Everyone admired the pet, and the boy's mother and I both remarked on how pretty it was.

His resentment against the animal began to show when others started admiring it. He suspected that they found it better-looking than its owner. I remember finding him squatting in front of a low mirror, holding the kid in his arms, and studying their reflections in the glass. After a few minutes of this, Suresh thrust the goat away. When he noticed that I was watching him, he got up and left the room without looking at me.

Two days later, when I called at the house, I found his mother looking very upset. I could see that she had been crying. But she seemed relieved to see me, and took me into the sitting room. When Suresh saw me, he got up from the floor and ran to the veranda.

'What's wrong?' I asked.

'It was the little goat,' she said. 'Suresh killed it.'

She told me how Suresh, in a sudden and uncontrollable rage, had thrown a brick at the kid, breaking its skull. What had upset her more than the animal's death was the fact that Suresh had shown no regret for what he had done.

'I'll talk to him,' I said, and went out to the veranda, but the boy had disappeared.

'He must have gone to the bazaar,' said his mother anxiously. 'He does that when he's upset. Sometimes I think he likes to be teased and beaten.'

He was not in the bazaar. I found him near the stream, lying flat on his belly in the soft mud, chasing tadpoles with a stick.

'Why did you kill the goat?' I asked.

He shrugged his shoulders.

'Did you enjoy killing it?'

He looked at me and smiled and nodded his head vigorously.

'How very cruel,' I said. But I did not mean it. I knew that his cruelty was no different from mine or anyone else's; only his was an untrammelled cruelty, primitive, as yet undisguised by civilizing restraints.

He took a penknife from his shirt pocket, opened it, and held it out to me by the blade. He pointed to his bare stomach and motioned me to thrust the blade into his belly. He had such a mournful look on his face (the result of having offended me and not in remorse for the goat sacrifice) that I had to burst out laughing.

'You are a funny fellow,' I said, taking the knife from him and throwing it into the stream. 'Come, let's have a swim.'

We swam all afternoon, and Suresh went home smiling. His mother and I conspired to keep the whole affair a secret from his father—who had not in any case been aware of the goat's presence.

Suresh seemed quite contented during the following weeks. And then I received a letter offering me a job in Delhi and I knew that I would have to take it, as I was earning very little by my writing at the time.

The boy's mother was disappointed, even depressed, when I told her I would be going away. I think she had grown quite fond of me. But the boy, always unpredictable, displayed no feeling at all. I felt a little hurt by his apparent indifference. Did our weeks of companionship mean nothing to him? I told myself that he probably did not realize that he might never see me again.

On the evening my train was to leave, I went to the house to say goodbye. The boy's mother made me promise to write to them, but Suresh seemed cold and distant, and refused to sit near me or take my hand. He made me feel that I was an outsider again—one of the mob throwing stones at odd and frightening people.

At eight o'clock that evening I entered a third-class compartment and, after a brief scuffle with several other travellers, succeeded in securing a seat near a window. It enabled me to look down the length of the platform.

The guard had blown his whistle and the train was about to leave when I saw Suresh standing near the station turnstile, looking up and down the platform.

'Suresh!' I shouted and he heard me and came hobbling along the platform. He had run the gauntlet of the bazaar during the busiest hour of the evening.

'I'll be back next year,' I called.

The train had begun moving out of the station, and as I waved to Suresh, he broke into a stumbling run, waving his arms in frantic, restraining gestures.

I saw him stumble against someone's bedding roll and fall sprawling on the ground. The engine picked up speed and the platform receded.

And that was the last I saw of Suresh, lying alone on the crowded platform, alone in the great grey darkness of the world, crooked and bent and twisted—the most beautiful boy in the world.

THE ROOM OF MANY COLOURS

Last week I wrote a story, and all the time I was writing it, I thought it was a good story; but when it was finished and I had read it through, I found that there was something missing, that it didn't ring true. So I tore it up. I wrote a poem, about an old man sleeping in the sun, and this was true, but it was finished quickly, and once again I was left with the problem of what to write next. And I remembered my father, who taught me to write; and I thought, why not write about my father, and about the trees we planted, and about the people I knew while growing up and about what happened on the way to growing up.

And so, like Alice, I must begin at the beginning, and in the beginning there was this red insect, just like a velvet button, which I found on the front lawn of the bungalow. The grass was still wet with overnight rain.

I placed the insect on the palm of my hand, and took it into the house to show my father.

'Look, Dad,' I said, 'I haven't seen an insect like this before. Where has it come from?'

'Where did you find it?' he asked.

'On the grass.'

'It must have come down from the sky,' he said. 'It must have come down with the rain.'

Later, he told me how the insect really happened to be there but I preferred his first explanation. It was more fun to have it dropping from the sky.

I was seven at the time, and my father was thirty-seven, but, right from the beginning, he made me feel that I was old enough to talk to him about everything—insects, people, trees, steam engines, King George, comics, crocodiles, the Mahatma, the Viceroy, America, Mozambique, and Timbuctoo. We took long walks together, explored old ruins, chased butterflies, and waved to passing trains.

My mother had gone away when I was four, and I had very dim memories of her. Most other children had their mothers with them, and I found it a bit strange that mine couldn't stay. Whenever I asked my father why she'd gone, he'd say, 'You'll understand when you grow up.' And if I asked him *where* she'd gone, he'd look troubled and say, 'I really don't know.' This was the only question of mine to which he didn't have an answer.

But I was quite happy living alone with my father; I had never known any other kind of life.

We were sitting on an old wall, looking out to sea at a couple of Arab dhows and a tramp steamer, when my father said, 'Would you like to go to sea one day?'

'Where does the sea go?' I asked.

'It goes everywhere.'

'Does it go to the end of the world?'

'It goes right around the world. It's a round world.'

'It can't be.'

'It is. But it's so big, you can't see the roundness. When a fly sits on a watermelon, it can't see right around the melon, can it? The melon must seem quite flat to the fly. Well, in comparison to the world, we're much, much smaller than the tiniest of insects.'

'Have you been around the world?' I asked.

'No, only as far as England. That's where your grandfather was born.'

'And my grandmother?'

'She came to India from Norway when she was quite small. Norway is a cold land, with mountains and snow, and the sea cutting deep into the land. I was there as a boy. It's very beautiful, and the people are good and work hard.'

'I'd like to go there.'

'You will, one day. When you are older, I'll take you to Norway.'

'Is it better than England?'

'It's quite different.'

'Is it better than India?'

'It's quite different.'

'Is India like England?'

'No, it's different.'

'Well, what does "different" mean?'

'It means things are not the same. It means people are different. It means the weather is different. It means trees and birds and insects are different.'

'Are English crocodiles different from Indian crocodiles?'

'They don't have crocodiles in England.'

'Oh, then it must be different.'

'It would be a dull world if it was the same everywhere,' said my father.

He never lost patience with my endless questioning. If he wanted a rest, he would take out his pipe and spend a long time lighting it. If this took very long I'd find something else to do. But sometimes I'd wait patiently until the pipe was drawing, and then return to the attack.

'Will we always be in India?' I asked.

'No, we'll have to go away one day. You see, it's hard to explain, but it isn't really our country.'

'Ayah says it belongs to the king of England, and the jewels in his crown were taken from India, and that when the Indians get their jewels back the king will lose India! But first they have to get the crown from the king, but this is very difficult, she says, because the crown is always on his head. He even sleeps wearing his crown!'

Ayah was my nanny. She loved me deeply, and was always filling my head with strange and wonderful stories. My father did not comment on Ayah's views. All he said was, 'We'll have to go away some day.'

'How long have we been here?' I asked.

'Two hundred years.'

'No, I mean us.'

'Well, you were born in India, so that's seven years for you.'

'Then can't I stay here?'

'Do you want to?'

'I want to go across the sea. But can we take Ayah with us?'

'I don't know, son. Let's walk along the beach.'

We lived in an old palace beside a lake. The palace looked like a ruin from the outside, but the rooms were cool and comfortable. We lived in one wing, and my father organized a small school in another wing. His pupils were the children of the raja and the raja's relatives. My father had started life in India as a tea planter, but he had been trained as a teacher and the idea of starting a school in a small state facing the Arabian Sea had appealed to him. The pay wasn't much, but we had a palace to live in, the latest 1938 model Hillman to drive about in, and a number of servants. In those days, of course, everyone had servants (although the servants did not have any!). Ayah was our own; but the cook, the bearer, the gardener, and the bhisti were all provided by the state. Sometimes I sat in the schoolroom with the other children (who were all much bigger than me), sometimes I remained in the house with Ayah, sometimes I followed the gardener, Dukhi, about the spacious garden.

Dukhi means 'sad', and though I never could discover if the gardener had anything to feel sad about, the name certainly suited him. He had grown to resemble the drooping weeds that he was always digging up with a tiny spade. I seldom saw him standing up. He always sat on the ground with his knees well up to his chin, and attacked the weeds from this position. He could spend all day on his haunches, moving about the garden simply by shuffling his feet along the grass.

I tried to imitate his posture, sitting down on my heels and putting my knees into my armpits, but could never hold the position for more than five minutes.

Time had no meaning in a large garden, and Dukhi never hurried. Life, for him, was not a matter of one year succeeding another, but of five seasons—winter, spring, hot weather, monsoon, and autumn—arriving and departing. His seedbeds had always to be in readiness for the coming season, and he did not look any further than the next monsoon. It was impossible to tell his age. He may have been thirty-six or eighty-six. He was either very young for his years or very old for them.

Dukhi loved bright colours, especially reds and yellows. He liked strongly scented flowers, like jasmine and honeysuckle. He couldn't understand my father's preference for the more delicately perfumed petunias and sweet peas. But I shared Dukhi's fondness for the common bright orange marigold, which is offered in temples and is used to make garlands and nosegays. When the garden was bare of all colour, the marigold would still be there, gay and flashy, challenging the sun.

Dukhi was very fond of making nosegays, and I liked to watch him at work. A sunflower formed the centrepiece. It was surrounded by roses, marigolds, and oleander, fringed with green leaves, and bound together with silver thread. The perfume was overpowering. The nosegays were presented to me or my father on special occasions, that is, on a birthday or to guests of my father's who were considered important.

One day I found Dukhi making a nosegay, and said, 'No one is coming today, Dukhi. It isn't even a birthday.'

'It is a birthday, Chota Sahib,' he said. 'Little Sahib' was the title he had given me. It wasn't much of a title compared to Raja Sahib, Diwan Sahib, or Burra Sahib, but it was nice to have a title at the age of seven.

'Oh,' I said, 'And is there a party, too?'

'No party.'

'What's the use of a birthday without a party? What's the use of a birthday without presents?'

'This person doesn't like presents—just flowers.'

'Who is it?' I asked, full of curiosity.

'If you want to find out, you can take these flowers to her. She lives right at the top of that far side of the palace. There are twenty-two steps to climb. Remember that, Chota Sahib, you take twenty-three steps and you will go over the edge and into the lake!'

I started climbing the stairs.

It was a spiral staircase of wrought iron, and it went round and round and up and up, and it made me quite dizzy and tired.

At the top I found myself on a small balcony, which looked out over the lake and another palace, at the crowded city and the distant harbour. I heard a voice, a rather high, musical voice, saying (in English), 'Are you a ghost?' I turned to see who had spoken but found the balcony empty. The voice had come from a dark room.

I turned to the stairway, ready to flee, but the voice said, 'Oh, don't go, there's nothing to be frightened of!'

And so I stood still, peering cautiously into the darkness of the room.

'First, tell me—are you a ghost?'

'I'm a boy,' I said.

'And I'm a girl. We can be friends. I can't come out there, so you had better come in. Come along, I'm not a ghost either—not yet, anyway!'

As there was nothing very frightening about the voice, I stepped into the room. It was dark inside, and, coming in from the glare, it took me some time to make out the tiny, elderly lady seated on a cushioned gilt chair. She wore a red sari, lots of coloured bangles on her wrists, and golden earrings. Her hair was streaked with white, but her skin was still quite smooth and unlined, and she had large and very beautiful eyes.

'You must be Master Bond!' she said. 'Do you know who I am?'

'You're a lady with a birthday,' I said, 'but that's all I know. Dukhi didn't tell me anymore.'

'If you promise to keep it secret, I'll tell you who I am. You see, everyone thinks I'm mad. Do you think so too?'

'I don't know.'

'Well, you must tell me if you think so,' she said with a chuckle. Her laugh was the sort of sound made by the gecko, a little wall lizard, coming from deep down in the throat. 'I have a feeling you are a truthful boy. Do you find it very difficult to tell the truth?'

'Sometimes.'

'Sometimes. Of course, there are times when I tell lies— lots of little lies—because they're such fun! But would you call me a liar? I wouldn't, if I were you, but *would* you?'

'Are you a liar?'

'I'm asking you! If I were to tell you that I was a queen—that I *am* a queen—would you believe me?'

I thought deeply about this, and then said, 'I'll try to believe you.'

'Oh, but you *must* believe me. I'm a real queen, I'm a rani! Look, I've got diamonds to prove it!' And she held out her hands, and there was a ring on each finger, the stones glowing and glittering in the dim light. 'Diamonds, rubies, pearls, and emeralds! Only a queen can have these!' She was most anxious that I should believe her.

'You must be a queen,' I said.

'Right!' she snapped. 'In that case, would you mind calling me, "Your Highness"?'

'Your Highness,' I said.

She smiled. It was a slow, beautiful smile. Her whole face lit up. 'I could love you,' she said. 'But better still, I'll give you something to eat. Do you like chocolates?'

'Yes, Your Highness.'

'Well,' she said, taking a box from the table beside her, 'these have come all the way from England. 'Take two. Only two, mind, otherwise the box will finish before Thursday, and I don't want that to happen because I won't get any more till Saturday. That's when Captain MacWhirr's ship gets in, the S. S. *Lucy*, loaded with boxes and boxes of chocolates!'

'All for you?' I asked in considerable awe.

'Yes, of course. They have to last at least three months. I get them from England. I get only the best chocolates. I like them with pink, crunchy fillings, don't you?'

'Oh, yes!' I exclaimed, full of envy.

'Never mind,' she said. 'I may give you one, now and then— if you're very nice to me! Here you are, help yourself....' She pushed the chocolate box towards me.

I took a silver-wrapped chocolate, and then just as I was thinking of taking a second, she quickly took the box away.

'No more!' she said. 'They have to last till Saturday.'

'But I took only one,' I said with some indignation.

'Did you?' She gave me a sharp look, decided I was telling the truth, and said graciously, 'Well, in that case you can have another.'

Watching the rani carefully, in case she snatched the box away again, I selected a second chocolate, this one with a green wrapper. I don't remember what kind of day it was outside, but I remember the bright green of the chocolate wrapper.

I thought it would be rude to eat the chocolates in front of a queen, so I put them in my pocket and said, 'I'd better go now. Ayah will be looking for me.'

'And when will you be coming to see me again?'

'I don't know,' I said.

'Your Highness.'

'Your Highness.'

'There's something I want you to do for me,' she said, placing one finger on my shoulder, and giving me a conspiratorial look. 'Will you do it?'

'What is it, Your Highness?'

'What is it? Why do you ask? A real prince never asks where or why or whatever, he simply does what the princess asks of him. When I was a princess—before I became a queen, that is—I asked a prince to swim across the lake and fetch me a lily growing on the other bank.'

'And did he get it for you?'

'He drowned halfway across. Let that be a lesson to you. Never agree to do something without knowing what it is.'

'But I thought you said…'

'Never mind what I *said*. It's what I say that matters!'

'Oh, all right,' I said, fidgeting to be gone. 'What is it you want me to do?'

'Nothing.' Her tiny rosebud lips pouted and she stared sullenly at a picture on the wall. Now that my eyes had grown used to the dim light in the room, I noticed that the walls were hung with portraits of stout rajas and ranis turbaned and bedecked in fine clothes. There were also portraits of Queen Victoria and King George V of England. And, in the centre of all this distinguished company, a large picture of Mickey Mouse.

'I'll do it if it isn't too dangerous,' I said.

'Then listen.' She took my hand and drew me towards her— what a tiny hand she had!—and whispered, 'I want a red rose. From the palace garden. But be careful! Don't let Dukhi, the gardener, catch you. He'll know it's for me. He knows I love roses. And he hates me! I'll tell you why, one day. But if he catches you, he'll do something terrible.'

'To me?'

'No, to himself. That's much worse, isn't it? He'll tie himself into knots, or lie naked on a bed of thorns, or go on a long fast with nothing to eat but fruit, sweets, and chicken! So you will be careful, won't you?'

'Oh, but he doesn't hate you,' I cried in protest, remembering the flowers he'd sent for her, and looking around I found that I'd been sitting on them. 'Look, he sent these flowers for your birthday!'

'Well, if he sent them for my birthday, you can take them back,' she snapped. 'But if he sent them for me...' and she suddenly softened and looked coy, 'then I might keep them. Thank you, my dear, it was a very sweet thought.' And she learnt forward as though to kiss me.

'It's late, I must go!' I said in alarm, and turning on my heels, ran out of the room and down the spiral staircase.

Father hadn't started lunch, or rather tiffin, as we called it then. He usually waited for me if I was late. I don't suppose he enjoyed eating alone.

For tiffin we usually had rice, a mutton curry (koftas or meatballs, with plenty of gravy, was my favourite curry), fried dal, and a hot lime or mango pickle. For supper we had English food—a soup, roast pork and fried potatoes, a rich gravy made by my father, and a custard or caramel pudding. My father enjoyed cooking, but it was only in the morning that he found time for it. Breakfast was his own creation. He cooked eggs in a variety of interesting ways, and favoured some Italian recipes which he had collected during a trip to Europe, long before I was born.

In deference to the feelings of our Hindu friends, we did not eat beef; but, apart from mutton and chicken, there was a plentiful supply of other meats—partridge, venison, lobster, and even porcupine!

'And where have you been?' asked my father, helping himself

to the rice as soon as he saw me come in.

'To the top of the old palace,' I said.

'Did you meet anyone there?'

'Yes, I met a tiny lady who told me she was a rani. She gave me chocolates.'

'As a rule, she doesn't like visitors.'

'Oh, she didn't mind me. But is she really a queen?'

'Well, she's the daughter of a maharaja. That makes her a princess. She never married. There's a story that she fell in love with a commoner, one of the palace servants, and wanted to marry him, but of course they wouldn't allow that. She became very melancholic, and started living all by herself in the old palace. They give her everything she needs, but she doesn't go out or have visitors. Everyone says she's mad.'

'How do they know?' I asked.

'Because she's different from other people, I suppose.'

'Is that being mad?'

'No. Not really, I suppose madness is not seeing things as others see them.'

'Is that very bad?'

'No,' said Father, who for once was finding it very difficult to explain something to me. 'But people who are like that—people whose minds are so different that they don't think, step by step, as we do, whose thoughts jump all over the place—such people are difficult to live with.'

'Step by step,' I repeated. 'Step by step.'

'You aren't eating,' said my father. 'Hurry up, and you can come with me to school today.'

I always looked forward to attending my father's classes. He did not take me to the schoolroom very often, because he wanted school to be a treat, to begin with, and then, later, the routine wouldn't be so unwelcome.

Sitting there with older children, understanding only half of what they were learning, I felt important and part grown-up. And of course I did learn to read and write, although I first learnt to read upside-down, by means of standing in front of the others' desks and peering across at their books. Later, when I went to school, I had some difficulty in learning to read the right way up; and even today I sometimes read upside-down, for the sake of variety. I don't mean that I read standing on my head; simply that I held the book upside-down.

I had at my command a number of rhymes and jingles, the most interesting of these being 'Solomon Grundy'.

Solomon Grundy,
Born on a Monday,
Christened on Tuesday,
Married on Wednesday,
Took ill on Thursday,
Worse on Friday,
Died on Saturday,
Buried on Sunday:
This is the end of
Solomon Grundy.

Was that all that life amounted to, in the end? And were we all Solomon Grundys? These were questions that bothered me at the time. Another puzzling rhyme was the one that went:

Hark, hark,
The dogs do hark,
The beggars are coming to town;
Some in rags,
Some in bags,
And some in velvet gowns.

This rhyme puzzled me for a long time. There were beggars

aplenty in the bazaar, and sometimes they came to the house, and some of them, did wear rags and bags (and some nothing at all) and the dogs did bark at them, but the beggar in the velvet gown never came our way.

'Who's this beggar in a velvet gown?' I asked my father.

'Not a beggar at all,' he said.

'Then why call him one?'

And I went to Ayah and asked her the same question, 'Who is the beggar in the velvet gown?'

'Jesus Christ,' said Ayah.

Ayah was a fervent Christian and made me say my prayers at night, even when I was very sleepy. She had, I think, Arab and Negro blood in addition to the blood of the Koli fishing community to which her mother had belonged. Her father, a sailor on an Arab dhow, had been a convert to Christianity. Ayah was a large, buxom woman, with heavy hands and feet and a slow, swaying gait that had all the grace and majesty of a royal elephant. Elephants for all their size are nimble creatures; and Ayah, too, was nimble, sensitive, and gentle with her big hands. Her face was always sweet and childlike.

Although a Christian, she clung to many of the beliefs of her parents, and loved to tell me stories about mischievous spirits and evil spirits, humans who changed into animals, and snakes who had been princes in their former lives.

There was the story of the snake who married a princess. At first, the princess did not wish to marry the snake, whom she had met in a forest, but the snake insisted, saying, 'I'll kill you if you won't marry me,' and of course that settled the question. The snake led his bride away and took her to a great treasure. 'I was a prince in my former life,' he explained. 'This treasure is yours.' And then the snake very gallantly disappeared.

'Snakes,' declared Ayah, 'are very lucky omens if seen early in the morning.'

'But what if the snake bites the lucky person?' I asked.

'He will be lucky all the same,' said Ayah with a logic that was all her own.

Snakes! There were a number of them living in the big garden, and my father had advised me to avoid the long grass. But I had seen snakes crossing the road (a lucky omen, according to Ayah) and they were never aggressive.

'A snake won't attack you,' said Father, 'provided you leave it alone. Of course, if you step on one it will probably bite.'

'Are all snakes poisonous?'

'Yes, but only a few are poisonous enough to kill a man. Others use their poison on rats and frogs. A good thing, too, otherwise during the rains the house would be taken over by the frogs.'

One afternoon, while Father was at school, Ayah found a snake in the bathtub. It wasn't early morning and so the snake couldn't have been a lucky one. Ayah was frightened and ran into the garden calling for help. Dukhi came running. Ayah ordered me to stay outside while they went after the snake.

And it was while I was alone in the garden—an unusual circumstance, since Dukhi was nearly always there—that I remembered the rani's request. On an impulse, I went to the nearest rose bush and plucked the largest rose, pricking my thumb in the process.

And then, without waiting to see what had happened to the snake (it finally escaped), I started up the steps to the top of the old palace.

When I got to the top, I knocked on the door of the rani's room. Getting no reply, I walked along the balcony until I reached another doorway. There were wooden panels around the door, with elephants, camels, and turbaned warriors carved into it. As the door was open, I walked boldly into the room then stood still in astonishment. The room was filled with a strange light. There were windows going right around the room, and each small windowpane was made of a different coloured glass. The sun that came through one window flung red and green and purple colours on the figure of the little rani who stood there with her face pressed to the glass.

She spoke to me without turning from the window. 'This is my favourite room. I have all the colours here. I can see a different world through each pane of glass. Come, join me!' And she beckoned to me, her small hand fluttering like a delicate butterfly.

I went up to the rani. She was only a little taller than me, and we were able to share the same windowpane.

'See, it's a red world!' she said.

The garden below, the palace and the lake, were all tinted red. I watched the rani's world for a little while and then touched her on the arm, and said, 'I have brought you a rose!'

She started away from me, and her eyes looked frightened. She would not look at the rose.

'Oh, why did you bring it?' she cried, wringing her hands. 'He'll be arrested now!'

'Who'll be arrested?'

'The prince, of course!'

'But *I* took it,' I said. 'No one saw me. Ayah and Dukhi were inside the house, catching a snake.'

'Did they catch it?' she asked, forgetting about the rose.

'I don't know. I didn't wait to see!'

'They should follow the snake, instead of catching it. It may lead them to a treasure. All snakes have treasures to guard.'

This seemed to confirm what Ayah had been telling me, and I resolved that I would follow the next snake that I met.

'Don't you like the rose, then?' I asked.

'Did you steal it?'

'Yes.'

'Good. Flowers should always be stolen. They're more fragrant then.'

Because of a man called Hitler, war had been declared in Europe and Britain was fighting Germany.

In my comic papers, the Germans were usually shown as blundering idiots; so I didn't see how Britain could possibly lose the war, nor why it should concern India, nor why it should be necessary for my father to join up. But I remember him showing me a newspaper headline which said:

BOMBS FALL ON BUCKINGHAM PALACE—
KING AND QUEEN SAFE

I expect that had something to do with it.

He went to Delhi for an interview with the RAF and I was left in Ayah's charge.

It was a week I remember well, because it was the first time I had been left on my own. That first night I was afraid—afraid of the dark, afraid of the emptiness of the house, afraid of the howling of the jackals outside. The loud ticking of the clock was the only reassuring sound: clocks really made themselves heard in those days! I tried concentrating on the ticking, shutting out other sounds and the menace of the dark, but it wouldn't work. I thought I heard a faint hissing near the bed, and sat up, bathed in perspiration, certain that a snake was in the room. I shouted for Ayah and she came running, switching on all the lights.

'A snake!' I cried. 'There's a snake in the room!'

'Where, baba?'

'I don't know where, but I *heard* it.'

Ayah looked under the bed, and behind the chairs and tables, but there was no snake to be found. She persuaded me that I must have heard the breeze whispering in the mosquito curtains.

But I didn't want to be left alone.

'I'm coming to you,' I said, and followed her into her small room near the kitchen.

Ayah slept on a low string cot. The mattress was thin, the blanket worn and patched up; but Ayah's warm and solid body made up for the discomfort of the bed. I snuggled up to her and was soon asleep.

I had almost forgotten the rani in the old palace and was about to pay her a visit when, to my surprise, I found her in the garden. I had risen early that morning, and had gone running barefoot over the dew-drenched grass. No one was about, but I startled a flock of parrots and the birds rose screeching from a banyan tree and wheeled away to some other corner of the palace grounds. I was just in time to see a mongoose scurrying across the grass with an egg in its mouth. The mongoose must have been raiding the poultry farm at the palace.

I was trying to locate the mongoose's hideout, and was on all fours in a jungle of tall cosmos plants when I heard the rustle of clothes, and turned to find the rani staring at me. She didn't ask me what I was doing there, but simply said: 'I don't think he could have gone in there.'

'But I saw him go this way,' I said.

'Nonsense! He doesn't live in this part of the garden. He lives in the roots of the banyan tree.'

'But that's where the snake lives,' I said

'You mean the snake who was a prince. Well, that's who I'm looking for!'

'A snake who was a prince!' I gaped at the rani.

She made a gesture of impatience with her butterfly hands, and said, 'Tut, you're only a child, you can't *understand*. The prince lives in the roots of the banyan tree, but he comes out early every morning. Have you seen him?'

'No. But I saw a mongoose.'

The rani became frightened. 'Oh dear, is there a mongoose in the garden? He might kill the prince!'

'How can a mongoose kill a prince?' I asked.

'You don't understand, Master Bond. Princes, when they die, are born again as snakes.'

'*All* princes?'

'No, only those who die before they can marry.'

'Did your prince die before he could marry you?'

'Yes. And he returned to this garden in the form of a beautiful snake.'

'Well,' I said, 'I hope it wasn't the snake the water carrier killed last week.'

'He killed a snake!' The rani looked horrified. She was quivering all over. 'It might have been the prince!'

'It was a brown snake,' I said.

'Oh, then it wasn't him.' She looked very relieved. 'Brown snakes are only ministers and people like that. It has to be a green snake to be a prince.'

'I haven't seen any green snakes here.'

'There's one living in the roots of the banyan tree. You won't kill it, will you?'

'Not if it's really a prince.'

'And you won't let others kill it?'

'I'll tell Ayah.'

'Good. You're on my side. But be careful of the gardener. Keep him away from the banyan tree. He's always killing snakes. I don't trust him at all.'

She came nearer and, leaning forward a little, looked into my eyes.

'Blue eyes—I trust them. But don't trust green eyes. And yellow eyes are evil.'

'I've never seen yellow eyes.'

'That's because you're pure,' she said, and turned away and hurried across the lawn as though she had just remembered a very urgent appointment.

The sun was up, slanting through the branches of the banyan tree, and Ayah's voice could be heard calling me for breakfast.

'Dukhi,' I said, when I found him in the garden later that day, 'Dukhi, don't kill the snake in the banyan tree.'

'A snake in the banyan tree!' he exclaimed, seizing his hose.

'No, no!' I said. 'I haven't seen it. But the rani says there's one. She says it was a prince in its former life, and that we shouldn't kill it.'

'Oh,' said Dukhi, smiling to himself. 'The rani says so. All right, you tell her we won't kill it.'

'Is it true that she was in love with a prince but that he died before she could marry him?'

'Something like that,' said Dukhi. 'It was a long time ago—before I came here.'

'My father says it wasn't a prince, but a commoner. Are you a commoner, Dukhi?'

'A commoner? What's that, Chota Sahib?'

'I'm not sure. Someone very poor, I suppose.'

'Then I must be a commoner,' said Dukhi.

'Were you in love with the rani?' I asked.

Dukhi was so startled that he dropped his hose and lost his balance; the first time I'd seen him lose his poise while squatting on his haunches.

'Don't say such things, Chota Sahib!'

'Why not?'

'You'll get me into trouble.'

'Then it must be true.'

Dukhi threw up his hands in mock despair and started collecting his implements.

'It's true, it's true!' I cried, dancing around him, and then I ran indoors to Ayah and said, 'Ayah, Dukhi was in love with the rani!'

Ayah gave a shriek of laughter, then looked very serious and put her finger against my lips.

'Don't say such things,' she said. 'Dukhi is of a very low caste. People won't like it if they hear what you say. And besides, the rani told you her prince died and turned into a snake. Well, Dukhi hasn't become a snake as yet, has he?'

True, Dukhi didn't look as though he could be anything but a gardener; but I wasn't satisfied with his denials or with Ayah's attempts to still my tongue. Hadn't Dukhi sent the rani a nosegay?

When my father came home, he looked quite pleased with himself.

'What have you brought for me?' was the first question I asked.

He had brought me some new books, a dartboard, and a train set; and in my excitement over examining these gifts, I forgot to ask about the result of his trip.

It was during tiffin that he told me what had happened and what was going to happen.

'We'll be going away soon' he said. 'I've joined the Royal Air Force. I'll have to work in Delhi.'

'Oh! Will you be in the war, Dad? Will you fly a plane?'

'No, I'm too old to be flying planes. I'll be forty years old in July. The RAF will be giving me what they call intelligence work, decoding secret messages and things like that and I don't suppose I'll be able to tell you much about it.'

This didn't sound as exciting as flying planes, but it sounded important and rather mysterious.

'Well, I hope it's interesting,' I said. 'Is Delhi a good place to live in?'

'I'm not sure. It will be very hot by the middle of April. And you won't be able to stay with me, Ruskin—not at first, anyway, not until I can get married quarters and then, only if your mother returns.... Meanwhile, you'll stay with your grandmother in Dehra.' He must have seen the disappointment on my face, because he quickly added, 'Of course, I'll come to see you often. Dehra isn't far from Delhi—only a night's train journey.'

But I was dismayed. It wasn't that I didn't want to stay with my grandmother, but I had grown so used to sharing my father's life and even watching him at work, that the thought of being separated from him was unbearable.

'Not as bad as going to boarding school,' he said. 'And that's the only alternative.'

'Not boarding school,' I said quickly, 'I'll run away from boarding school.'

'Well, you won't want to run away from your grandmother. She's very fond of you. And if you come with me to Delhi, you'll be alone all day in a stuffy little hut while I'm away at work. Sometimes I may have to go on tour—then what happens?'

'I don't mind being on my own.' And this was true. I had already grown accustomed to having my own room and my own trunk and my own bookshelf and I felt as though I was about to lose these things.

'Will Ayah come too?' I asked.

My father looked thoughtful. 'Would you like that?'

'Ayah must come,' I said firmly. 'Otherwise I'll run away.'

'I'll have to ask her,' said my father.

Ayah, it turned out, was quite ready to come with us. In fact, she was indignant that Father should have considered leaving her behind. She had brought me up since my mother went away, and she wasn't going to hand over charge to any upstart aunt or governess. She was pleased and excited at the prospect of the move, and this helped to raise my spirits.

'What is Dehra like?' I asked my father.

'It's a green place,' he said. 'It lies in a valley in the foothills of the Himalaya, and it's surrounded by forests. There are lots of trees in Dehra.'

'Does grandmother's house have trees?'

'Yes. There's a big jackfruit tree in the garden. Your grandmother planted it when I was a boy. And there's an old banyan tree, which is good to climb. And there are fruit trees, litchis, mangoes, papayas.'

'Are there any books?'

'Grandmother's books won't interest you. But I'll be bringing you books from Delhi whenever I come to see you.'

I was beginning to look forward to the move. Changing houses had always been fun. Changing towns ought to be fun, too.

A few days before we left, I went to say goodbye to the rani.

'I'm going away,' I said.

'How lovely!' said the rani. 'I wish I could go away!'

'Why don't you?'

'They won't let me. They're afraid to let me out of the palace.'

'What are they afraid of, Your Highness?'

'That I might run away. Run away, far, far away, to the land where the leopards are learning to pray.'

Gosh, I thought, she's really quite crazy…. But then she was silent, and started smoking a small hookah.

She drew on the hookah, looked at me, and asked, 'Where is your mother?'

'I haven't one.'

'Everyone has a mother. Did yours die?'

'No. She went away.'

She drew on her hookah again and then said, very sweetly, 'Don't go away….'

'I must,' I said. 'It's because of the war.'

'What war? Is there a war on? You see, no one tells me anything.'

'It's between us and Hitler,' I said.

'And who is Hitler?'

'He's a German.'

'I knew a German once, Dr Schreinherr, he had beautiful hands.'

'Was he an artist?'

'He was a dentist.'

The rani got up from her couch and accompanied me out on to the balcony. When we looked down at the garden, we could see Dukhi weeding a flower bed. Both of us gazed down at him in silence, and I wondered what the rani would say if I asked her if she had ever been in love with the palace gardener. Ayah had told me it would be an insulting question, so I held my peace. But as I walked slowly down the spiral staircase, the rani's voice came after me.

'Thank him,' she said. 'Thank him for the beautiful rose.'

FRIENDS OF MY YOUTH

1
SUDHEER

Friendship is all about doing things together. It may be climbing a mountain, fishing in a mountain stream, cycling along a country road, camping in a forest clearing, or simply travelling together and sharing the experiences that a new place can bring.

On at least two of these counts, Sudheer qualified as a friend, albeit a troublesome one, given to involving me in his adolescent escapades.

I met him in Dehra soon after my return from England. He turned up at my room, saying he'd heard I was a writer and did I have any comics to lend him?

'I don't write comics,' I said; but there were some comics lying around, left over from my own boyhood collection so I gave these to the lanky youth who stood smiling in the doorway, and he thanked me and said he'd bring them back. From my window I saw him cycling off in the general direction of Dalanwala.

He turned up again a few days later and dumped a large pile of new-looking comics on my desk. 'Here are all the latest,' he announced. 'You can keep them for me. I'm not allowed to read comics at home.'

It was only weeks later that I learnt he was given to pilfering comics and magazines from the town's bookstores. In no time at all, I'd become a receiver of stolen goods!

My landlady had warned me against Sudheer and so had one or two others. He had acquired a certain notoriety for having been expelled from his school. He had been in charge

164

of the library, and before a consignment of newly acquired books could be registered and library stamped, he had sold them back to the bookshop from which they had originally been purchased. Very enterprising but not to be countenanced in a very pukka public school. He was now studying in a municipal school, too poor to afford a library.

Sudheer was an amoral scamp all right, but I found it difficult to avoid him, or to resist his undeniable and openly affectionate manner. He could make you laugh. And anyone who can do that is easily forgiven for a great many faults.

One day he produced a couple of white mice from his pockets and left them on my desk.

'You keep them for me,' he said. 'I'm not allowed to keep them at home.'

There were a great many things he was not allowed to keep at home. Anyway, the white mice were given a home in an old cupboard, where my landlady kept unwanted dishes, pots and pans, and they were quite happy there, being fed on bits of bread or chapatti, until one day I heard shrieks from the storeroom, and charging into it, found my dear stout landlady having hysterics as one of the white mice sought refuge under her blouse and the other ran frantically up and down her back.

Sudheer had to find another home for the white mice. It was that, or finding another home for myself.

Most young men, boys, and quite a few girls used bicycles. There was a cycle hire shop across the road, and Sudheer persuaded me to hire cycles for both of us. We cycled out of town, through tea gardens and mustard fields, and down a forest road until we discovered a small, shallow river where we bathed and wrestled on the sand. Although I was three or four years older than Sudheer, he was much the stronger, being about six feet tall and broad in the shoulders. His parents had come from Bhanu, a rough-and-ready district on the North West Frontier, as a result of the partition of the country. His father ran a small press situated behind the Sabzi Mandi and brought out a weekly newspaper called the *Frontier Times*.

We came to the stream quite often. It was Sudheer's way of playing truant from school without being detected in the bazaar or at the cinema. He was sixteen when I met him, and eighteen when we parted, but I can't recall that he ever showed any interest in his school work.

He took me to his home in the Karanpur bazaar, then a stronghold of the Bhanu community. The Karanpur boys were an aggressive lot and resented Sudheer's friendship with an angrez. To avoid a confrontation, I would use the back alleys and side streets to get to and from the house in which they lived. Sudheer had been overindulged by his mother, who protected him from his father's wrath. Both parents felt I might have an 'improving' influence on their son, and encouraged our friendship. His elder sister seemed more doubtful. She felt he was incorrigible, beyond redemption, and that I was not much better, and she was probably right.

The father invited me to his small press and asked me if I'd like to work with him. I agreed to help with the newspaper for a couple of hours every morning. This involved proofreading and editing news agency reports. Uninspiring work, but useful.

Meanwhile, Sudheer had got hold of a pet monkey, and he carried it about in the basket attached to the handlebar of his bicycle. He used it to ingratiate himself with the girls. 'How sweet! How pretty!' they would exclaim, and Sudheer would get the monkey to show them its tricks.

After some time, however, the monkey appeared to be infected by Sudheer's amorous nature, and would make obscene gestures which were not appreciated by his former admirers. On one occasion, the monkey made off with a girl's dupatta. A chase ensued, and the dupatta retrieved, but the outcome of it all was that Sudheer was accosted by the girl's brothers and given a black eye and a bruised cheek. His father took the monkey away and returned it to the itinerant juggler who had sold it to the young man.

Sudheer soon developed an insatiable need for money. He wasn't getting anything at home, apart from what he pinched from his mother and sister, and his father urged me not to give the boy any money. After paying for my boarding and lodging I had very little to spare, but Sudheer seemed to sense when a money order or cheque arrived, and would hang around, spinning tall tales of great financial distress until, in order to be rid of him, I would give him five to ten rupees. (In those days, a magazine payment seldom exceeded fifty rupees.)

He was becoming something of a trial, constantly interrupting me in my work, and even picking up confectionery from my landlady's small shop and charging it to my account. I had stopped going for bicycle rides. He had wrecked one of the cycles and the shopkeeper held me responsible for repairs.

The sad thing was that Sudheer had no other friends. He did not go in for team games or for music or other creative pursuits which might have helped him to move around with people of his own age group. He was a loner with a propensity for mischief. Had he entered a bicycle race, he would have won easily. Forever eluding a variety of pursuers, he was extremely fast on his bike. But we did not have cycle races in Dehra.

And then, for a blessed two or three weeks, I saw nothing of my unpredictable friend.

I discovered later that he had taken a fancy to a young schoolteacher, about five years his senior, who lived in a hostel up at Rajpur. His cycle rides took him in that direction. As usual, his charm proved irresistible, and it wasn't long before the teacher and the acolyte were taking rides together down lonely forest roads. This was all right by me, of course, but it wasn't the norm with the middle-class matrons of small-town India, at least not in 1957. Hostel wardens, other students, and naturally Sudheer's parents, were all in a state of agitation. So I wasn't surprised when Sudheer turned up in my room to announce that he was on his way to Nahan, to study at an Inter college there.

Nahan was a small hill town about sixty miles from Dehra. Sudheer was banished to the home of his mama, an uncle who was a sub-inspector in the local police force. He had promised to see that Sudheer stayed out of trouble.

Whether he succeeded or not, I could not tell, for a couple of months later I gave up my rooms in Dehra and left for Delhi. I lost touch with Sudheer's family, and it was only several years later, when I bumped into an old acquaintance, that I was given news of my erstwhile friend.

He had apparently done quite well for himself. Taking off for Calcutta, he had used his charm and his fluent English to land a job as an assistant on a tea estate. Here he had proved quite efficient, earning the approval of his manager and employers. But his roving eye soon got him into trouble. The women working in the tea gardens became prey to his amorous and amoral nature. Keeping one mistress was acceptable. Keeping several was asking for trouble. He was found dead early one morning, with his throat cut.

2
THE ROYAL CAFE SET

Dehra was going through a slump in those days, and there wasn't much work for anyone—least of all for my neighbour, Suresh Mathur, an income tax lawyer, who was broke for two reasons. To begin with, there was not much work going around, as those with taxable incomes were few and far between. Apart from that, when he did get work, he was slow and half-hearted about getting it done. This was because he seldom got up before eleven in the morning, and by the time he took a bus down from Rajpur and reached his own small office (next door to my rooms), or the income tax office a little further on, it was lunchtime and all the tax officials were out. Suresh would then repair to the Royal Cafe for a beer or two (often at my expense) and this would stretch into a gin and tonic, after which he would stagger up to his first-floor office and collapse on the sofa for an afternoon nap. He would wake up at six, after the income tax office had closed.

I occupied two rooms next to his office, and we were on friendly terms, sharing an enthusiasm for the humorous works of P.G. Wodehouse. I think he modelled himself on Bertie Wooster, for he would often turn up wearing mauve or yellow socks or a pink shirt and a bright green tie—enough to make anyone in his company feel quite liverish. Unlike Bertie Wooster, he did not have a Jeeves to look after him and get him out of various scrapes. I tried not to be too friendly, as Suresh was in the habit of borrowing lavishly from all his friends, conveniently forgetting to return the amounts. I wasn't well off and could ill afford the company of a spendthrift friend. Sudheer was trouble enough.

Dehra, in those days, was full of people living on borrowed money or no money at all. Hence, the large number of disconnected telephone and electric lines. I did not have electricity myself, simply because the previous tenant had taken off, leaving me with outstandings of over a thousand rupees, then a princely sum. My monthly income seldom exceeded five hundred rupees. No matter. There was plenty of kerosene available, and the oil lamp lent a romantic glow to my literary endeavours.

Looking back, I am amazed at the number of people who were quite broke. There was William Matheson, a Swiss journalist, whose remittances from Zurich never seemed to turn up; my landlady, whose husband had deserted her two years previously; Mr Madan, who dealt in second-hand cars which no one wanted; the owner of the corner restaurant, who sat in solitary splendour

surrounded by empty tables; and the proprietor of the Ideal
Book Depot, who was selling off his stock of unsold books and
becoming a departmental store. We complain that few people
buy or read books today, but I can assure you that there were
even fewer customers in the fifties and sixties. Only doctors,
dentists, and the proprietors of English schools were making
money.

Suresh spent whatever cash came his way, and borrowed
more. He had an advantage over the rest of us—he owned an old
bungalow, inherited from his father, up at Rajpur in the foothills,
where he lived alone with an old manservant. And owning a
property gave him some standing with his creditors. The grounds
boasted of a mango and litchi orchard, and these he gave out
on contract every year, so that his friends did not even get to
enjoy some of his produce. The proceeds helped him to pay his
office rent in town, with a little left over to give small amounts
on account to the owner of the Royal Cafe.

If a lawyer could be hard up, what chance had a journalist?
And yet, William Matheson had everything going for him from
the start, when he came out to India as an assistant to Von
Hesseltein, correspondent for some of the German papers. Von
Hesseltein passed on some of the assignments to William, and
for a time, all went well. William lived with Von Hesseltein and
his family, and was also friendly with Suresh, often paying for the
drinks at the Royal Cafe. Then William committed the folly (if
not the sin) of having an affair with Von Hesseltein's wife. Von
Hesseltein was not the understanding sort. He threw William out
of the house and stopped giving him work.

William hired an old typewriter and set himself up as
a correspondent in his own right, living and working from
a room in the Doon Guest House. At first he was welcome
there, having paid a three-month advance for room and board.
He bombarded the Swiss and German papers with his articles,

but there were very few takers. No one in Europe was really interested in India's five-year plans, or Corbusier's Chandigarh, or the Bhakra Nangal Dam. Book publishing in India was confined to textbooks, otherwise William might have published a vivid account of his experiences in the French Foreign Legion. after two or three rums at the Royal Cafe, he would regale us with tales of his exploits in the Legion, before and after the siege of Dien Bien Phu. Some of his stories had the ring of truth, others (particularly his sexual exploits) were obviously tall tales; but I was happy to pay for the beer or coffee in order to hear him spin them out.

Those were glorious days for an unknown freelance writer. I was realizing my dream of living by my pen, and I was doing it from a small town in north India, having turned my back on both London and New Delhi. I had no ambitions to be a great writer, or even a famous one, or even a rich one. All I wanted to do was *write*. And I wanted a few readers and the occasional cheque so I could carry on living my dream.

The cheques came along in their own desultory way—fifty rupees from *The Weekly*, or thirty-five from *The Statesman* or the same from *Sport and Pastime*, and so on—just enough to get by, and to be the envy of Suresh Mathur, William Matheson, and a few others, professional people who felt that I had no business earning more than they did. Suresh even declared that I should have been paying tax, and offered to represent me, his other clients having gone elsewhere.

And there was old Colonel Wilkie, living on a small pension in a corner room of the White House Hotel. His wife had left him some years before, presumably because of his drinking, but he claimed to have left her because of her obsession with moving the furniture—it seems she was always shifting things about, changing rooms, throwing out perfectly sound tables and chairs, and replacing them with fancy stuff picked up here and there. If he took a liking to a particular easy chair and showed signs of settling down in it, it would disappear the next day to be replaced by something horribly ugly and uncomfortable.

'It was a form of mental torture,' said Colonel Wilkie, confiding in me over a glass of beer on the White House veranda. 'The sitting room was cluttered with all sorts of ornamental junk and flimsy side tables, so that I was constantly falling over the damn things. It was like a minefield! And the mines were never in the same place. You've noticed that I walk with a limp?'

'First World War?' I ventured. 'Wounded at Ypres? Or was it Flanders?'

'Nothing of the sort,' snorted the Colonel. 'I did get one or two flesh wounds but they were nothing as compared to the damage inflicted on me by those damned shifting tables and chairs. Fell over a coffee table and dislocated my shoulder. Then broke an ankle negotiating a stool that was in the wrong place. Bookshelf fell on me. Tripped on a rolled-up carpet. Hit by a curtain rod. Would you have put up with it?'

'No,' I had to admit.

'Had to leave her, of course. She went off to England. Send her an allowance. Half my pension! All spent on furniture!'

'It's a superstition of sorts, I suppose. Collecting things.'

The Colonel told me that the final straw was when his favourite spring bed had suddenly been replaced by a bed made up of hard wooden slats. It was sheer torture trying to sleep on it, and he had left his house and moved into the White House Hotel as a permanent guest.

Now he couldn't allow anyone to touch or tidy up anything in his room. There were beer stains on the tablecloth, cobwebs on his family pictures, dust on his books, empty medicine bottles on his dressing table, and mice nesting in his old, discarded boots. He had gone to the other extreme and wouldn't have anything changed or moved in his room.

I didn't see much of the room because we usually sat out on the veranda, waited upon by one of the hotel bearers, who came over with bottles of beer that I dutifully paid for, the Colonel having exhausted his credit. I suppose he was in his late sixties then. He never went anywhere, not even for a walk in the compound. He blamed this inactivity on his gout, but it was really inertia and an unwillingness to leave the precincts of the bar, where he could cadge the occasional drink from a sympathetic guest. I am that age now, and not half as active as I used to be, but there are people to live for, and tales to tell, and I keep writing. It is important to keep writing.

Colonel Wilkie had given up on life. I suppose he could have gone off to England, but he would have been more miserable there, with no one to buy him a drink (since he wasn't likely to reciprocate), and the possibility of his wife turning up again to rearrange the furniture.

3
'BIBIJI'

My landlady was a remarkable woman, and this little memoir of Dehra in the 1950s would be incomplete without a sketch of hers.

She would often say, 'Ruskin, one day you must write my life story,' and I would promise to do so. And although she really deserves a book to herself, I shall try to do justice to her in these few pages.

She was, in fact, my Punjabi stepfather's first wife. Does that sound confusing? It was certainly complicated. And you might well ask, why on earth were you living with your stepfather's first wife instead of your stepfather and mother?

The answer is simple. I got on rather well with this rotund, well-built lady, and sympathized with her predicament. She had been married at a young age to my stepfather, who was something of a playboy and who ran the photographic saloon he had received as part of her dowry. When he left her for my mother, he sold the saloon and gave his first wife part of the premises. In order to sustain herself and two small children, she started a small provision store and thus became Dehra's first lady shopkeeper.

I had just started freelancing from Dehra and was not keen on joining my mother and stepfather in Delhi. When 'Bibiji'—as I called her—offered me a portion of her flat on very reasonable terms, I accepted without hesitation and was to spend the next two years above her little shop on Rajpur Road. Almost fifty years later, the flat is still there, but it is now an ice cream parlour! Poetic justice, perhaps.

'Bibiji' sold the usual provisions. Occasionally, I lent a helping hand and soon learnt the names of the various lentils arrayed before us—moong, malka, masoor, arhar, channa, rajma, etc. She bought her rice, flour and other items wholesale from the mandi, and sometimes I would accompany her on an early morning march to the mandi (about two miles distant) where we would load a handcart with her purchases. She was immensely strong and could lift sacks of wheat or rice that left me gasping. I can't say I blame my rather skinny stepfather for staying out of her reach.

She had a helper, a Bihari youth, who would trundle the cart back to the shop and help with the loading and unloading. Before opening the shop (at around 8 a.m.) she would make our breakfast—parathas with my favourite shalgam pickle, and in winter, a delicious kanji made from the juice of red carrots. When the shop opened, I would go upstairs to do my writing while she conducted the day's business.

Sometimes she would ask me to help her with her accounts, or in making out a bill, for she was barely literate. But she was an astute shopkeeper; she knew instinctively who was good for credit and who was strictly nakad (cash). She would also warn me against friends who borrowed money without any intention of returning it; warnings that I failed to heed. Friends in perpetual need there were aplenty—Sudheer, William, Suresh, and a couple of others—and I am amazed that I didn't have to borrow, too, considering the uncertain nature of my income. Those little cheques and money orders from magazines did not always arrive in time. But sooner or later something *did* turn up. I was very lucky.

Bibiji had a friend, a neighbour, Mrs Singh, an attractive woman in her thirties who smoked a hookah and regaled us with tales of ghosts and chudails from her village near Agra. We did not see much of her husband who was an excise inspector. He was busy making money.

Bibiji and Mrs Singh were almost inseparable, which was quite understandable in view of the fact that both had absentee husbands. They were really happy together. During the day Mrs Singh would sit in the shop, observing the customers. And afterwards she would entertain us with clever imitations of the more odd or eccentric among them. At night, after the shop was closed, Bibiji and her friend would make themselves comfortable on the same cot (creaking beneath their combined weights), wrap themselves in a razai or blanket, and invite me to sit on the next charpai and listen to their yarns or tell them a few of my own. Mrs Singh had a small son, not very bright, who was continually eating laddoos, jalebis, barfis, and other sweets. Quite appropriately, he was called Laddoo. And I believe he grew into one.

Bibiji's son and daughter were then at a residential school. They came home occasionally. So did Mr Singh, with more sweets for his son. He did not appear to find anything unusual in his wife's intimate relationship with Bibiji. His mind was obviously on other things.

Bibiji and Mrs Singh both made plans to get me married. When I protested, saying I was only twenty-three, they said I was old enough. Bibiji had an eye on an Anglo-Indian schoolteacher who sometimes came to the shop, but Mrs Singh turned her down, saying she had very spindly legs. Instead, she suggested the daughter of the local padre, a glamorous-looking, dusky beauty, but Bibiji vetoed the proposal, saying the young lady used too much make-up and already displayed too much fat around the waistline. Both agreed that I should marry a plain-looking girl who could cook, use a sewing machine, and speak a little English.

'And be strong in the legs,' I added, much to Mrs Singh's approval.

They did not know it, but I was enamoured by Kamla, a girl from the hills, who lived with her parents in quarters behind the flat. She was always giving me mischievous glances with her dark, beautiful, expressive eyes. And whenever I passed her on the landing, we exchanged pleasantries and friendly banter; it was as though we had known each other for a long time. But she was already betrothed, and that too to a much older man, a widower, who owned some land outside the town. Kamla's family was poor, her father was in debt, and it was to be a marriage of convenience. There was nothing much I could do about it— landless, and without prospects—but after the marriage had taken place and she had left for her new home, I befriended her younger brother and through him sent her my good wishes from time to time. She is just a distant memory now, but a bright one, like a forget-me-not blooming on a bare rock. Would I have married her, had I been able to? She was simple, unlettered; but I might have taken the chance.

Those two years on Rajpur Road were an eventful time, what with the visitations of Sudheer, the company of William and Suresh, the participation in Bibiji's little shop, the evanescent friendship with Karma. I did a lot of writing and even sold a few stories here and there; but the returns were modest, barely adequate. Everyone was urging me to try my luck in Delhi. And so I bid goodbye to sleepy little Dehra (as it then was) and took a bus to the capital. I did no better there as a writer, but I found a job of sorts and that kept me going for a couple of years.

But to return to Bibiji, I cannot just leave her in limbo. She continued to run her shop for several years, and it was only failing health that forced her to close it. She sold the business and went to live with her married daughter in New Delhi. I saw her from time to time. In spite of high blood pressure, diabetes, and eventually blindness, she lived on into her eighties. She was always glad to see me, and never gave up trying to find a suitable bride for me.

The last time I saw her, shortly before she died, she said, 'Ruskin, there is this widow—lady who lives down the road and comes over sometimes. She has two children but they are grown up. She feels lonely in her big house. If you like, I'll talk to her. It's time you settled down. And she's only sixty.'

'Thanks, Bibiji,' I said, holding both ears. 'But I think I'll settle down in my next life.'

ON FAIRY HILL

Those little green lights that I used to see, twinkling away on Pari Tibba—there had to be a scientific explanation for them, I was sure. After dark we see or hear many things that seem mysterious, irrational. And then by the clear light of day we find that the magic, the mystery has an explanation after all.

But I did see those lights occasionally—late at night, when I walked home from town to my little cottage at the edge of the forest. They moved too fast for them to be torches or lanterns carried by people. And as there were no roads on Pari Tibba, they could not have been cycle or cart lamps. Someone told me there was phosphorus in the rocks, and that this probably accounted for the luminous glow emanating from the hillside late at night. Possibly; but I was not convinced.

My encounter with the little people happened by the light of day.

One morning, early in April, purely on an impulse I decided to climb to the top of Pari Tibba and look around for myself. It was springtime in the Himalayan foothills. The sap was rising—in the trees, in the grass, in the wild flowers, in my own veins. I took the path through the oak forest, down to the little steam at the bottom of the hill, and then up the steep slope of Pari Tibba, hill of the fairies.

It was quite a scramble getting to the top. The path ended at the stream. After that, I had to clutch at brambles and tufts of grass to make the ascent. Fallen pine needles, slippery underfoot, made it difficult to get a foothold. But finally I made it to the top—a grassy plateau fringed by pines and a few wild medlar trees now clothed in white blossom.

It was a pretty spot. And as I was hot and sweaty, I removed most of my clothing and lay down under a medlar to rest. The climb had been quite tiring. But a fresh breeze soon brought me back to life. It made a soft humming sound in the pines. And the grass, sprinkled with yellow buttercups, buzzed with the sound of crickets and grasshoppers.

After some time I stood up and surveyed the scene. To the north, Landour with its rusty red-roofed cottages; to the south, the wide valley and a silver stream flowing towards the Ganga. To the west, rolling hills, patches of forest, and a small village tucked into a fold of the mountain.

Disturbed by my presence, a barking deer ran across the clearing and down the opposite slope. A band of long-tailed blue magpies rose from the oak trees, glided across the knoll and settled in another strand of oaks.

I was alone. Alone with the wind and the sky. It had probably been months, possibly years, since any human had passed that way. The soft lush grass looked most inviting. I lay down again on the sun-warmed sward. Pressed and bruised by my weight, catmint and clover gave out a soft fragrance. A ladybird climbed up my leg and began to explore my body. A swarm of white butterflies fluttered around me.

I slept.

I have no idea how long I slept, but when I awoke it was to experience an unusual, soothing sensation all over my limbs, as though they were being gently stroked with rose petals.

All lethargy gone, I opened my eyes to find a little girl—or was it a woman?—about two inches high, sitting cross-legged on my chest and studying me intently. Her hair fell in long black tresses. Her skin was the colour of honey. Her firm little breasts were like tiny acorns. She held a buttercup, larger than her hand, and with it she was stroking my tingling flesh.

I was tingling all over. A sensation of sensual joy surged through my limbs.

A tiny boy—or man—completely naked, now joined the elfin girl, and they held hands and looked into my eyes, smiling, their teeth little pearls, their lips soft petals of apricot blossom. Were these the nature spirits, the flower fairies I had often dreamt of? I raised my head and saw that there were scores of little people all over me—exploring my legs, thighs, waist and arms. Delicate, caring, gentle, caressing creatures. They wanted to love me!

Some of them were lavishing me with dew or pollen or some soft essence. I closed my eyes. Waves of pure physical pleasure swept over me. I had never known anything like it. My limbs turned to water. The sky revolved around me, and I must have fainted.

When I awoke, perhaps an hour later, the little people had gone. A fragrance of honeysuckle lingered in the air. A deep rumble overhead made me look up. Dark clouds had gathered, threatening rain. Had the thunder frightened them away, to their abode beneath the rocks and tree roots? Or had they simply tired of sporting with a strange newcomer? Mischievous they were; for when I looked around for my clothes I could not find them anywhere.

A wave of panic surged over me. I ran here and there, looking behind shrubs and tree trunks, but to no avail. My clothes had disappeared, along with the fairies—if, indeed, they were fairies!

It began to rain. Large drops cannoned off the dry rocks. Then it hailed and soon the slope was covered with ice. There was no shelter. Naked, I ran down the path to the stream. There was no one to see me—only a wild mountain goat, speeding away in the opposite direction. Gusts of wind slashed rain and hail across my face and body. Panting and shivering, I took shelter beneath an overhanging rock until the storm had passed. By then it was almost dusk and I was able to ascend the path to my cottage without encountering anyone, apart from a band of startled langurs, who chattered excitedly on seeing me.

I couldn't stop shivering, so I went straight to bed. I slept a deep, dreamless sleep and woke up the next morning with a high fever.

Mechanically I dressed, made myself some breakfast and tried to get through the morning's chores. When I took my temperature I found it was a hundred and four. So I swallowed a tablet and went back to bed.

There I lay until late afternoon, when the postman's knocking woke me. I left my letters unopened on my desk (that in itself was unusual) and returned to my bed.

The fever lasted almost a week and left me weak and half-starved. I couldn't have climbed Pari Tibba again, even if I'd wanted to; but I reclined on my window seat and looked at the clouds drifting over that desolate hill. Desolate it seemed, and yet strangely inhabited. When it grew dark, I waited for those little green fairy lights to appear; but these, it seemed, were now to be denied to me.

And so I returned to my desk, my typewriter, my newspaper articles and correspondence. It was a lonely period in my life. My marriage hadn't worked out: my wife, fond of high society and averse to living with an unsuccessful writer in a remote cottage in the woods, was following her own, more successful career in Mumbai. I had always been rather half-hearted in my approach to making money, whereas she had always wanted more and more of it. She left me—left me with my books and my dreams....

Had it all been a dream, that strange episode on Pari Tibba? Had an overactive imagination conjured up those aerial spirits, those siddhas of the upper air? Or were they underground people, living deep within the bowels of the hill? If I was going to keep my sanity I knew I had better get on with the more mundane aspects of living—such as going into town to buy my groceries, mending the leaking roof, paying the electricity bill, plodding up to the post office and remembering to deposit the odd cheque that came my way. All the mundane things that made life so dull and dreary.

The truth is, what we commonly call life is not life at all.

Its routine and settled ways are the curse of life and we will do almost anything to get away from the trivial, even if it is only for a few hours of forgetfulness in alcohol, drugs, forbidden sex or golf. Some of us would even go underground with the fairies, those little people who have sought refuge in Mother Earth from mankind's killing ways; for they are as vulnerable as butterflies and flowers. All things beautiful are easily destroyed.

I am sitting at my window in the gathering dark, penning these stray thoughts, when I see them coming—hand in hand, walking on a swirl of mist, radiant, suffused with all the colours of the rainbow. For a rainbow has formed a bridge from them, from Pari Tibba, to the edge of my window.

I am ready to go, to love and be loved, in their secret lairs or in the upper air—far from the stifling confines of the world in which we toil....

Come, fairies, carry me away, to love me as you did that summer's day!

THE OLD SUITCASE

The autobiography of my suitcase is, in many respects, my own autobiography.

I bought it in Jersey, in the Channel Islands, in 1952, and for well over sixty-five years it has given shelter to so many of my personal effects—socks, underwear, shirts, trousers; books, notebooks, pens, paper, passport; and in recent years (when, like its owner, it is showing signs of wear and tear): a receptacle for old manuscripts, photographs, newspaper cuttings, publisher's contracts, and the flotsam of a lifetime of putting pen to paper.

For the last few years the suitcase had lain under my bed, so forgotten that the mice had managed to get in, building a nest from old newspapers; and I was woken one night by the squealing of baby mice—several of them. I was about to evict the family when I remembered the times when I had been evicted from lodgings, so I allowed them a respite of several days—a sort of stay order—before tipping the lot into an empty flowerpot and hoping for the best.

The suitcase was in a sad condition, but I was loath to throw it away. You don't throw away old friends. Or do you? There are all-weather friends and there are fair-weather friends, and it can take time to tell one from the other. The old suitcase had been with one long enough to be called both friend and philosopher, and so I hung on to it.

It was a very cheap suitcase—the cheapest I could find in that Woolworth's Store in Jersey, when I was eighteen and ready to try my luck in London. I had spent a year in Jersey, living with my aunt's family and working as a junior clerk in the

Public Health Department. Late evening I'd sit down at my small portable typewriter (bought with the help of a loan from Mr Bromley, a kind senior clerk) and work on the novel that I was writing—the novel that was to become *The Room on the Roof*, but I was keen to move to London, where there were publishers and writers and bookshops and theatres, and I was saving something out of my weekly wage of three pounds in order to make that dream a reality.

I had saved about twelve pounds when a decision to leave was forced upon me as result of a quarrel I had with my uncle, a good man but somewhat set in his way of thinking.

I used to keep a diary at the time, and I'd made the mistake of leaving it on my desk near the typewriter in the attic room where I worked. My uncle, prowling around while I was out at work, had come across and read some entries in which I had expressed dissatisfaction with his narrow-mindedness and extreme political views. He confronted me with the diary. He accused me of being an ingrate and a 'nigger lover' (his words) and suggested that I leave his house.

So, of course, I took up his suggestion, gave a week's notice to the Public Health Department, and packed my belongings. Jersey was not for me.

But I needed a suitcase—and a cheap one. The tin trunk I had brought from India was unsuitable for travelling about in England, where you had to manage your own luggage. The suitcase I found was very light—made of some sort of reinforced hardboard—and I did not expect it to last very long. But it was big enough for my few belongings, and it cost two pounds and a few shillings.

And so, with my new suitcase in my right hand, and the typewriter in my left hand, I boarded the ferry for Southampton, and eight hours later found myself on the train to London—without a job, without a home to go to, and with a half-written novel as my only asset.

⌇

The gales of Jersey were exchanged for the fog of London. March is probably the most dismal month in that hardy city—fog outside, and indoors the smell of leaking gas. Continuous drizzle. Aspidistras growing in dark corners of boarding-house entrance halls. The sun a distant memory. I cursed myself for leaving India.

An old school friend put me up in his small room for almost a month. He loved cooking, and the room was always fall of the fragrance of curries and spices. I found a job and a room of my own, and typewriter, suitcase, and I ascended the stairs to a tiny attic room in a boarding house in Glenmore Road.

It was a depressing little room, but I was out most of the day, working in an office in distant Soho, or wandering about looking for cheap cafés, living off beans on toast or 'meat and two veg'—the staple chow in the ABC restaurants. When I had money to spare I went to the cinema. Everyone smoked in those days, and it was difficult to see the screen through the haze of smoke that drifted through the hall.

I left Glenmore Road for Haverstock Hill, my suitcase getting heavier with the few books that I had been acquiring. At night I worked on my novel—the first draft written by hand, the second draft typed out on my little portable.

Diana Athill, a partner in the firm of Andre Deutsch, and about fifteen years my senior befriended me and had me over for dinner on several occasions. She gave me an old raincoat—we were about the same height—and out of gratitude I showed her how to make a curry. I think it was more of a stew than a curry, but we managed to consume it.

Then the three friends—suitcase, typewriter, and budding author—moved to Tooting, in South London.

Why Tooting?

Well, I'd fallen in love with this wonderful girl from Vietnam.

She was a student and her name was Vu-Phuong, meaning 'like the wind', and true enough, she came and went like the wind.

She was sweet company, and for several weeks we spent a lot of time together—strolling in Kensington Gardens, wandering through the hothouses in Kew, even going to the opera. It was my suggestion that we go to the opera. The cheaper seats were right at the back of the huge opera house, and we couldn't hear much of the singing, not even the rollicking Toreador song (it was Carmen)—it was much better on gramophone records!

On a rainy day in June we joined the crowds on the streets, watching Queen Elizabeth's coach pass by in all its splendour. Vu had a pretty umbrella and I had Diana Athill's raincoat, so we did not mind the rain.

And then, unaccountably, Vu stopped seeing me. She even changed her lodgings without giving me her new address. I tried to trace her, but without any success. Then I received a note from her saying she was returning to her home in Hanoi. The Vietnam War was at its height, and Hanoi was part of Communist-held territory. It was possible that she was under pressure to avoid contact with 'Westerners'. I was no Westerner, but how were her political bosses to know that? Heartbroken, I left Tooting—how I hated Tooting!—and returned to the more familiar streets of Belsize Park.

I told Diana of my unhappy plight—I would often confide in her—and to cheer me up she took me to St Paul's Cathedral to hear Yehudi Menuhin, the great violinist, give a recital. It was a moving experience, and for once I felt grateful to London for giving me the opportunity to hear great music.

⌣

Another kind of music assailed me when I made friends with a bunch of West Indians, newly arrived in England. They invited me to a calypso party in a flat in Brixton (right next to the prison), and the dancing and revelry continued till dawn. Unthinking, I invited them to hold their next party in my bedsitter (now a fairly spacious one) in Belsize Park. The party was a great success, the building shuddered to its foundations as the rum flowed and the dancing grew frenetic, and the next day my landlord gave me twenty-four-hours' notice to leave the premises.

I lugged my suitcase and typewriter down the road to Swiss Cottage, where a kindly Jewish landlady (my third Jewish landlady) took me in and gave me a pleasant room with a large window which let in the sunlight on those few occasions when the sun came out. She even gave me a good breakfast. But she warned me against having parties in the room. And no lady visitors. And no pin-ups on the walls. Down came Eartha Kitt.

I was quite happy in Swiss Cottage, but after nearly four years away from India I felt it was time to go home.

'No job for you here,' my mother had warned me. 'And you won't make any money from writing. Better stay in England.'

But I was not to be put off. Home is where the heart is, and my heart was still in the foothills of Dehra.

After much dithering, Diana and Andre Deutsch gave me a cheque for fifty pounds as an advance against my novel, which had finally been accepted. This was the standard advance in those days. Publication was still a year off, but I did not feel like hanging around in London any longer. The fare to Bombay—by the cheapest passenger liner, the M. S. *Batory*, a Polish ship—was just under forty pounds. I bought a ticket, gave a week's notice to my employer, thanked Diana for her many kindnesses, and bought a second suitcase.

This new suitcase cost more than the old one, and was quite flashy, but it was not to last as long. The cheap hardboard suitcase had accompanied me all over London, from one boarding house to another, and had attached itself to me like an unwanted stray, knowing no one else would keep it.

The M. S. *Batory* had a reputation for being unlucky, and even before it sailed half the crew had sought political asylum in the UK. But it had a good bar, serving Polish vodka, and only one passenger fell overboard in the course of the voyage.

At Gibraltar I went ashore and bought several bottles of perfume from an Indian trader. These, I thought, would make suitable presents for friends and family. At Port Said I went ashore and had my pocket picked; fortunately I'd kept most of my money in the old suitcase. At Aden I went ashore and did nothing; there was nothing to do and nothing to see. At Bombay I stepped ashore with my suitcases and was met by a couple of young customs officials and told to open them. I did so, and they took away all my bottles of perfume. Contraband, they said.

Happy homecoming!

'What will they do with it?' I asked a fellow passenger.

'Give it all to their girlfriends this evening,' he said knowingly.

At least they left my typewriter alone. And suitcases, typewriter, and I arrived in Dehradun without further mishap. I had no presents for anyone, but I was welcomed back anyway.

And so began three years of freelancing, bombarding every magazine and newspaper in the land with stories, articles, and anything they would publish and pay for! The little typewriter broke down from all the strain, the letter 'b' breaking off; being irreplaceable, I had to go through all my typescripts and fill in the 'b's' by hand. Stories and articles would only be considered if typed, so I had no choice but to go through with this chore, cursing all the time, the letter 'b' being most appropriate for this purpose: 'Bugger the bloody B!' In all my years of writing, I have never used swear words in print—and now here I am doing just that!

While my typewriter was getting a battering, the suitcase was enjoying a well-earned rest. It was put to use again when I moved to Delhi for three or four years, a period when my creative efforts were at their lowest ebb. As a writer I am greatly influenced by my surroundings and environment, and the Delhi (or rather, New Delhi) of the 1960s failed to get my creative juices flowing.

There was only one thing to do—pack up, and take to the hills.

It was a wise move although not always a restful one. Landlords, leaking roofs, crumbling hillsides, and water shortages all involved moving from one dwelling to another—Maplewood Lodge, Wayside Cottage (on the old Kipling Road), a flat near the Mall, then up to Landour's Prospect Point, and down again to Ivy Cottage! The old suitcase was kept fairly busy, now used more as a receptacle for books and papers. The latches had rusted away and I had to use a length of rope to close the suitcase; but it held up wonderfully well, although it was just reinforced hardboard.

For several years it was located under my bed, and whenever I came across some interesting relic, by way of an old magazine or newspaper, I would store it away for reference. My collection included the *Madras Mail Annual* of 1926, an issue of *The Statesman* (1936, I think) reporting on the horrors of the Quetta earthquake, and a copy of *Life* (1947) carrying a feature on the changes that were taking place in India at the time of Independence. This had a picture of me, looking very angelic, saying my prayers in the school chapel of Bishop Cotton School, Simla, referred to in the article as the 'Eton of the East'. I think I was chosen for the picture partly because I looked angelic and partly because I was one of the handful of English-looking boys left in the school. But there was nothing angelic about me when I was thirteen, just as there is nothing angelic about me now.

Over a period of time the mice had managed to gnaw their way through the fabric of the suitcase and had made a neat little home for themselves among my souvenirs. As they did no great damage, I left them alone, live and let live always having been my motto.

Then last month we had a terrible storm. The window burst open, the glass fell out, the rain came pouring into the room, and by morning the suitcase was half-full of water. The mice had already gone, but everything made of paper had been ruined and had to be thrown away.

The suitcase was put out to dry on the veranda, but it did not look as though it would recover.

'Shall I throw it away?' asked Beena, my granddaughter. 'It's falling to pieces.'

Do you throw away an old friend just because he's a cripple and of no use to anyone anymore? For over sixty-four years that cheap hardboard suitcase had been my constant companion, a witness to all my struggles, my successes, my failures, my follies.

'No, we can't throw it away,' I said. 'Put it in the attic, fill it with all those pastries I'm not supposed to eat, and let the mice make merry!'

THE PLAYING FIELDS OF SIMLA

It had been a lonely winter for a twelve-year-old boy. I hadn't really got over my father's untimely death two years previously; nor had I as yet reconciled myself to my mother's marriage to the Punjabi gentleman who dealt in second-hand cars. The three-month winter break over, I was almost happy to return to my boarding school in Simla—that elegant hill station once celebrated by Kipling and soon to lose its status as the summer capital of the Raj in India.

It wasn't as though I had many friends at school. I had always been a bit of a loner, shy and reserved, looking out only for my father's rare visits—on his brief leaves from RAF duties—and to my sharing his tent or air force hutment outside Delhi or Karachi. Those unsettled but happy days would not come again. I needed a friend but it was not easy to find one among a horde of rowdy, pea-shooting fourth formers, who carved their names on desks and stuck chewing gum on the class teacher's chair. Had I grown up with other children, I might have developed a taste for schoolboy anarchy; but, in sharing my father's loneliness after his separation from my mother, I had turned into a premature adult. The mixed nature of my reading—Dickens, Richmal Crompton, Tagore, and *Champion* and *Film Fun* comics—probably reflected the confused state of my life. A book reader was rare even in those pre-electronic times. On rainy days most boys played cards or Monopoly, or listened to Artie Shaw on the wind-up gramophone in the common room.

After a month in the fourth form I began to notice a new boy, Omar, and then only because he was a quiet, almost taciturn person who took no part in the form's feverish attempts to imitate the Marx Brothers at the circus. He showed no resentment at the prevailing anarchy, nor did he make a move to participate in it. Once he caught me looking at him, and he smiled ruefully, tolerantly. Did I sense another adult in the class? Someone who was a little older than his years?

Even before we began talking to each other, Omar and I developed an understanding of sorts, and we'd nod almost respectfully to each other when we met in the classroom corridors or the environs of dining hall or dormitory. We were not in the same house. The house system practised its own form of apartheid, whereby a member of, say, Curzon House was not expected to fraternize with someone belonging to Rivaz or Lefroy! Those public schools certainly knew how to clamp you into compartments. However, these barriers vanished when Omar and I found ourselves selected for the School Colts' hockey team— Omar as a fullback, I as goalkeeper. I think a defensive position suited me by nature. In all modesty I have to say that I made a good goalkeeper, both at hockey and football. And fifty years on, I am still keeping goal. Then I did it between goalposts, now I do it off the field—protecting a family, protecting my independence as a writer....

The taciturn Omar now spoke to me occasionally, and we combined well on the field of play. A good understanding is needed between goalkeeper and fullback. We were on the same wavelength. I anticipated his moves, he was familiar with mine. Years later, when I read Conrad's *The Secret Sharer,* I thought of Omar.

It wasn't until we were away from the confines of school, classroom and dining hall that our friendship flourished. The hockey team travelled to Sanawar on the next mountain range, where we were to play a couple of matches against our old rivals, the Lawrence Royal Military School. This had been my father's old school, but I did not know that in his time it had also been a military orphanage. Grandfather, who had been a private foot soldier—of the likes of Kipling's Mulvaney, Otheris, and Learoyd—had joined the Scottish Rifles after leaving home at the age of seventeen. He had died while his children were still very young, but my father's more rounded education had enabled him to become an officer.

Omar and I were thrown together a good deal during the visit to Sanawar, and in our more leisurely moments, strolling undisturbed around a school where we were guests and not pupils, we exchanged life histories and other confidences. Omar, too, had lost his father—had I sensed that before?—shot in some tribal encounter on the Frontier, for he hailed from the lawless lands beyond Peshawar. A wealthy uncle was seeing to Omar's education. The RAF was now seeing to mine.

We wandered into the school chapel, and there I found my father's name—A. A. Bond—on the school's roll of honour board: old boys who had lost their lives while serving during the two World Wars.

'What did his initials stand for?' asked Omar.

'Aubrey Alexander.'

'Unusual names, like yours. Why did your parents call you Ruskin?'

'I am not sure. I think my father liked the works of John Ruskin, who wrote on serious subjects like art and architecture. I don't think anyone reads him now. They'll read me, though!' I had already started writing my first book. It was called *Nine Months* (the length of the school term, not a pregnancy), and it described some of the happenings at school and lampooned a few of our teachers. I had filled three slim exercise books with this premature literary project, and I allowed Omar to go through them. He must have been my first reader and critic. 'They're very interesting,' he said, 'but you'll get into trouble if someone finds them. Especially Mr Oliver.' And he read out an offending verse:

Olly, Olly, Olly, with his balls on a trolley,
and his arse all painted green!

I have to admit it wasn't great literature. I was better at
hockey and football. I made some spectacular saves, and we won
our matches against Sanawar. When we returned to Simla, we
were school heroes for a couple of days and lost some of our
reticence; we were even a little more forthcoming with other boys.
And then Mr Fisher, my housemaster, discovered my literary opus,
Nine Months, under my mattress, and took it away and read it
(as he told me later) from cover to cover. Corporal punishment
then being in vogue, I was given six of the best with a springy
malacca cane, and my manuscript was torn up and deposited in
Fisher's waste-paper basket. All I had to show for my efforts were
some purple welts on my bottom. These were proudly displayed
to all who were interested, and I was a hero for another two days.

'Will you go away too when the British leave India?' Omar
asked me one day.

'I don't think so,' I said. 'My stepfather is Indian.'

'Everyone is saying that our leaders and the British are
going to divide the country. Simla will be in India, Peshawar
in Pakistan!'

'Oh, it won't happen,' I said glibly. 'How can they cut up
such a big country?' But even as we chatted about the possibility,
Nehru and Jinnah and Mountbatten and all those who mattered
were preparing their instruments for major surgery.

Before their decision impinged on our lives and everyone
else's, we found a little freedom of our own—in an underground
tunnel that we discovered below the third flat.

It was really part of an old, disused drainage system, and when
Omar and I began exploring it, we had no idea just how far it
extended. After crawling along on our bellies for some twenty
feet, we found ourselves in complete darkness. Omar had brought
along a small pencil torch, and with its help we continued writhing

forward (moving backwards would have been quite impossible) until we saw a glimmer of light at the end of the tunnel. Dusty, musty, very scruffy, we emerged at last on to a grassy knoll, a little way outside the school boundary.

It's always a great thrill to escape beyond the boundaries that adults have devised. Here we were in unknown territory. To travel without passports—that would be the ultimate in freedom!

But more passports were on their way and more boundaries.

Lord Mountbatten, viceroy and governor-general-to-be, came for our Founder's Day and gave away the prizes. I had won a prize for something or the other, and mounted the rostrum to receive my book from this towering, handsome man in his pinstripe suit. Bishop Cotton's was then the premier school of India, often referred to as the 'Eton of the East'. Viceroys and governors had graced its functions. Many of its boys had gone on to eminence in the civil services and armed forces. There was one 'old boy' about whom they maintained a stolid silence—General Dyer, who had ordered the massacre at Amritsar and destroyed the trust that had been building up between Britain and India.

Now Mountbatten spoke of the momentous events that were happening all around us—the War had just come to an end, the United Nations held out the promise of a world living in peace and harmony, and India, an equal partner with Britain, would be among the great nations....

A few weeks later, Bengal and Punjab provinces were bisected. Riots flared up across northern India, and there was a great exodus of people crossing the newly drawn frontiers of Pakistan and India. Homes were destroyed, thousands lost their lives.

The common room radio and the occasional newspaper kept us abreast of events, but in our tunnel, Omar and I felt immune from all that was happening, worlds away from all the pillage, murder and revenge. And outside the tunnel, on the pine knoll below the school, there was fresh untrodden grass, sprinkled with clover and daisies, the only sounds the hammering of a woodpecker, the distant insistent call of the Himalayan barbet. Who could touch us there?

'And when all the wars are done,' I said, 'a butterfly will still be beautiful.'

'Did you read that somewhere?'

'No, it just came into my head.'

'Already you're a writer.'

'No, I want to play hockey for India or football for Arsenal. Only winning teams!'

'You can't win forever. Better to be a writer.'

When the monsoon rains arrived, the tunnel was flooded, the drain choked with rubble. We were allowed out to the cinema to see Lawrence Olivier's *Hamlet*, a film that did nothing to raise our spirits on a wet and gloomy afternoon—but it was our last picture that year, because communal riots suddenly broke out in Simla's Lower Bazaar, an area that was still much as Kipling had described it—'a man who knows his way there can defy all the police of India's summer capital'—and we were confined to school indefinitely.

One morning after chapel, the headmaster announced that the Muslim boys—those who had their homes in what was now Pakistan—would have to be evacuated, sent to their homes across the border with an armed convoy.

The tunnel no longer provided an escape for us. The bazaar was out of bounds. The flooded playing field was deserted. Omar and I sat on a damp wooden bench and talked about the future in vaguely hopeful terms; but we didn't solve any problems. Mountbatten and Nehru and Jinnah were doing all the solving.

It was soon time for Omar to leave—he along with some fifty other boys from Lahore, Pindi and Peshawar. The rest of us—Hindus, Christians, Parsis—helped them load their luggage into the waiting trucks. A couple of boys broke down and wept. So did our departing school captain, a Pathan who had been known for his stoic and unemotional demeanour. Omar waved cheerfully to me and I waved back. We had vowed to meet again someday.

The convoy got through safely enough. There was only one casualty—the school cook, who had strayed into an off-limits area in the foothill town of Kalka and been set upon by a mob. He wasn't seen again.

Towards the end of the school year, just as we were all getting ready to leave for the school holidays, I received a letter from Omar. He told me something about his new school and how he missed my company and our games and our tunnel to freedom. I replied and gave him my home address, but I did not hear from him again. The land, though divided, was still a big one, and we were very small.

Some seventeen or eighteen years later I did get news of Omar, but in an entirely different context. India and Pakistan were at war and in a bombing raid over Ambala, not far from Simla, a Pakistani plane was shot down. Its crew died in the crash. One of them, I learnt later, was Omar.

Did he, I wonder, get a glimpse of the playing fields we knew so well as boys?

Perhaps memories of his schooldays flooded back as he flew over the foothills. Perhaps he remembered the tunnel through which we were able to make our little escape to freedom.

But there are no tunnels in the sky.

MY FATHER'S TREES IN DEHRA

Our trees still grow in Dehra. This is one part of the world where trees are a match for man. An old pipal may be cut down to make way for a new building; two pipal trees will sprout from the walls of the building. In Dehra the air is moist and the soil hospitable to seeds and probing roots. The valley of Dehradun lies between the first range of the Himalayas and the smaller but older Shivalik range. Dehra is an old town, but it was not in the reign of Rajput princes or Mughal kings that it really grew and flourished; it acquired a certain size and importance with the coming of the British and Anglo-Indian settlers. The English have an affinity with trees, and in the rolling hills of Dehra they discovered a retreat which, in spite of snakes and mosquitoes, reminded them, just a little bit, of England's green and pleasant land.

The mountains to the north are austere and inhospitable; the plains to the south are flat, dry and dusty. But Dehra is green. I look out of the train window at daybreak to see the sal and shisham trees sweep by majestically, while trailing vines and great clumps of bamboo give the forest a darkness and density which add to its mystery. There are still a few tigers in these forests, only a few, and perhaps they will survive, to stalk the spotted deer and drink at forest pools.

I grew up in Dehra. My grandfather built a bungalow on the outskirts of the town at the turn of the century. The house was sold a few years after Independence. No one knows me now in Dehra, for it is over twenty years since I left the place, and my boyhood friends are scattered and lost. And although the India of Kim is no more, and the Grand Trunk Road is now a procession of trucks instead of a slow-moving caravan of horses and camels, India is still a country in which people are easily lost and quickly forgotten.

From the station I can take either a taxi or a snappy little scooter rickshaw (Dehra had neither before 1950), but because I am on an unashamedly sentimental pilgrimage, I take a tonga, drawn by a lean, listless pony, and driven by a tubercular old Muslim man in a shabby green waistcoat. Only two or three tongas stand outside the station. There were always twenty or thirty here in the 1940s when I came home from boarding school to be met at the station by my grandfather; but the days of the tonga are nearly over, and in many ways this is a good thing, because most tonga ponies are overworked and underfed. Its wheels squeaking from lack of oil and its seat slipping out from under me, the tonga drags me through the bazaars of Dehra. A couple of miles of this slow, funereal pace makes me impatient to use my own legs, and I dismiss the tonga when we get to the small Dilaram bazaar.

It is a good place from which to start walking.

The Dilaram bazaar has not changed very much. The shops are run by a new generation of bakers, barbers and banias, but professions have not changed. The cobblers belong to the lower castes, the bakers are Muslims, the tailors are Sikhs. Boys still fly kites from the flat rooftops, and women wash clothes on the canal steps. The canal comes down from Rajpur and goes underground here, to emerge about a mile away.

I have to walk only a furlong to reach my grandfather's house. The road is lined with eucalyptus, jacaranda and laburnum trees. In the compounds there are small groves of mangoes, litchis and papayas. The poinsettia thrusts its scarlet leaves over garden walls. Every veranda has its bougainvillea creeper, every garden its bed of marigolds. Potted palms, those symbols of Victorian snobbery, are popular with Indian housewives. There are a few houses, but most of the bungalows were built by 'old India hands' on their retirement from the army, the police or the railways. Most of the present owners are Indian businessmen or government officials.

I am standing outside my grandfather's house. The wall has been raised, and the wicket gate has disappeared. I cannot get a clear view of the house and garden. The nameplate identifies the owner as Major General Saigal; the house has had more than one owner since my grandparents sold it in 1949.

On the other side of the road there is an orchard of litchi trees. This is not the season for fruit, and there is no one looking after the garden. By taking a little path that goes through the orchard, I reach higher ground and gain a better view of our old house.

Grandfather built the house with granite rocks taken from the foothills. It shows no sign of age. The lawn has disappeared, but the big jackfruit tree, giving shade to the side veranda, is still there. On this tree I spent my afternoons, absorbed in my Magnets, Champions and Hotspurs, while sticky mango juice trickled down my chin. (One could not eat the jackfruit unless it was cooked into a vegetable curry.) There was a hole in the bole of the tree in which I kept my pocket knife, top, catapult and any badges or buttons that could be saved from my father's RAF tunics when he came home on leave. There was also an Iron Cross, a relic of World War I, given to me by my grandfather. I have managed to keep the Iron Cross, but what did I do with my top and catapult? Memory fails me. Possibly they are still in the hole in the jackfruit tree; I must have forgotten to collect them when we went away after my father's death. I am seized by a whimsical urge to walk in at the gate, climb into the branches of the jackfruit tree and recover my lost possessions. What would the present owner, the major general (retired), have to say if I politely asked permission to look for a catapult left behind more than twenty years ago?

An old man is coming down the path through the litchi trees.

He is not a major general but a poor street vendor. He carries a small tin trunk on his head, and walks very slowly. When he sees me, he stops and asks me if I will buy something. I can think of nothing I need, but the old man looks so tired, so very old, that I am afraid he will collapse if he moves any further along the path without resting. So I ask him to show me his wares. He cannot get the box off his head by himself, but together we manage to set it down in the shade, and the old man insists on spreading its contents on the grass: bangles, combs, shoelaces, safety pins, cheap stationery, buttons, pomades, elastic and scores of other household necessities.

When I refuse buttons because there is no one to sew them on for me, he plies me with safety pins. I say no, but as he moves from one article to another, his querulous, persuasive voice slowly wears down my resistance, and I end up buying envelopes, a letter pad (pink roses on bright blue paper), a one-rupee fountain pen guaranteed to leak and several yards of elastic. I have no idea what I will do with the elastic, but the old man convinces me that I cannot live without it.

Exhausted by the effort of selling me a lot of things I obviously do not want, he closes his eyes and leans back against the trunk of a litchi tree. For a moment I feel rather nervous. Is he going to die sitting here beside me? He sinks to his haunches and puts his chin on his hands. He only wants to talk.

'I am very tired, Huzoor,' he says. 'Please do not mind if I sit here for a while.'

'Rest for as long as you like,' I say. 'That's a heavy load you've been carrying.'

He comes to life at the chance of a conversation and says, 'When I was a young man, it was nothing. I could carry my box up from Rajpur to Mussoorie by the bridle path—seven steep miles! But now I find it difficult to cover the distance from the station to Dilaram bazaar.'

'Naturally. You are quite old.'

'I am seventy, sahib.'

'You look very fit for your age,' I say this to please him; he looks frail and brittle. 'Isn't there someone to help you?' I ask.

'I had a servant boy last month, but he stole my earnings and ran off to Delhi. I wish my son was alive—he would not have permitted me to work like a mule for a living—but he was killed in the riots in 1947.'

'Have you no other relatives?'

'I have outlived them all. That is the curse of a healthy life. Your friends, your loved ones, all go before you, and at the end you are left alone. But I must go too, before long. The road to the bazaar seems to grow longer every day. The stones are harder. The sun is hotter in the summer, and the wind much colder in the winter. Even some of the trees that were there in my youth have grown old and have died. I have outlived the trees.'

He has outlived the trees. He is like an old tree himself, gnarled and twisted. I have a feeling that if he falls asleep in the orchard, he will strike root here, sending out crooked branches. I can imagine a small bent tree wearing a black waistcoat, a living scarecrow.

He closes his eyes again, but goes on talking.

'The English memsahibs would buy great quantities of elastic. Today it is ribbons and bangles for the girls, and combs for the boys. But I do not make much money. Because I cannot walk very far. How many houses do I reach in a day? Ten, fifteen. But twenty years ago I could visit more than fifty houses. That makes a difference.'

'Have you always been here?'

'Most of my life, Huzoor. I was here before they built the motor road to Mussoorie. I was here when the sahibs had their own carriages and ponies and the memsahibs their own rickshaws. I was here before there were any cinemas. I was here when the

Prince of Wales came to Dehradun.... Oh, I have been here a long time, Huzoor. I was here when that house was built,' he says, pointing with his chin towards my grandfather's house. 'Fifty, sixty years ago it must have been. I cannot remember exactly. What is ten years when you have lived seventy? But it was a tall, red-bearded sahib who built that house. He kept many creatures as pets. A kachwa (turtle) was one of them. And there was a python which crawled into my box one day and gave me a terrible fright. The sahib used to keep it hanging from his shoulders, like a garland. His wife, the burra mem, always bought a lot from me—lots of elastic. And there were sons, one a teacher, another in the air force, and there were always children in the house. Beautiful children. But they went away many years ago. Everyone has gone away.'

I do not tell him that I am one of the 'beautiful children', I doubt if he will believe me. His memories are of another age, another place, and for him there are no strong bridges into the present.

'But others have come,' I say.

'True, and that is as it should be. That is not my complaint. My complaint—should God be listening—is that I have been left behind.'

He gets slowly to his feet and stands over his shabby tin box, gazing down at it with a mixture of disdain and affection. I help him to lift and balance it on the flattened cloth on his head. He does not have the energy to turn and make a salutation of any kind, but, setting his sights on the distant hills, he walks down the path with steps that are shaky and slow but still wonderfully straight.

I wonder how much longer he will live. Perhaps a year or two, perhaps a week, perhaps an hour. It will be an end of living, but it will not be death. He is too old for death; he can only sleep; he can only fall gently, like an old, crumpled brown leaf.

I leave the orchard. The bend in the road hides my grandfather's house. I reach the canal again. It emerges from under a small culvert, where maidenhair ferns grow in the shade. The water, coming from a stream in the foothills, rushes along with a familiar sound; it does not lose its momentum until the canal has left the gently sloping streets of the town.

There are new buildings on this road, but the small police station is housed in the same old lime-washed bungalow. A couple of off-duty policemen, partly uniformed but with their pyjamas on, stroll hand in hand on the grass verge. Holding hands (with persons of the same sex, of course) is common practice in northern India, and denotes no special relationship.

I cannot forget this little police station. Nothing very exciting ever happened in its vicinity until, in 1947, communal riots broke out in Dehra. Then, bodies were regularly fished out of the canal and dumped on a growing pile in the station compound. I was only a boy, but when I looked over the wall at that pile of corpses, there was no one who paid any attention to me. They were too busy to send me away. At the same time they knew that I was perfectly safe. While Hindus and Muslims were at each other's throats, a white boy could walk the streets in safety. No one was any longer interested in the Europeans.

The people of Dehra are not violent by nature, and the town has no history of communal discord. But when refugees from partitioned Punjab poured into Dehra in the thousands, the atmosphere became charged with tension. These refugees, many of them Sikhs, had lost their homes and livelihoods; many had seen their loved ones butchered. They were in a fierce and vengeful frame of mind. The calm, sleepy atmosphere of Dehra was shattered during two months of looting and murder. Those Muslims who could get away, fled. The poorer members of the community remained in a refugee camp until the holocaust was over, then they returned to their former occupations, frightened and deeply mistrustful. The old box-man was one of them.

I cross the canal and take the road that will lead me to the riverbed. This was one of my father's favourite walks. He, too, was a walking man. Often, when he was home on leave, he would say, 'Ruskin, let's go for a walk,' and we would slip off together and walk down to the riverbed or into the sugarcane fields or across the railway lines and into the jungle.

On one of these walks (this was before Independence), I remember him saying, 'After the war is over, we'll be going to England. Would you like that?'

'I don't know,' I said. 'Can't we stay in India?'

'It won't be ours anymore.'

'Has it always been ours?' I asked.

'For a long time,' he said, 'over two hundred years. But we have to give it back now.'

'Give it back to whom?' I asked. I was only nine.

'To the Indians,' said my father.

The only Indians I had known till then were my ayah, the cook, the gardener and their children, and I could not imagine them wanting to be rid of us. The only other Indian who came to the house was Dr Ghose, and it was frequently said of him that he was more English than the English. I could understand my father better when he said, 'After the war, there'll be a job for me in England. There'll be nothing for me here.'

The war had at first been a distant event, but somehow it kept coming closer. My aunt, who lived in London with her two children, was killed with them during an air raid, then my father's younger brother died of dysentery on the long walk out from Burma. Both these tragic events depressed my father. Never in good health (he had been prone to attacks of malaria), he looked more worn and wasted every time he came home. His personal life was far from being happy, as he and my mother had separated, she to marry again. I think he looked forward a great deal to the days he spent with me; far more than I could have realized at the time. I was someone to come back to, someone for whom things could be planned, someone who could learn from him.

Dehra suited him. He was always happy when he was among trees, and this happiness communicated itself to me. I felt like drawing close to him. I remember sitting beside him on the veranda steps when I noticed the tendril of a creeping vine that was trailing near my feet. As we sat there, doing nothing in particular—in the best gardens, time has no meaning—I found that the tendril was moving almost imperceptibly away from me and towards my father. Twenty minutes later it had crossed the veranda steps and was touching his feet. This, in India, is the sweetest of salutations.

There is probably a scientific explanation for the plant's behaviour—something to do with the light and warmth on the veranda steps—but I like to think that its movements were motivated simply by affection for my father. Sometimes, when I sat alone beneath a tree, I felt a little lonely or lost. As soon as my father rejoined me, the atmosphere lightened, the tree itself became more friendly.

Most of the fruit trees round the house were planted by father, but he was not content with planting trees in the garden. On rainy days we would walk beyond the riverbed, armed with cutting and saplings and then we would amble through the jungle, planting flowering shrubs between the sal and shisham trees.

'But no one ever comes here,' I protested the first time. 'Who is going to see them?'

'Some day,' he said, 'someone may come this way…. If people keep cutting trees instead of planting them, there'll soon be no forests left at all, and the world will just be one vast desert.'

The prospect of a world without trees became a sort of nightmare for me (and one reason why I shall never want to live on a treeless moon), and I assisted my father in his tree planting with great enthusiasm.

'One day the trees will move again,' he said. 'They've been standing still for thousands of years. There was a time when they could walk about like people, but someone cast a spell on them and rooted them to one place. But they're always trying to move—see how they reach out with their arms!'

We found an island, a small rocky island in the middle of a dry riverbed. It was one of those riverbeds, so common in the foothills, which are completely dry in the summer but flooded during the monsoon rains. The rains had just begun, and the stream could still be crossed on foot, when we set out with a number of tamarind, laburnum and coral tree saplings and cuttings. We spent the day planting them on the island, then ate our lunch there, in the shelter of a wild plum.

My father went away soon after that tree planting. Three months later, in Calcutta, he died.

I was sent to boarding school. My grandparents sold the house and left Dehra. After school, I went to England. Years passed, my grandparents died, and when I returned to India, I was the only member of the family in the country.

And now I am in Dehra again, on the road to the riverbed.

The houses with their trim gardens are soon behind me, and I am walking through fields of flowering mustard, which make a carpet of yellow blossoms stretching away towards the jungle and the foothills.

The riverbed is dry at this time of the year. A herd of skinny cattle graze on the short brown grass at the edge of the jungle. The sal trees have been thinned out. Could our trees have survived? Will our island be there, or has some flash flood during a heavy monsoon washed it away completely?

As I look across the dry watercourse, my eye is caught by the spectacular red plumes of the coral blossom. In contrast with the dry, rocky riverbed, the little island is a green oasis. I walk across to the trees and notice that a number of parrots have come to live in them. A koel challenges me with a rising 'who-are-you, who-are-you....'

But the trees seem to know me. They whisper among themselves and beckon me nearer. And, looking around, I find that other trees and wild plants and grasses have sprung up under the protection of the trees we planted.

They have multiplied. They are moving. In this small forgotten corner of the world, my father's dreams are coming true and the trees are moving again.

THE FIGHT

Ranji had been less than a month in Rajpur when he discovered the pool in the forest. It was the height of summer, and his school had not yet opened, and, having as yet made no friends in this semi-hill station, he wandered about a good deal by himself into the hills and forests that stretched away interminably on all sides of the town. It was hot, very hot, at that time of year, and Ranji walked about in his vest and shorts, his brown feet white with the chalky dust that flew up from the ground. The earth was parched, the grass brown, the trees listless, hardly stirring, waiting for a cool wind or a refreshing shower of rain.

It was on such a day—a hot, tired day—that Ranji found the pool in the forest. The water had a gentle translucency, and you could see the smooth round pebbles at the bottom of the pool. A small stream emerged from a cluster of rocks to feed the pool. During the monsoon, this stream would be a gushing torrent, cascading down from the hills, but during the summer it was barely a trickle. The rocks, however, held the water in the pool, and it did not dry up like the pools in the plains.

When Ranji saw the pool, he did not hesitate to get into it. He had often gone swimming, alone or with friends, when he had lived with his parents in a thirsty town in the middle of the Rajputana desert. There, he had known only sticky, muddy pools, where buffaloes wallowed and women washed clothes. He had never seen a pool like this—so clean and cold and inviting. He threw off all his clothes, as he had done when he went swimming in the plains, and leapt into the water. His limbs were supple, free of any fat, and his dark body glistened in patches of sunlit water.

The next day he came again to quench his body in the cool waters of the forest pool. He was there for almost an hour, sliding in and out of the limpid green water, or lying stretched out on the smooth yellow rocks in the shade of broad-leaved sal trees. It was while he lay thus, naked on a rock, that he noticed another boy standing a little distance away, staring at him in a rather hostile manner. The other boy was a little older than Ranji, taller, thickset, with a broad nose and thick, red lips. He had only just noticed Ranji, and he stood at the edge of the pool, wearing a pair of bathing shorts, waiting for Ranji to explain himself.

When Ranji did not say anything, the other called out, 'What are you doing here, Mister?'

Ranji, who was prepared to be friendly, was taken aback at the hostility of the other's tone.

'I am swimming,' he replied. 'Why don't you join me?'

'I always swim alone,' said the other. 'This is my pool, I did not invite you here. And why are you not wearing any clothes?'

'It is not your business if I do not wear clothes. I have nothing to be ashamed of.'

'You skinny fellow, put on your clothes.'

'Fat fool, take yours off.'

This was too much for the stranger to tolerate. He strode up to Ranji, who still sat on the rock and, planting his broad feet firmly on the sand, said (as though this would settle the matter once and for all), 'Don't you know I am a Punjabi? I do not take replies from villagers like you!'

'So you like to fight with villagers?' said Ranji. 'Well, I am not a villager. I am a Rajput!'

'I am a Punjabi!'

'I am a Rajput!'

They had reached an impasse. One had said he was a Punjabi, the other had proclaimed himself a Rajput. There was little else that could be said.

'You understand that I am a Punjabi?' said the stranger, feeling that perhaps this information had not penetrated Ranji's head.

'I have heard you say it three times,' replied Ranji.

'Then why are you not running away?'

'I am waiting for *you* to run away!'

'I will have to beat you,' said the stranger, assuming a violent attitude, showing Ranji the palm of his hand.

'I am waiting to see you do it,' said Ranji.

'You will see me do it,' said the other boy.

Ranji waited. The other boy made a strange, hissing sound. They stared each other in the eye for almost a minute. Then the Punjabi boy slapped Ranji across the face with all the force he could muster. Ranji staggered, feeling quite dizzy. There were thick red finger marks on his cheek.

'There you are!' exclaimed his assailant. 'Will you be off now?'

For answer, Ranji swung his arm up and pushed a hard, bony fist into the other's face.

And then they were at each other's throats, swaying on the rock, tumbling on to the sand, rolling over and over, their legs and arms locked in a desperate, violent struggle. Gasping and cursing, clawing and slapping, they rolled right into the shallows of the pool.

Even in the water the fight continued as, spluttering and covered with mud, they groped for each other's head and throat. But after five minutes of frenzied, unscientific struggle, neither boy had emerged victorious. Their bodies heaving with exhaustion, they stood back from each other, making tremendous efforts to speak.

'Now—now do you realize—I am a Punjabi?' gasped the stranger.

'Do you know I am a Rajput?' said Ranji with difficulty.

They gave a moment's consideration to each other's answers,

and in that moment of silence there was only their heavy breathing and the rapid beating of their hearts.

'Then you will not leave the pool?' said the Punjabi boy.

'I will not leave it,' said Ranji.

'Then we shall have to continue the fight,' said the other.

'All right,' said Ranji.

But neither boy moved, neither took the initiative.

The Punjabi boy had an inspiration.

'We will continue the fight tomorrow,' he said. 'If you dare to come here again tomorrow, we will continue this fight, and I will not show you mercy as I have done today.'

'I will come tomorrow,' said Ranji. 'I will be ready for you.'

They turned from each other then and, going to their respective rocks, put on their clothes, and left the forest by different routes.

When Ranji got home, he found it difficult to explain the cuts and bruises that showed on his face, legs and arms. It was difficult to conceal the fact that he had been in an unusually violent fight, and his mother insisted on his staying at home for the rest of the day. That evening, though, he slipped out of the house and went to the bazaar, where he found comfort and solace in a bottle of vividly coloured lemonade and a banana leaf full of hot, sweet jalebis. He had just finished the lemonade when he saw his adversary coming down the road. His first impulse was to turn away and look elsewhere, his second to throw the lemonade bottle at his enemy. But he did neither of these things. Instead, he stood his ground and scowled at his passing adversary. And the Punjabi boy said nothing either, but scowled back with equal ferocity.

The next day was as hot as the previous one. Ranji felt weak and lazy and not at all eager for a fight. His body was stiff and sore after the previous day's encounter. But he could not refuse the challenge. Not to turn up at the pool would be an acknowledgement of defeat. From the way he felt just then, he knew he would be beaten in another fight. But he could not acquiesce in his own defeat. He must defy his enemy to the last, or outwit him, for only then could he gain his respect. If he surrendered now, he would be beaten for all time; but to fight and be beaten today left him free to fight and be beaten again. As long as he fought, he had a right to the pool in the forest.

He was half hoping that the Punjabi boy would have forgotten the challenge, but these hopes were dashed when he saw his opponent sitting, stripped to the waist, on a rock on the other side of the pool. The Punjabi boy was rubbing oil on his body, massaging it into his broad thighs. He saw Ranji beneath the sal trees, and called a challenge across the waters of the pool.

'Come over on this side and fight!' he shouted.

But Ranji was not going to submit to any conditions laid down by his opponent.

'Come *this* side and fight!' he shouted back with equal vigour.

'Swim across and fight me here!' called the other. 'Or perhaps you cannot swim the length of this pool?'

But Ranji could have swum the length of the pool a dozen times without tiring, and here he would show the Punjabi boy his superiority. So, slipping out of his vest and shorts, he dived straight into the water, cutting through it like a knife, and surfaced with hardly a splash. The Punjabi boy's mouth hung open in amazement.

'You can dive!' he exclaimed.

'It is easy,' said Ranji, treading water, waiting for a further challenge. 'Can't you dive?'

'No,' said the other. 'I jump straight in. But if you will tell me how, I will make a dive.'

'It is easy,' said Ranji. 'Stand on the rock, stretch your arms out and allow your head to displace your feet.'

The Punjabi boy stood up, stiff and straight, stretched out

his arms, and threw himself into the water. He landed flat on his belly, with a crash that sent the birds screaming out of the trees.

Ranji dissolved into laughter.

'Are you trying to empty the pool?' he asked, as the Punjabi boy came to the surface, spouting water like a small whale.

'Wasn't it good?' asked the boy, evidently proud of his feat.

'Not very good,' said Ranji. 'You should have more practice. See, I will do it again.'

And pulling himself up on a rock, he executed another perfect dive. The other boy waited for him to come up, but, swimming under water, Ranji circled him and came upon him from behind.

'How did you do that?' asked the astonished youth.

'Can't you swim under water?' asked Ranji.

'No, but I will try it.'

The Punjabi boy made a tremendous effort to plunge to the bottom of the pool and indeed he thought he had gone right down, though his bottom, like a duck's, remained above the surface.

Ranji, however, did not discourage him.

'It was not bad,' he said. 'But you need a lot of practice.'

'Will you teach me?' asked his enemy.

'If you like, I will teach you.'

'You must teach me. If you do not teach me, I will beat you. Will you come here every day and teach me?'

'If you like,' said Ranji. They had pulled themselves out of the water, and were sitting side by side on a smooth grey rock.

'My name is Suraj,' said the Punjabi boy. 'What is yours?'

'It is Ranji.'

'I am strong, am I not?' asked Suraj, bending his arm so that a ball of muscle stood up stretching the white of his flesh.

'You are strong,' said Ranji. 'You are a real pehelwan.'

'One day I will be the world's champion wrestler,' said Suraj, slapping his thighs, which shook with the impact of his hand.

He looked critically at Ranji's hard, thin body. 'You are quite strong yourself,' he conceded. 'But you are too bony. I know, you people do not eat enough. You must come and have your food with me. I drink one seer of milk every day. We have got our own cow! Be my friend, and I will make you a pehelwan like me! I know—if you teach me to dive and swim under water, I will make you a pehelwan! That is fair, isn't it?'

'That is fair!' said Ranji, though he doubted if he was getting the better of the exchange.

Suraj put his arm around the younger boy and said, 'We are friends now, yes?'

They looked at each other with honest, unflinching eyes, and in that moment love and understanding were born.

'We are friends,' said Ranji.

The birds had settled again in their branches, and the pool was quiet and limpid in the shade of the sal trees.

'It is our pool,' said Suraj. 'Nobody else can come here without our permission. Who would dare?'

'Who would dare?' said Ranji, smiling with the knowledge that he had won the day.

WHEN THE GUAVAS ARE RIPE

Guava trees are easy to climb. And guavas are good to eat. So it's little wonder that an orchard of guava trees is a popular place with boys and girls.

Just across the road from Ranji's house, on the other side of a low wall, was a large guava orchard. The monsoon rains were almost over. It was a warm humid day in September, and the guavas were ripening, turning from green to gold—no longer hard, but growing soft and sweet and juicy.

The schools were closed because of a religious festival. Ranji's father was at work. Ranji's mother was enjoying an afternoon siesta on a cot in the backyard. His grandmother was busy teaching her pet parrot to recite a prayer.

'I feel like getting into those guava trees,' said Ranji to himself. 'It's months since I climbed a tree.'

He was soon across the road and over the wall and into the trees. He chose a tree that grew in the middle of the orchard, where it was unlikely that he would be disturbed, then he climbed swiftly into its branches. A cluster of guavas swung just above him. He reached up for one of them, but to his surprise he found himself clutching a small bare foot which had suddenly been thrust through the foliage.

Having caught the foot, Ranji did not let go. Instead he pulled hard on it. There was a squeal and someone came toppling down on him. Ranji found himself clutching at arms and legs. Together they crashed through a couple of branches and landed with a thud on the soft ground beneath the tree.

Ranji and the intruder struggled fiercely. They rolled about on the grass. Ranji tried a judo hold—without any success.

Then he saw that his opponent was a girl. It was his friend and neighbour, Koki.

'It's you!' he gasped.

'It's me,' said Koki. 'And what are *you* doing here?'

'Get your knee out of my stomach, and I'll tell you.'

When he recovered his breath, he said, 'I just felt like climbing a tree.'

'So did I.'

He stared at her. There was guava juice at the corners of her mouth and on her chin.

'Are the guavas good?' he asked.

'Quite sweet, in this tree,' said Koki. 'You find another tree for yourself, Ranji. There must be thirty or forty trees to choose from.'

'And all going to waste,' said Ranji. 'Look, some of the guavas have been spoilt by the birds.'

'Nobody wants them, it seems.'

Koki climbed back into her tree, and Ranji obligingly walked a little further and climbed another tree. After a few polite exchanges they fell silent, their attention given over entirely to the eating of guavas.

'I've eaten five,' said Koki after some time.

'You'd better stop.'

'You're only saying that because you've just started.'

'Well, three's enough for me.'

'I'm getting a tummy ache, I think.'

'I warned you. Come on, I'll take you home. We can come back tomorrow. There are still lots of guavas left. Hundreds!'

'I don't think I want to eat any more,' said Koki.

She felt better the next day—so well, in fact, that Ranji found her leaning on the gate, waiting for him to join her. She was accompanied by her small brother, Teju, who was only six and very mischievous.

'How are you feeling today?' asked Ranji.

'Hungry,' said Koki.

'Why did you bring your brother?'

'He wants to start climbing trees.'

Soon they were in the orchard. Ranji and Koki helped Teju into the branches of one of the smaller trees and then made for other trees, disturbing a party of parrots who flew in circles around the orchard, screaming their protests.

Two boys and a girl talking to each other from three different trees can make quite a lot of noise, and it wasn't only the birds who were disturbed. Though they did not know it, the orchard belonged to a wealthy property dealer and he employed a watchman, whose duty was to keep away birds, children, monkeys, flying foxes and other fruit-eating pests. But on a hot, sultry afternoon Gopal, the watchman, could not resist taking a nap. He was stretched out under a shady jackfruit tree, snoring so loudly that the flies that had been buzzing around him felt that a storm was brewing and kept their distance.

He woke to the sound of voices raised high in glee. Sitting up, he brushed a ladybird from his long moustache, then seized his lathi.

'Who's there?' he shouted, struggling to his feet.

There was a sudden silence in the trees.

'Who's there?' he called again.

No answer.

'I must have been dreaming,' he muttered, and was preparing to lie down and take another nap when Teju, who had been watching him, burst into laughter.

'Ho!' shouted the watchman, coming to life again.

'Thieves! I'll settle you!' And he began striding towards the centre of the orchard, boasting all the time of his physical prowess. 'I am not afraid of thieves, bandits, or wild beasts! I'll have you know that I was once the wrestling champion of an entire district of Dehra. Come on out and fight me if you dare!'

'Run!' hissed Koki, scrambling down her tree.

'Run!' shouted Ranji, as though it were a cricket match.

Teju was so startled by the sudden activity that he tumbled out of his tree and began crying, and Ranji and Koki had to go to his aid.

The sight of an enormous ex-wrestler bearing down on them was enough to make Teju stop crying and get to his feet. Then all three were fleeing across the grove, the watchman a little way behind them, waving his lathi and shouting at the top of his voice. Although he was an ex-wrestler (or perhaps because of it) he could not run very fast, and was still huffing and puffing some twenty metres behind them when they climbed up and over the wall. He could not climb walls either.

They ran off in different directions before returning home.

⌒

The next day, Ranji met Koki and Teju at the far end of the road.

'Is he there?' asked Koki.

'I haven't seen him. But he must be around somewhere.'

'Maybe he's gone for his lunch. We'll just walk past and take a quick look.'

The three of them strolled casually down the road. Koki said the gardens were looking very pretty. Teju gazed admiringly at a boy flying a kite from a rooftop. Ranji kept one eye on the road and one eye on the orchard wall. A squirrel ran along the top of the wall; the parrots were back in the guava trees.

They moved closer to the wall. Ranji leaned casually against it and Koki began to pick little daisies growing at the edge of the road. Teju, unable to hide his curiosity, pulled himself up on the wall and looked over. At the same time Gopal, the watchman, who had been hiding behind the wall waiting for them, stood up slowly and glared fiercely at Teju.

Teju gulped, but he did not flinch. He was looking straight into the watchman's red angry eyes.

'And what can I do for you?' said Gopal.

'I was just looking,' said Teju.

'At what?'

'At the view.'

Gopal was a little baffled. They looked just like the children he'd chased away yesterday, but he couldn't be sure. They didn't *look* guilty. But did children ever look guilty?

'There's a better view from the other side of the road,' he said gruffly. 'Now be off!'

'What lovely guavas,' said Koki, smiling sweetly. There weren't many people who could resist that smile!

'True,' said Ranji, with the air of one who was an expert on guavas and all things good to eat. 'They are just the right size and colour. I don't think I've seen better. But they'll be spoilt by the birds if you don't gather them soon.'

'It's none of your business,' said the watchman.

'Just look at his muscles,' said Teju, trying a different approach. 'He's really strong!'

Gopal looked pleased for once. He was proud of his former prowess, even though he was now rather flabby around the waist.

'You look like a wrestler,' said Ranji.

'I *am* a wrestler,' said Gopal.

'I told you so,' said Koki. 'What else could he be?'

'I'm a retired wrestler,' said Gopal.

'You don't look retired,' said Teju, fast learning that flattery can get you almost anywhere.

Gopal swelled with pride; such admiration hadn't come his way for a long time. To Koki he looked like a bullfrog swelling up, but she thought it better not to say so.

'Do you want to see my muscles?' he asked.

'Yes, yes!' they cried. 'Do show us!'

Gopal peeled off his shirt and thumped his chest. It sounded like a drum. They were really impressed. Then he bent his elbow and his biceps stood up like cricket balls.

'You can touch them,' he said generously.

Teju poked a finger into Gopal's biceps.

'Mister Universe!' he exclaimed.

Gopal glowed all over. He liked these children. How intelligent they were! Not everyone had the sense to appreciate his strength, his manliness, his magnificent physique!

'Climb over the wall and join me,' he said. 'Come sit on the grass and I'll tell you about the time when I was a wrestling champion.'

Over the wall they came, and sat politely on the grass. Gopal told them about some of his exploits, how he had vanquished a world-famous wrestler in five seconds flat, and how he had saved a carload of travellers from drowning by single-handedly dragging their car out of a river. They listened patiently. Then Teju mentioned that he was feeling hungry.

'Hungry?' said Gopal. 'Why didn't you tell me before? I'll bring you some guavas, that's all there is to eat here. I know which tree has the best ones. And they're all going to rot if no one eats them—no one's buying the crop this year, the owner's price is too high!'

Gopal hurried off and soon returned with a basket full of guavas.

'Help yourselves,' he said. 'But don't eat too many, you'll get sick.'

So they munched guavas and listened to Gopal tell them about the time he was waylaid by three bandits and how he threw them all into the village pond.

'Will you come again tomorrow?' asked Gopal eagerly, when

the guavas were finished and the children got up to leave. 'Come tomorrow and I'll tell you another story.'

'We'll come tomorrow,' said Teju, looking at all the guava trees laden with fruit.

Somehow it seemed very important to Gopal that they should come again. It was lonely in the orchard. Koki sensed this, and said, 'We like your stories.'

'They are good stories,' said Ranji, even if they were not entirely true, he thought....

They climbed over the wall and waved goodbye to Gopal.

They came again the next day.

And even when the guava season was over and Gopal had nothing to offer them but his stories, they went to see him because by that time they had grown to like him.

THE FOUR FEATHERS

Our school dormitory was a very long room with about thirty beds, fifteen on either side of the room. This was good for pillow fights. Class VI would take on Class VII (the two senior classes in our prep school) and there would be plenty of space for leaping, struggling small boys, pillows flying, feathers flying, until there was a cry of 'Here comes Fishy!' or 'Here comes Olly!' and either Mr Fisher, the headmaster, or Mr Oliver, the senior master, would come striding in, cane in hand, to put an end to the general mayhem. Pillow fights were allowed, up to a point; nobody got hurt. But parents sometimes complained if, at the end of the term, a boy came home with a pillow devoid of cotton-wool or feathers.

In that last year at prep school in Simla, there were four of us who were close friends—Bimal, whose home was in Bombay; Riaz, who came from Lahore; Brian, who hailed from Vellore; and your narrator, who lived wherever his father (then in the Air Force) was posted.

We called ourselves 'Four Feathers'—the feathers signifying that we were companions in adventure, comrades in arms, knights of the round table, etc. Bimal adopted a peacock's feather as his emblem; he was always a bit showy. Riaz chose a falcon's feather—although we couldn't find one. Brian and I were at first offered crows' feathers, but we protested vigorously and threatened a walkout. Finally, I settled for a parrot's feather (taken from Mr Fisher's pet parrot), and Brian found a woodpecker's, which suited him, as he was always knocking things about.

Bimal was all thin legs and arms, so light and frisky that at times he seemed to be walking on air. We called him 'Bambi', after the delicate little deer in the Disney film. Riaz, on the other hand, was a sturdy boy, good at games but not very studious; but always good-natured, always smiling. Brian was a dark, good-looking boy from the south; he was just a little spoilt—hated being given out in a cricket match and would refuse to leave the crease!—but he was affectionate and a loyal friend. I was the 'scribe'—good at inventing stories in order to get out of scrapes—but hopeless at sums, my highest marks being 22 out of 100.

On Sunday afternoons, when there were no classes or organized games, we were allowed to roam about on the hillside below the school. The Four Feathers would laze about on the short summer grass, sharing the occasional food parcel from home, reading comics (sometimes a book), and making plans for the long winter holidays. My father, who collected everything from stamps to seashells to butterflies, had given me a butterfly net and urged me to try and catch a rare species which, he said, was found only near Chhota Simla. He described it as a large purple butterfly with yellow and black borders on its wings. A 'purple emperor', I think it was called. As I wasn't very good at identifying butterflies, I would chase anything that happened to flit across the school grounds, usually ending up with common 'red admirals', 'clouded yellows', or 'cabbage whites'. But that 'purple emperor'—that rare specimen being sought by collectors the world over—proved elusive. I would have to seek my fortune in some other line of endeavour.

One day, scrambling about among the rocks and thorny bushes below the school, I almost fell over a small bundle lying in the shade of a young spruce tree. On taking a closer look, I discovered that the bundle was really a baby, wrapped up in a tattered old blanket.

'Feathers, feathers!' I called, 'Come here and look. A baby's been left here!'

The feathers joined me, and we all stared down at the infant, who was fast asleep.

'Who would leave a baby on the hillside?' asked Bimal of no one in particular.

'Someone who doesn't want it,' said Brian.

'And hoped some good people would come along and keep it,' said Riaz.

'A panther might have come along instead,' I said. 'Can't leave it here.'

'Well, we'll just have to adopt it,' said Bimal.

'We can't adopt a baby,' said Brian.

'Why not?'

'We have to be married.'

'We don't.'

'Not us, you dope. The grown-ups who adopt babies.'

'Well, we can't just leave it here for grown-ups to come along,' I said.

'We don't even know if it's a boy or a girl,' said Riaz.

'Makes no difference. A baby's a baby. Let's take it back to school.'

'And keep it in the dormitory?'

'Of course not. Who's going to feed it? Babies need milk. We'll hand it over to Mrs Fisher. She doesn't have a baby.'

'Maybe she doesn't want one. Look, it's beginning to cry. Let's hurry!'

Riaz picked up the wide-awake and crying baby and gave it to Bimal who gave it to Brian who gave it to me. The Four Feathers marched up the hill to school with a very noisy baby.

'Now it has done potty in the blanket,' I complained, 'and some of it is on my shirt.'

'Never mind,' said Bimal. 'It's in a good cause. You're a Boy Scout, remember. You're supposed to help people in distress.'

The headmaster and his wife were in their drawing room,

enjoying their afternoon tea and cakes. We trudged in and Bimal announced, 'We've got something for Mrs Fisher.'

Mrs Fisher took a look at the bundle in my arms and let out a shriek. 'What have you brought here, Bond?'

'A baby, Ma'am. I think it's a girl. Do you want to adopt it?'

Mrs Fisher threw up her arms in consternation and turned to her husband. 'What are we to do, Frank? These boys are impossible. They've picked up someone's child!'

'We'll have to inform the police,' said Mr Fisher, reaching for the telephone, 'we can't have lost babies in the school.'

Just then there was a commotion outside, and a wild-eyed woman, her clothes dishevelled, entered at the front door accompanied by several menfolk from one of the villages. She ran towards us, crying out, 'My baby, my baby! Mera bachcha! You've stolen my baby!'

'We found it on the hillside,' I stammered.

'That's right,' said Brian. 'Finders keepers!'

'Quiet, Adams,' said Mr Fisher, holding up his hand for order and addressing the villagers in a friendly manner. 'These boys found the baby alone on the hillside and brought it here before—before—'

'Before the hyenas got it,' I put in.

'Quite right, Bond. And why did you leave your child alone?' he asked the woman.

'I put her down for five minutes so that I could climb the plum tree and collect the plums. When I came down, the baby had gone! But I could hear it crying up on the hill. I called the menfolk and we came here looking for it.'

'Well, here's your baby,' I said, thrusting it into her arms. By then I was glad to be rid of it! 'Look after it properly in future.'

'Kidnapper!' she screamed at me.

Mr Fisher succeeded in mollifying the villagers. 'These boys are good scouts,' he told them. 'It's their business to help people.'

'Scout Law Number Three, sir,' I added. 'To be useful and helpful.'

And then the headmaster turned the tables on the villagers. 'By the way, these plum trees belong to the school. So do the peaches and apricots. Now I know why they've been disappearing so fast!'

The villagers, a little chastened, went their way. Mr Fisher reached for his cane. From the way he fondled it I knew he was itching to use it on our bottoms.

'No, Frank,' said Mrs Fisher, intervening on our behalf. 'It was really very sweet of them to look after that baby. And look at Bond—he's got baby-goo all over his clothes.'

'So he has. Go and take a bath, all of you. And what are you grinning about, Bond?' asked Mr Fisher.

'Scout Law Number Eight, sir. A scout smiles and whistles under all difficulties.'

And so ended the first adventure of the Four Feathers.

THE THIEF'S STORY

I was still a thief when I met Romi. And though I was only fifteen years old, I was an experienced and fairly successful hand. Romi was watching a wrestling match when I approached him. He was about twenty-five and he looked easy-going, kind, and simple enough for my purpose. I was sure I would be able to win the young man's confidence.

'You look a bit of a wrestler yourself,' I said. There's nothing like flattery to break the ice!

'So do you,' he replied, which put me off for a moment because at that time I was rather thin and bony.

Well,' I said modestly, 'I do wrestle a bit.'

What's your name?'

'Hari Singh,' I lied. I took a new name every month, which kept me ahead of the police and former employers.

After these formalities Romi confined himself to commenting on the wrestlers, who were grunting, gasping, and heaving each other about. When he walked away, I followed him casually.

'Hello again,' he said.

I gave him my most appealing smile. 'I want to work for you,' I said.

'But I can't pay you anything—not for some time, anyway.'

I thought that over for a minute. Perhaps I had misjudged my man. 'Can you feed me?' I asked.

'Can you cook?'

'I can cook,' I lied again.

'If you can cook, then maybe I can feed you.'

He took me to his room over the Delhi Sweet Shop and told me I could sleep on the balcony. But the meal I cooked that night must have been terrible because Romi gave it to a stray dog and told me to be off.

But I just hung around, smiling in my most appealing way, and he couldn't help laughing.

Later, he said never mind, he'd teach me to cook. He also taught me to write my name and said he would soon teach me to write whole sentences and to add figures. I was grateful. I knew that once I could write like an educated person, there would be no limit to what I could achieve.

It was quite pleasant working for Romi. I made tea in the morning and then took my time buying the day's supplies, usually making a profit of two or three rupees. I think he knew I made a little money this way, but he didn't seem to mind.

Romi made money by fits and starts. He would borrow one week, lend the next. He kept worrying about his next cheque, but as soon as it arrived he would go out and celebrate. He wrote for the *Delhi* and *Bombay* magazines: a strange way to make a living.

One evening he came home with a small bundle of notes, saying he had just sold a book to a publisher. That night I saw him put the money in an envelope and tuck it under the mattress.

I had been working for Romi for almost a month and, apart from cheating on the shopping, had not done anything big in my real line of work. I had every opportunity for doing so. I could come and go as I pleased, and Romi was the most trusting person I had ever met.

That was why it was so difficult to rob him. It was easy for me to rob a greedy man. But robbing a nice man could be a problem. And if he doesn't notice he's being robbed, then all the spice goes out of the undertaking!

Well, it's time I got down to some real work, I told myself. If I don't take the money, he'll only waste it on his so-called friends. After all, he doesn't even give me a salary.

Romi was sleeping peacefully. A beam of moonlight reached over the balcony and fell on his bed. I sat on the floor, considering the situation. If I took the money, I could catch the 10.30 express to Lucknow. Slipping out of my blanket, I crept over to the bed.

My hand slid under the mattress, searching for the notes. When I found the packet, I drew it out without a sound. Romi sighed in his sleep and turned on his side. Startled, I moved quickly out of the room.

Once on the road, I began to run. I had the money stuffed into a vest pocket under my shirt. When I'd gotten some distance from Romi's place, I slowed to a walk and, taking the envelope from my pocket, counted the money. Seven hundred rupees in fifties. I could live like a prince for a week or two!

When I reached the station, I did not stop at the ticket office (I had never bought a ticket in my life) but dashed straight on to the platform. The Lucknow Express was just moving out. The train had still to pick up speed and I should have been able to jump into one of the compartments, but I hesitated—for some reason I can't explain—and I lost the chance to get away.

When the train had gone, I found myself standing alone on the deserted platform. I had no idea where to spend the night. I had no friends, believing that friends were more trouble than help. And I did not want to arouse curiosity by staying at one of the small hotels nearby. The only person I knew really well was the man I had robbed. Leaving the station, I walked slowly through the bazaar.

In my short career, I had made a study of people's faces after they had discovered the loss of their valuables. The greedy showed panic; the rich showed anger; the poor, resignation. But I knew that Romi's face when he discovered the theft would show only a touch of sadness—not for the loss of money, but for the loss of trust.

The night was chilly—November nights can be cold in northern India—and a shower of rain added to my discomfort. I sat down in the shelter of the clock tower. A few beggars and vagrants lay beside me, rolled up tight in their blankets. The clock showed midnight. I felt for the notes; they were soaked through.

Romi's money. In the morning, he would probably have given me five rupees to go to the movies, but now I had it all: no more cooking meals, running to the bazaar, or learning to write sentences.

Sentences! I had forgotten about them in the excitement of the theft. Writing complete sentences, I knew, could one day bring me more than a few hundred rupees. It was a simple matter to steal. But to be a really big man, a clever and respected man, was something else. I should go back to Romi, I told myself, if only to learn to read and write.

I hurried back to the room feeling very nervous, for it is much easier to steal something than to return it undetected.

I opened the door quietly, then stood in the doorway in clouded moonlight. Romi was still asleep. I crept to the head of the bed, and my hand came up with the packet of notes. I felt his breath on my hand. I remained still for a few moments. Then my fingers found the edge of the mattress, and I slipped the money beneath it.

I awoke late the next morning to find that Romi had already made the tea. He stretched out a hand to me. There was a fifty-rupee note between his fingers. My heart sank.

'I made some money yesterday,' he said. 'Now I'll be able to pay you regularly.'

My spirits rose. But when I took the note, I noticed that it was still wet from the night's rain.

So he knew what I'd done. But neither his lips nor his eyes revealed anything.

'Today we'll start writing sentences,' he said.

I smiled at Romi in my most appealing way. And the smile came by itself, without any effort.

THE WINDOW

When Amir was thirteen, he decided that he was old enough to have a room of his own.

'What for?' asked his mother.

'The kids make too much noise,' he said, referring to his younger brothers and sisters. 'I can't study.'

'Well, if you really want to study, you can have your own room,' said his grandfather, who owned the old building. 'There's the room on the roof.'

So Amir took the room on the roof. It was a long, low building with large cracks in the walls from which peepul trees were growing. Amir's grandfather said he couldn't afford to have it repaired. There were a number of tenants in the building and they were paying rents that had been fixed forty years back, when rents were very low, so there wasn't much money coming in. Amir's father had a tailor's shop in the bazaar, but that didn't make much money either. The building had a flat roof, with just the one small room—called a barsati—opening on to it. From the window of his room Amir looked out upon a world quite different from the world below.

The banyan tree, just opposite, was his, and its inhabitants his subjects. There were two squirrels, several mynahs, a crow and, at night, a pair of flying foxes. The squirrels were busy in the afternoon, the birds in the morning and evening, the flying foxes at night. Amir wasn't very busy. He'd look at his books now and then, but decided that it wasn't a very good year for studying. There was much more to learn from looking out of his window.

At first he felt lonely in the room. But then he discovered the power of the window. It looked out on the banyan tree and the mango grove, on the rather untidy garden, on the broad path running past the building, and out over the roofs of other houses, over roads and fields, as far as the horizon. The path was a busy one: fruit and vegetable vendors came and went, as did the toy seller and the balloon man, their wares strung on poles; there were boys on cycles, babies in prams, schoolgirls chattering, housewives quarrelling, old men gossiping...all passed his way, the way of his window.

Early that summer a tonga came rattling and jingling down the path and stopped in front of the building. A girl and an elderly lady got down, while a servant unloaded their luggage. They went into the house and the tonga moved off.

The next day the girl looked up from the garden and saw Amir at the window.

She had black hair that came to her shoulders. Her eyes were black, like her hair, and just as shiny. She must have been about eleven years old.

'Hello,' said Amir.

She looked up at him suspiciously. 'Who are you?' she asked.

'I am a ghost.'

She laughed, and her laugh had a gay, mocking quality, 'You look like one!'

Amir didn't think her remark was very funny, but he had asked for it.

'What are you doing up there?' she asked.

'Practising magic,' he said.

She laughed again but this time without the mockery. 'I don't believe you,' she said.

'Why don't you come up and see for yourself?'

She came round to the steps and began climbing them slowly, cautiously. When she entered the room, she stared at Amir and said: 'Where's your magic?'

'Come here,' he said, and he took her to the window and showed her his world.

She said nothing, just stared out of the window. Then she turned and smiled at Amir, and they were friends.

He only knew that she was called Chummo, and that she had come with her aunt for the summer months. He did not need to know any more about her, and she did not need to know any more about him except that he wasn't really a ghost.

She came up the steps nearly every day and joined Amir at the window. There was a lot of excitement to be had in the world of the window, especially when the monsoon rains arrived.

At the first rumblings, women would rush outside to retrieve their washing from the clothesline and, if there was a breeze, to chase a few garments across the compound. When the rain came, it came with a vengeance, making a bog of the garden and a river of the path.

A cyclist would come riding furiously down the path, an elderly gentleman would be having difficulty with his umbrella, naked toddlers would be frisking about in the rain. Sometimes Amir would run out on the roof and shout and dance in the rain. And the rain would come through the open door and window of the room, flooding the floor and making an island of the bed.

But the window was more fun than anything else.

'It's like a film,' said Chummo. 'The window is the screen, the world outside is the picture.'

Soon the mangoes were ripe and Chummo was in the branches of the mango tree as often as she was at Amir's window. Amir was supposed to be deep in study, so any forays into the mango tree on his part would not have pleased his grandfather. But from the window he had a good view of the tree, and he could speak to Chummo from about the same level. She brought him unripe mangoes, and they ate far too many of them and had tummy aches for the rest of the day.

'Let's make a garden on the roof,' said Chummo.

'How do we do that?' asked Amir.

'It's easy. We bring up mud and bricks and make the flower beds. Then we plant the seeds. We'll grow all sorts of flowers.'

'The roof will fall in,' said Amir.

'Never mind,' said Chummo.

They spent two days carrying buckets of mud up the steps to the roof and laying out the flower beds. It was hard work, but Chummo did most of it. When the beds were ready, they had a planting ceremony. But apart from a few small plants collected from the garden below, they had only one kind of seed—pumpkin.

'I can't eat pumpkins,' said Amir.

'Have you ever met anyone who likes pumpkins?' asked Chummo.

'No. Everyone hates them.'

'True. And yet people keep on growing them, and selling them, and forcing children to eat them.'

'They just do it to make us suffer,' said Amir.

'True. We'll present our pumpkins to our enemies.'

So they planted the pumpkin seeds in the mud and felt proud of themselves.

But the following night it rained very heavily, and in the morning they discovered that everything—except the bricks—had been washed away.

So they returned to the window.

A mynah had been in a fight and the feathers had been knocked off its head. A bougainvillea creeper that had been climbing the wall had sent a long green shoot in through the window.

Chummo said, 'Now we can't shut the window without spoiling the creeper.'

'Then we won't close the window,' said Amir.

And they let the creeper into the room.

The rains passed and an autumn wind came whispering through the branches of the banyan tree. There were red leaves on the ground and the wind picked them up and blew them about so that they looked like butterflies. Amir would watch the sunrise, the sky all red until the first rays splashed the windowsill and crept up the walls of the room. And in the evening Chummo and Amir would watch the sun go down in a sea of fluffy clouds. Sometimes the clouds were pink, sometimes orange; they were nearly always coloured clouds, framed in the window.

'I'm going tomorrow,' said Chummo one evening.

Amir was too surprised to say anything.

'You stay here all the time, don't you?' she said.

Amir nodded.

'When I come again next year, you'll still be here, won't you?'

'I suppose so,' said Amir.

In the morning the tonga was at the door, and the servant, the aunt, and Chummo were in it. Amir was at his window. Chummo waved up to him. Then the driver flicked the pony's reins, the tonga creaked and rattled, the bell jingled. Down the path and through the compound gate went the tonga, and all the time Chummo waved.

When the tonga was out of sight, Amir took the spray of bougainvillea and pushed it out of the room. Then he closed the window. It would be opened only when the spring and Chummo came again.

DUST ON THE MOUNTAINS

Winter came and went, without so much as a drizzle. The hillside was brown all summer and the fields were bare. The old plough that was dragged over the hard ground by Bisnu's lean oxen made hardly any impression. Still, Bisnu kept his seeds ready for sowing. A good monsoon, and there would be plenty of maize and rice to see the family through the next winter.

Summer went its scorching way, and a few clouds gathered on the south-western horizon.

'The monsoon is coming,' announced Bisnu.

His sister Puja was at the small stream, washing clothes. 'If it doesn't come soon, the stream will dry up,' she said. 'See, it's only a trickle this year. Remember when there were so many different flowers growing here on the banks of the stream? This year there isn't one.'

'The winter was dry. It did not even snow,' said Bisnu. 'I cannot remember another winter when there was no snow,' said his mother. 'The year your father died, there was so much snow the villagers could not light his funeral pyre for hours. And now there are fires everywhere.' She pointed to the next mountain, half-hidden by the smoke from a forest fire. At night they sat outside their small house, watching the fire spread. A red line stretched right across the mountain. Thousands of Himalayan trees were perishing in the flames. Oaks, deodars, maples, pines; trees that had taken hundreds of years to grow. And now a fire started carelessly by some campers had been carried up the mountain with the help of the dry grass and strong breeze.

There was no one to put it out. It would take days to die down by itself.

'If the monsoon arrives tomorrow, the fire will go out,' said Bisnu, ever the optimist. He was only twelve, but he was the man in the house; he had to see that there was enough food for the family and for the oxen, for the big black dog and the hens.

There were clouds the next day but they brought only a drizzle. 'It's just the beginning,' said Bisnu as he placed a bucket of muddy water on the steps.

'It usually starts with a heavy downpour,' said his mother. But there were to be no downpours that year. Clouds gathered on the horizon but they were white and puffy and soon disappeared.

True monsoon clouds would have been dark and heavy with moisture. There were other signs—or lack of them—that warned of a long dry summer. The birds were silent, or simply absent. The Himalayan barbet, which usually heralded the approach of the monsoon with strident calls from the top of a spruce tree, hadn't been seen or heard. And the cicadas, which played a deafening overture in the oaks at the first hint of rain, seemed to be missing altogether.

Puja's apricot tree usually gave them a basket full of fruit every summer. This year it produced barely a handful of apricots, lacking juice and flavour. The tree looked ready to die, its leaves curled up in despair. Fortunately there was a store of walnuts, and a binful of wheat grain and another of rice stored from the previous year, so they would not be entirely without food; but it looked as though there would be no fresh fruit or vegetables. And there would be nothing to store away for the following winter.

Money would be needed to buy supplies in Tehri, some thirty miles distant. And there was no money to be earned in the village.

'I will go to Mussoorie and find work,' announced Bisnu. 'But Mussoorie is a two-day journey by bus,' said his mother. 'There is no one there who can help you. And you may not get any work.'

'In Mussoorie there is plenty of work during the summer. Rich people come up from the plains for their holidays. It is full of hotels and shops and places where they can spend their money.'

'But they won't spend any money on you.'

'There is money to be made there. And if not, I will come home. I can walk back over the Nag Tibba mountain. It will take only two and a half days and I will save the bus fare!'

'Don't go, Bhai,' pleaded Puja.

'There will be no one to prepare your food—you will only get sick.'

But Bisnu had made up his mind so he put a few belongings in a cloth shoulder bag, while his mother prised several rupee coins out of a cache in the wall of their living room. Puja prepared a special breakfast of parathas and an egg scrambled with onions, the hen having laid just one for the occasion. Bisnu put some of the parathas in his bag. Then, waving goodbye to his mother and sister, he set off down the road from the village. After walking for a mile, he reached the highway where there was a hamlet with a bus stop. A number of villagers were waiting patiently for a bus. It was an hour late but they were used to that. As long as it arrived safely and got them to their destination, they would be content. They were patient people. And although Bisnu wasn't quite so patient, he too had learnt how to wait—for late buses and late monsoons.

II

Along the valley and over the mountains went the little bus with its load of frail humans. A little misjudgment on the part of the driver, and they would all be dashed to pieces on the rocks far below.

'How tiny we are,' thought Bisnu, looking up at the towering peaks and the immensity of the sky. 'Each of us no more than a raindrop... And I wish we had a few raindrops!'

There were still fires burning to the north but the road went south, where there were no forests anyway, just bare brown hillsides. Down near the river there were small paddy fields but unfortunately rivers ran downhill and not uphill, and there was no inexpensive way in which the water could be brought up the steep slopes to the fields that depended on rainfall.

Bisnu stared out of the bus window at the river running far below. On either bank huge boulders lay exposed, for the level of the water had fallen considerably during the past few months. 'Why are there no trees here?' he asked aloud, and received the attention of a fellow passenger, an old man in the next seat who had been keeping up a relentless dry coughing. Even though it was a warm day, he wore a woollen cap and had an old muffler wrapped about his neck.

'There were trees here once,' he said. 'But the contractors took the deodars for furniture and houses. And the pines were tapped to death for resin. And the oaks were stripped of their leaves to feed the cattle—you can still see a few tree skeletons if you look hard—and the bushes that remained were finished off by the goats!'

'When did all this happen?' asked Bisnu.

'A few years ago. And it's still happening in other areas, although it's forbidden now to cut trees. The only forests that remain are in remote places where there are no roads.' A fit of coughing came over him, but he had found a good listener and was eager to continue. 'The road helps you and me to get about but it also makes it easier for others to do mischief. Rich men from the cities come here and buy up what they want—land, trees, people!'

'What takes you to Mussoorie, Uncle?' asked Bisnu politely. He always addressed elderly people as uncle or aunt. 'I have a cough that won't go away. Perhaps they can do something for it at the hospital in Mussoorie. Doctors don't like coming to villages, you know—there's no money to be made in villages. So we must go to the doctors in the towns. I had a brother who could not be cured in Mussoorie. They told him to go to Delhi. He sold his buffaloes and went to Delhi, but there they told him it was too late to do anything. He died on the way back. I won't go to Delhi. I don't wish to die amongst strangers.' 'You'll get well, Uncle,' said Bisnu.

'Bless you for saying so. And you—what takes you to the big town?'

'Looking for work—we need money at home.'

'It is always the same. There are many like you who must go out in search of work. But don't be led astray. Don't let your friends persuade you to go to Bombay to become a film star! It is better to be hungry in your village than to be hungry on the streets of Bombay. I had a nephew who went to Bombay. The smugglers put him to work selling afeem (opium) and now he is in jail. Keep away from the big cities, boy. Earn your money and go home.'

'I'll do that, Uncle. My mother and sister will expect me to return before the summer season is over.'

The old man nodded vigorously and began coughing again. Presently he dozed off. The interior of the bus smelt of tobacco smoke and petrol fumes and as a result Bisnu had a headache. He kept his face near the open window to get as much fresh air as possible, but the dust kept getting into his mouth and eyes.

Several dusty hours later the bus got into Mussoorie, honking its horn furiously at everything in sight. The passengers, looking dazed, got down and went their different ways. The old man trudged off to the hospital.

Bisnu had to start looking for a job straightaway. He needed a lodging for the night and he could not afford even the cheapest of hotels. So he went from one shop to another, and to all the little restaurants and eating places, asking for work—anything in exchange for a bed, a meal and a minimum wage. A boy at one of the sweet shops told him there was a job at the Picture

Palace, one of the town's three cinemas. The hill station's main road was crowded with people, for the season was just starting. Most of them were tourists who had come up from Delhi and other large towns.

The street lights had come on, and the shops were lighting up, when Bisnu presented himself at the Picture Palace.

III

The man who ran the cinema's tea stall had just sacked the previous helper for his general clumsiness. Whenever he engaged a new boy (which was fairly often) he started him off with the warning: 'I will be keeping a record of all the cups and plates you break, and their cost will be deducted from your salary at the end of the month.'

As Bisnu's salary had been fixed at fifty rupees a month, he would have to be very careful if he was going to receive any of it.

'In my first month,' said Chittru, one of the three tea stall boys, 'I broke six cups and five saucers, and my pay came to three rupees! Better be careful!'

Bisnu's job was to help prepare the tea and samosas, serve these refreshments to the public during intervals in the film, and later wash up the dishes. In addition to his salary, he was allowed to drink as much tea as he wanted or could hold in his stomach. But the sugar supply was kept to a minimum.

Bisnu went to work immediately and it was not long before he was as well-versed in his duties as the other two tea boys, Chittru and Bali. Chittru was an easy-going, lazy boy who always tried to place the brunt of his work on someone else's shoulders. But he was generous and lent Bisnu five rupees during the first week. Bali, besides being a tea boy, had the enviable job of being the poster boy. As the cinema was closed during the mornings, Bali would be busy either pushing the big poster board around Mussoorie, or sticking posters on convenient walls.

'Posters are very useful,' he claimed. 'They prevent old walls from falling down.'

Chittru had relatives in Mussoorie and slept at their house. But both Bisnu and Bali were on their own and had to sleep at the cinema. After the last show the hall was locked up, so they could not settle down in the expensive seats as they would have liked! They had to sleep on a dirty mattress in the foyer, near the ticket office, where they were often at the mercy of icy Himalayan winds.

Bali made things more comfortable by setting his poster board at an angle to the wall, which gave them a little alcove where they could sleep protected from the wind. As they had only one blanket each, they placed their blankets together and rolled themselves into a tight warm ball.

During shows, when Bisnu took the tea around, there was nearly always someone who would be rude and offensive. Once when he spilt some tea on a college student's shoes, he received a hard kick on the shin. He complained to the tea stall owner, but his employer said, 'The customer is always right. You should have got out of the way in time!'

As he began to get used to this life, Bisnu found himself taking an interest in some of the regular customers.

There was, for instance, the large gentleman with the soup-strainer moustache, who drank his tea from the saucer. As he drank, his lips worked like a suction pump, and the tea, after a brief agitation in the saucer, would disappear in a matter of seconds. Bisnu often wondered if there was something lurking in the forests of that gentleman's upper lip, something that would suddenly spring out and fall upon him! The boys took great pleasure in exchanging anecdotes about the peculiarities of some of the customers.

Bisnu had never seen such bright, painted women before. The girls in his village, including his sister Puja, were good-looking and often sturdy; but they did not use perfumes or make-up like these more prosperous women from the towns of the plains. Wearing expensive clothes and jewellery, they never gave Bisnu more than a brief, bored glance. Other women were more inclined to notice him, favouring him with kind words and a small tip when he took away the cups and plates. He found he could make a few rupees a month in tips; and when he received his first month's pay, he was able to send some of it home.

Chittru accompanied him to the post office and helped him to fill in the money order form. Bisnu had been to the village school, but be wasn't used to forms and official paperwork. Chittru, a town boy, knew all about them, even though he could just about read and write.

Walking back to the cinema, Chittru said, 'We can make more money at the limestone quarries.'

'All right, let's try them,' said Bisnu.

'Not now,' said Chittru, who enjoyed the busy season in the hill station. 'After the season—after the monsoon.'

But there was still no monsoon to speak of, just an occasional drizzle which did little to clear the air of the dust that blew up from the plains. Bisnu wondered how his mother and sister were faring at home. A wave of homesickness swept over him. The hill station, with all its glitter, was just a pretty gift box with nothing inside.

One day in the cinema Bisnu saw the old man who had been with him on the bus. He greeted him like a long lost friend. At first the old man did not recognize the boy, but when Bisnu asked him if he had recovered from his illness, the old man remembered and said, 'So you are still in Mussoorie, boy. That is good. I thought you might have gone down to Delhi to make more money.' He added that he was a little better and that he was undergoing a course of treatment at the hospital. Bisnu brought him a cup of tea and refused to take any money for it; it could be included in his own quota of free tea. When the show was over, the old man went his way and Bisnu did not see him again.

In September the town began to get empty. The taps were running dry or giving out just a trickle of muddy water. A thick mist lay over the mountain for days on end, but there was no rain. When the mists cleared, an autumn wind came whispering through the deodars.

At the end of the month the manager of the Picture Palace gave everyone a week's notice, a week's pay, and announced that the cinema would be closing for the winter.

IV

Bali said, 'I'm going to Delhi to find work. I'll come back next summer. What about you, Bisnu, why don't you come with me? It's easier to find work in Delhi.'

'I'm staying with Chittru,' said Bisnu.

'We may work at the quarries.'

'I like the big towns,' said Bali. 'I like shops and people and lots of noise. I will never go back to my village. There is no money there, no fun.'

Bali made a bundle of his things and set out for the bus stand. Bisnu bought himself a pair of cheap shoes, for his old ones had fallen to pieces. With what was left of his money, he sent another money order home. Then he and Chittru set out for the limestone quarries, an eight-mile walk from Mussoorie.

They knew they were nearing the quarries when they saw clouds of limestone dust hanging in the air. The dust hid the next mountain from view. When they did see the mountain, they found that the top of it was missing—blasted away by dynamite to enable the quarries to get at the rich strata of limestone rock below the surface.

The skeletons of a few trees remained on the lower slopes. Almost everything else had gone—grass, flowers, shrubs, birds, butterflies, grasshoppers, ladybirds. A rock lizard popped its head out of a crevice to look at the intruders. Then, like some prehistoric survivor, it scuttled back into its underground shelter. 'I used to come here when I was small,' announced Chittru cheerfully.

'Were the quarries here then?'

'Oh, no. My friends and I—we used to come for the strawberries. They grew all over this mountain. Wild strawberries, but very tasty.'

'Where are they now?' asked Bisnu, looking around at the devastated hillside.

'All gone,' said Chittru. 'Maybe there are some on the next mountain.'

Even as they approached the quarries, a blast shook the hillside. Chittru pulled Bisnu under an overhanging rock to avoid the shower of stones that pelted down on the road. As the dust enveloped them, Bisnu had a fit of coughing. When the air cleared a little, they saw the limestone dump ahead of them.

Chittru, who was older and bigger than Bisnu, was immediately taken on as a labourer; but the quarry foreman took one look at Bisnu and said, 'You're too small. You won't be able to break stones or lift those heavy rocks and load them into the trucks. Be off, boy. Find something else to do.'

He was offered a job in the labourers' canteen, but he'd had enough of making tea and washing dishes. He was about to turn round and walk back to Mussoorie when he felt a heavy hand descend on his shoulder. He looked up to find a grey-bearded, turbanned Sikh looking down at him in some amusement.

'I need a cleaner for my truck,' he said. 'The work is easy, but the hours are long.'

Bisnu responded immediately to the man's gruff but jovial manner.

'What will you pay?' he asked.

'Fifteen rupees a day, and you'll get food and a bed at the depot.'

'As long as I don't have to cook the food,' said Bisnu. The truck driver laughed. 'You might prefer to do so, once you've tasted the depot food. Are you coming on my truck? Make up your mind.'

'I'm your man,' said Bisnu; and waving goodbye to Chittru, he followed the Sikh to his truck.

V

A horn blared, shattering the silence of the mountains, and the truck came round a bend in the road. A herd of goats scattered to left and right.

The goatherds cursed as a cloud of dust enveloped them, and then the truck had left them behind and was rattling along the bumpy, unmetalled road to the quarries.

At the wheel of the truck, stroking his grey moustache with one hand, sat Pritam Singh. It was his own truck. He had never allowed anyone else to drive it. Every day he made two trips to the quarries, carrying truckloads of limestone back to the depot at the bottom of the hill. He was paid by the trip and he was always anxious to get in two trips every day. Sitting beside him was Bisnu, his new cleaner. In less than a month Bisnu had become an experienced hand at looking after trucks, riding in them, and even sleeping in them. He got on well with Pritam, the grizzled, fifty-year-old Sikh, who boasted of two well-off sons— one a farmer in Punjab, the other a wine merchant in far-off London. He could have gone to live with either of them, but his sturdy independence kept him on the road in his battered old truck.

Pritam pressed hard on his horn. Now there was no one on the road—neither beast nor man—but Pritam was fond of the sound of his horn and liked blowing it. He boasted that it was the loudest horn in northern India. Although it struck terror into the hearts of all who heard it—for it was louder than the trumpeting of an elephant—it was music to Pritam's ears.

Pritam treated Bisnu as an equal and a friendly banter had grown between them during their many trips together.

'One more year on this bone-breaking road,' said Pritam, 'and then I'll sell my truck and retire.'

'But who will buy such a shaky old truck?' asked Bisnu. 'It will retire before you do!'

'Now don't be insulting, boy. She's only twenty years old—there are still a few years left in her!' And as though to prove it he blew the horn again. Its strident sound echoed and re-echoed down the mountain gorge. A pair of wildfowl burst from the bushes and fled to more silent regions.

Pritam's thoughts went to his dinner. 'Haven't had a good meal for days.'

'Haven't had a good meal for weeks,' said Bisnu, although in fact he looked much healthier than when he had worked at the cinema's tea stall.

'Tonight I'll give you a dinner in a good hotel. Tandoori chicken and rice pilaf.'

He sounded his horn again as though to put a seal on his promise. Then he slowed down, because the road had become narrow and precipitous, and trotting ahead of them was a train of mules.

As the horn blared, one mule ran forward, another ran backward. One went uphill, another went downhill. Soon there were mules all over the place. Pritam cursed the mules and the mule drivers cursed Pritam; but he had soon left them far behind.

Along this range, all the hills were bare and dry. Most of the forest had long since disappeared.

'Are your hills as bare as these?' asked Pritam. 'No, we still have some trees,' said Bisnu. 'Nobody has started blasting the hills as yet. In front of our house there is a walnut tree which gives us two baskets of walnuts every year. And there is an apricot

tree. But it was a bad year for fruit. There was no rain. And the
stream is too far away.'

'It will rain soon,' said Pritam. 'I can smell rain. It is coming
from the north. The winter will be early.'

'It will settle the dust.'

Dust was everywhere. The truck was full of it. The leaves
of the shrubs and the few trees were thick with it. Bisnu could
feel the dust under his eyelids and in his mouth. And as they
approached the quarries, the dust increased. But it was a different
kind of dust now—whiter, stinging the eyes, irritating the nostrils.

They had been blasting all morning.

'Let's wait here,' said Pritam, bringing the truck to a halt.
They sat in silence, staring through the windscreen at the scarred
cliffs a little distance down the road. There was a sharp crack of
explosives and the hillside blossomed outwards. Earth and rocks
hurtled down the mountain.

Bisnu watched in awe as shrubs and small trees were flung
into the air. It always frightened him—not so much the sight
of—the rocks bursting asunder, as the trees being flung aside and
destroyed. He thought of the trees at home—the walnut, the
chestnuts, the pines—and wondered if one day they would suffer
the same fate, and whether the mountains would all become a
desert like this particular range. No trees, no grass, no water—
only the choking dust of mines and quarries.

VI

Pritam pressed hard on his horn again, to let the people at the
site know that he was approaching. He parked outside a small
shed where the contractor and the foreman were sipping cups
of tea. A short distance away, some labourers, Chittru among
then, were hammering at chunks of rock, breaking them up into
manageable pieces. A pile of stones stood ready for loading; while
the rock that had just been blasted lay scattered about the hillside.

'Come and have a cup of tea,' called out the contractor. 'I can't hang about all day,' said Pritam. 'There's another trip to make—and the days are getting shorter. I don't want to be driving by night.'

But he sat down on a bench and ordered two cups of tea from the stall. The foreman strolled over to the group of labourers and told them to start loading. Bisnu let down the grid at the back of the truck. Then, to keep himself warm, he began helping Chittru and the men with the loading.

'Don't expect to be paid for helping,' said Sharma, the contractor, for whom every rupee spent was a rupee off his profits.

'Don't worry,' said Bisnu. 'I don't work for contractors, I work for friends.'

'That's right,' called out Pritam.

'Mind what you say to Bisnu—he's no one's servant!'

Sharma wasn't happy until there was no space left for a single stone. Then Bisnu had his cup of tea and three of the men climbed on the pile of stones in the open truck.

'All right, let's go!' said Pritam. 'I want to finish early today Bisnu and I are having a big dinner!'

Bisnu jumped in beside Pritam, banging the door shut. It never closed properly unless it was slammed really hard. But it opened at a touch.

'This truck is held together with sticking plaster,' joked Pritam.

He was in good spirits. He started the engine, and blew his horn just as he passed the foreman and the contractor.

'They are deaf in one ear from the blasting,' said Pritam. 'I'll make them deaf in the other ear!'

The labourers were singing as the truck swung round the sharp bends of the winding road. The door beside Bisnu rattled on its hinges. He was feeling quite dizzy.

'Not too fast,' he said.

'Oh,' said Pritam. 'About my driving?'

'It's just today,' said Bisnu uneasily.

'You're getting old,' said Pritam. 'And since when did you become nervous?'

'It's a feeling, that's all.'

'That's your trouble.'

'I suppose so,' said Bisnu.

Pritam was feeling young, exhilarated. He drove faster. As they swung round a bend, Bisnu looked out of his window.

All he saw was the sky above and the valley below. They were very near the edge; but it was usually like that on this narrow mountain road.

After a few more hairpin bends, the road descended steeply to the valley. Just then a stray mule ran into the middle of the road. Pritam swung the steering wheel over to the right to avoid the mule, but here the road turned sharply to the left. The truck went over the edge.

As it tipped over, hanging for a few seconds on the edge of the cliff, the labourers leapt from the back of the truck. It pitched forward, and as it struck a rock outcrop, the loose door burst open. Bisnu was thrown out.

The truck hurtled forward, bouncing over the rocks, turning over on its side and rolling over twice before coming to rest against the trunk of a scraggly old oak tree. But for the tree, the truck would have plunged several hundred feet down to the bottom of the gorge.

Two of the labourers sat on the hillside, stunned and badly shaken. The third man had picked himself up and was running back to the quarry for help.

Bisnu had landed in a bed of nettles. He was smarting all over, but he wasn't really hurt; the nettles had broken his fall. His first impulse was to get up and run back to the road. Then he realized that Pritam was still in the truck.

Bisnu skidded down the steep slope, calling out, 'Pritam Uncle, are you all right?'

There was no answer.

VII

When Bisnu saw Pritam's arm and half his body jutting out of the open door of the truck, he feared the worst. It was a strange position, half in and half out. Bisnu was about to turn away and climb back up the hill, when he noticed that Pritam had opened a bloodied and swollen eye. It looked straight up at Bisnu.

'Are you alive?' whispered Bisnu, terrified.

'What do you think?' muttered Pritam. He closed his eye again. When the contractor and his men arrived, it took them almost an hour to get Pritam Singh out of the wreckage of the truck, and another hour to get him to the hospital in the next big town. He had broken bones, fractured ribs and a dislocated shoulder. But the doctors said he was repairable—which was more than could be said for the truck.

'So the truck's finished,' said Pritam, between groans when Bisnu came to see him after a couple of days. 'Now I'll have to go home and live with my son. And what about you, boy? I can get you a job on a friend's truck.'

'No,' said Bisnu, 'I'll be going home soon.'

'And what will you do at home?'

'I'll work on my land. It's better to grow things on the land, than to blast things out of it.'

They were silent for some time.

'There is something to be said for growing things,' said Pritam. 'But for that tree, the truck would have finished up at the foot of the mountain, and I wouldn't be here, all bandaged up and talking to you. It was the tree that saved me. Remember that, boy.'

'I'll remember, and I won't forget the dinner you promised me, either.'

It snowed during Bisnu's last night at the quarries. He slept on the floor with Chittru, in a large shed meant for the labourers. The wind blew the snowflakes in at the entrance; it whistled down the deserted mountain pass. In the morning Bisnu opened his eyes to a world of dazzling whiteness. The snow was piled high against the walls of the shed, and they had some difficulty getting out. Bisnu joined Chittru at the tea stall, drank a glass of hot sweet tea, and ate two stale buns. He said goodbye to Chittru and set out on the long march home. The road would be closed to traffic because of the heavy snow, and he would have to walk all the way.

He trudged over the hills all day, stopping only at small villages to take refreshment. By nightfall he was still ten miles from home.

But he had fallen in with other travellers, and with them he took shelter at a small inn. They built a fire and crowded round it, and each man spoke of his home and fields and all were of the opinion that the snow and rain had come just in time to save the winter crops. Someone sang, and another told a ghost story. Feeling at home already, Bisnu fell asleep listening to their tales. In the morning they parted and went their different ways. It was almost noon when Bisnu reached his village. The fields were covered with snow and the mountain stream was in spate. As he climbed the terraced fields to his house, he heard the sound of barking, and his mother's big black mastiff came bounding towards him over the snow. The dog jumped on him and licked his arms and then went bounding back to the house to tell the others.

Puja saw him from the courtyard and ran indoors shouting, 'Bisnu has come, my brother has come!'

His mother ran out of the house, calling, 'Bisnu, Bisnu!'

Bisnu came walking through the fields, and he did not hurry, he did not run; he wanted to savour the moment of his return, with his mother and sister smiling, waiting for him in front of the house.

There was no need to hurry now. He would be with them for a long time, and the manager of the Picture Palace would have to find someone else for the summer season.... It was his home, and these were his fields! Even the snow was his. When the snow melted he would clear the fields, and nourish them, and make them rich.

He felt very big and very strong as he came striding over the land he loved.

FROM SMALL BEGINNINGS

And the last puff of the day-wind brought from the unseen
villages the scent of damp wood-smoke, hot cakes, dripping
undergrowth, and rotting pine-cones. That is the true smell of
the Himalayas, and if once it creeps into the blood of a man,
that man will at the last, forgetting all else,
return to the hills to die.

—Rudyard Kipling

On the first clear September day, towards the end of the rains, I visited the pine knoll, my place of peace and power.

It was months since I'd last been there. Trips to the plains, a crisis in my affairs, involvements with other people and their troubles, and an entire monsoon had come between me and the grassy, pine-topped slope facing the Hill of Fairies (Pari Tibba to the locals). Now I tramped through late monsoon foliage— tall ferns, bushes festooned with flowering convolvulus—and crossed the stream by way of its little bridge of stones before climbing the steep hill to the pine slope.

When the trees saw me, they made as if to turn in my direction. A puff of wind came across the valley from the distant snows. A long-tailed blue magpie took alarm and flew noisily out of an oak tree. The cicadas were suddenly silent. But the trees remembered me. They bowed gently in the breeze and beckoned me nearer, welcoming me home. Three pines, a straggling oak and a wild cherry. I went among them and acknowledged their welcome with a touch of my hand against their trunks—the cherry's smooth and polished; the pine's patterned and whorled;

the oak's rough, gnarled, full of experience. He'd been there longest, and the wind had bent his upper branches and twisted a few, so that he looked shaggy and undistinguished. But like the philosopher who is careless about his dress and appearance, the oak has secrets, a hidden wisdom. He has learnt the art of survival!

While the oak and the pines are older than me and have been here many years, the cherry tree is exactly seven years old. 1 know, because I planted it.

One day I had this cherry seed in my hand, and on an impulse I thrust it into the soft earth, and then went away and forgot all about it. A few months later I found a tiny cherry tree in the long grass. I did not expect it to survive. But the following year it was two feet tall. And then some goats ate its leaves and a grass cutter's scythe injured the stem, and I was sure it would wither away. But it renewed itself, sprang up even faster, and within three years it was a healthy, growing tree, about five feet tall.

I left the hills for two years—forced by circumstances to make a living in Delhi—but this time I did not forget the cherry tree. I thought about it fairly often, sent telepathic messages of encouragement in its direction. And when, a couple of years ago, I returned in the autumn, my heart did a somersault when I found my tree sprinkled with pale pink blossom. (The Himalayan cherry flowers in November.) And later, when the fruit was ripe, the tree was visited by finches, tits, bulbuls and other small birds, all come to feast on the sour, red cherries.

Last summer I spent a night on the pine knoll, sleeping on the grass beneath the cherry tree. I lay awake for hours, listening to the chatter of the stream and the occasional *tonk-tonk* of nightjars, and watching through the branches overhead, the stars turning in the sky. And I felt the power of the sky and the earth, and the power of a small cherry seed....

And so when the rains are over, this is where I come, that I might feel the peace and power of this place.

This is where I will write my stories. I can see everything from here—my cottage across the valley; behind and above me, the town and the bazaar, straddling the ridge; to the left, the high mountains and the twisting road to the source of the great river; below me, the little stream and the path to the village; ahead, the Hill of Fairies and the fields beyond; the wide valley below, and another range of hills and then the distant plains. I can even see Prem Singh in the garden, putting the mattresses out in the sun.

From here he is just a speck on the far hill, but I know it is Prem by the way he stands. A man may have a hundred disguises, but in the end it is his posture that gives him away. Like my grandfather, who was a master of disguise and successfully roamed the bazaars as fruit vendor or basket maker. But we could always recognize him because of his pronounced slouch.

Prem Singh doesn't slouch, but he has this habit of looking up at the sky (regardless of whether it's cloudy or clear), and at the moment he's looking at the sky.

Eight years with Prem. He was just a sixteen-year-old boy when I first saw him, and now he has a wife and child.

I had been in the cottage for just over a year…. He stood on the landing outside the kitchen door. A tall boy, dark, with good teeth and brown, deep-set eyes, dressed smartly in white drill—his only change of clothes. Looking for a job. I liked the look of him, but—

'I already have someone working for me,' I said.

'Yes, sir. He is my uncle.'

In the hills, everyone is a brother or an uncle.

'You don't want me to dismiss your uncle?'

'No, sir. But he says you can find a job for me.'

'I'll try. I'll make inquiries. Have you just come from your village?'

'Yes. Yesterday I walked ten miles to Pauri. There I got a bus.'

'Sit down. Your uncle will make some tea.'

He sat down on the steps, removed his white keds, wriggled his toes. His feet were both long and broad, large feet but not ugly. He was unusually clean for a hill boy. And taller than most.

'Do you smoke?' I asked.

'No, sir.'

'It is true,' said his uncle. 'He does not smoke. All my nephews smoke but this one. He is a little peculiar, he does not smoke—neither beedi nor hookah.'

'Do you drink?'

'It makes me vomit.'

'Do you take bhang?'

'No, Sahib.'

'You have no vices. It's unnatural.'

'He is unnatural, sahib,' said his uncle.

'Does he chase girls?'

'They chase him, Sahib.'

'So he left the village and came looking for a job.' I looked at him. He grinned, then looked away and began rubbing his feet.

'Your name is…?'

'Prem Singh.'

'All right, Prem, I will try to do something for you.'

I did not see him for a couple of weeks. I forgot about finding him a job. But when I met him again, on the road to the bazaar, he told me that he had got a temporary job in the Survey, looking after the surveyor's tents.

'Next week we will be going to Rajasthan,' he said.

'It will be very hot. Have you been in the desert before?'

'No, sir.'

'It is not like the hills. And it is far from home.'

'I know. But I have no choice in the matter. I have to collect some money in order to get married.'

In his region there was a bride price, usually of two thousand rupees.

'Do you have to get married so soon?'

'I have only one brother and he is still very young. My mother is not well. She needs a daughter-in-law to help her in the fields and the house, and with the cows. We are a small family, so the work is greater.'

Every family has its few terraced fields, narrow and stony, usually perched on a hillside above a stream or river. They grow rice, barley, maize, potatoes—just enough to live on. Even if their produce is sufficient for marketing, the absence of roads makes it difficult to get the produce to the market towns. There is no money to be earned in the villages, and money is needed for clothes, soap, medicines, and for recovering the family jewellery from the moneylenders. So the young men leave their villages to find work, and to find work they must go to the plains. The lucky ones get into the army. Others enter domestic service or take jobs in garages, hotels, wayside tea shops, schools....

In Mussoorie the main attraction is the large number of schools which employ cooks and bearers. But the schools were full when Prem arrived. He'd been to the recruiting centre at Roorkee, hoping to get into the army; but they found a deformity in his right foot, the result of a bone broken when a landslip carried him away one dark monsoon night. He was lucky, he said, that it was only his foot and not his head that had been broken.

He came to the house to inform his uncle about the job and to say goodbye. I thought, another nice person I probably won't see again; another ship passing in the night, the friendly twinkle of its lights soon vanishing in the darkness. I said 'Come again', held his smile with mine so that I could remember him better, and returned to my study and my typewriter. The typewriter is the repository of a writer's loneliness. It stares unsympathetically back at him every day, doing its best to be discouraging. Maybe I'll go back to the old-fashioned quill pen and marble inkstand; then I can feel like a real writer—Balzac or Dickens—scratching away into the endless reaches of the night.... Of course, the days and nights are seemingly shorter than they need to be! They must be, otherwise why do we hurry so much and achieve so little, by the standards of the past....

Prem goes, disappears into the vast faceless cities of the plains, and a year slips by, or rather I do, and then here he is again, thinner and darker and still smiling and still looking for a job. I should have known that hillmen don't disappear altogether. The spirit-haunted rocks don't let their people wander too far, lest they lose them forever.

I was able to get him a job in the school. The headmaster's wife needed a cook. I wasn't sure if Prem could cook very well but I sent him along and they said they'd give him a trial. Three days later the headmaster's wife met me on the road and started gushing all over me. She was the type who gushed.

'We're so grateful to you! Thank you for sending me that lovely boy. He's so polite. And he cooks very well. A little too hot for my husband, but otherwise delicious—just delicious! He's a real treasure—a lovely boy.' And she gave me an arch look—the famous look which she used to captivate all the good-looking young prefects who became prefects, it was said, only if she approved of them.

I wasn't sure that she didn't want something more than a cook, and I only hoped that Prem would give every satisfaction.

He looked cheerful enough when he came to see me on his off day.

'How are you getting on?' I asked.

'Lovely,' he said, using his mistress's favourite expression.

'What do you mean—lovely? Do they like your work?'

'The memsahib likes it. She strokes me on the cheek whenever she enters the kitchen. The sahib says nothing. He takes medicine after every meal.'

'Did he always take medicine—or only now that you're doing the cooking?'

'I am not sure. I think he has always been sick.'

He was sleeping in the headmaster's veranda and getting sixty rupees a month. A cook in Delhi got a hundred and sixty. And a cook in Paris or New York got ten times as much. I did not say as much to Prem. He might ask me to get him a job in New York. And that would be the last I saw of him! He, as a cook, might well get a job making curries off-Broadway; I, as a writer, wouldn't get to first base. And only my Uncle Ken knew the secret of how to make a living without actually doing any work. But then, of course, he had four sisters. And each of them was married to a fairly prosperous husband. So Uncle Ken divided his year among them. Three months with Aunt Ruby in Nainital. Three months with Aunt Susie in Kashmir. Three months with my mother (not quite so affluent) in Jamnagar. And three months in the Vet Hospital in Bareilly, where Aunt Mabel ran the hospital for her veterinary husband. In this way he never overstayed his welcome. A sister can look after a brother for just three months at a time and no more. Uncle K had it worked out to perfection.

But I had no sisters and I couldn't live forever on the royalties of a single novel. So I had to write others. So I came to the hills.

The hillmen go to the plains to make a living. I had to come to the hills to try and make mine.

'Prem,' I said, 'why don't you work for me?'

'And what about my uncle?'

'He seems ready to desert me any day. His grandfather is ill, he says, and he wants to go home.'

'His grandfather died last year.'

'That's what I mean—he's getting restless. And I don't mind if he goes. These days he seems to be suffering from a form of sleeping sickness. I have to get up first and make his tea....'

Sitting here under the cherry tree, whose leaves are just beginning to turn yellow, I rest my chin on my knees and gaze across the valley to where Prem moves about in the garden. Looking back over the seven years he has been with me, I recall some of the nicest things about him. They come to me in no particular order—just pieces of cinema—coloured slides slipping across the screen of memory....

Prem rocking his infant son to sleep—crooning to him, passing his large hand gently over the child's curly head—Prem following me down to the police station when I was arrested (on a warrant from Bombay, charging me with writing an allegedly obscene short story!), and waiting outside until I reappeared, his smile, when I found him in Delhi, his large, irrepressible laughter, most in evidence when he was seeing an old Laurel and Hardy movie.

Of course, there were times when he could be infuriating, stubborn, deliberately pig-headed, sending me little notes of resignation—but I never found it difficult to overlook these little acts of self-indulgence. He had brought much love and laughter into my life, and what more could a lonely man ask for?

It was his stubborn streak that limited the length of his stay in the headmaster's household. Mr Good was tolerant enough. But Mrs Good was one of those women who, when they are pleased with you, go out of their way to help, pamper and flatter, but when displeased, become vindictive, going out of their way to harm or destroy. Mrs Good sought power—over her husband, her dog, her favourite pupils, her servant... She had absolute power over the husband and the dog, partial power over her slightly bewildered pupils, and none at all over Prem, who missed the subtleties of her designs upon his soul. He did not respond to her mothering, or to the way in which she tweaked him on the cheeks, brushed against him in the kitchen and made admiring remarks about his looks and physique. Memsahibs, he knew, were not for him. So he kept a stony face and went diligently about his duties. And she felt slighted, put in her place. Her liking turned to dislike. Instead of admiring remarks, she began making disparaging remarks about his looks, his clothes, his manners. She found fault with his cooking. No longer was it 'lovely'. She even accused him of taking away the dog's meat and giving it to a poor family living on the hillside—no more heinous crime could be imagined! Mr Good threatened him with dismissal. So Prem became stubborn. The following day he withheld the dog's food altogether, threw it down the khud where it was seized upon by innumerable strays, and went off to the pictures.

That was the end of his job. 'I'll have to go home now,' he told me. 'I won't get another job in this area. The mem will see to that.'

'Stay a few days,' I said.

'I have only enough money with which to get home.'

'Keep it for going home. You can stay with me for a few days, while you look around. Your uncle won't mind sharing his food with you.'

His uncle did mind. He did not like the idea of working for his nephew as well; it seemed to him no part of his duties. And he was apprehensive that Prem might get his job.

So Prem stayed no longer than a week.

Here on the knoll the grass is just beginning to turn October yellow. The first clouds approaching winter cover the sky. The trees are very still. The birds are silent. Only a cricket keeps singing on the oak tree. Perhaps there will be a storm before evening. A storm like the one in which Prem arrived at the cottage with his wife and child—but that's jumping too far ahead....

After he had returned to his village, it was several months before I saw him again. His uncle told me he had taken up a job in Delhi. There was an address. It did not seem complete, but I resolved that when I was next in Delhi I would try to see him.

The opportunity came in May, as the hot winds of summer blew across the plains. It was the time of year when people who can afford it, try to get away to the hills. I dislike New Delhi at the best of times, and I hate it in summer. People compete with each other in being bad-tempered and mean. But I had to go down—I don't remember why, but it must have seemed very necessary at the time—and I took the opportunity to try and see Prem.

Nothing went right for me. Of course the address was all wrong, and I wandered about in a remote, dusty, treeless colony called Vasant Vihar (Spring Garden) for over two hours, asking all the domestic servants I came across if they could put me in touch with Prem Singh of Village Koli, Pauri Garhwal. There were innumerable Prem Singhs, but apparently none who belonged to Village Koli. I returned to my hotel and took two days to recover from heatstroke before returning to Mussoorie, thanking God for mountains!

And then the uncle gave notice. He'd found a better-paid job in Dehradun and was anxious to be off. I didn't try to stop him.

For the next six months I lived in the cottage without any help. I did not find this difficult. I was used to living alone. It wasn't service that I needed but companionship. In the cottage it was very quiet. The ghosts of long-dead residents were sympathetic but unobtrusive. The song of the whistling thrush was beautiful, but I knew he was not singing for me. Up the valley came the sound of a flute, but I never saw the flute player. My affinity was with the little red fox who roamed the hillside below the cottage. I met him one night and wrote these lines:

> As I walked home last night
> I saw a lone fox dancing
> In the cold moonlight.
> I stood and watched—then

took the low road, knowing
the night was his by right.
Sometimes, when words ring true,
I'm like a lone fox dancing
In the morning dew.

During the rains, watching the dripping trees and the mist climbing the valley, I wrote a great deal of poetry. Loneliness is of value to poets. But poetry didn't bring me much money, and funds were low. And then, just as I was wondering if I would have to give up my freedom and take a job again, a publisher bought the paperback rights of one of my children's stories, and I was free to live and write as I pleased—for another three months!

That was in November. To celebrate, I took a long walk through the Landour bazaar and up the Tehri road. It was a good day for walking; and it was dark by the time I returned to the outskirts of the town. Someone stood waiting for me on the road above the cottage. I hurried past him.

If I am not for myself,
Who will be for me?
And if I am not for others,
What am I?
And if not now, when?

I startled myself with the memory of these words of Hillel, the ancient Hebrew sage. I walked back to the shadows where the youth stood, and saw that it was Prem.

'Prem!' I said. 'Why are you sitting out here, in the cold? Why did you not go to the house?'

'I went, sir, but there was a lock on the door. I thought you had gone away.'

'And you were going to remain here, on the road?'

'Only for tonight. I would have gone down to Dehra in the morning.'

'Come, let's go home. I have been waiting for you. I looked for you in Delhi, but could not find the place where you were working.'

'I have left them now.'

'And your uncle has left me. So will you work for me now?'

'For as long as you wish.'

'For as long as the gods wish.'

We did not go straight home, but returned to the bazaar and took our meal in the Sindhi Sweet Shop—hot puris and strong sweet tea.

We walked home together in the bright moonlight. I felt sorry for the little fox dancing alone.

That was twenty years ago, and Prem and his wife and three children are still with me. But we live in a different house now, on another hill.

THE NIGHT TRAIN AT DEOLI

When I was at college I used to spend my summer vacations in Dehra, at my grandmother's place. I would leave the plains early in May and return late in July. Deoli was a small station about thirty miles from Dehra. It marked the beginning of the heavy jungles of the Indian Terai.

The train would reach Deoli at about five in the morning when the station would be dimly lit with electric bulbs and oil lamps, and the jungle across the railway tracks would just be visible in the faint light of dawn. Deoli had only one platform, an office for the stationmaster, and a waiting room. The platform boasted a tea stall, a fruit vendor, and a few stray dogs; not much else because the train stopped there for only ten minutes before rushing on into the forests.

Why it stopped at Deoli, I don't know. Nothing ever happened there. Nobody got off the train and nobody got on. There were never any coolies on the platform. But the train would halt there a full ten minutes and then a bell would sound, the guard would blow his whistle, and presently Deoli would be left behind and forgotten.

I used to wonder what happened in Deoli behind the station walls. I always felt sorry for that lonely little platform and for the place that nobody wanted to visit. I decided that one day I would get off the train at Deoli and spend the day there just to please the town.

I was eighteen, visiting my grandmother, and the night train stopped at Deoli. A girl came down the platform selling baskets.

It was a cold morning and the girl had a shawl thrown across her shoulders. Her feet were bare and her clothes were old but she was a young girl, walking gracefully and with dignity.

When she came to my window, she stopped. She saw that I was looking at her intently, but at first she pretended not to notice. She had pale skin, set off by shiny black hair and dark, troubled eyes. And then those eyes, searching and eloquent, met mine.

She stood by my window for some time and neither of us said anything. But when she moved on, I found myself leaving my seat and going to the carriage door. I stood waiting on the platform looking the other way. I walked across to the tea stall. A kettle was boiling over a small fire, but the owner of the stall was busy serving tea somewhere on the train. The girl followed me behind the stall.

'Do you want to buy a basket?' she asked. 'They are very strong, made of the finest cane....'

'No,' I said, 'I don't want a basket.'

We stood looking at each other for what seemed a very long time, and she said, 'Are you sure you don't want a basket?'

'All right, give me one,' I said, and took the one on top and gave her a rupee, hardly daring to touch her fingers.

As she was about to speak, the guard blew his whistle. She said something, but it was lost in the clanging of the bell and the hissing of the engine. I had to run back to my compartment. The carriage shuddered and jolted forward.

I watched her as the platform slipped away. She was alone on the platform and she did not move, but she was looking at me and smiling. I watched her until the signal box came in the way and then the jungle hid the station. But I could still see her standing there alone....

I stayed awake for the rest of the journey. I could not rid my mind of the picture of the girl's face and her dark, smouldering eyes.

But when I reached Dehra the incident became blurred and distant, for there were other things to occupy my mind. It was only when I was making the return journey, two months later, that I remembered the girl.

I was looking out for her as the train drew into the station, and I felt an unexpected thrill when I saw her walking up the platform. I sprang off the footboard and waved to her.

When she saw me, she smiled. She was pleased that I remembered her. I was pleased that she remembered me. We were both pleased, and it was almost like a meeting of old friends.

She did not go down the length of the train selling baskets but came straight to the tea stall. Her dark eyes were suddenly filled with light. We said nothing for some time but we couldn't have been more eloquent.

I felt the impulse to put her on the train there and then, and take her away with me. I could not bear the thought of having to watch her recede into the distance of Deoli station. I took the baskets from her hand and put them down on the ground. She put out her hand for one of them, but I caught her hand and held it.

'I have to go to Delhi,' I said.

She nodded. 'I do not have to go anywhere.'

The guard blew his whistle for the train to leave, and how I hated the guard for doing that.

'I will come again,' I said. 'Will you be here?'

She nodded again and, as she nodded, the bell clanged and the train slid forward. I had to wrench my hand away from the girl and run for the moving train.

This time I did not forget her. She was with me for the remainder of the journey and for long after. All that year she was a bright, living thing. And when the college term finished, I packed in haste and left for Dehra earlier than usual. My grandmother would be pleased at my eagerness to see her.

I was nervous and anxious as the train drew into Deoli, because I was wondering what I should say to the girl and what

I should do. I was determined that I wouldn't stand helplessly before her, hardly able to speak or do anything about my feelings.

The train came to Deoli, and I looked up and down the platform but I could not see the girl anywhere.

I opened the door and stepped off the footboard. I was deeply disappointed and overcome by a sense of foreboding. I felt I had to do something and so I ran up to the stationmaster and said, 'Do you know the girl who used to sell baskets here?'

'No, I don't,' said the stationmaster. 'And you'd better get on the train if you don't want to be left behind.'

But I paced up and down the platform and stared over the railings at the station yard. All I saw was a mango tree and a dusty road leading into the jungle. Where did the road go? The train was moving out of the station and I had to run up the platform and jump for the door of my compartment. Then, as the train gathered speed and rushed through the forests, I sat brooding in front of the window.

What could I do about finding a girl I had seen only twice, who had hardly spoken to me, and about whom I knew nothing—absolutely nothing—but for whom I felt a tenderness and responsibility that I had never felt before?

My grandmother was not pleased with my visit after all, because I didn't stay at her place more than a couple of weeks. I felt restless and ill at ease. So I took the train back to the plains, meaning to ask further questions of the stationmaster at Deoli.

But at Deoli there was a new stationmaster. The previous man had been transferred to another post within the past week. The new man didn't know anything about the girl who sold baskets. I found the owner of the tea stall, a small, shrivelled-up man, wearing greasy clothes, and asked him if he knew anything about the girl with the baskets.

'Yes, there was such a girl here. I remember quite well,' he said.

'But she has stopped coming now.'

'Why?' I asked. 'What happened to her?'

'How should I know?' said the man. 'She was nothing to me.'

And once again I had to run for the train.

As Deoli platform receded, I decided that one day I would have to break journey there, spend a day in the town, make inquiries, and find the girl who had stolen my heart with nothing but a look from her dark, impatient eyes.

With this thought I consoled myself throughout my last term in college. I went to Dehra again in the summer and when, in the early hours of the morning, the night train drew into Deoli station, I looked up and down the platform for signs of the girl, knowing I wouldn't find her but hoping just the same.

Somehow, I couldn't bring myself to break journey at Deoli and spend a day there. (If it was all fiction or a film, I reflected, I would have got down and cleared up the mystery and reached a suitable ending to the whole thing.) I think I was afraid to do this.

I was afraid of discovering what really happened to the girl. Perhaps she was no longer in Deoli, perhaps she was married, perhaps she had fallen ill....

In the last few years I have passed through Deoli many times, and I always look out of the carriage window half expecting to see the same unchanged face smiling up at me. I wonder what happens in Deoli, behind the station walls. But I will never break my journey there. I prefer to keep hoping and dreaming and looking out of the window up and down that lonely platform, waiting for the girl with the baskets.

I never break my journey at Deoli, but I pass through as often as I can.

THE FUNERAL

'I don't think he should go,' said Aunt M.

'He's too young,' concurred Aunt B. 'He'll get upset and probably throw a tantrum. And you know Padre Lal doesn't like having children at funerals.'

The boy said nothing. He sat in the darkest corner of the darkened room, his face revealing nothing of what he thought and felt. His father's coffin lay in the next room, the lid fastened forever over the tired, wistful countenance of the man who had meant so much to the boy. Nobody else had mattered—neither uncles nor aunts nor fond grandparents. Least of all the mother who was hundreds of miles away with another husband. He hadn't seen her since he was four—that was just over five years ago—and he did not remember her very well.

The house was full of people—friends, relatives, neighbours. Some had tried to fuss over him but had been discouraged by his silence, the absence of tears. The more understanding of them had kept their distance.

Scattered words of condolence passed back and forth like dragonflies in the wind. 'Such a tragedy!'

'Only forty.'

'No one realized how serious it was.'

'Devoted to the child.'

It seemed to the boy that everyone who mattered in the hill station was present. And for the first time they had the run of the house for his father had not been a sociable man. Books, music, flowers and his stamp collection had been his main preoccupations, apart from the boy.

A small hearse, drawn by a hill pony, was led in at the gate and several able-bodied men lifted the coffin and manoeuvred it into the carriage. The crowd drifted away. The cemetery was about a mile down the road and those who did not have cars would have to walk the distance.

The boy stared through a window at the small procession passing through the gate. He'd been forgotten for the moment— left in care of the servants, who were the only ones to stay behind. Outside it was misty. The mist had crept up the valley and settled like a damp towel on the face of the mountain. Everyone was wet although it hadn't rained.

The boy waited until everyone had gone and then he left the room and went out onto the veranda. The gardener, who had been sitting in a bed of nasturtiums, looked up and asked the boy if he needed anything. But the boy shook his head and retreated indoors. The gardener, looking aggrieved because of the damage done to the flower beds by the mourners, shambled off to his quarters. The sahib's death meant that he would be out of a job very soon. The house would pass into other hands. The boy would go to an orphanage. There weren't many people who kept gardeners these days. In the kitchen, the cook was busy preparing the only big meal ever served in the house. All those relatives, and the padre too, would come back famished, ready for a sombre but nevertheless substantial meal. He, too, would be out of a job soon; but cooks were always in demand.

The boy slipped out of the house by a back door and made his way into the lane through a gap in a thicket of dog roses. When he reached the main road, he could see the mourners wending their way around the hill to the cemetery. He followed at a distance.

It was the same road he had often taken with his father during their evening walks. The boy knew the name of almost every plant and wildflower that grew on the hillside. These, and various birds and insects, had been described and pointed out to him by his father.

Looking northwards, he could see the higher ranges of the Himalayas and the eternal snows. The graves in the cemetery were so laid out that if their incumbents did happen to rise one day, the first thing they would see would be the glint of the sun on those snow-covered peaks. Possibly the site had been chosen for the view. But to the boy it did not seem as if anyone would be able to thrust aside those massive tombstones and rise from their graves to enjoy the view. Their rest seemed as eternal as the snows. It would take an earthquake to burst those stones asunder and thrust the coffins up from the earth. The boy wondered why people hadn't made it easier for the dead to rise. They were so securely entombed that it appeared as though no one really wanted them to get out.

'God has need of your father....' With those words a well-meaning missionary had tried to console him.

And had God, in the same way, laid claim to the thousands of men, women and children who had been put to rest here in these neat and serried rows? What could he have wanted them for? Of what use are we to God when we are dead, wondered the boy.

The cemetery gate stood open but the boy leant against the old stone wall and stared down at the mourners as they shuffled about with the unease of a batsman about to face a very fast bowler. Only this bowler was invisible and would come up stealthily and from behind.

Padre Lal's voice droned on through the funeral service and then the coffin was lowered—down, deep down. The boy was surprised at how far down it seemed to go! Was that other, better world down in the depths of the earth? How could anyone, even a Samson, push his way back to the surface again? Superman did it in comics but his father was a gentle soul who wouldn't fight too hard against the earth and the grass and the roots of tiny trees. Or perhaps he'd grow into a tree and escape that way! 'If ever I'm put away like this,' thought the boy, 'I'll get into the root of a plant and then I'll become a flower and then maybe a bird will come and carry my seed away.... I'll get out somehow!'

A few more words from the padre and then some of those present threw handfuls of earth over the coffin before moving away.

Slowly, in twos and threes, the mourners departed. The mist swallowed them up. They did not see the boy behind the wall. They were getting hungry.

He stood there until they had all gone. Then he noticed that the gardeners or caretakers were filling in the grave. He did not know whether to go forward or not. He was a little afraid. And it was too late now. The grave was almost covered.

He turned and walked away from the cemetery. The road stretched ahead of him, empty, swathed in mist. He was alone. What had his father said to him once? 'The strongest man in the world is he who stands alone.'

Well, he was alone, but at the moment he did not feel very strong.

For a moment he thought his father was beside him, that they were together on one of their long walks. Instinctively he put out his hand, expecting his father's warm, comforting touch. But there was nothing there, nothing, no one....

He clenched his fists and pushed them deep down into his pockets. He lowered his head so that no one would see his tears. There were people in the mist but he did not want to go near them for they had put his father away.

'He'll find a way out,' the boy said fiercely to himself. 'He'll get out somehow!'

THE BIG RACE

Dawn crept quietly over the sleeping town. Only a cock was aware of it, and crowed. Koki heard a soft tapping on the windowpane, and immediately sat up in bed. She was ten years old. Her hair fell about her shoulders in a disorderly fashion and there were slight shadows under her dark eyes, but she was wide awake and listening. The tapping was repeated.

Koki got out of bed and tiptoed across to the window and unlatched it. Ranji was standing outside, looking somewhat disgruntled.

'Come on,' he said. 'It's nearly time.'

Koki put her finger to her lips, for she did not want her parents and grandmother to wake up.

'You go and tell Bhim,' she whispered. 'I'll meet you at the maidan.'

Ranji hurried off in the direction of Bhim's house, and Koki turned from the window and went to the dressing table. She combed her hair carelessly and tied it roughly with a ribbon. She was excited and in a hurry, and had slept in her dress, which was very crushed. Now she was ready to leave.

Very quietly, she pulled open a dressing table drawer, and brought out a cardboard box in which were punctured little holes. She opened the lid of the box to see if Rajkumari was all right.

Rajkumari, a dumpy rhino beetle, was asleep on the core of an apple. Koki did not disturb her. She closed the box and barefoot crept out of the house through the back door.

As soon as she was outside, Koki broke into a run. She did not stop running until she reached the maidan.

On the maidan, the slanting rays of the early morning sun

were just beginning to make emeralds of the dewdrops. Later in the day the grass would dry and be prickly to the feet, but now it was cool and soft. A group of boys had gathered at one corner of the maidan, talking excitedly, and among them were Ranji and Bhim, a lanky, bespectacled boy of fourteen. Koki was the only girl among them.

Bhim's beetle was the favourite for the race. It was a large bamboo beetle, with a slim body and long, slender legs, rather like its master's. It was called 2001. Ranji's beetle was a stone carrier with what looked like a very long pair of whiskers. It was appropriately named Moocha. Koki's beetle was not half as big as the other two. Though she did not know how to tell its sex, she was sure it was a female and had called it Rajkumari.

There were only three entries. Strictly speaking, betting wasn't allowed, but the boys made a few quiet bets among themselves. The prize was a giant insect (there was some disagreement as to whether it was a beetle or an outsize cockroach), which was meant to enable the winner to breed larger racing beetles.

There was some confusion when Ranji's Moocha escaped from his box and took a preliminary canter over the grass; but he was soon caught and returned to his enclosure. Moocha appeared to be in good form, in fact he would be tough competition for Bhim's 2001.

The course was about two metres long, the tracks fifteen centimetres wide. The tracks were fenced with strips of cardboard so that the contestants did not get in each other's way or leave the course altogether. They were held at the starting post by another piece of cardboard, which would be placed behind them as soon as the race began—just to make sure that no one backed out.

A little Sikh boy in a yellow pyjama-suit was acting as starter, and he kept blowing his whistle for order and attention. When the onlookers saw that the race was about to begin, they fell silent. The little Sikh boy then announced the rules of the race—

the contestants were not to be touched during the race, or blown at from behind, or enticed forward with bits of food. They could, however, be cheered on as loudly as anyone wished.

Moocha and 2001 were already at the starting post, but Koki was giving Rajkumari a few words of advice. Rajkumari seemed reluctant to leave her apple core and needed to be taken forcibly to the starting post.

There was further delay when Moocha and 2001 got their horns and whiskers entangled. They had to be separated and calmed down before being placed in their respective tracks. The race was about to start.

Koki knelt on the grass, very quiet and serious, looking from Rajkumari to the finishing line and back again. Ranji was biting his fingernails. Bhim's glasses had clouded over, and he had to keep taking them off and wiping them on his shirt. There was a hush amongst the dozen or so spectators.

'Pee-ee-eeep!' The little Sikh boy blew his whistle.

They were off!

Or rather, Moocha and 2001 were off. Rajkumari was still at the starting post, wondering what had happened to her apple core.

Everyone was cheering madly, and Ranji was jumping up and down, and Bhim's glasses had been knocked off. Moocha was going at a spanking rate. 2001 wasn't taking a great deal of interest in the proceedings, but he was moving, and anything could happen in a race like this.

Koki was on the verge of tears. All the coaching she had given Rajkumari seemed to be of no avail. Her beetle was still looking bewildered and hurt.

'Stop sulking,' said Koki. 'I won't keep you if you don't try.'

Then Moocha stopped suddenly, less than a metre from the finishing line. He seemed to be having trouble with his whiskers, and kept twitching them this way and that. 2001 was catching up slowly but surely, and both Ranji and Bhim were shouting themselves hoarse. Nobody paid any attention to Rajkumari, who was considered to be out of the race; but Koki was using all her willpower to get her racer going.

As 2001 approached Moocha, he seemed to sense his rival's trouble and stopped to find out what was the matter. They could not see each other over the cardboard fence, but otherwise appeared to be communicating very well. Ranji and Bhim were becoming quite frantic in their efforts to rally their faltering steeds, and the cheering on all sides was deafening.

Rajkumari, goaded with rage and frustration at having been deprived of her apple core, now took it into her head to make a bid for liberty and new pastures, and rushed forward in great style.

Koki shouted with joy, but the others did not notice the new challenge until Rajkumari had drawn level with her conferring rivals. There was a gasp from the crowd as Rajkumari strode across the finishing line in record time.

Everyone cheered the gallant outsider. Ranji and Bhim very sportingly shook Koki's hand, congratulating her on Rajkumari's victory. The little Sikh boy in the yellow pyjama-suit blew his whistle for silence and presented Koki with her prize.

Koki gazed in rapture at the new beetle—or was it a cockroach? She stroked its back with her thumb. The insect didn't seem to mind. Then, lest Rajkumari should feel jealous, Koki closed the prize box and, picking up her victorious beetle, returned her to the apple core.

The crowd began to break up. Ranji decided that he would trim Moocha's whiskers before the next race, and Bhim thought 2001 was in need of a special diet.

'Just wait till next Sunday,' said Ranji. 'Then watch my Moocha leave the rest of you standing!'

Bhim said nothing. He looked very thoughtful. There were

some new training methods which he was going to try out for next time.

Koki walked home, a cardboard box under each arm. Her thoughts were busy with the future. She would breed beetles (or would they be cockroaches?) until she had a stable of about twenty. Her racers would win every event, both here and in the next town. They might make her famous. Beetle racing would become a national sport!

Meanwhile, she was happy, and Rajkumari was happy on the apple core, and the new insect was just being an insect and did not know and did not care about anything except how to get out of that wretched box.

THE PROSPECT OF FLOWERS

Fern Hill, The Oaks, Hunter's Lodge, The Parsonage, The Pines, Dumbarnie, Mackinnon's Hall, and Windermere. These are the names of some of the old houses that still stand on the outskirts of one of the smaller Indian hill stations. Most of them have fallen into decay and ruin. They are very old, of course—built over a hundred years ago by Britons who sought relief from the searing heat of the plains. Today's visitors to the hill stations prefer to live near the markets and cinemas, and many of the old houses, set amidst oak and maple and deodar, are inhabited by wild cats, bandicoots, owls, goats, and the occasional charcoal burner or mule driver.

But amongst these neglected mansions stands a neat, whitewashed cottage called Mulberry Lodge. And in it, up to a short time ago, lived an elderly English spinster named Miss Mackenzie.

In years Miss Mackenzie was more than 'elderly', being well over eighty. But no one would have guessed it. She was clean, sprightly, and wore old-fashioned but well-preserved dresses. Once a week, she walked the two miles to town to buy butter and jam and soap and sometimes a small bottle of eau de cologne.

She had lived in the hill station since she had been a girl in her teens, and that had been before the First World War. Though she had never married, she had experienced a few love affairs and was far from being the typical frustrated spinster of fiction. Her parents had been dead thirty years; her brother and sister were also dead. She had no relatives in India, and she lived on a small pension of forty rupees a month and the gift parcels that were sent out to her from New Zealand by a friend of her youth.

Like other lonely old people, she kept a pet—a large black cat with bright yellow eyes. In her small garden she grew dahlias, chrysanthemums, gladioli, and a few rare orchids. She knew a great deal about plants and about wild flowers, trees, birds, and insects. She had never made a serious study of these things, but having lived with them for so many years had developed an intimacy with all that grew and flourished around her.

She had few visitors. Occasionally, the padre from the local church called on her, and once a month the postman came with a letter from New Zealand or her pension papers. The milkman called every second day with a litre of milk for the lady and her cat. And sometimes she received a couple of eggs free, for the egg seller remembered a time when Miss Mackenzie, in her earlier prosperity, had bought eggs from him in large quantities. He was a sentimental man. He remembered her as a ravishing beauty in her twenties when he had gazed at her in round-eyed, nine-year-old wonder and consternation.

Now it was September and the rains were nearly over, and Miss Mackenzie's chrysanthemums were coming into their own. She hoped the coming winter wouldn't be too severe because she found it increasingly difficult to bear the cold.

One day, as she was pottering about in her garden, she saw a schoolboy plucking wild flowers on the slope above the cottage.

'Who's that?' she called. 'What are you up to, young man?'

The boy was alarmed and tried to dash up the hillside, but he slipped on pine needles and came slithering down the slope on to Miss Mackenzie's nasturtium bed.

When he found there was no escape, he gave a bright disarming smile and said, 'Good morning, Miss.'

He belonged to the local English-medium school and wore a bright red blazer and a red and black striped tie. Like most polite Indian schoolboys, he called every woman 'miss'.

'Good morning,' said Miss Mackenzie severely. 'Would you

mind moving out of my flower bed?'

The boy stepped gingerly over the nasturtiums and looked up at Miss Mackenzie with dimpled cheeks and appealing eyes. It was impossible to be angry with him.

'You're trespassing,' said Miss Mackenzie.

'Yes, Miss.'

'And you ought to be in school at this hour.'

'Yes, Miss.'

'Then what are you doing here?'

'Picking flowers, Miss.' And he held up a bunch of ferns and wild flowers.

'Oh,' Miss Mackenzie was disarmed. It was a long time since she had seen a boy taking an interest in flowers, and, what was more, playing truant from school in order to gather them.

'Do you like flowers?' she asked.

'Yes, Miss. I'm going to be a botan—a botantist?'

'You mean a botanist.'

'Yes, Miss.'

'Well, that's unusual. Most boys at your age want to be pilots or soldiers or perhaps engineers. But you want to be a botanist. Well, well. There's still hope for the world, I see. And do you know the names of these flowers?'

'This is a bukhilo flower,' he said, showing her a small golden flower. 'That's a Pahari name. It means puja or prayer. The flower is offered during prayers. But I don't know what this is....'

He held out a pale pink flower with a soft, heart-shaped leaf.

'It's a wild begonia,' said Miss Mackenzie. 'And that purple stuff is salvia, but it isn't wild. It's a plant that escaped from my garden. Don't you have any books on flowers?'

'No, Miss.'

'All right, come in and I'll show you a book.'

She led the boy into a small front room, which was crowded with furniture and books and vases and jam jars, and offered him a chair. He sat awkwardly on its edge. The black cat immediately leapt on to his knees, and settled down on them, purring loudly.

'What's your name?' asked Miss Mackenzie, as she rummaged through her books.

'Anil, Miss.'

'And where do you live?'

'When school closes, I go to Delhi. My father has a business.'

'Oh, and what's that?'

'Bulbs, miss.'

'Flower bulbs?'

'No, electric bulbs.'

'Electric bulbs! You might send me a few, when you get home. Mine are always fusing, and they're so expensive, like everything else these days. Ah, here we are!' She pulled a heavy volume down from the shelf and laid it on the table. *'Flora Himaliensis,* published in 1892, and probably the only copy in India. This is a very valuable book, Anil. No other naturalist has recorded so many wild Himalayan flowers. And let me tell you this, there are many flowers and plants which are still unknown to the fancy botanists who spend all their time with microscopes instead of in the mountains. But perhaps, *you'll* do something about that, one day.'

'Yes, Miss.'

They went through the book together, and Miss Mackenzie pointed out many flowers that grew in and around the hill station while the boy made notes of their names and seasons. She lit a stove and put the kettle on for tea. And then the old English lady and the small Indian boy sat side by side over cups of hot sweet tea, absorbed in a book on wild flowers.

'May I come again?' asked Anil, when finally he rose to go.

'If you like,' said Miss Mackenzie. 'But not during school hours. You mustn't miss your classes.'

After that, Anil visited Miss Mackenzie about once a week,

and nearly always brought a wild flower for her to identify. She found herself looking forward to the boy's visits—and sometimes, when more than a week passed and he didn't come, she was disappointed and lonely and would grumble at the black cat.

Anil reminded her of her brother, when the latter had been a boy. There was no physical resemblance. Andrew had been fair-haired and blue-eyed. But it was Anil's eagerness, his alert, bright look and the way he stood—legs apart, hands on hips, a picture of confidence—that reminded her of the boy who had shared her own youth in these same hills.

And why did Anil come to see her so often? Partly because she knew about wild flowers, and he really did want to become a botanist. And partly because she smelt of freshly baked bread, and that was a smell his own grandmother had possessed. And partly because she was lonely and sometimes a boy of twelve can sense loneliness better than an adult. And partly because he was a little different from other children.

By the middle of October, when there was only a fortnight left for the school to close, the first snow had fallen on the distant mountains. One peak stood high above the rest, a white pinnacle against the azure-blue sky. When the sun set, this peak turned from orange to gold to pink to red.

'How high is that mountain?' asked Anil.

'It must be over twelve thousand feet,' said Miss Mackenzie.

'About thirty miles from here, as the crow flies. I always wanted to go there, but there was no proper road. At that height, there'll be flowers that you don't get here—the blue gentian and the purple columbine, the anemone and the edelweiss.'

'I'll go there one day,' said Anil.

'I'm sure you will, if you really want to.'

The day before his school closed, Anil came to say goodbye to Miss Mackenzie.

'I don't suppose you'll be able to find many wild flowers in Delhi,' she said. 'But have a good holiday.'

'Thank you, Miss.'

As he was about to leave, Miss Mackenzie, on an impulse, thrust the *Flora Himaliensis* into his hands.

'You keep it,' she said. 'It's a present for you.'

'But I'll be back next year, and I'll be able to look at it then. It's so valuable.'

'I know it's valuable and that's why I've given it to you. Otherwise it will only fall into the hands of the junk dealers.'

'But, Miss....'

'Don't argue. Besides, I may not be here next year.'

'Are you going away?'

'I'm not sure. I may go to England.'

She had no intention of going to England; she had not seen the country since she was a child, and she knew she would not fit in with the life of post-war Britain. Her home was in these hills, among the oaks and maples and deodars. It was lonely, but at her age it would be lonely anywhere.

The boy tucked the book under his arm, straightened his tie, stood stiffly to attention and said, 'Goodbye, Miss Mackenzie.' It was the first time he had spoken her name.

Winter set in early and strong winds brought rain and sleet, and soon there were no flowers in the garden or on the hillside. The cat stayed indoors, curled up at the foot of Miss Mackenzie's bed. Miss Mackenzie wrapped herself up in all her old shawls and mufflers, but still she felt the cold. Her fingers grew so stiff that she took almost an hour to open a can of baked beans. And then it snowed and for several days; the milkman did not come. The postman arrived with her pension papers, but she felt too tired to take them up to town to the bank.

She spent most of the time in bed. It was the warmest place. She kept a hot-water bottle at her back, and the cat kept her feet warm. She lay in bed, dreaming of the spring and summer months. In three months' time the primroses would be out, and with the coming of spring the boy would return.

One night the hot-water bottle burst, and the bedding was soaked through. As there was no sun for several days, the blanket remained damp. Miss Mackenzie caught a chill and had to keep to her cold, uncomfortable bed. She knew she had a fever but there was no thermometer with which to take her temperature. She had difficulty in breathing.

A strong wind sprang up one night, and the window flew open and kept banging all night. Miss Mackenzie was too weak to get up and close it, and the wind swept the rain and sleet into the room. The cat crept into the bed and snuggled close to its mistress's warm body. But towards morning that body had lost its warmth and the cat left the bed and started scratching about on the floor.

As a shaft of sunlight streamed through the open window, the milkman arrived. He poured some milk into the cat's saucer on the doorstep, and the cat leapt down from the windowsill and made for the milk.

The milkman called a greeting to Miss Mackenzie, but received no answer. Her window was open and he had always known her to be up before sunrise. So he put his head in at the window and called again. But Miss Mackenzie did not answer. She had gone away to the mountain where the blue gentian and purple columbine grew.

GRACIE

Show me the way to go home,
I'm tired and I want to go to bed,
I had a little drink but an hour ago,
And it's gone right to my head....

A group of British soldiers, a little drunk, were singing in the middle of the road. It was almost midnight. And yes, it was World War II. But it wasn't a street in Paris or Naples or Rangoon—it was Rajpur Road in Dehradun, then a small town tucked away in the Doon Valley some 200 miles north of New Delhi.

The soldiers were on leave. Not home leave, because they were still far from home—but a break from active duty on the warfront, from the fighting in Burma and the Far East. Dehradun had been designated a 'recreational centre' for Allied troops. Unfortunately, we in Dehra could provide little by way of recreation for these restless young men, who were looking for something more than food and drink.

Coming down the street from the other end of town were a group of American soldiers. They too were engaged in a sing-song. 'Sweet Rosie O'Grady' or something very Irish. They had more money to throw around, as they were better paid than the British soldiers. There was no love lost between these 'allies'. Someone made an insulting gesture and remark, and soon there was a brawl in the middle of the road.

Looking down at them from the balcony of our flat above the road, I asked my mother: 'Has World War III begun?'

'It looks like it,' she said.

'Who's winning?'

A couple of soldiers were already flat on the ground.

'The military police. Here they come!'

A jeep-load of military police, British and American, drove up, and showed their solidarity in the midst of hostilities by rounding up the drunken brigade and carrying them off to barracks.

Silence descended on Rajpur Road, and I went back to bed.

⁓

It was the winter of 1944–45, a few months after I'd lost my father, and I was back in Dehra for the winter holidays. My mother and stepfather were always moving from one house or flat to another (usually under pressure from the landlord), and that year we had a flat in Astley Hall, right in the centre of town.

Astley Hall and its environs were having something of a boom during the war years, due mainly to the presence of several thousand Allied troops stationed outside Dehradun. Casinos, cafes, and dance halls had sprung up in this otherwise sedate centre of town, and every evening they would be filled to capacity with rowdy roistering soldiers who had survived the fighting but who might well have to return to active duty before long.

To avoid bar fights and street brawls, the Americans were allowed into town three days a week, the British three days a week, and the Italian prisoners of war once a week.

The Italians were the best behaved. They were, after all, war prisoners and confined to a prison camp six days in the week. Nor did they have money to throw around, so they made a little pocket money by selling postage stamps and handmade toys.

The American soldiers had unlimited supplies of chewing gum, and these they distributed freely amongst the children of the locality. Naturally this made them the most popular of the visiting soldiers.

The British did not have much to offer by way of surplus

rations, but one young corporal, more educated than his fellows, gave me three well-thumbed paperbacks in the Collins Crime Club Series, and through them I made my first acquaintance with the works of Agatha Christie, Edgar Wallace, and Peter Cheyney. As a result I became a lifelong addict of the crime novel.

This same young corporal took more than a casual interest in one of our neighbours, a girl called Gracie, who lived in the next flat with her elder sister, a schoolteacher. Gracie was just seventeen or eighteen, a very pretty girl of mixed English, Portuguese, Burmese, and Indian descent. A terrific combination of genes and hereditary traits. And physically she had inherited the best of all worlds. No one could have been lovelier. Coffee-coloured, sloe-eyed, with glossy black hair and full inviting lips, she had only to walk down the street for heads to turn in her direction. At ten, I was madly in love with her.

Gracie had a good singing voice—sweet and low and a little husky—and she had been engaged by bandmaster Billy Cotton to sing a few numbers during the late evening dances and cabaret shows at the Casino, Dehra's very own 'night club'. We had never had a night club before the war, and as far as I know there hasn't been one after Independence—not yet, anyway. But in those jolly wartime years, with everyone panting for a little pleasure, the Casino provided music, dance, food and drink, and a 'magic show'.

For the Casino was owned by 'Mustafa Pasha' (real name Roshan Kapoor), one of the country's foremost conjurers and magicians.

Every evening, for an hour, he'd put on a magic show, doing card tricks, taking rabbits out of hats, paper streamers out of his mouth, and egg out of his customers' pockets. He climaxed it by sawing his teenaged daughter in half. She was none the worse for it, naturally.

When the magic show was over, the singing and dancing

commenced, and so did the boozing. By midnight the place was in an uproar, chairs flying about, tables overturned, one or two soldiers flat on their backs—knocked out by drink or one of their comrades. The enemy would have loved it.

Gracie would evade the last lurching warrior, slip out from beneath his grasping arms, and leave the Casino by the back entrance. One of the cooks, a local boy, would escort her home.

Gracie received two hundred rupees a month for singing to the troops, which was what her sister got for teaching little children to read and write. Gracie sang at a night club, her sister (I forget her name) taught at a convent. And yet, Gracie was the brighter of the two. She had more conversation, more wit, more joie-de-vivre.

And we had one thing in common—we both enjoyed chaat.

Every evening a chaatwallah would come around to the Astley Hall shops and flats, preparing chaat on the spot. Served on large green leaves, the chaat and kachalu, flavoured with lemon juice, tamarind juice, chillies and garam masala, was almost an addiction. I did not always have enough pocket money, cheap though it was, but Gracie would call me over and make sure I had as much chaat as I could consume. Corporal Allen did not approve of the chaat, but would occasionally give me a rupee and tell me to run off and buy toffees, so that he could have Gracie to himself for ten or fifteen minutes. I did not care for toffees, but I would keep the rupee and come back after five minutes to find them kissing on the veranda.

The corporal was a little too refined for the Casino, and contented himself with taking Gracie to the pictures. We had three cinemas showing English or American films—the Orient, the Odeon, and the Hollywood. Once Gracie took me to the pictures—it was a sentimental drama called *Always in My Heart*—and we held hands throughout the show. I had got the better of Corporal Allen that day.

At the Casino, Gracie sang sentimental ballads such as 'Smoke Gets in Your Eyes' and 'White Christmas', and although Dehra did not get a white Christmas, we got a white New Year on the evening of 31 December.

My mother was in bed, having that week given birth to my baby brother. I was knocking a football around on the parade ground with Bhim and Ranbir and some of the local boys when, to everyone's delight and consternation, it began to snow. As far as we knew it had never snowed in Dehra, so it was a unique, almost freakish event. We ran about, shouting in excitement while it continued snowing, so that by late evening the town was covered with a glistening white mantle. I ran home, breathless with excitement, and told my mother it was snowing outside.

'Don't try to make a fool of me,' she said 'I'm not in the mood for your silly jokes.'

So I went outside and broke off a branch of the litchi tree. The leaves were covered with snow. I took indoors and showed it to my mother, and she said, 'the last time it snowed here was around forty years ago—1905, the year your grandparents were married. It was snowing outside St Thomas's church just as they were taking their marriage vows.'

'They must have seen it as a good sign,' I said.

'Well, they were married for thirty years until your grandfather died.'

'And they had lots of children.'

'Five girls and one spoilt brat of a boy—your Uncle Ken. But I was the youngest and they spoilt me too.'

⁓

That night, New Year's Eve, there was a grand dance at the Casino, and Gracie persuaded my mother to allow me to go along with her. I was to sit in a corner of the dance hall and avoid fraternizing with the partying soldiers.

It was an eventful evening. The snowfall had made New Year's Eve even more special, and the dance hall was crowded, mostly with high-spirited soldiers, but there were also a few of the local gentry and their families.

Mustafa Pasha, uttering magical incantations, went through his usual routine, which was always popular—and this was followed by three or four sentimental ballads sung by Gracie to the accompaniment of Billy Cotton's four-piece band. Gracie wasn't a great singer, but her freshness, energy, and sensuality always brought the house down—as it did that New Year's Eve.

I had a small table to myself in a corner of the dance hall, and Gracie saw to it that I was well supplied with my favourite fish fingers, chips, gulab jamuns, and Vimto—the last, a raspberry-flavoured soft drink that was very popular during the war years. Whatever happened to Vimto? Killed off, no doubt, by all the colas and fizzy drinks that came in later.

Between songs, Gracie would come over to see if I was all right. I must have been the only boy in a roomful of adults. The soldiers whistled and called to Gracie to come over to their table for a change, but she simply smiled good-naturedly and went back to the rostrum to give a fair imitation of Lena Horne. She had the same sultry presence as the famous blues singer.

At midnight the lights went out and everyone began to sing 'Auld Lang Syne'.

Should old acquaintance be forgot
and never brought to mind...?
We'll drink a cup of kindness yet,
for auld lang syne....

Gracie was standing beside me, singing, and I stood up and took her hand. I loved listening to her singing. My own voice was ragged and tuneless and I thought it best not to inflict it on others.

'Come, Ruskin, give me a kiss,' said Gracie, leaning over me, and I suddenly found my lips pressed against hers in what was, till then, the most magical moment of my life. It was the first time I'd been kissed full on the lips, and I wanted that kiss to go on forever.

But the lights came on, and we drew apart, and everyone shouted 'HAPPY NEW YEAR!' The band struck up again and Gracie sang 'The White Cliffs of Dover', which made the British soldiers very maudlin and homesick.

At two in the morning I accompanied Gracie back to our adjoining flats, but there were no further kisses, as by then we had been joined by Corporal Allen who had missed the party but had turned up to escort us home. I found myself fervently wishing that he'd be sent back to Burma or wherever the fighting was going on.

I have to admit that Gracie did not see me in the same romantic light that I saw her. She looked upon me as a younger brother, and treated me with the openness and light-hearted affection that she would have bestowed on a brother, had there been one.

'Press my back, will you, Ruskin?' she pleaded more than once. 'I can hardly stand straight.'

Most willingly did I oblige, knowing full well that I would not have been assigned this delicious task had I been an adult. I might well have grown up to be a physiotherapist had my holidays not come to an end.

On more than one occasion Gracie changed her dress in front of me, and I saw her lovely breasts and supple waist and thighs as she studied herself in the mirror, almost oblivious of my presence.

I noticed a long scar on her lower abdomen and asked her how she'd got it.

'Oh, when I was in school up in Mussoorie,' she said. 'Dr Butcher removed my appendix.'

'Dr Butcher! Was he a butcher or a doctor?'

'He was the civil surgeon. And he had a thing about appendixes. If you went to him with a tummy ache, he cut you open and took out your appendix. He said it was at the root of all our problems! He had so much difficulty finding mine that he had to make an extra-large cut.'

'Can I touch it?'

'Of course. It doesn't hurt now.'

I ran my finger along her scar. I found it quite thrilling to be touching her like that.

'You don't have to stop at the scar,' said Gracie with a laugh. 'You can touch other places too.'

But I was too shy to be making further explorations. For a ten-year-old, the scar was more fascinating than her hips or her navel. But it put me on terms of close familiarity. Even Corporal Allen hadn't seen her scar, or so she assured me!

My boarding school was in Simla, a day and a night's train journey from Dehra, so when my three-month-long winter holidays were over and I returned to school, I knew it would be nine long months before I came home to Dehra.

In that time a lot could happen, and it generally did. For one thing, the war ended and all the soldiers went home—to England or America or wherever they'd come from. A few war brides went with them. A few illegitimate children were left behind in various countries. Also, everyone knew that India's independence was just around the corner, and the Anglo-Indians and the 'country-born' British were beginning to pack their bags.

When I came home to Dehra in the winter of 1945–46, the

Casino, the dance hall and cafes had vanished, and the town was going through something of a slump.

'Where's Gracie?' I asked my mother, as soon as I was home.

'Gracie's in England. She married that baby-faced corporal who used to hang around her all the time. But her sister's still here, teaching at the convent. Do you want some help with your maths?'

'No.' There was nothing romantic about maths.

Mustafa Pasha was missing too. He had moved to Bombay, where he was making a fortune.

I can't say I missed anyone very much. At eleven, I had my priorities, and they were the four Cs—the cinemas, comics, chaat, and Crime Club thrillers, all in that order. With the exception of the chaat, I had, till then, absorbed very little of Indian culture. It was the same with most Anglo-Indian boys of my age. They went to hill schools and came home to railway colonies and Saturday night dance parties. Some of them excelled at hockey and made it to the Olympics. I played football and occasionally cricket, and the boys I played with were the children of Indian shopkeepers or clerks—boys who, when they grew up, would be the backbone of the prosperous middle class.

Sometimes I accompanied Bhim or Ranbir to a Hindi movie, but most the time I haunted English cinemas which were still running, although to smaller audiences.

Dehra–Simla, Simla–Dehra, and the years slipped by, and before I knew it I was a young man just out of school and without any prospects. I suppose I could have gone to the local college, or joined the army (the truly Indian Army, the British having left three years previously), or possibly got a job on a tea estate; but none of these prospects thrilled me. I wanted to be a happy writer, even though readers were in short supply in 1950s India.

Sensibly, my mother packed me off to the UK. I had to take a job there, of course. There was no one to see me through a college or university. Even the Regent Street polytechnic was beyond my means. In any case, I was not interested in acquiring a degree. Any kind of work would do, provided I could sit down in my bedsitter over the weekends, sometimes at night, and work on the novel that I had resolved to finish.

For three months I worked in a grocery store, then moved up in the social hierarchy by taking a job as an accounts clerk in a firm making photographic goods and accessories. It was boring work—simple arithmetic, really—but it allowed my mind to wander in various other directions. And the pay packet, a basic wage of five pounds a week, covered my living expenses.

It was a lonely life. Every evening I would return to my cold and silent room, turn on the gas, make myself a marmite sandwich, and sit down to work on my literary opus.

Just occasionally I would go to a cinema or theatre, or take a meal in a cheap restaurant. Sometimes, late at night, I would walk about the city—London's streets were comparatively safe in those days, although occasionally there were gang fights and hold-ups.

The prostitutes would stand, as they always did, every ten yards down the left-hand side of the road, keeping to fixed pitches for the sale of their overripe wares. It was difficult to find one who was under thirty.

Whenever I came out of a cinema in the Piccadilly area, I would walk past them, feigning indifference; but I would steal covert glances at these women, hoping to see someone young and pretty. At eighteen, I was anxious to lose my virginity and prove my manhood. At eighteen, time seems to be passing very swiftly. Any day, I used to think, I shall be old, too old for love, too old for sex, too old for an affair. Young men in the office spoke of their dalliance with flirtatious girls, of sexual adventures in their teens. I had nothing to boast about. I was still an innocent—untried as a lover—and I felt that this was something that had to be remedied.

Late one evening, as I passed a young woman who was a little different from the others—sultry-looking, with Asiatic features—I stopped and looked back, and she smiled and gave me the usual line: 'Come along, darling, I'll give you a good time.' And summoning up a little courage, I went along, hoping for a good time the first time.

She took me down a side street, to a seedy-looking lodging house, and up some stairs to her room—where, without ado, she thrust a large biscuit tin at me. Only it didn't contain biscuits, it held condoms.

'You'd better use one,' she said.

Not the most romantic way to get going, but she was obviously in a hurry—other customers were waiting!

I tried fondling her, stroking her breasts, but she said there wasn't time for all that. She pulled up her dress. She had varicose veins—probably from too much street-walking. She pulled down her knickers, and that was when I saw the scar.

I could not have mistaken the scar—Dr Butcher's over-eager attempt to locate an appendix.

'Gracie?' I stammered.

She looked hard at me then, and recognition flooded her painted face. Under the heavy make-up, it was Gracie. And I was no longer a ten-year-old. I was an awkward young man trying to prove his manhood.

Desire had died in me the minute I recognized the girl I used to know; all the freshness and romance and youth had vanished, leaving her a well-paid chattel for the gratification of lonely, loveless men.

And all I could say was, 'What happened to Corporal Allen?'

Well, it appeared that Corporal Allen had ditched Gracie soon after they had arrived in Britain. He had been posted in West Berlin, where he had taken up with a fräulein. Gracie had tried to put her talents as a singer to good use, but torch singers were cheaper by the dozen, and she was unable to break into show business. She spent a year working in a garment factory on a basic wage. An engaging young pimp had persuaded her and a couple of other attractive girls to join a West End brothel, and there she was now, still fighting fit although a little battle worn. But she had saved some money.

'In a year or two I'll retire from this racket and start a little boarding house near the sea. Down on the south coast. It's warmer there. I do miss India, though. How's my sister?'

'She's fine. Might start her own school soon. Don't you write to her?'

'Will do, one of these days.'

I got up to leave. I might have had a crush on Gracie when I was a boy, but I couldn't possibly make love to her now. It would be like having sex with a close relative.

'You don't have to go,' she said. 'We can sit and talk.'

'You must have other engagements.'

'No,' she said. 'As soon as you've gone I'll be out on the streets again, trying to hook someone.'

'You're a good hooker. You hooked me all right.'

She laughed then. And her laughter was still the same— unforced, genuine. Some things don't change.

'Is this your first time, then?'

I nodded. 'You were the only girl on the street who had any appeal for me. Perhaps, subconsciously, I recognized you. But it was only when I saw that old scar of yours that I knew....'

'And now?'

'No, not now. I couldn't.'

'But you'll come again?'

'We'll meet again.'

There was a loud knocking on the door.

'My landlady,' said Gracie, and went to the door. A formidable-looking madam was waiting outside.

'You've been a long time, dearie.' She looked me up and down. 'Just out of school, too, by the looks of him.'

'He's just leaving.'

'And there's a gentleman in my parlour who's asking for you. Seems he took a fancy to you the last time he was here. Oldish, but well-heeled.'

'I'll be down in a jiffy.'

Gracie gave me a hug and kissed me on the cheek. As I stepped into the street, the strains of an old song floated after me. It came from someone's record-player in one of the apartments. Vera Lynn. But it might have been Gracie....

We'll meet again,
don't know where,
don't know when,
but we'll meet again,
some sunny day....

We never met again. Life took me in another direction. It usually does. But I hope Gracie saved enough to start a little boarding house in some sunny seaside resort. She deserved something better than a brothel.

THE CHERRY TREE

One day, when Rakesh was six, he walked home from the Mussoorie bazaar eating cherries. They were a little sweet, a little sour; small, bright red cherries which had come all the way from the Kashmir Valley.

Here in the Himalayan foothills where Rakesh lived, there were not many fruit trees. The soil was stony, and the dry cold winds stunted the growth of most plants. But on the more sheltered slopes there were forests of oak and deodar.

Rakesh lived with his grandfather on the outskirts of Mussoorie, just where the forest began. His father and mother lived in a small village fifty miles away, where they grew maize and rice and barley in narrow terraced fields on the lower slopes of the mountain. But there were no schools in the village, and Rakesh's parents were keen that he should go to school. As soon as he was of school-going age, they sent him to stay with his grandfather in Mussoorie.

Grandfather was a retired forest ranger. He had a little cottage outside the town.

Rakesh was on his way home from school when he bought the cherries. He paid fifty paise for the bunch. It took him about half an hour to walk home, and by the time he reached the cottage there were only three cherries left.

'Have a cherry, Grandfather,' he said, as soon as he saw his grandfather in the garden.

Grandfather took one cherry and Rakesh promptly ate the other two. He kept the last seed in his mouth for some time, rolling it round and round on his tongue until all the tang had gone. Then he placed the seed on the palm of his hand and studied it.

'Are cherry seeds lucky?' asked Rakesh.

'Of course.'

'Then I'll keep it.'

'Nothing is lucky if you put it away. If you want luck, you must put it to some use.'

'What can I do with a seed?'

'Plant it.'

So Rakesh found a small spade and began to dig up a flower bed.

'Hey, not there,' said Grandfather. 'I've sown mustard in that bed. Plant it in that shady corner where it won't be disturbed.'

Rakesh went to a corner of the garden where the earth was soft and yielding. He did not have to dig. He pressed the seed into the soil with his thumb and it went right in.

Then he had his lunch and ran off to play cricket with his friends and forgot all about the cherry seed.

When it was winter in the hills, a cold wind blew down from the snows and went whoo-whoo-whoo through the deodar trees, and the garden was dry and bare. In the evenings Grandfather told Rakesh stories—stories about people who turned into animals, and ghosts who lived in trees, and beans that jumped and stones that wept—and in turn Rakesh would read to him from the newspaper, Grandfather's eyesight being rather weak. Rakesh found the newspaper very dull—especially after the stories—but Grandfather wanted all the news....

They knew it was spring when the wild duck flew north again, to Siberia. Early in the morning, when he got up to chop wood and light a fire, Rakesh saw the V-shaped formation streaming northwards, the calls of the birds carrying clearly through the thin mountain air.

One morning in the garden, he bent to pick up what he thought was a small twig and found to his surprise that it was well rooted. He stared at it for a moment, then ran to fetch

Grandfather, calling, 'Dada, come and look, the cherry tree has come up!'

'What cherry tree?' asked Grandfather, who had forgotten about it.

'The seed we planted last year—look, it's come up!'

Rakesh went down on his haunches, while Grandfather bent almost double and peered down at the tiny tree. It was about four inches high.

'Yes, it's a cherry tree,' said Grandfather. 'You should water it now and then.'

Rakesh ran indoors and came back with a bucket of water.

'Don't drown it!' said Grandfather.

Rakesh gave it a sprinkling and circled it with pebbles.

'What are the pebbles for?' asked Grandfather.

'For privacy,' said Rakesh.

He looked at the tree every morning but it did not seem to be growing very fast. So he stopped looking at it—except quickly, out of the corner of his eye. And, after a week or two, when he allowed himself to look at it properly, he found that it had grown—at least an inch!

That year the monsoon rains came early and Rakesh plodded to and from school in raincoat and gumboots. Ferns sprang from the trunks of trees, strange-looking lilies came up in the long grass, and even when it wasn't raining the trees dripped, and mist came curling up the valley. The cherry tree grew quickly in this season.

It was about two feet high when a goat entered the garden and ate all the leaves. Only the main stem and two thin branches remained.

'Never mind,' said Grandfather, seeing that Rakesh was upset. 'It will grow again; cherry trees are tough.'

Towards the end of the rainy season new leaves appeared on the tree. Then a woman cutting grass scrambled down the hillside, her scythe swishing through the heavy monsoon foliage. She did not try to avoid the tree: one sweep, and the cherry tree was cut in two.

When Grandfather saw what had happened, he went after the woman and scolded her; but the damage could not be repaired.

'Maybe it will die now,' said Rakesh.

'Maybe,' said Grandfather.

But the cherry tree had no intention of dying.

By the time summer came round again, it had sent out several new shoots with tender green leaves. Rakesh had grown taller too. He was eight now, a sturdy boy with curly black hair and deep black eyes. Blackberry eyes, Grandfather called them.

That monsoon Rakesh went home to his village, to help his father and mother with the planting and ploughing and sowing. He was thinner but stronger when he came back to Grandfather's house at the end of the rains, to find that the cherry tree had grown another foot. It was now up to his chest.

Even when there was rain, Rakesh would sometimes water the tree. He wanted it to know that he was there.

One day he found a bright green praying mantis perched on a branch, peering at him with bulging eyes. Rakesh let it remain there. It was the cherry tree's first visitor.

The next visitor was a hairy caterpillar, who started making a meal of the leaves. Rakesh removed it quickly and dropped it on a heap of dry leaves.

'They're pretty leaves,' said Rakesh. 'And they are always ready to dance. If there's a breeze.'

After Grandfather had come indoors, Rakesh went into the garden and lay down on the grass beneath the tree. He gazed up through the leaves at the great blue sky; and turning on his side, he could see the mountain striding away into the clouds. He was still lying beneath the tree when the evening shadows crept across the garden. Grandfather came back and sat down beside

Rakesh, and they waited in silence until the stars came out and the nightjar began to call. In the forest below, the crickets and cicadas began tuning up; and suddenly the tree was full of the sounds of insects.

'There are so many trees in the forest,' said Rakesh. 'What's so special about this tree? Why do we like it so much?'

'We planted it ourselves,' said Grandfather. 'That's why it's special.'

'Just one small seed,' said Rakesh, and he touched the smooth bark of the tree that had grown. He ran his hand along the trunk of the tree and put his finger to the tip of a leaf. 'I wonder,' he whispered, 'is this what it feels to be God?'

GETTING GRANNY'S GLASSES

Granny could hear the distant roar of the river and smell the pine needles beneath her feet, and feel the presence of her grandson, Mani; but she couldn't see the river or the trees; and of her grandson she could only make out his fuzzy hair, and sometimes, when he was very close, his blackberry eyes and the gleam of his teeth when he smiled.

Granny wore a pair of old glasses; she'd been wearing them for well over ten years, but her eyes had grown steadily weaker, and the glasses had grown older and were now scratched and spotted, and there was very little she could see through them. Still, they were better than nothing. Without them, everything was just a topsy-turvy blur.

Of course, Granny knew her way about the house and the fields, and on a clear day she could see the mountains—the mighty Himalayan snow peaks—striding away into the sky; but it was felt by Mani and his father that it was high time Granny had her eyes tested and got herself new glasses.

'Well, you know we can't get them in the village,' said Granny.

Mani said, 'You'll have to go to the eye hospital in Mussoorie. That's the nearest town.'

'But that's a two-day journey,' protested Granny. 'First I'd have to walk to Nain Market, twelve miles at least, spend the night there at your Uncle's place, and then catch a bus for the rest of the journey! You know how I hate buses. And it's ten years since I walked all the way to Mussoorie. That was when I had these glasses made.'

'Well, it's still there,' said Mani's father.

'What is still there?'

'Mussoorie.'

'And the eye hospital?'

'That too.'

'Well, my eyes are not too bad, really,' said Granny, looking for excuses. She did not feel like going far from the village; in particular, she did not want to be parted from Mani. He was eleven and quite capable of looking after himself, but Granny had brought him up ever since his mother had died when he was only a year old. She was his Nani (maternal grandmother), and had cared for boy and father, and cows and hens and household, all these years, with great energy and devotion.

'I can manage quite well,' she said. As long as I can see what's right in front of me, there's no problem. I know you got a ball in your hand, Mani; please don't bounce it off the cow.'

'It's not a ball, Granny; it's an apple.'

'Oh, is it?' said Granny, recovering quickly from her mistake. 'Never mind, just don't bounce it off the cow. And don't eat too many apples!'

'Now listen,' said Mani's father sternly, 'I know you don't want to go anywhere. But we're not sending you off on your own. I'll take you to Mussoorie.'

'And leave Mani here by himself? How could you even think of doing that?'

'Then I'll take you to Mussoorie,' said Mani eagerly. 'We can leave Father on his own, can't we? I've been to Mussoorie before, with my school friends. I know where we can stay. But—' He paused a moment and looked doubtfully from his father to his grandmother. 'You wouldn't be able to walk all the way to Nain, would you, Granny?'

'Of course I can walk,' said Granny. 'I may be going blind, but there's nothing wrong with my legs!'

That was true enough. Only day before they'd found Granny

in the walnut tree, tossing walnuts, not very accurately, into a large basket on the ground.

'But you're seventy, Granny.'

'What has that got to do with it? And besides, it's downhill to Nain.'

'And uphill coming back.'

'Uphill's easier!' said Granny.

Now that she knew Mani might be accompanying her, she was more than ready to make the journey.

The monsoon rains had begun, and in front of the small stone house a cluster of giant dahlias reared their heads. Mani had seen them growing in Nain and had brought some bulbs home. 'These are big flowers, Granny,' he'd said. 'You'll be able to see them better.'

She could indeed see the dahlias, splashes of red and yellow against the old stone of the cottage walls.

Looking at them now, Granny said, 'While we're in Mussoorie, we'll get some seeds and bulbs. And a new bell for the white cow. And a pullover for your father. And shoes for you. Look, there's nothing much left of the ones you're wearing.'

'Now just a minute,' said Mani's father. 'Are you going there to get your eyes tested, or are you going on a shopping expedition? I've got only a hundred rupees to spare. You'll have to manage with that.'

'We'll manage,' said Mani. 'We'll sleep at the bus shelter.'

'No, we won't,' said Granny. 'I've got fifty rupees of my own. We'll stay at a hotel!'

Early next morning, in a light drizzle, Granny and Mani set out on the path to Nain.

Mani carried a small bedding roll on his shoulder; Granny carried a large cloth shopping bag and an umbrella. The path went through fields and around the brow of the hill and then began to wind here and there, up and down and around, as though it had a will of its own and no intention of going anywhere in particular. Travellers new to the area often left the path, because they were impatient or in a hurry, and thought there were quicker, better ways of reaching their destinations. Almost immediately they found themselves lost. For it was a wise path and a good path, and had found the right way of crossing the mountains after centuries of trial and error.

'Whenever you feel tired, we'll take a rest,' said Mani.

'We've only just started out,' said Granny. 'We'll rest when you're hungry!'

They walked at a steady pace, without talking too much. A flock of parrots whirled overhead, flashes of red and green against the sombre sky. High in a spruce tree a barbet called monotonously. But there were no other sounds, except for the hiss and gentle patter of the rain.

Mani stopped to pick wild blackberries from a bush. Granny wasn't fond of berries and didn't slacken her pace. Mani had to run to catch up with her. Soon his lips were purple with the juice from the berries.

The rain stopped and the sun came out. Below them, the light green of the fields stood out against the dark green of the forests, and the hills were bathed in golden sunshine.

Mani ran ahead.

'Can you see all right, Granny?' he called.

'I can see the path and I can see your white shirt. That's enough for now.'

'Well, watch out, there are some mules coming down the road.'

Granny stepped aside to allow the mules to pass. They clattered by, the mule-driver urging them on with a romantic song; but the last mule veered toward Granny and appeared to be heading straight for her. Granny saw it just in time. She knew that mules and ponies always preferred going around objects, if they could see what lay ahead of them, so she held out her open umbrella and the mule cantered round it without touching her.

Granny and Mani ate their light meal on the roadside, in the shade of a whispering pine, and drank from a spring a little further down the path.

By late afternoon they were directly above Nain.

'We're almost there,' said Mani. 'I can see the temple near Uncle's house.'

'I can't see a thing,' said Granny.

'That's because of the mist. There's a thick mist coming up the valley.'

It started raining heavily as they entered the small market town on the banks of the river. Granny's umbrella was leaking badly. But they were soon drying themselves in Uncle's house, and drinking glasses of hot sweet milky tea.

Mani got up early the next morning and ran down the narrow street to bathe in the river. The swift but shallow mountain river was a tributary of the sacred Ganges, and its waters were held sacred too. As the sun rose, people thronged the steps leading down to the river, to bathe or pray or float flower offerings downstream.

As Mani dressed, he heard the blare of a bus horn. There was only one bus to Mussoorie. He scampered up the slope, wondering if they'd miss it. But Granny was waiting for him at the bus stop. She had already bought their tickets.

The motor road followed the course of the river, which thundered a hundred feet below. The bus was old and rickety, and rattled so much that the passengers could barely hear themselves speaking.

One of them was pointing to a spot below, where another bus had gone off the road a few weeks back, resulting in many casualties.

The driver appeared to be unaware of the accident. He drove

at some speed, and whenever he went round a bend, everyone in the bus was thrown about. In spite of all the noise and confusion, Granny fell asleep; her head resting against Mani's shoulder.

Suddenly the bus came to a grinding halt. People were thrown forward in their seats. Granny's glasses fell off and had to be retrieved from the folds of someone else's umbrella.

'What's happening?' she asked. 'Have we arrived?'

'No, something is blocking the road,' said Mani.

'It's a landslide!' exclaimed someone, and all the passengers put their heads out of the windows to take a look.

It was a big landslide. Sometime in the night, during the heavy rain, earth and trees and bushes had given way and come crashing down, completely blocking the road. Nor was it over yet. Debris was still falling. Mani saw rocks hurtling down the hill and into the river.

'Not a suitable place for a bus stop,' observed Granny, who couldn't see a thing.

Even as she spoke, a shower of stones and small rocks came clattering down on the roof of the bus. Passengers cried out in alarm. The driver began reversing, as more rocks came crashing down.

'I never did trust motor roads,' said Granny.

The driver kept backing until they were well away from the landslide. Then everyone tumbled out of the bus. Granny and Mani were the last to get down.

They were told that it would take days to clear the road, and most of the passengers decided to return to Nain with the bus. But a few bold spirits agreed to walk to Mussoorie, taking a shortcut up the mountain which would bypass the landslide.

'It's only ten miles from here by the footpath,' said one of them. 'A stiff climb, but we can make it by evening.'

Mani looked at Granny. 'Shall we go back?'

'What's ten miles?' said Granny. 'We did that yesterday.'

So they started climbing a narrow path, little more than a goat track, which went steeply up the mountainside. But there was much huffing and puffing, and pausing for breath and by the time they got to the top of the mountain Granny and Mani were on their own. They could see a few stragglers far below; the rest had retreated to Nain.

Granny and Mani stood on the summit of the mountain. They had it all to themselves. Their village was hidden by the range to the north. Far below rushed the river. Far above circled a golden eagle.

In the distance, on the next mountain, the houses of Mussoorie were white specks on the dark green hillside.

'Did you bring any food from Uncle's house?' asked Mani.

'Naturally,' said Granny. 'I knew you'd soon be hungry. There are pakoras and buns, and peaches from Uncle's garden.'

'Good!' said Mani, forgetting his tiredness. 'We'll eat as we go along. There's no need to stop.'

'Eating or walking?'

'Eating, of course. We'll stop when you're tired, Granny.'

'Oh, I can walk forever,' said Granny, laughing. 'I've been doing it all my life. And one day I'll just walk over the mountains and into the sky. But not if it's raining. This umbrella leaks badly.'

Down again they went, and up the next mountain, and over bare windswept hillsides, and up through a dark gloomy deodar forest. And then just as it was getting dark, they saw the lights of Mussoorie twinkling ahead of them.

As they came nearer, the lights increased, until presently they were in a brightly lit bazaar, swallowed up by crowds of shoppers, strollers, tourists and merrymakers. Mussoorie seemed a very jolly sort of place for those who had money to spend. Jostled in the crowd, Granny kept one hand firmly on Mani's shoulder so that she did not lose him.

They asked around for the cheapest hotel. But there were no

cheap hotels. So they spent the night in a dharamshala adjoining the temple, where other pilgrims had taken shelter.

Next morning, at the eye hospital, they joined a long queue of patient patients. The eye specialist, a portly man in a suit and tie who himself wore glasses, dealt with the patients in a brisk but kind manner. After an hour's wait, Granny's turn came.

The doctor took one horrified look at Granny's glasses and dropped them in a wastebasket. Then he fished them out and placed them on his desk and said, 'On second thought, I think I'll send them to a museum. You should have changed your glasses years ago. They've probably done more harm than good.'

He examined Granny's eyes with a strong light, and said, 'Your eyes are very weak, but you're not going blind. We'll fit you up with a stronger pair of glasses.' Then he placed her in front of a board covered with letters in English and Hindi, large and small, and asked Granny if she could make them out.

'I can't even see the board,' said Granny.

'Well, can you see me?' asked the doctor.

'Some of you,' said Granny.

'I want you to see all of me,' said the doctor, and he balanced a wire frame on Granny's nose and began trying out different lenses.

Suddenly Granny could see much better. She saw the board and the biggest letters on it.

'Can you see me now?' asked the doctor.

'Most of you,' said Granny. And then added, by way of being helpful: 'There's quite a lot of you to see.'

'Thank you,' said the doctor. 'And now turn around and tell me if you can see your grandson.'

Granny turned, and saw Mani clearly for the first time in many years.

'Mani!' she exclaimed, clapping her hands with joy. 'How nice you look! What a fine boy I've brought up! But you do need a haircut. And a wash. And buttons on your shirt. And a new pair of shoes. Come along to the bazaar!'

'First have your new glasses made,' said Mani, laughing. 'Then we'll go for shopping!'

A day later they were in a bus again, although no one knew how far it would be able to go. Sooner or later they would have to walk.

Granny had a window seat, and Mani sat beside her. He had new shoes and Granny had a new umbrella and they had also bought a thick woollen Tibetan pullover for Mani's father. And seeds and bulbs and a cowbell.

As the bus moved off, Granny looked eagerly out of the window. Each bend in the road opened up new vistas for her, and she could see many things that she hadn't seen for a long time—distant villages, people working in the fields, milkmen on the road, two dogs rushing along beside the bus, monkeys in the trees, and, most wonderful of all, a rainbow in the sky.

She couldn't see perfectly, of course, but she was very pleased with the improvement.

'What a large cow!' she remarked, pointing at a beast grazing on the hillside.

'It's not a cow, Granny,' said Mani. 'It's a buffalo.'

Granny was not to be discouraged. 'Anyway, I saw it,' she insisted.

While most of the people on the bus looked weary and bored, Granny continued to gaze out of the window, discovering new sights.

Mani watched for some time and listened to her excited chatter. Then his head began to nod. It dropped against Granny's shoulder, and remained there, comfortably supported. The bus swerved and jolted along the winding mountain road, but Mani was fast asleep.

SUNFLOWERS

Magic. It's all around us.

Take this little seed. It's a sunflower seed. I thrust it into the soil—the rich soil of mother earth. I sprinkle a little water over the topsoil. Ten days or two weeks later, a tiny green plant has sprung up, as if from nowhere. It grows rapidly, much faster than you or I. In a couple of months it's a tall, full-grown plant, as tall as you or me. Another month, and it sends forth a big yellow sunflower. The flower-head is full of seeds. That one bloom has produced hundreds of sunflower seeds—each one capable of producing more sunflowers—gardens, fields full of sunflowers! And the oil from the seeds makes our food nutritious and palatable.

Sunflowers are easy to grow. And a field full of sunflowers is an inspiring sight. Especially after a shower of rain. Then they glitter like gold.

IN SEARCH OF WILD FLOWERS

During those early years in Mussoorie, when I lived in a cottage far from other houses, one of my pleasures was roaming the hillside in search of wild flowers. They were at their best, in the spring and late September, towards the end of the monsoon rains. In the spring and early summer there were dog-roses, St John's Wort, buttercups, traveller's joy—flowers that are common in England, where the climate is very similar to that of the lower Himalayas—and in autumn, wild ginger, wild geraniums, ground orchids, sky-blue commelinas…. I knew the names of many wild flowers from having read the nature stories and memoirs of Richard Jefferies (*The Story of My Heart*, *Wood Magic*) and the short stories of H. E. Bates ('Alexander', 'My Uncle Silas'), in which the English countryside plays so large a part.

There was plenty for me to explore and discover on the grassy slopes below my cottage, Maplewood. There were trees too—maples, oaks, walnuts, horse-chestnuts, wild cherry. The cherry trees blossomed in November, just when it seemed the flowering season was over. Their pale pink petals brightened up the drab early winter hillsides.

Down near the little stream—a twenty-minute scramble from the cottage—there were ferns, several varieties, clusters of them flourishing in shady places. And they were there all the year round, for they knew just where to settle down, in shady and sheltering nooks protected from wind, frost, and too much sunshine.

Plants can be as fussy as humans—sometimes more so!

Most plants dislike windy places, hot or cold. The wind takes the moisture out of their leaves and stems. We stay out of the wind too. People who live in windy places have furrows across their faces. Like plants, we need shelter and just the right about of sun and shade.

LEGEND

The Supreme Artist, the great gardener who had fashioned this planet into something beautiful, decided to give names to the thousands of different flowers that flourished on our mountains, valleys, and plains. But he failed to notice one little flower, a tiny sky-blue flower growing in a rocky niche on a hillside. The flower ran after its Creator, crying 'Don't forget me, kind sir, I want a name too!' The good gardener apologized, saying 'You are very special, little one. And you shall have a name. We'll call you Forget-me-not!'

THE HOLLY TREE

Oh, I am green in winter-time,
when other trees are brown;
of all the trees—so went the rhyme—
the holly bears the crown.

Many years ago, a holly tree grew near the cottage, and every December, at Christmas time, it would give us branches adorned with scarlet berries. Then the builders came and the road-makers, and the holly tree disappeared. But I am told there are a couple of holly trees on the other side of the mountain, in a shady grove. I must bestir myself, stretch my old bones, and go in search of them.

For there's no tree so loved and merry
as the scarlet Holly Berry.

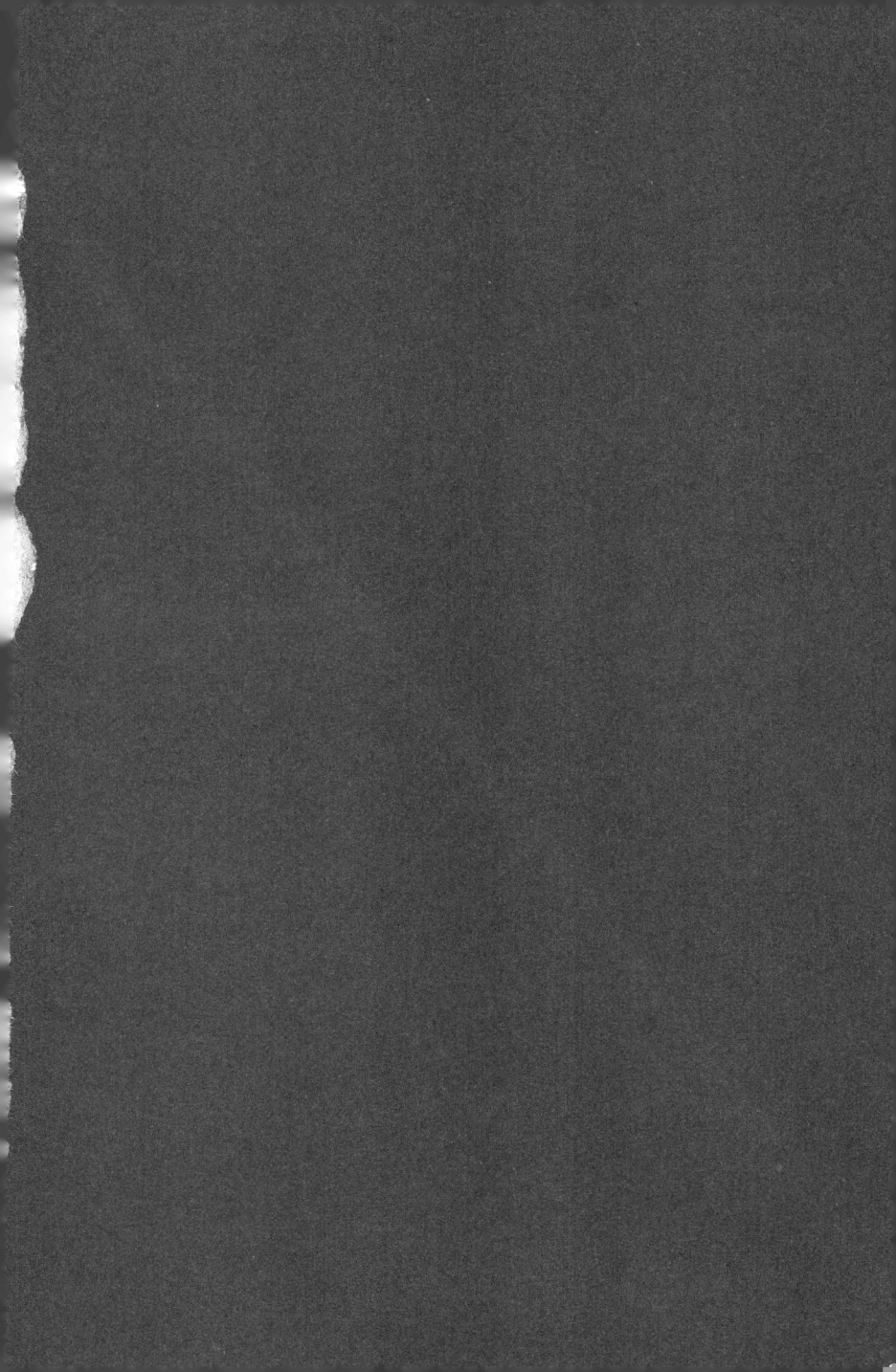